Sophia Dickinson Cobb

Hillsboro' Farms

Sophia Dickinson Cobb

Hillsboro' Farms

ISBN/EAN: 9783337326319

Printed in Europe, USA, Canada, Australia, Japan

Cover: Foto ©Andreas Hilbeck / pixelio.de

More available books at **www.hansebooks.com**

HILLSBORO' FARMS.

BY

SOPHIA DICKINSON COBB.

BOSTON:
LEE AND SHEPARD.
1869.

Stereotyped at the Boston Stereotype Foundry,
19 Spring Lane.

PREFACE.

THIS little book does not claim to have any special moral or mission. Its author has not aimed, through it, to teach anything, or to prove anything. She has but looked on nature and life in some of their quiet and little-noticed phases, and, loving what she saw there, has tried, upon her modest canvas, to paint it. If her readers shall find the picture true, her object will be gained.

HILLSBORO' FARMS.

CHAPTER I.

It is just possible that the good township of Hillsboro' may not be found laid down, with that designation, upon any of the maps; but this trifling circumstance will not prevent some who may read these pages from recognizing dear and familiar scenes; and they will need no map or gazetteer to tell them in which of the six New England States it is, or what is the name of its county. The town lies on a succession of long swells, the last diminishing undulations of a distant mountain range. To the west, through Edgehill, rise wild and picturesque hills, crowned with storm-beaten forests, and seamed with many a rocky rent and chasm; while beyond, sharp and blue in the morning light, or purple with the haze of sunset, are actual mountains. To the east the face of the country is tame by contrast, being an alternation of forest and farm for half a county's width. The eye ranges over miles of rolling woodland, chequered at intervals by silver river courses, and dotted here and there with what seem, at this distance, but clusters of white specks, but which in reality are busy villages, surrounded by acres on acres of the richest farming land of New England. A feeling of lonely

(7)

remoteness impresses the traveller who for the first time
journeys over the unfrequented roads of Hillsboro'—a feeling which yet can hardly become dreariness, even where
the farm-houses are most thinly scattered.　The evidences
of thrift and homely comfort, of abundance, and, in many
instances, of positive wealth, are everywhere too apparent
to admit an aspect of dreariness; and, moreover, the traces
of a still, but vigorous and almost vivid life, are everywhere
present in the picture.　The farms are, for the most part,
large, and the homes of the owners widely separated, only
rarely gathering in clusters of two or three, "Hillsboro'
Centre," the only village in the township, being but a collection of half a dozen dwelling-houses grouped about a
church, a post-office, a variety store, and a blacksmith's shop.
A very pleasing effect in the landscape is produced by the
prevailing taste among the farmers for red and yellow in
the color of their houses.　White may do very well amid
the greenness of the short, glowing summer; but through
the long, windy springs and sombre, decaying autumns,
these specks of brilliant coloring on the wide, gray hill-
sides, give a wonderful warmth and character to the picture.

The farmers, honest souls, are probably but little actuated
by ideas concerning tone or harmony of color.　Red and
and yellow are cheap paints; but we will not quarrel with
the cause so long as the effect is so satisfactory.

Hillsboro' really shows to best advantage in the summer;
but nowhere does the autumn come more softly, or with
a more pensive loveliness, stealing on the traces of summer with a mournful glory almost rivalling the beauty it
displaces.　Something of this charm lingered even to a
day in the late November of the year 185-.　The day was

warm for the season, the air soft and dry, with no bright
sunshine, and, in place of blue sky, that silvery curtain of
thin gray cloud, which is no forerunner of storm, and
which gives to all objects in the landscape a magical
clearness and distinctness of outline that clear sunshine cannot produce. The woods were bare and leafless; silent, too, but for the occasional rustle of a late-
falling leaf, or the murmur of the quiet autumn wind. The
fields had lost their last shade of green, even in the warm,
sheltered hollows; and, though the cattle still dotted the
hill-side, it was only the sheep that cropped the short brown
stubble.

Half way up the eastern slope of one of the longest
swells described, and about three miles from the " Centre,"
lies the farm of David Page. The house stands a little
back from the highway, and the unenclosed sward in front
comes up in a sharp, well-defined line to the road-side, its
surface unbroken save by a single huge butternut tree,
whose spreading branches almost sweep the ground. The
dwelling itself is a large, rambling, roomy structure, built
of wood, and neatly painted red, suggestive, at the first
glance, of wide, low-browed rooms and deep fireplaces, and
having always, even on a gray day like this, a cheery, sun-
shiny look, that seems to emanate from the life within.
Under the front windows you may see, in the summer
time, a brilliant display of sweet-williams, London pride,
and prince's feather; and on either side the broad, flat,
unhewn stone which forms the doorstep, glow, in the long
June days, the blood-red peonies. To the right of the
door, a gate between two great lilac trees leads to the
orchard, lying on the upward slope above the house. It

is a pleasant orchard, stone-walled, with the frost-faded grass under foot smooth as a carpet, and the long, straight rows of ancient apple trees, from whose brown branches the last yellow leaves have fallen. At the eastern end of the house is another door, which is the one in commonest use by the family, the front door being seldom opened except in summer. A curving, well-trodden foot-path leads up to it from the road, and before it the grassy slope runs down to the garden fence. Beside this fence, and between the long rows of currant bushes and the border of sunflowers, stands a line of bee-hives, around which, through all the long summer days, sounds a drowsy murmur from the "pollen-dusted bees," as they come and go from great beds of balm and sage, or hover over the gaudy borders where blossom tiger lilies, tall hollyhocks, and monkshood, with, now and then, the more delicate faces of sweet-peas and carnations. Now all this summer glory is vanished; still is the busy hive, faded and despoiled the garden walks, where a hen, with a late brood of overgrown, long-legged chickens, is allowed to scratch at pleasure. Near the garden gate stands the well, its wooden curb and platform weather-stained and mossy with the rains of many years. An empty bucket dangles from the long pole, and the heavy sweep, when put in motion, has a creaking groan that may be heard far down the valley. Around the worn platform and up through its seams the grass grows always thick and tall. Wonderfully clear, cool, and sweet is the water far down below, in whose smooth mirror are reflected all aspects of the heavens — the bright summer cloud, the driving storm-rack, the blue sky, and by night the slow procession of the stars.

In the rear of the house are the great barns, which, with their clustering sheds and out-buildings, make almost a village of themselves. From the open barn doors comes forth now a heavy, thundering sound, not precisely the "dull thunder of alternate flails," but a sound of kindred significance. It is the steady, prolonged jar of a huge threshing machine, where two tired horses plod wearily on in an endless treadmill journey. The yellow waves of straw flow out through the wide doors, and overflow even the high stone wall of the barn-yard. Standing knee-deep in the golden tide, and wiping his hot forehead with a bandanna handkerchief as he leans upon his pitchfork, is the farmer to whom all this homely wealth belongs — a strong, active-looking man, with a keen, shrewd face, a merry gray eye, and a large mouth which would seem to like smiling, it does that so much more readily than anything else. A prosperous and thrifty farmer is David Page, not positively rich, but what our people call "fore-handed;" that is, having a large, productive farm, not a debt in the world, and here and there small sums of money well invested. This autumn day finds him engaged in finishing up the more important labors of the year. When the threshing is done there will ensue a period of comparative leisure.

As Mr. Page replaced the hat upon his head, and, with a word or two to his workmen, turned again to his labor, a youth came slowly towards him out of the barn. He was a well-built young fellow of about seventeen, with a slow, deliberate manner of doing everything, which, without savoring really of indolence, was yet in marked contrast to the farmer's wiry energy. He had an intelligent

face, round and ruddy, and a pair of blue eyes running
over with boyish drollery. This was Mr. Page's youngest
son; in fact, the only son now remaining to him, all the
others having sought and found homes of their own in the
great West.

"Come, Heman, spry is the word, if we are going to get
this job off our hands to-night."

"Gorry, father! perhaps you see how it's going to be
done, but I don't."

"O, you will see shortly. Here, give Ezra a hand now
with them bags."

The youth heaved with a will.

"Well, Mr. Page," said one of the men, "we are pretty
well on time to-day. There goes the last bushel, and Amos
is taking off the horses this minute."

"That's better than I expected, Walker. A good day's
work, and the heaviest barley I ever raised. Plague on
those girls!" he added to himself, in a lower tone; "I wish
they had staid away. No getting anything out of that
boy when they are round."

A gay voice from the hill-side called Heman by name,
and two young girls were seen coming slowly down over
the crisp grass from the strip of beech wood that crested
the hill. Heman answered the call, and, as if to verify his
father's words, went and leaned on the farm-yard gate,
watching the approach of the two with bright and rather
admiring eyes. The new-comers justified his admiration.
The elder was about seventeen, and might have stood for
the embodiment of fresh youthful life. She carried a gray
straw hat in her hand, and a shawl was falling carelessly
from her shoulders, as with glowing cheek she walked

along, regardless of the autumn air. Her round, pliant
figure, graceful as a birch sapling, was set off to the best
advantage by a softly fitting gown of mulberry-colored
merino. She had a pure, innocent face, full of the wilful
spirit and gay daring of a child, a great abundance of fine
chestnut hair, which had an inclination to droop in heavy
masses round a small head, a low, well-formed forehead,
with clearly-defined but delicate eyebrows, and beautiful,
dewy, violet eyes, shaded by long, curving lashes. She
had also, what is a rare beauty in the human face, a handsome nose; it was small and straight, making a not too
abrupt angle with the brow, and giving to the face a degree of character and energy it might not have taken from
the sweet spirited mouth alone. Add to this a manner
frank and gay, at times a little shy, and always a good deal
wilful, and you have Lucy Fraser as all Hillsboro' know
her. Her companion, Lydia Page, was some two years
younger—a thin, sallow girl, with a bright, saucy face, and
a pair of sparkling black eyes. She was at that transition
period of a girl's life when it is impossible to decide if two
or three years will transform her into a beauty, or leave
her hopelessly plain. David Page had married the elder
sister of Lucy's father, and these two girls were, therefore,
cousins. They were near neighbors, sworn allies, and inseparable companions. Lucy Fraser being without brother
or sister, Heman and Lydia had sustained, as nearly as
possible such relations to her; and the affection which
united them was close and strong.

Mr. Page was not mistaken in his expectation that the
arrival of these new-comers would interfere with his son's
devotion to the task in hand. The girls came down to

where Heman stood awaiting them. They were full of
eager announcements and questions, and all three were
shortly quite absorbed in the discussion of some one of
those innumerable topics of weighty interest with which
young people of their age are usually occupied. The
farmer's ears could catch the continuous murmur of their
pleasant, youthful voices, and now and then a ringing peal
of girlish laughter, as some dry sally of Heman's provoked the merriment of his companions. Presently he left
his work and came towards them.

"Here," cried Lucy, "comes uncle David; and I know,
by his looks, he is going to send us away. O, uncle, what
will you give us to come in there and help you fill the
bags?"

"I will give you two chatterboxes twice as much to go
into the house, and leave this lazy boy to do his work."

"Heman *is* lazy, uncle David; I have often told him so;
and it is a very bad fault."

"I can't help it, Lucy; it's something that runs in the
Page blood, you see."

"If you were not quite so tall, sir," answered his father,
laughing, "I would stir the Page blood in you with a good
birch stick."

"Don't stand on ceremony, father, if you feel disposed
to lay on," retorted the imperturbable Heman; and, satisfied with having got, as he usually did, the last word, he
moved off to his work.

"Now, girls," said Mr. Page, "I want you to go down to
the house and ask Hannah to have supper ready for the
men by half past four. They are about through with
the thrashing, and will want to start for home in good
season."

"And O, uncle, is it really all settled about your going?"

"We'll talk about that by and by. Run along, now, and don't forget your errand before you get to the house."

The girls made a wide circuit around the barns and sheds, and came up through the garden to the house. They loitered all the way, feeling, unconsciously, the influence of all the quiet beauty around them, and lingered, even on the threshold, to look back for a moment ere they sought the duller atmosphere within.

The door by which they entered opened into a square entry, having the sitting-room on the left hand and the kitchen upon the right. The former was a large, square room, of cheerful aspect, and conveying, the instant you entered it, an impression of exquisite neatness. A bright fire, burning in an ample fireplace, diffused a pleasant warmth, tempered, this fine afternoon, by an open window; a serviceable rag carpet, woven in brilliant stripes, covered the floor; the tall brass andirons were polished like mirrors, and the knit cotton "tidies" on the chair-backs were of a snowy whiteness. The furniture was plain and old-fashioned — a birch table, a tall mahogany secretary, curtained behind its glass door with faded green silk, one or two chintz-covered arm-chairs, and a settee with pillows in ornamental (?) patchwork. Yet there was a wonderful air of comfort pervading the apartment, and the genial, warm-hearted atmosphere which always prevailed there made it one of the most attractive in the neighborhood.

At one of the front windows, busy with putting the last stitches to a fine white shirt for her father, sat Hannah Page, the farmer's eldest child. Long the virtual, Hannah had, since the death of her mother, five years before, been

the actual head of her father's family, his thoughtful
companion, and almost the parent of her young brother
and sister.   Hannah was no longer young; indeed, she
was a year or two on the wrong side of thirty — if that
respectable age, strictly speaking, admits of a right or
wrong side.   Her erect, active figure was clad with careful
neatness, her brown hair brushed to a satin smoothness.
The most partial and affectionate of her friends were not
accustomed to call Hannah Page pretty; but her face was
full of character and sense.   Her clear, well-opened eyes
were keen and honest, and had a steadfast, cordial glance,
which at once invited confidence and insured support.
Round the corners of her rather large mouth lurked a
shrewd yet genial smile, and her voice was exceedingly
pleasant, notwithstanding it was a little loud and slightly
imperative.

As I have already said, the wife of Mr. Page had been
the elder sister of Lucy's father.   The father of Mrs. Page,
and the grandfather of all these young people, "Old Captain Fraser," as he was commonly called, had been a
sailor from his boyhood.   When scarcely more than one
and twenty he had married a pretty Hillsboro' girl, and,
yielding to the entreaties of his bride and her family,
bought a handsome farm in her native town, and settled
down, as he then thought, for life.   But the quiet routine
of a Hillsboro' farmer's existence did not suit the restless
energy of his spirit.   He chafed and pined for the freedom
of the sea, and for the old life of enterprise and adventure
which he had abandoned.   At the end of three years he
came to the conclusion that he could no longer endure so
uncongenial a lot; and, settling a brother of his wife's in

his home to look after his family and his interests, he departed for "just one more voyage." But when the one voyage was completed, there seemed equally good reason for another, and then for a dozen more; and so the years came and went, bringing him, apparently, no nearer to the end of his wanderings. Many were the changes, however, which their passage brought to his quiet home among the hills. His daughter grew to womanhood, married, and had children of her own, to be danced upon his knee in his frequent visits to Hillsboro. His son became a tall young man, and took upon himself the control and care of his mother's household; and then he, too, married and brought a young wife to the old home. At length the captain's family grew urgent that he should leave what they had ever regarded as a most unsettled mode of life, and return permanently to them. He put them off from year to year, with now an excuse and now a promise, well knowing he must yield at last, but dreading bitterly the time when age and infirmity should compel him to renounce the career of activity and change he loved so well. About eight years before the time with which we have to do, an accident had hastened what otherwise might have been some time longer deferred. A fractured leg rendered the old man quite helpless for some months; and though at the end of a year he was entirely recovered, and hale and hearty as ever, yet his feelings had undergone a change. He had found life in his son's family much more pleasant than he had dreamed; and so, at last, he settled up his affairs, saw his beloved ship sail under a new captain, and returned to Hillsboro' to — as he expressed it — begin in earnest to be an old man. That this had not proved to him

2

a more difficult undertaking was owing, in a great measure,
to his little granddaughter, Lucy, who, at the time of his
return to Hillsboro', was about nine years old. Sensible
elderly people shook their heads, and declared that Lucy
Fraser was sure to be spoiled; and, indeed, they had the
probabilities on their side. An only child, she had been
petted and indulged from infancy; but when her grandfather became a member of the family, the others seemed
to half resign their claims upon ,her; and thenceforward,
by a sort of tacit understanding, she belonged to the old
man. She was his constant companion, his pet, his play-
thing, and his darling. He forestalled, if possible, all her
wishes, and indulged her most absurd whims. One thing
only he denied her — permission ever to leave him. In
return for her grandfather's half indulgent, half tyrannical
affection, Lucy gave a love which was much of the same
kind. She knew no sacrifice too great to be cheerfully
made for his sake; yet at the same time she coaxed and tor-
mented him into a compliance with her plans, till he declared
that he was a slave to her caprices, and that she ruled him
with a rod of iron. Lucy was now seventeen, and the most
admired girl in Hillsboro'. Handsome and high-spirited,
the only child of one of the richest farmers in the neighborhood, and the undoubted heiress of her grandfather,
whose fortune, for that modest community, was large, cordially liked, though a little envied by all the girls who
were her companions, and admired by all the beaus within
a circuit of a dozen miles — was it any matter of wonder
if Lucy Fraser was a little spoiled, self-willed, and vain?

Hannah looked up from her work, with a pleasant greeting, as the two young girls came in. "Where have you
two been all this long afternoon?" she said.

" O, everywhere," answered Lucy; " down by the brook, and through the hollow, and up among the beeches. It is splendid in the woods to-day; and we have been to all the nice places it will soon be too cold to go to. I believe I am almost tired. What was it, Lydia, that uncle David asked us to tell Hannah ? "

" To have supper ready for the thrashers by half past four. Shall I go and tell Debby ? "

" Yes; but tell her she need not get our supper now. We will have it at the usual time."

Lydia went out, and Lucy, pushing Hannah's work away, sat down on the deep window-seat beside her cousin, and began idly unwinding the spools of cotton, and turning into confusion the other contents of Miss Page's well-ordered work-basket. When she had marked the initials of her name with rows of pins on Hannah's pincushion, and watched a while the neat and rapid fingers of the latter at their work, she broke out, suddenly, —

" Hannah, are you always just so busy? Do you never stop working ? "

" Well, dear, there is usually something to keep me busy; and then I more than half believe in Satan's having always some mischief ready for idle hands."

" Dear me! what a world of mischief he must have for mine!" cried Lucy, looking down at the pretty hands which now lay clasped in her lap.

Hannah smiled. " I wasn't thinking of yours," she said. " Perhaps they do not do as much mischief as some, though they are responsible for enough, in all conscience. The truth is, Lucy, you have always been a kind of a stumbling-block to me."

"I, Hannah? What do you mean?"

"I mean," said Hannah, gravely, "that you are a standing contradiction to all my rules and principles. It is against reason and common sense, I dare say; but sometimes I think there may be uses in the world for which such idle ne'er-do-weels as you are better fitted than ordinary, useful people."

"Of course there are, Hannah. What do you suppose would become of grandpa if I were a steady, industrious girl, always busy with the housework, like Desire Sharpe? He would have nobody to stir him up."

"I think he might live through it if you were a trifle more industrious. Hand me that gusset on the chair beside you; yes, that is it. Now just pick me out some buttons, and I will have this shirt finished in a few minutes. Then the last of father's things will be done."

"And then will he be all ready to start?"

"Yes, he will be ready; but whether he will start or not is another thing."

"But I thought it was all settled that he was to go as soon as the thrashing was done."

"Well, that was the plan. William and Ellen keep writing to know when they can expect him; and last night we had a letter from Robert, promising to meet him in Cincinnati the twenty-ninth."

"Why doesn't he go, then?"

"O, as the time comes near, he hates to leave us alone for all winter. He thinks we shall be lonesome without him, and that Heman is only a boy, not fit to have charge of everything."

"Pshaw! Heman is as fit to have charge of a farm as

half the men; and, if he isn't enough of himself, I'll come down and help him."

"You had better make that offer to your uncle, Lucy; he will feel quite safe then."

"So I shall, Hannah; and you will see that he will think something of it, if you don't. Everybody does not consider me such a baby."

The journey which the cousins were discussing was one which Mr. Page had long had in contemplation, for the purpose of paying a visit to his two elder sons, who were settled in Ohio. It had been arranged that he should leave home as soon as possible after the fall work was done, and spend the whole winter with these children in the West. But as the time drew near, he began, as Hannah said, to hesitate about leaving his family so long alone. He had great confidence in Heman, yet he thought the lad almost too young to be the only manly protector of his sisters; though all the time the farmer knew quite well that there was very little likelihood of any protection being needed by them. Still he felt uneasy, and would decide on nothing, though the preparations for his journey went on.

The day's work was done, the threshers were gone, and silence and darkness had settled over the great closed barns. Inside the farm-house the fire blazed cheerily, the candles were lighted, and the family gathered around the well-spread supper-table. This was always a pleasant meal at the Pages', and Lucy's presence usually made it a merry one. There was a cheerful confusion of young voices and laughter, in the midst of which the father sat smiling and content. Presently Lucy recalled the subject

of her conversation with Hannah, and appealed to her
uncle to know if he were really decided on not going to
Ohio.

"Not exactly decided, Lucy. I hardly know what to do
about leaving Hannah and the children alone, though."

"But, uncle, Heman is almost eighteen, — at least, he
will be eighteen next summer, — and I am sure he can
take care of himself and the girls too. - Besides, there are
father and grandfather close by."

"True they are not far off; but of what use would they
be in the long, stormy nights? It would be pretty dismal,
Lucy — pretty dismal."

"But I mean to come down here and stay with the girls,
uncle. I am sure that that would help matters."

"It would help a little, in more ways than one; for if
you were here I should know your grandfather would be
on hand most of the time. But you could never get his
consent to such a plan."

"O, I shall persuade him. Think, Lydia," she added,
enthusiastically, "how splendid it will be to stay all winter, and go to school together every day, and study our
lessons together in the evenings."

"Great deal of study evenings there would be," remarked Heman, rather disrespectfully; but no one took
any notice of him.

Lydia was not sanguine with regard to her cousin's plan.
"You know, Lucy," she said, "grandpa hardly allows you
out of his sight. When you wanted to go to Windham
this fall to see Mary Elliot, you had to take the time when
he was gone to New York for a week."

"Well, at least I can try what virtue there is in teasing.

Perhaps I can make him say yes, for the sake of getting rid of me. I shall tell him it is so much nearer to the school-house, you know. But you have not told me yet who is to teach the school this winter."

"I heard," said Heman, "that Sam Warren had applied for it again this year."

"Sam Warren!" ejaculated Lydia and Lucy in a breath, and with the same scornful accent.

"I don't believe the deacon means to engage him," continued Heman. "But I don't see why Lucy should object to him," he added, slyly; "Sam was more partial to her last winter than to any scholar he had."

"Now, Heman, don't be a goose."

"But you remember, Lucy, he was up to your house three or four evenings in a week."

"I ought to remember it," pouted the beauty; "I think grandpa and I underwent enough from his visits."

"O, Lucy," cried Lydia, laughing, "do you remember the night you hid in the clothes-press to get out of Sam's way, and had to stay there more than two hours?"

"Does she hide in the clothes-press when Ben Miller comes?" asked Heman, slyly.

"I never knew her to," laughed Lydia; and Lucy's cheek was mantled with a faint, conscious blush, as she rose from the table, declaring that she heard a horse outside, and knew that Jerry had come for her.

CHAPTER II.

A QUIET fortnight crept away. Mr. Page, urged on all
sides, had made his final preparations and departed on his
long-projected journey, leaving the regency of his domestic
kingdom in Hannah's faithful hands. The latter assumed
the new responsibility, as she did everything else, in a tranquil, matter-of-course sort of way, that made little of any
description of burden.

It was Saturday afternoon, and the work of the week
was nearly done. About the large, cheerful kitchen everything was in the most perfect order. The spotless floor;
the high mantel-piece, whereon were ranged the iron can-
dlesticks and snuffers, a shot-pouch, a tobacco-box, and
sundry collections of choice garden seeds; the very row
of chairs set primly against the wall,—proclaimed the tidy
housekeeper. The atmosphere was fragrant with delicious
odors from the Saturday's baking, which had just emerged
from the oven, and was cooling on the dressers. The room
was empty now, and silent but for the contented purring
of a cat beside the stove, and the ticking of the tall wooden
clock behind the door.

Hannah stood in the east door, watching her brother
and sister as they seated themselves in an open wagon,
behind a strong bay horse, preparatory to setting forth on
an expedition, half of fun, half of business, down among the

valley farms. The last arrangements made, and the last injunction given to forget none of the errands, and to be back before dark, Heman turned his horse's head down the descent, leaving the elder sister standing alone in the doorway. Hannah watched them as they wound slowly down the hill and along the valley; and when they were quite out of sight she still remained, gazing far away over the sunny landscape, held, half unconsciously to herself, by its stillness and tranquil beauty. It was a rare day for New England, bordering as it did so closely upon the winter, yet suggesting, with its calm airs and hazy sunshine, the transient splendors of the Indian summer. The gray, leafless forests rimmed the horizon, showing like outline pictures against the pale blue sky. An almost solemn stillness brooded over hill, and wood, and field. Through the slumbrous air the few occasional sounds came mellowed to the ear, filling the mind with vague, unreal images, and suggesting shadowy possibilities, with dim hints and revelations of something beyond our daily common sphere, something which comes to us familiar, but broken and indistinct as the fragments of a dream. On the brown hill-sides and through the wide fields there was no sign of life, save here and there a thin, pale wreath of smoke from some hidden farm-house chimney. At intervals a crow, with long and lazy flight, sailed by, and disappeared in the dim horizon. The distant bark of a dog for a moment broke the stillness, or from far down the valley came the strokes of a woodcutter's axe.

While Hannah stood dreamily enjoying the scene, the charmed silence was broken by the slow reverberation of distant wheels over the frozen ground. Nearer and nearer, now deadened by some intervening swell, now rising louder than before, a long, undulating wave of sound rolled over the sleeping hill-side, broken at last, like spray, into a thousand sharpened echoes. Suddenly the sound ceased, and Hannah, her reverie abruptly ended, looked up, and saw a horse and wagon standing in the road opposite the house. In the vehicle were an elderly man and a young girl, the latter already preparing to alight. Shading her eyes with her hand, Hannah went down to the road-side.

"Good afternoon, grandfather. Aren't you coming in? Let me take your basket, Lucy."

"Not to-day, Hannah," replied the old man, as Lucy sprang lightly out. "Where are the children?"

"They have just gone down the middle road; did you want them?"

"I thought perhaps Lydia might like to ride down to the Centre with me, as it is a fine afternoon."

"Heman has gone to the Centre to get a few things at the store; and Lydia went with him as far as Mr. Perkins's, and was going to walk back."

"Come up into the wagon again, Lucy," said the captain, "and visit Hannah another day. I don't want to ride alone."

"How can I, grandpa, with this old bonnet on?"

"O, if you bring up your old bonnet, I have not another word to say. That is a final argument always. I do hope, Hannah, that you will see to it that Lydia's head is not so stuffed with nonsense and vanity as this child's is."

"Be sure, grandpa, you remember my last vanity — five yards of velvet ribbon, four inches wide: now, please don't forget."

"You see she is incorrigible, Hannah," said the old man, smiling more in pride than rebuke on the saucy girl, as he gathered up his reins and drove away.

Hannah turned towards the house, and Lucy followed her to the kitchen. She threw off her bonnet and shawl, and sat down in the sunshine by the window.

"Take your things into the sitting-room," said her cousin, "and I will be in there in a minute."

"Why not let us stay here, Hannah? I think this is the pleasantest room in the house."

"Well, dear, if you like it, we will stay here, and I will bring down the rug I was braiding. It *does* rather litter the sitting-room carpet."

Left to herself, Lucy turned to the window, and sat looking up the slope into the orchard, where the afternoon sun was falling pleasantly through the gnarled and leafless boughs. There was a thoughtful expression on her bright face quite unusual. Lucy Fraser was seldom thoughtful. Like every impressible girl of seventeen, she indulged at times in absorbed and delicious reverie; but her life had been too entirely one of sensations, she lived too completely in the pleasure of the passing hour, to have learned to think. She was intelligent, and, in a solid, unornamental way, extremely well educated. From her grandfather, too, she had managed to derive a great deal of general information on a variety of subjects, but her knowledge of life, her interests, her sympathies, and her ideas were bounded by the Hillsboro' horizon. Had she been less happy, or less secluded from the world, her active intelligence might have found something limited and unsatisfying in her life. Even as it was, she was sometimes vaguely

conscious of its incompleteness; but the feeling was soon
forgotten in some fresh enjoyment. Perhaps it was a dim
consciousness of this kind which gave to-day the shade of
unusual seriousness to the bright young face; perhaps —
such things are possible — there already rested upon her
the advancing shadow of some new influence which was to
mould her life. When her cousin reëntered the room, she
looked up as one who calls his thoughts back from a great
distance, and said, —

"So uncle David is really gone, Hannah. How you
must miss him!"

"Yes, we miss him a good deal, of course; and it seems
rather lonesome since the hired man and Deborah are
gone, as it leaves only the children and me."

"But I thought you intended to keep the man all winter."

"There will be nothing for him to do, and if I take the
master to board, I don't want two men to wait upon."

"The master, Hannah! Have you promised to board
the schoolmaster?"

"Yes; I found father would feel a great deal easier
about us if he knew there was a man in the house; and on
the whole, when the long winter nights come, I shall feel
better myself not to be alone with the children. So, as the
choice lay between Ezra and the schoolmaster, I took the
master, and told Deacon Sharpe he might bring him."

"I suppose he must come, then; but he will be im-
mensely in the way. I had planned to have such a good
time this winter, just you and I, and Lydia and Heman!"

"Why, Lucy! Have your father and mother really consented to let you stay with us?"

"O, they said yes long ago; the trouble was all with grandpa. But last night he told me, if my heart was really set on staying with you and Lydia, I might. But, the dear old fox! he hedged his consent all round with conditions. I haven't the faintest idea what they were, and there were dozens of them; but I accepted every one, sure he would remember them if I couldn't. It was good of him, Hannah — was it not? for I am sure he will miss me badly; perhaps not so much since grandma is so feeble, for he spends most of his time with her."

"That reminds me to ask, How is grandma to-day?"

"Much as usual. The doctor called this morning. He says she is quite out of danger, and with care will rally and be as well as for several years. But about boarding this man, Hannah — I don't like it at all."

"Perhaps we shall find him very pleasant, Lucy."

"And perhaps he will prove just such a disagreeable oaf as Sam Warren."

"*I* never thought Sam so very disagreeable."

"Then I don't know what you could have been thinking of, Hannah. To be sure he never undertook to be in love with you, and that may make a difference."

"Possibly it may," replied her cousin, laughing. "But they say Sam is dreadfully disappointed at not getting the school again this year; says he hasn't been fairly treated, and runs down the new master at a great rate — thinks we shall have no kind of a school."

"Well, at any rate, all the girls have made up their minds to have a real good time this winter. Mother says I shall soon be too old to go to school, and must improve my time; and that is what I mean to do."

"I am afraid you will be sorry some day, Lucy, that you don't improve your time to more purpose."

"I do, Hannah; I have the best time I possibly can."

"You know that is not what I mean. You don't try to improve your mind as you ought, and you will be sorry for it some day. Mark that. You will not always live at home, but will have to go out into the world, and think and act for yourself."

"I shall take grandpa along for any severe thinking I may have to do. But I should like to know, Hannah Page, how a little mathematics, more or less, is to help me in thinking and acting for myself?"

"You know every one says habits of thought and study strengthen the mind and sober the judgment."

"Strength of mind and sober judgment are just what I don't like. They make people solemn, and conceited, and stupid, and disagreeable, and I hate them."

"But you like Mary Elliot, and she knows more than any girl you ever knew."

"O, yes; but we like Mary because she is so gay and so good; not because she is so very wise."

"But Mary is just as much at home with very polite and educated people as she is with us plain folks."

"I know it, Hannah; but Mary is different from most girls. At Windham she sees a great many grand people, for the Elliots, though they are poor, are among the best families there, and Mary cares about pleasing them. When I was at Mrs. Elliot's this fall, I saw a good many of Mary's friends, and I suppose of course they were very nice; but I enjoyed myself better when we were alone, nobody but Mary, Miles, and their mother."

"I suppose you did not like Mary's friends because they were rational people, and had something sensible to say."

"Possibly; but I know *one* sensible person I do like, even when she scolds me for not having a ray of sense myself. When I have enjoyed myself a little more, Hannah, I mean to turn sober and rational as — as you are. Now tell me, when is the master coming?"

"I expect him to-night. Just come and look at the room I have got ready for him."

Laying down her work, Hannah led the way through the sitting-room and across the front entry to the door of the parlor, which she threw open. The parlor was a large, low-ceiled room, with a handsome, home-made carpet in broad, shaded stripes of brown and green covering the floor. The furniture was old-fashioned, spider-legged mahogany and hair-cloth, bought for Mrs. Page by her father at the time of her marriage. It was in a wonderful state of preservation, and Hannah Page's parlor was regarded as one of the most sumptuous in Hillsboro'. Between the front windows stood a card-table, — never used for play, — on which were displayed a number of books in brilliant bindings, laid in prim little piles of three or four, the family miniatures, and a small basket made of shells. The last contained cards bearing the names of various friends and acquaintances of the family. Some of these were enriched with emblematic devices, such as hearts transfixed with arrows, yoked doves, Cupids, and the like, while others showed choice selections of poetry, testifying to the undying nature of the giver's regard. On the mantel-piece was a pretty collection of shells, corals, and sea-fans, a figure in plaster of the infant Samuel, and some China toys. On

the wall above, framed in resplendent gilt, was the most
cherished work of art in the possession of the family. This
was a landscape done in water-colors, the work of Mrs.
Page when a young lady, and a pupil at the Colchester
Female Seminary. It was supposed to represent a scene
in Scotland, and in it were depicted a castle, a bridge, a
foaming waterfall, distant mountains, rocks, a sunset, trees,
two men, a boat, and a dog. Mrs. Page had all her life
viewed this painting with secret satisfaction; while her
husband and children openly expressed their admiration,
believing it unsurpassed as a work of art, and a faithful
representation of nature in the land of rocks and heather.

As Hannah pushed open the shutter, admitting the afternoon sunshine, the gay carpet was seen to be covered in
the centre with a square of green baize, upon which were
arranged a good-sized table and a large chintz-cushioned
arm-chair.

"Why, Hannah! You are not going to give him the
parlor. You will want it yourself."

"No; we seldom have a fire in it after Thanksgiving;
and I thought if he had this room and the little bedroom
next it, he would be quite on one side, and out of the way
of everything. Then we can have our nice quiet time by
ourselves, as much as if he were not here."

"So we can; and now it is all arranged, I am impatient
to have him come, for I want to see what he is like."

When the cousins returned to the kitchen, the short
afternoon was already wearing to a close. The shadows
were lengthening, and the light on the distant mountains
growing cold. Already the chill gray of evening was
creeping up from the valley. Lucy threw a shawl over

her shoulders, and saying she would walk and meet Lydia, went away down the hill, singing softly to herself. At first her step was quick and her song gay, as she tripped along with her eyes bent on the ground; but insensibly the one grew slower, and the other died upon her lips. Lower and lower into the shadow she descended; deeper and deeper grew the cloud of reverie that inwrapped her. What were the fancies that floated through her brain it would be hard to tell, of such unsubstantial stuff are the dreams of youth; but doubtless they drew their coloring in some degree from the pensive beauty of the hour and scene. She had walked for perhaps half a mile when she met her cousin returning, and her pretty day-dream was abandoned for eager, girlish gossip. Lydia was full of news.

"I have been to the Perkins's, Lucy. Phœbe and Laura have just got home, and they are both going to school this winter."

"I am glad of it."

"Yes; and the Smiley girls, too, and Fan Miller, and Ben."

"Is Ben Miller going?"

"He told Laura so. He says it is his last chance, for he will be twenty-one in the spring. I wonder who that is coming behind us."

The sound of wheels close at hand had caught Lucy's ear also, and turning, she immediately recognized the fat, easy-going horse and comfortable wagon of Deacon Sharpe, the district school agent. Seated in the wagon was the deacon himself, and beside him a slender young man wrapped in a loose overcoat. The glimpse the girls had

3

in passing revealed a pleasant face, lighted by smiling, dark-blue eyes. Lucy had got her wish; she had seen what the new teacher was like. As the wagon passed on, the deacon was saying to his companion, —

"Them two girls will be scholars of yourn, I reckon."

"Indeed! Who are they?"

"Wal, one of 'em is David Page's darter — lives right up here where you are a-goin' to board; and t'other is Squire Robert Fraser's gal. Good many nice folks in this deestrict."

"That must be the master, Lucy," said Lydia, in a whisper. "Does he look as you expected?"

"I don't know; I had not thought much about him."

CHAPTER III.

THE next morning broke fair and sunny, with promise of rivalling in serene beauty its predecessors. But, as the day advanced, a gray shadow dimmed without obscuring the sunshine, and the air assumed a chill, which penetrated almost imperceptibly. As the morning wore on, from various directions, laden with sober, church-going farmers and their families, came numerous wagons, rolling slowly, and with far-resounding wheels, over the frozen ground towards the place of worship. This was the district school-house, a lonely-looking, square, red building, standing some sixty rods down the hill from the home of the Pages. As the vehicles were discharged of their occupants at the door, the horses were led away to the adjoining fences, where, with bridles off, and covered with blankets, they were supplied with hay brought for that purpose under the wagon-seats, and fed quietly thereon, while their owners were feeding on the bread of life within. About the door were gathered in the sunshine little knots of hard-handed, stoop-shouldered men, discussing the weather, the crops, and other topics of common interest; and on the doorsteps, and just within the small entry, a group of the young men and girls of the neighborhood were talking in lively but subdued tones. An occasional irrepressible laugh was quickly smothered in a handkerchief, and accompanied by an apprehensive glance towards the inner door, through which was visible a cluster of matrons seated around the stove. It was still early for the service; but your real country congregation is never late. Its members are afflicted with no fashionable terrors of being too early. It is, on the contrary, the intention, particularly of the younger portion, to be at least half an hour before service time. To this class of worshippers the morning chat and the interval between the services are often the only occasions afforded, for weeks together, for pleasant intercourse and the exercise of social feeling.

Conspicuous among the youthful loiterers was a very pretty girl of eighteen, with a round, good-humored face, dressed with some pretensions to style, and having the air of one who felt herself of consequence in her little set. And, indeed, Miss Laura Perkins, being a beauty and acknowledged belle, had a right to plume herself upon her social consequence. She stood just within the entry, talking with a tall, athletic, sun-burned young fellow, who leaned against the door beside her. Despite the evidences of country breeding, there was something in the appearance of this young man which was very attractive — something at once modest and manly. Ben Miller — once or twice before referred to in this history — was a universal favorite. Good looks, good temper, and a kind of frank gallantry of spirit which he possessed, are traits which find acknowledgment everywhere. On this occasion Miss Laura had brought the whole battery of her charms to bear upon him, and, by her engaging smiles, sought to prevent numerous quick glances up the long hill, down which Lucy Fraser must come on her way to meeting. It was well understood among the young people that Ben Miller admired Lucy more than any girl in Hillsboro'; but of the extent of her regard for him neither he nor they could so well determine. That her father and mother liked him was plain, and it was also plain that Lucy allowed his admiration, and permitted him oftenest to be her escort to the various merrymakings in the neighborhood. But she seemed to enjoy herself just as well when he was absent. She was glad to see him when he came, but she never smiled the less when he went. Sometimes, indeed, she would seem to prefer him, but the next hour would nearly break his heart by her indifference.

Ben had at length become so much interested in Miss Laura's lively chatter, that he failed to observe the chaise of Squire Fraser descending the hill, or to see Lucy, as it came opposite her uncle's, alight and go in, leaving her father and mother to continue on their way without her. He was startled, a moment after, by a low exclamation from his young sister Fanny, who stood near: —

"There is Mrs. Robert Fraser; and, I declare, she has got on a splendid new set of furs."

Ben turned so quickly as to nearly lose his balance, standing as he did on the threshold. His feeling of annoyance at not seeing the bright face he looked for was not lessened by the remark from Sarah Smiley, a tall, red-haired girl, —

"La! Ben Miller, you needn't break your neck. Lucy isn't with 'em."

A subdued titter ran round the circle, and Laura said, with the amiable desire to cover Ben's embarrassment, —

"The boys told me last night that the master had come. Did you see him, Ben?"

"I saw somebody with the deacon."

"That was him," said Sarah Smiley, who, like Mrs. Squeers, was no grammarian. "The deacon told our folks he had been to fetch him over. I wonder if he will come to meeting."

The people were now passing in and taking their places, for the minister, a little, withered, pious-looking old man, had entered and seated himself in the desk. Just behind the preacher, and quite unperceived till they reached the door, came Hannah Page and Lucy, and with them the new teacher. They had had a pleasant walk, judging by their animated faces. As they entered, Lucy bestowed a little smile of recognition on the group of idlers, of whom she had often made one, but, without pausing, proceeded with Hannah into the school-room. Ben Miller's eyes followed them uneasily, and, as he saw the stranger seat himself by Lucy, he experienced the first pang of real jealousy which she had ever caused him.

The house filled rapidly, and, while the preacher read the hymn in a thin, nasal voice, and the choir sang it to the droning accompaniment of a bass-viol, the new teacher had leisure to observe his future pupils, and they, in turn, to survey him.

Ralph Fanshaw, the "new master," was a young man from Colchester, the large county town, some fifteen miles away. Of good family and well connected, his youth had been spent in the enjoyment of some wealth. He had received an expensive education, but in early manhood, just as his college course was closing, he had found himself with his own energies alone to depend on. In this emergency he had turned, as so many of our young men do, to teaching as a means of support while studying a profession. It had been a rather uncongenial life to a somewhat indolent man with quiet tastes; but, persevered in, it had now nearly brought success. In the spring he would be admitted to the bar and to a partnership with Mr. Burke, an old family friend at Colchester, with whom he had been studying. It was with the feeling of satisfaction which we have in a task nearly accomplished that he entered for the last time upon the duties of a teacher; and he experienced a pleasant sense of rest as he floated into the quiet haven that was to shelter him for the winter. The little world of Hillsboro' surveyed him on that Sunday morning, and decided that it should like him; and, indeed, with a rather attractive person, and quiet, refined manners, he seldom failed to please. Contact with the world and jostling with rude natures had not marred a certain gentle urbanity, which was with him as much character as manner, and indicated something of the cultivated home atmosphere in which his youth had been passed.

While the droning voice of the preacher discoursed of heaven and the final rest of the saints, and while the elders listened and nodded, and their juniors listened and exchanged, under cover of the benches, telegraphic signals which in no wise related to what the good man was saying, Lucy sat between Hannah and Fanshaw, and listened even more attentively than usual to the words of the preacher, with now and then, it is possible, a thought of the pleasant, courteous stranger beside her, whom she had met for the first time the evening before. When the service was ended she declined going home with her mother, and, to Ben Miller's inexpressible relief, also declined Hannah's invitation to return with them, preferring a ramble through the brown fields with her young companions. It was a delightful walk, over the wide, frosty hill-side, notwithstanding the pale sunshine and the chill air. Lucy never seemed more gentle and kind, and poor foolish Ben felt himself repaid for weeks of indifference. When the young people returned, Lucy found her cousins already seated, and the service just commencing. One glance sufficed to show her that Fanshaw was not there; and, as she accompanied her father directly home at the close of the meeting, she did not see him again that night.

As for Fanshaw, he passed the afternoon alone in his room, arranging his books, writing, and preparing to be very comfortable for the next three or four months. So employed, the hours slipped away imperceptibly, and dusk came on. Going to the window, he perceived that a great change had befallen the day since he walked to church in the morning. Where all was then bright and sunny lowered now a dark and threatening sky. Over the bleak hills swept a moaning, chilly wind, while now and then fell fine, sharp flakes of snow. The whole landscape looked dreary and desolate in the extreme; and it was with a feeling of relief that he obeyed Hannah's summons to tea, and sought the light and warmth of the sitting-room.

As they lingered round the table, Fanshaw asked, —

"Where is Miss Lucy to-night? Did she not return from church with you?"

"No; she went right home from meeting. She always reads to her grandfather Sunday afternoon. I will say for Lucy, wild as she is, she never forgets her grandfather."

"Is she wild? I should hardly have thought it."

"I am afraid she is. Fine weather is the only thing she ever seems to feel any anxiety about."

"She is an only child, I think you said."

"Yes; and that accounts for a good deal."

"Certainly; the spoiling of only children has come to be a proverb."

"I don't want you to suppose I think Lucy quite spoiled," answered Hannah, jealous for her favorite; "she is a good girl, and capable, too; but everything comes so easy to her that she never applies herself."

"Indolent, perhaps."

"No, O, no, indeed! but so thoughtless! She doesn't seem to care for the things other girls care for. She would rather ride about the country with her grandfather, or follow her father over the farm, — anything sooner than stay quietly in the house and attend to her work or her books, as she ought. I love Lucy myself, almost as well as I do my own sister, and for that very reason I am anxious for her. Life is not all a summer day to be enjoyed."

"My dear Miss Page, you are inclined to look too much at the dismal realities of life. If trials should ever come, I am confident your young cousin will prove equal to them. Indeed, I am by no means certain that the anxious, careful ones are those who meet with most fortitude the shocks of life. These elastic natures bend for the time, but the others break soonest. Will Miss Lucy be a scholar of mine?"

"Yes; and Lucy is a good scholar — better than most girls of her age; though such a perfect child so far as any sense of responsibility goes."

"I hope you are not relying on me to impress her with any such sense of responsibility," answered Fanshaw, laughing.

"I *do* hope you will be able to steady her a little. Any one she takes a fancy to has great influence with her. Mary Elliot, who kept our school last summer, was a great advantage to Lucy for that reason."

"I may not be so fortunate as Miss Elliot. But I am wondering why my young friend Lydia, here, is no more an object of your solicitude."

"Well, for the matter of that, there are several reasons. Instead of being an only child, Lydia is one of five. She hasn't the expectations Lucy has, nor has she been flattered so much. Her bringing up has been altogether different, and she has a steadier head naturally."

"Well done, Hannah Page!" exclaimed Lydia. "That is the first time I ever heard you own my merits."

Fanshaw and Hannah both laughed, and the former, rising from the table, returned to his own room.

He put down his lamp, and, pushing open the shutter, looked out. The snow beat sharply on the window pane, and, far as his eye could penetrate through the gloom, the ground was white. It was winter now in earnest.

CHAPTER IV.

ONE bright winter evening, when Fanshaw had been several weeks domesticated with the Pages, Hannah's little family were gathered around the fire in the comfortable sitting-room. On one side of the hearth Hannah herself, with her knitting-work in her hand, sat slowly rocking in a large arm-chair, and watching the bright coals as they fell. The time was past with her when she could see strange prophetic pictures in the glowing embers; yet, practical and unimaginative as she now seemed, our Hannah had had her romance and her dreams. Opposite her, on the other side of the fire, were Heman and Lydia, the former holding on his extended hands a huge skein of blue yarn, which his sister was slowly winding. At a small table, which was drawn near the centre of the room, sat Lucy Fraser, with an open book in her hand, from which she was reading aloud, her sweet tones falling pleasantly upon the quiet of the room. Near her, Mr. Fanshaw, leaning indolently back in his chair, listened while he contemplated with dreamy, half-shut eyes, the lovely face of his pupil.

The few weeks which had elapsed since Lucy first knew Fanshaw had been outwardly uneventful, yet they had really wrought changes that would be visible for long. He was the first young man of education and culture whom she

had ever known, and for the first time she felt and regretted
her own deficiencies. She was conscious of new and vague
aspirations arising in her soul, and of an interest before un-
felt, not alone in her studies, but in the intellectual pur-
suits and the wider sphere of thought of her new friend.
She had met him at a time in her life which was most
decisive, a period when the higher and better traits of her
mind and character could be easily quickened into activity; or when the waters of a placid and contented, though
most incomplete existence, might as easily flow over them
forever. A slight impetus now, in any direction, might
change the whole after-current of her life. Fanshaw had
from the first been interested in Lucy, and his conversation
with Hannah having led him to study her more closely
than he might have otherwise done, he was not slow in
perceiving the rich promise of her yet unformed character.
Her unusual beauty, too, could not well be without its influence, and her bright, engaging temper, even her pretty
wilfulness and coquetry, attracted him greatly; so that,
with their constant and familiar intercourse, and the absence of all society, he found himself giving a good deal of
his time, and a great many of his thoughts also, to his
charming pupil. He lent her books, and often of an evening he read aloud to the family; but it was always to
Lucy he turned with comment or in admiration of what he
read. He arranged French lessons, which occupied an
hour of almost every evening, and were often prolonged in
pleasant talk, in which he sought to draw out the shy and
reserved mind of the young girl. All this was very charming, but it was just possible that it might be dangerous to
both. To Lucy such companionship was new and most

delightful; and what man of average vanity could be insensible to the delicate flattery of implicit confidence and innocent admiration?

> " 'Comme un vague chant, dont expire
> Le lointain et dernier accord;
> Comme une musique cessée
> Qui n'est plus que dans la pensée,
> Et que l'oreille écoute encore,' "

read Lucy, as she closed the book. "Is it not beautiful, Mr. Fanshaw?"

"Very beautiful; but I was listening, just then, to your accent. It is excellent — much better, indeed, than mine. Pray who has hitherto been your teacher?"

"I never really studied enough to signify," answered Lucy, blushing at his praise. "While Mary Elliot was teaching our school, last summer, I recited a few lessons to her; but it is grandpa who has taught me all I know."

"Ah! does Captain Fraser speak French?"

"Yes; he speaks it beautifully. He has been in France a great deal; indeed, his dearest friend is an old French sea captain. Hannah," she added, "do you remember that man? He came to see grandpa once, years ago."

"Yes; I remember him perfectly. A droll, black, little old man. What was his name, Lucy?"

"It was Lascaux — André Lascaux. He has a granddaughter, Julie, just my age; and, do you know, she sent me, not long ago, a bracelet woven of her hair, — such pretty, black hair, — and the sweetest letter! I want to send her something in return; but I cannot think of anything half pretty enough. Bless me! here it is half past seven o'clock; and I must go home and back to-night."

"Did I not say that if you would wait and read a lesson, I would go with you?" said Fanshaw, rising and gathering up the books.

"You said so; but it is not necessary. I am not at all afraid."

"I presume not; but it is too late to go alone. I will put away these books while you bring your hood and shawl."

It was a clear, starlight night, keen and frosty — one of those nights when the stars twinkle sharply, and the snow treads under foot with a short, crisp sound; when the blood comes tingling to the cheeks, and the first breath of the chill air cuts like a knife. Fanshaw drew his companion's arm closely within his own, and they commenced the long ascent towards Lucy's home, their quick, regular footsteps for some time the only sound that broke the stillness. Their way led for some distance up the long hill towards the west; but when it reached the point where the road began to fall into the valley beyond, they turned directly to the north. Here the road was still ascending, though more gently and gradually than before, and at the end of half a mile they reached the pleasant home of the Frasers. It was a large, handsome, white farm-house, with old-fashioned square roof, and green doors and blinds. In summer, roses and flowering shrubs clustered about the windows, and graceful, plumy elms flung their shadows on the sward in front. The surrounding farm lay on the sunny south-western slope of the hill, and this, with the large orchards clustering in the rear, gave the house a warm and sheltered appearance, while, from its elevated situation, it commanded a view over a magnificent reach of country.

Both Lucy and Fanshaw had found their long walk extremely pleasant. Their conversation had fallen, as it frequently did now, into a strain exceedingly confidential and unreserved. A mingling of half-sportive sentiment and half-serious jest, with now and then touches of deeper and more earnest feeling, it was just the kind of talk an inexperienced girl, like Lucy, finds so fascinating, but which, of all idle indulgences, is among the most dangerous.

As they drew near the house, Lucy's favorite Newfoundland, Carlo, came bounding down the path, barking joyously, and thrusting his great muzzle into the little hand his mistress held out to him. At the doorstep Lucy dropped her companion's arm, and, springing forward, opened the door, exclaiming, gayly, —

> "'On Heaven and on thy lady call,
> And enter our enchanted hall!'"

Fanshaw had lent her "The Lady of the Lake" the week before. He answered in the same strain, —

> "'My hope, my trust, my heaven must be,
> My gentle guide, in following thee.'"

The sitting-room into which Lucy led the way was a large apartment, softly carpeted, richly curtained, full of warmth and light. All the appointments and surroundings of Lucy's home were far handsomer and more expensive than any of her neighbors possessed, though the habits and manners of the family were as simple and unpretending as those of the humblest. Captain Fraser and his son were the only occupants of the room. The former stood squarely on the hearth-rug, with his back to the fire, and his hands clasped under his coat-skirts, talking to his son, who, in an arm-chair beside the fire, was slowly and very carefully paring an apple. The captain was a tall and powerfully-built old man, as erect as at twenty-five, with a massive head, and bold, square-cut features, bronzed with the suns of many years. His eyes were keen and brilliant, their undimmed fire almost belying the story of age told by his iron-gray hair and beard. His manner was *brusque*, but kindly; and it had the coolness and self-possession of one who had dealt much with the great, busy world, and known men in masses and under a variety of aspects. He had a hearty, ringing voice, imperative and decided, like his granddaughter Hannah's, and a laugh it was impossible not to join with.

Squire Robert Fraser resembled his father in that he was tall and large; but he had a fair, florid face, with serious, blue eyes, a head slightly bald, and a grave, deliberate manner, more primitive than the old man's, and with a flavor of the hills in it. There was a mild air of consequence about him, natural to the most prominent man, on the score of wealth and intelligence, in Hillsboro'. He held many offices of trust in his town and county, was a justice of the peace, and had represented his district for several years in the state legislature.

The old man greeted Fanshaw's entrance with a friendly nod, and, while his son rose and cordially welcomed the schoolmaster, turned to Lucy with a kind of growl.

"Well, young lady," he said; "don't you think you have been some time getting to see your father and me?"

"Now, grandpa," answered Lucy, untying her hood and drawing close to his side, "you must be very glad to see me, and very civil; for I have taken a great deal of pains to come and see you to-night."

"A vast deal of pains, to be sure! Here it is eight o'clock, and you were to have been here by seven."

"But I had to read a French lesson."

"A French lesson? Ah, well! that reminds me. But come now, child, and see your grandmother." And, with his arm over Lucy's shoulder, he drew her away out of the room.

In a cheerful and luxurious apartment above stairs they found old Mrs. Fraser, a thin, shadowy-looking woman, sitting, propped with cushions, in an arm-chair by the fire. She turned her pale face towards them as they entered, and greeted Lucy with a sweet smile, and a look of pleasure brightening in her soft eyes. The captain took the arm-chair that always stood beside his wife's; Lucy seated herself upon his knee, and was soon busy recounting, for her grandmother's entertainment, all the events of the day. Mrs. Robert Fraser, who had been occupied about the room in arrangements for the comfort of the invalid, smoothed her hair, laid aside her large linen apron, and hurried out to welcome the schoolmaster, ever an honored guest in rural districts.

"Do you like the new teacher, Lucy?" asked the old lady.

"O, yes; we all like him," answered her grandchild,

4

rather hastily; "and I am learning very fast. You can't think how hard I study, grandma."

"I hope you do, dear; school time is short at best. Dear me! it seems such a little time since you were a baby in my arms; and now you are as old as your aunt Lydia was when she was married."

"Do you want me to get married, grandma, just because I am old enough?"

"I don't know who would be simpleton enough to take you," growled her grandfather.

"Ah!" exclaimed Lucy, turning round and stroking his gray mustache with her pretty hand; "I am sure, sir, my chance is as good as yours was; and yet you found a very intelligent woman who was willing to take you. And she has endured her lot with you all these years without complaining."

The old man's voice changed as he replied, "My child, you will be blessed indeed if your choice shall bring you half the happiness mine has given me."

Lucy raised the thin, wrinkled hand of the invalid tenderly to her lips, and silence fell for a few minutes on the little group. Presently the captain opened a drawer in the table near him, and took out a small package, which he put into Lucy's hand. With eager curiosity she removed the wrapper, when there appeared a pretty jewel-case of purple morocco.

"O, grandpa! what is it — something for me?"

"Look and see," he answered.

Lucy opened the case, and revealed, reposing on its satin cushion, a beautiful comb and ear-rings of richly-wrought Etruscan gold. On the inside of the cover of the casket were engraved the words, "Lucy to Julie."

"Ah, how lovely!" cried Lucy. "The very thing I should have chosen to send to her, only I never should have thought of it."

Quickly arraying herself in the ornaments, she ran to the glass to see the effect. But, after a very brief survey, she said, shaking her head gravely, —

"No; I do not think they amount to much in my red-brown locks; but with her smooth, black hair, they will be charming. Pray, how are we ever to send them, grandpa?"

"I will see to that. What you have to do is to brush up your French, and write Mademoiselle Julie a letter to go along with your gift."

Lucy promised, and just then her mother came in to say that it was time to go. Bidding the old people an affectionate good night, she followed to the sitting-room, where Fanshaw still sat talking with the master of the house. Both gentlemen looked up as the mother and daughter entered, Squire Fraser's face beaming with an expression of affectionate pride, while Fanshaw's calm blue eyes looked involuntary admiration. Mrs. Fraser was a pretty, delicate woman, not so tall or so striking as her daughter, but with a peculiarly soft and gentle grace. As for Lucy, she looked unusually lovely this evening. There was a soft, happy fire in her eyes, and a color like a damask rose in her cheek — a color that may have deepened slightly as her glance met that of the schoolmaster.

They walked home at a quick pace. They had gone some distance when Fanshaw perceived, for the first time, that the little hand which lay on his arm was uncovered. "Why, Lucy, where is your glove?" he exclaimed, taking her hand in his.

"I could not find it when we came out, and would not stop to look for it."

"How cold it is!" he continued, drawing off his own glove and taking the numb little fingers in his warm ones. "You shall wear my gloves now."

"No; O, no!" said Lucy, attempting to withdraw her hand; "I can wrap it in my shawl."

"And slip on this icy hill for your pains. You shall do no such thing; you shall wear this glove."

"I will not, Mr. Fanshaw; indeed, I will have my own way sometimes," she answered, folding her arms in her shawl, and springing a few steps from his side.

They walked a few yards in silence; then Fanshaw asked, in a low voice, and without approaching her, "Lucy, will you come back and take this glove, and my arm?"

"No, Mr. Fanshaw," in a tone of gay defiance.

"I will not wear it, if you will not."

"If you choose to freeze your fingers, it is nothing to me."

"Lucy!"

"Well, Mr. Fanshaw."

"Don't you wish to oblige me?"

"I wish to please myself more."

Fanshaw saw that it was of no use; so, crossing to her side, without further preface or ceremony, he took the hand which she had for a moment withdrawn from her shawl, put on the glove, then drew the hand through his arm, still holding it firmly, and saying, as he did so, "Can you really refuse me such a trifle, Lucy?"

Lucy did not reply, but she ceased to resist; indeed, for the first time in her life she found a pleasure in yielding.

But not another word was spoken during the remainder of their walk.

They found Hannah sitting by the fire, where they had left her; but "the children" were gone to bed, the tables and chairs were set primly back against the wall, and her knitting-work lay folded upon her lap.

"Laura Perkins and Sarah Smiley have been here since you went out," she said, addressing Lucy.

"To see me?"

"Yes; Dan Wilcox was with them, and they want you all to go down to Zenas Brown's to-morrow night to a surprise party. Some of the girls are going down to spend the afternoon, so that Statira and the boys may be sure to be at home."

"Of course I shall go. Mr. Fanshaw, do you hear? Hannah has an invitation for us to a surprise party."

"'Us'? Does the invitation include me?"

"Certainly," said Hannah. "They said you would be expected, of course."

"In that case I shall regard the plan very favorably. It seems to meet your cordial approbation, Miss Lucy," he said, smiling down at her, where she sat on a low stool by the hearth, her shawl and furs lying in a little heap by her side. She looked up shyly, and a faint blush deepened on her cheek as her eye met his. He had lighted his bed-room candle, and, as Lucy made no reply, he remarked that it was not fair to keep Miss Page up any longer, and bade the cousins good night.

When he was gone, Hannah carefully covered the fire, bolted the doors, and made various preparations for the night, while Lucy, drawing out her comb, let fall her lovely

hair about her shoulders, and sat idly passing her fingers
over its shining length, her eyes fixed dreamily on the dull
glow of the buried coals. She seemed quite unmindful of
the lateness of the hour, till Hannah lighted her candle,
and, laying a hand gently on her head, said, —

"Come, dear; it is very late."

Lucy picked up her things, kissed her cousin, and went
thoughtfully up stairs to the room where Lydia lay asleep.
As she was folding her shawl to put it away, Fanshaw's
glove fell out of its folds upon the floor. She stooped
quickly to pick it up, while a bright color flushed her
cheek. She held the glove irresolutely for a moment; then,
glancing at the bed where her cousin lay, she cautiously
opened a drawer of the bureau, laid the glove carefully in,
and, turning the key, drew it from the lock, and put it in
her pocket. She then quickly made her preparations for
bed, and in a few minutes was fast asleep beside the unconscious Lydia.

CHAPTER V.

It cannot be denied that on the next day, the older of Fanshaw's scholars — those, so to speak, who had made their entrance into society — were more occupied with the party in prospect than with grammars and blackboard exercises. Large gatherings, such as this promised to be, are not very frequent in country districts, and create a corresponding excitement when they do occur. The hours of school dragged somewhat wearily, and many pairs of wistful eyes followed the sun in its slow transit over the hacked and worm-eaten benches, till it faded, flickered, and finally vanished behind the near summits of Edgehill. But at length the signal was given, and the seats cleared as if by magic, leaving Fanshaw sitting alone in the wide, still room so lately filled with the eager, repressed life of childhood and youth. He closed his desk, locked the door, and walked musingly home in the quick-falling winter twilight, humming to himself an old tune, and thinking of a great many things, but, most of all, of charming Lucy Fraser. Not sentimentally, nor very ardently, but kindly, and a little softly. The kind of life he was leading was making it dangerously easy for the young man to substitute, insensibly, a tender regard for the friendly interest he had from the first felt in his lovely pupil. He was, to an extent, idle and unoccupied; and idleness and propinquity are the secret of half the love affairs in this world. She was beautiful, and he was impressible; and at this time, a day, a week, or an hour might turn the wavering balance, and decide the future for both.

An hour later Fanshaw came into the sitting-room, and found Lucy ready dressed for the evening. She wore a dress of dark-blue merino, of the shade favored by the Empress Maria Louisa. A frill of narrow lace edged the neck, closing low at the throat with a small brooch. A gold chain was wound several times around her neck, and from it depended a rich cross of the same material — a gift from her grandfather, and a favorite ornament. Her hair, drawn smoothly back, leaving uncovered the delicate temples and small ears, was gathered into a graceful mass of braids and curls at the back of the head. She looked very lovely, Fanshaw thought, as he carefully folded her gay Scotch plaid about her shoulders, while Hannah held ready a large, old-fashioned cape and little muff of glossy gray fur, which had belonged to Mrs. Page, and had been brought home, on some long-ago voyage, by the captain, from St. Petersburg.

The night was clear and starry, much milder than the preceding, and their horse strong and fleet. They were alone, Heman and Lydia having gone forward half an hour before. Their road lay for a mile down the eastern slope of the hill, then, turning south, wound through the valley, where the silence was broken into numberless echoes by the clear ringing sleigh-bells. In summer a pretty brook wound, with many a coquettish whirl and eddy, through this valley, crossing and recrossing the highway at frequent intervals. Now thick snow and ice lay over it, and the little wooden bridges gave hollow responses to the horse's hoofs. ` Here had Lucy, from her childhood, gathered the earliest spring flowers; here, in sheltered nooks, before the snows were gone, bloomed the Mayflower, best beloved of all New England children; here flamed, in sultry August days, the tall scarlet cardinals, and, when the autumn came, the fiery golden-rod and bright purple asters glowed along the brook-side. Emerging into more open country, they passed frequent farm-houses, whose lights shone out cheerfully over the snowy fields; and now and then a furious cur from some cottage doorstep darted out, and pursued them with far-resounding bark.

At length they approached the scene of the evening's festivities. It was a large, yellow farm-house, with an old-fashioned, gambrel roof, and four tall, gaunt Lombardy poplars standing, like grim sentinels, in front. Lights gleamed from numerous windows, and the collection of sleighs in the back yard proved that the invitations to the party had not been slighted.

Lucy and Fanshaw were met at the door by Laura Perkins and Statira Brown. Lucy followed the latter up stairs, leaving Fanshaw to be presented to the company by Laura; for, in gatherings of this description, the self-constituted committee of arrangements act, in a great measure, the part of hosts. Laura conducted the stranger to the sitting-room, where were assembled the older members of the family, she taking it for granted that the schoolmaster would prefer the society of the graver persons present.

Zenas Brown — a red-faced, good-natured looking man — rose, as they entered, to welcome his guest and introduce him to the group round the fireplace. On one side the chimney was old Mrs. Brown, the farmer's mother, a little, withered woman, wrinkled and dry, and beside her her daughter Sally, a spinster, apparently but few years less ancient, who, bolt upright in her chair, sat knitting, with a grimness and industry which seemed, as plain as words, to say, "*I* was never young and gay, and, in my opinion, it is the height of folly for those who are to enjoy themselves." One or two quiet, middle-aged neighbors, and the farmer's wife, were also of the group.

The last of the circle "introduced" was a young man of about eight and twenty. He sat with his elbow resting on his knee, and in his hand the long iron poker, with which he had been emphasizing a recent remark on the blazing forestick. He wore a suit of snuff-colored cloth, which told a plain story of the itinerant tailoress who, with goose and shears, circulates annually through country neighborhoods. His hands were large and red, and his hair had also a glowing hue. His sharp features and small gray eyes expressed some intelligence and more conceit. This person was no other than Sam Warren, of whom mention has been made as a rejected applicant for the school in which Fanshaw was engaged. The host, as he mentioned their names, made some remark, intended to be facetious, to the effect that he "had heard it said that two of a trade could never agree."

"I am sure, Mr. Brown," returned Fanshaw, with great suavity, "that we shall prove honorable exceptions to that rule."

Never having heard of Sam Warren, and knowing no reason why they should disagree, nor suspecting that the

immense dignity assumed by his new acquaintance was
intended for his benefit, Fanshaw offered his hand with an
air at once pleasant and cordial. It was accepted with a
lofty condescension, at which he could with difficulty repress a smile. So petty and trivial was Sam's nature, so
active the feeling of small envy and spite with which he
regarded the man who had succeeded where he had failed,
that Fanshaw's smiling demeanor seemed to him the inso-
lent assurance of success, and he hated him accordingly,
his dislike manifesting itself for the present in scornful
silence.

After the weather and the state of the roads had been
fully discussed, old Mrs. Brown, who had been attentively
studying the schoolmaster over her spectacles, said, —

"They say you come from Colchester way. Was your
father John Fanshaw?"

"He was. Did you know him?"

"No; I never see him but once — at the time he was
married. So you are John's son. Then your mother must
have been a Brandon."

"My mother was Amelia Brandon: you knew her, perhaps."

"Wal, not a great deal. She was a long time after my
day. But I always lived neighbor to her folks till I was
married. I remember your grandfather well, and you
look a wonderful sight like him. I remember, too, when
your mother was married. I was home then on a visit,
and it must ha' been nigh upon thirty year ago. She was
called the handsomest bride that ever went out of West-
field."

"My mother is still a handsome woman."

"The Brandons was all good-lookin'. Wal I mind how they used to look of a Sunday — five tall, handsome sons following their mother. She was a widow years and years. Ralph — that was your grandfather — he married a Foster, and lived on the old place. Who has it now?"

"It has shared the fate of many old homesteads: it is in the hands of strangers. My uncle was obliged to sell, and he offered it in turn to every member of the family. Some, like my mother, could not afford to buy it, and those who could found it too remote to be a desirable home; so the dear old acres went out of the family."

"Wal," returned Mrs. Brown, after a short pause, "there's some folks don't seem to care a button for the place where they've lived all their lives. Here's my son, Zenas, now; he gets a fancy every now and then to go out West. I tell him to go, if he wants to; but he will never get me and Sally to go with him. I have lived here goin' on sixty year. I have buried my husband and five children from this house: and here I mean to end my days."

"Miss Brown," began Sam Warren, breaking silence for the first time, turning in his chair, and crossing one leg over the other, — "Miss Brown, what you say is very natural, you being a woman and advanced in years; but for a young man who means to make a figure in the world, this staying right by the old place is no way to do it. Besides, it fosters aristocracy and family pride. The more I see of the world, the more I am convinced that the aristocracy of this country has got to give way before the march of intellect among the common people they have despised so long."

This remark was so palpably levelled at Fanshaw,

that the latter, though scarcely able to repress a smile, replied, —

"I was not aware that we had in this country any class so privileged as to be objectionable as an aristocracy. A few families there may be, who, with a slight show of justice, pride themselves on their descent; and for the rest, a dozen years of wealth make an aristocrat nowadays — a very harmless and inoffensive kind of aristocracy, and one that must be very comfortable, too."

"I can't say I think any aristocracy harmless," retorted Sam, with some asperity. "I believe in all men being equal; and no man has a right to look down on another. And I foresee," he continued, with an oratorical wave of his hand, "if the common people don't make an effort to vindicate their equality, they will be trodden under foot by an idle and haughty aristocracy, equal in tyranny to any in the old world."

Fanshaw suspected that Sam had got started on a favorite topic; and, not wishing to be subjected to an oration, he drew a little girl who was playing about the room to his side, and began talking with her. But his intended diversion failed of its end. Sam was fairly launched upon a theme with which he was accustomed to hold admiring audiences, and it was impossible to stop him so long as a listener remained.

Meantime the spacious kitchen presented a much more animated spectacle. The room was filled with youthful figures, and the din of gay voices rivalled the ancient confusion of Babel. Later there was to be dancing; but Mike Hennessey, the Irish fiddler, would not arrive till after eight, and something must be done in the interval. A game of

blind-man's-buff had been proposed, and Statira Brown
had produced a crimson silk handkerchief; but eyes to be
blindfolded were less easily found.

"You may tie it on my eyes if you'll promise me one
thing," called out Ben Miller from a corner.

"I promise whatever you please, Ben. Come here and
have it on."

"You must hear what I want first."

"Well, let us know."

"I want it fairly understood that I may kiss the first
girl I catch," answered Ben, with a smile that showed his
white teeth.

"We promise! we promise!" laughed a dozen gay voices.
"He is welcome to kiss us if he can catch us."

Ben came forward, and, shutting his bright eyes, sub-
mitted them to the handkerchief. He was in high spirits,
for, though Lucy had declined his escort to the party, and
had appeared attended by Fanshaw,—whom Ben regarded
with some fear as a possible rival, — still, since their appearance the latter had not once sought her side, and Ben himself had secured the promise of her hand for the first dance.
This world had seemed a rather dismal place to Ben that
evening as he drove his young sister Fanny to Mr. Brown's.
But Lucy had come, and smiled, and given him her soft
little hand, and said she was glad to see him, and at once
a warm glow diffused itself over everything. He became
reconciled to the world and all mankind, including the
schoolmaster, and assured himself, for the hundredth time,
that it was the most natural thing in life for Fanshaw to
be attentive to Lucy, living in the same house with her,
and there was no reason why he should make himself miserable on that account.

Now, indeed, the fun grew fast and furious. Ben was light of foot, and, blinded as he was, they found it difficult to elude his nimble pursuit. There appeared to be some witchery in the game, however, for, though he seemed constantly on the point of success, he as constantly failed. It is possible that, if one had watched him narrowly, there might have been detected a method in his failure. Lucy all the time had flitted round the outside of the room, carefully avoiding the inner circle of more eager players, her gay laugh mingling occasionally with the general confusion. She had just made up her mind to slip off and join some of the older girls in the parlor, when a door against which she was leaning opened. It created a little stir among those near, forcing Lucy into the middle of the room. For a moment she forgot the game, and at that moment Ben approached her with outstretched hands. She saw her danger, and attempted to escape by passing under his arms; but, with a quickness which argued little for the efficiency of the blindfolding, Ben caught her with his left arm as she was passing under his right. "Ah! Lucy Fraser, I have you!" he exclaimed, drawing his arm more firmly around her waist, while with his disengaged hand he tried to untie the handkerchief.

Alas for poor Ben! While he labored to undo the knot Statira had so carefully tied, Lucy remained for a second so quiet that he unconsciously loosened his hold slightly, when, quick as thought, she darted from his restraining arm, and was away across the room, sheltering herself behind the brawny figure of Ed Brown.

Though rather crestfallen, Ben received the raillery of his companions with great good-nature. He laughed with the rest, as he threw down the handkerchief, exclaiming, "Come, Lucy, if I lost a first-rate chance, I certainly caught you; and you must have your eyes blinded now."

Lucy declared her readiness to take her turn at the game. Her pursuit was a little more timid than Ben's had been, though not at all wanting in spirit. She was not very successful, and her cheeks were growing quite red in the excitement, when Fanshaw and Mrs. Brown came in from the entry. At one side of the kitchen was a door leading to a store-room adjoining. The floor of the store-room was considerably below the level of the kitchen, and the two rooms were connected by a steep, though short, flight of steps. The door, which swung *out* from the kitchen, had stood ajar all the evening. Lucy was beginning to grow a little tired, and to wish the game ended, when one of the girls, coming in front of her, teasingly caught for a second her extended hands, then, dropping them, sprang lightly to one side. Lucy darted confidently forward, her hands touched the door of the store-room, there was a startled exclamation from Statira and her mother, echoed by a sharp cry and a fall, and Lucy disappeared from sight.

There was an instant's pause before the company realized what had happened; but in that instant Fanshaw, whose eyes had been on Lucy at the moment, darted forward, and, before Mrs. Brown or her daughter reached the spot, he was kneeling by her side, supporting her almost senseless form in his arms. Half stunned, blind, and bewildered, she lay motionless, her head resting on Fanshaw's breast, while Statira, with trembling fingers, sought to remove the handkerchief from her eyes. Her young companions crowded round, some offering assistance and others in mute dismay. Ben Miller, with a face as white as Lucy's, brought water, in which Statira dipped her fingers and bathed the poor girl's forehead and temples. Lucy opened her eyes and looked round with a surprised, uncertain air, not fairly conscious of what had happened. Encountering the anxious gaze of Fanshaw, recollection seemed to dawn slowly upon her mind, for a faint color stole back to her cheeks, and, closing her eyes, she turned her head slightly away.

"Lucy, are you hurt?" he asked, in a tone of tender solicitude that made Ben Miller shut his teeth very hard.

Pushing back the damp hair from her forehead, Lucy attempted to rise from her recumbent posture. "No," she said, "I believe I am not hurt — only frightened. Did I fall?"

"Yes, you slipped right off the stairs," answered Statira, "and frightened us half to death. We thought you must be killed. Are you sure it didn't hurt you?"

"No, I am not hurt," repeated Lucy, rising, with Fanshaw's assistance, a little unsteadily, to her feet. "I will go up to the parlor, if you please, and sit down."

"Let me carry you," exclaimed Fanshaw and Ben Miller, in a breath.

"No, indeed! O, no. I can walk."

"You had better let one of 'em carry you, dear; you may be a little light-headed when you come to walk," suggested Mrs. Brown, anxiously.

"You had better not attempt walking, Lucy," urged Fanshaw.

"Then Ed Brown shall carry me. Won't you, Ed?"

she declared, with a sudden return to wilfulness, which went to show that she was not very seriously injured.

Ed Brown came forward smiling, secretly pleased at the little beauty's preference. He took her in his strong arms as lightly as if she had been a child; and she, shutting her eyes, drooped her head languidly on his big shoulder, while he carried her up the stairs to the parlor, and laid her gently on the sofa they had prepared for her. Fanshaw and Ben Miller both followed, the former amused at the way in which Lucy had avoided giving preference to either of them, and Ben gratified that, since he had not been allowed to be of service, the schoolmaster was no more fortunate than himself.

After so inopportune a check, the tide of enjoyment did not at once resume its flow; and the accident might have proved a serious damper to the gayety of the evening, had not Mike Hennessey happily arrived at this juncture. At the first note of his violin sounding through the rooms, Lucy raised her head and looked round. Most of the company had returned to the kitchen. Ben Miller was sitting near the front of her sofa, idly turning over a book. Statira and another young girl stood by the fire, talking with Fanshaw. At the sound of the music Statira came to the sofa.

"Well, Lucy," she said, "what do you think about dancing?"

"I shan't try just yet. Perhaps in an hour I may feel more like it. But, dear Statira, I cannot consent to your staying with me. Mr. Fanshaw, don't you dance?"

"I used to, and, if Miss Brown is willing to be my partner, think perhaps I could again.

He soon after left the room with the two girls, and Ben Miller alone now remained. Ben came up to Lucy's side.

"You must go, too," she said, smiling. "You have lost your first partner; but you will not mind that, I dare say."

"I thought, at one time, I had lost more than a dance. O, Lucy!" he began, in a husky voice, bending towards her, and taking her hand.

"Don't, Ben, don't!" she interrupted, quickly withdrawing it. "There, go and find another partner; and, if you are good, perhaps I will dance with you by and by."

Ben would have demurred at so summary a dismissal; but Mrs. Brown came in to mend the fire and see that Lucy wanted for nothing; so his opportunity was lost.

Left to herself, Lucy lay a long time with closed eyes, the strains of Mike's violin and the measured steps of the dancers beating unheeded in her ears. Though not sleeping, she was but vaguely conscious of what was passing around her. Indeed, since her accident, since the moment when she opened her eyes to meet the tender gaze of Fanshaw fixed upon her, and felt herself supported in his arms, everything in her mind had been dim and misty. In the confusion of images and impressions that floated through her brain, she saw and felt nothing distinctly; but she lay in a state of dreamy and delicious languor, conscious only of a pervading sense of tranquil but ineffable happiness, the source of which she never sought to find. The time passed quite unremarked. The members of the family, Heman and Lydia, came now and then to look at her, and went away unnoticed. Ben Miller looked in, thought her sleeping, and went softly out. After a time, Fanshaw, who had been dancing with great spirit and

energy, came to the side of her sofa, and stood looking
down at her still face. Its exquisite loveliness had never
so struck him before. He had always thought her beautiful; but to-night there was an added charm — something
about the lips and on the fair brow which he was unable
to read or define. It puzzled him; and he fell into a
thoughtful study of the face before him. While he gazed,
Lucy opened her eyes, and looked up.

"Can you forgive me for waking you?" he said. "I
think I must have disturbed a beautiful dream."

"I was not dreaming. What made you think so?"

"You had a look which seemed to belong to dreams.
But are you quite recovered, Lucy?" he added, taking her
hand, which drooped idly beside the sofa. "Poor child!
your hand trembles like a leaf. I fear you are suffering
more than you will admit."

"Indeed, no, Mr. Fanshaw; I am very well now; and,
if my hand trembles, it is only from the fright."

"I must try and believe you; but I trust, Lucy, you will
never give us ten minutes of such cruel anxiety again."

Lucy looked away for a minute, and then said, while a
faint little smile flickered round the corners of her lips,
"Are you sure you suffered so very deeply?"

"How can I convince you?"

"I don't care to be convinced."

"Lucy, I think you are recovering."

She laughed softly. There was a little pause, and then
he asked, —

"Shall I take you home to Hannah now? I think her
care will be better for you than anything else to-night."

"Yes, I am willing to go, and soon, if you please."

"We will go at once; and I will find Mrs. Brown, and tell her of your wishes."

Mrs. Brown warmly protested against Lucy's leaving. Ed should take her up in the morning; and it was much better for her to stay all night. Lucy mildly persisted; so her wraps were brought, and the horse led to the door. In the entry she found Heman and Ben Miller.

"Don't stay late, Heman," she said. "Good night, Ben," giving him her hand. "Remember, my promise holds good for another time. I am sorry not to keep it to-night."

Fanshaw and Ed Brown wrapped the furs warmly around her; the former took his seat by her side, and, with a comprehensive "good night," they drove away. The clear, cold air somewhat revived Lucy; still, their homeward drive was rather silent. The surprise party might seem to have proved a failure to her; but she did not regard it so. On the contrary, her sense of quiet enjoyment, as they drove along, exchanging only now and then a few low words, was keen and full. She exacted a promise from Fanshaw that he would not mention her accident to Hannah that night, as it would only make her needlessly anxious.

CHAPTER VI.

On reaching home they found that a visitor had arrived in their absence. As they entered the sitting-room, a young lady rose from beside the fire, where she sat talking with Hannah, and turned towards the door. With an eager cry of pleasure, Lucy sprang forward.

"Mary! dear Mary Elliot!" she exclaimed, warmly embracing the stranger.

There was a confusion of welcomes and explanations, eager questions and only half answers, during which Fanshaw was entirely forgotten. Naturally he occupied the time with observing the new-comer, of whom he had heard so much. He saw a small, slight girl, with a manner which struck him even then as being remarkably high bred. She was at least five years older than Lucy, and that young lady's whole lifetime older in experience and knowledge of the world. Her face was not strictly handsome; but, with its delicate, clear-cut features, brilliant dark eyes, and pale olive complexion, showing no trace of red except in the lips, it was certainly an attractive one. It was a face to which the smile came quick and sparkling, and yet one on which it was impossible to look without seeing that its owner had known grave and serious cares; and the charming sweetness of her smile could not wholly veil a certain half-defiant pride which flashed at times through every speaking feature. For there was in this girl, behind the acquired patience which she had won out of the conflict of life, a certain fiery and vehement discontent — an un-uttered, yet never silenced, protest against the adverse circumstances which walled her in.

After a time Hannah found an opportunity to introduce Fanshaw to Miss Elliot. She met him with a frank and graceful greeting, alluded, with a smile, to his successorship to her own old field of labor, and then turned again to Lucy, as if he had passed quite out of her mind.

"Yes, Lucy, I had nearly convinced myself that this visit to Hillsboro' must be given up, when Miles came home to stay a few weeks, and so obviated the difficulty about leaving our mother alone. Then last night Mr. Spencer came in, and insisted that he should regard it as a favor to be allowed to go several miles out of his way, on a cold winter evening, to bring me here; and, as I wished very much to think he spoke the truth, I believed him, and here I am. And now, had you a nice party? and were there numbers of young people there whom I know?"

"Yes, Mary, it was a pleasant party. All the girls were there; and we left Heman and Lydia dancing as if their lives depended on it."

"Now I look at you, Lucy, I think you must have danced yourself tired. You look positively pale. Is it so, Mr. Fanshaw? Has she danced every set for the evening?"

"On the contrary, I think she has not danced at all."

"Not danced at all!" exclaimed Hannah. "Are you sick, Lucy?"

"O, no. I was rather tired when I went away; and my head aches a little."

"You do look pale, as Mary says. I think you had better go right to bed. Mary is going to stay a good while, and you will have plenty of time for long talks, if you don't sit up for one to-night."

Mary began to gather up her things, and presently moved with Hannah to the other side of the room. Lucy remained sitting by the fire, her head resting a little languidly upon her hand. Fanshaw lighted his candle, and, bending over her chair, asked, in a low voice, —

"Are you really doing quite right in not telling Hannah of your fall? I fear you are suffering now."

"O, no: my head aches a little, but it will be better in the morning; and there is no need to frighten her."

"As you please; but I shall be very anxious. Good night."

His fingers touched hers lightly for a moment; and, bidding Hannah and Miss Elliot also good night, he left the room.

When the girls reached the chamber which Hannah had prepared for them, they loitered slowly over their preparations for bed, talking, as girls love to do, upon half a hundred things. Even after Lucy had dropped the extinguisher over the candle, they still lingered beside the warm stove. At length Mary said, —

"So that Mr. Fanshaw down stairs wields the rod of empire in my place. Do you like him?"

A week before, Lucy had anticipated seeing Mary, and telling her all about her new friend; but now a sudden reserve possessed her, and she answered, quietly, —

"Yes; we all like him very much indeed."

"Does it always take him so long to say good night as it did just now?"

Lucy laughed — a little, light laugh, whose carelessness was well assumed.

"I must tell you about that, Mary. I fell and hurt myself rather badly at Mrs. Brown's to-night; and I made him promise not to tell Hannah. But you all talked about my looking pale, and that nonsense; and I suppose he thought I was nearly dead, for he tried to persuade me to tell her, and have something done."

"O! was that all?"

"This headache of mine is certainly enough," returned Lucy, in a languid tone.

"Poor little head! I never dreamed it could ache," said Mary, caressingly stroking Lucy's long hair.

"Why should not my head ache as well as other people's?"

"It must, I suppose; yet I never associate you with any of the common ills of life; they do not belong to you in the least. But come, we are disobeying the good Hannah in sitting here so long."

The morning was well advanced when the two girls came down stairs; and they were still loitering over a late breakfast when Captain Fraser entered. He greeted Mary — of whom he was very fond — with almost boisterous delight, and presently carried off both the girls to spend the day with him. There was something in the atmosphere of Lucy's home which was especially grateful and pleasant to Mary. Her own home surroundings had a character of scant, faded, threadbare gentility, which, even aside from any sense of discomfort or inconvenience, was a perpetual offence to her. Contrasted with the genial, large-hearted hospitality of the Frasers, the prodi-

gal, almost sumptuous, comfort, and the happy, affectionate content of which everything was so eloquent, her own
seemed even more pinched, barren, and unattractive. For
the girl had a taste for luxury, and a love of elegance and
beauty, which craved gratification, though they found
little. Mary had early been left an orphan; and at an
age which, if not childhood, certainly is not womanhood,
had been obliged to turn her face resolutely from all
which in youth promises and allures, to become the support of others. Her father — a clergyman in the formal,
old-fashioned village of Windham, where she still lived —
had, in early life, married, against the wishes, indeed,
against the positive commands, of the young lady's father,
the daughter of a very rich man. Mr. Dwight had never
forgiven his daughter — had never seen her since her marriage; and Mrs. Elliot was fully aware that he had made
his will, and that she and her children were entirely left
out of its provisions. This knowledge had troubled her
little during her husband's lifetime; but when he suddenly died, leaving her with two children, and nothing but
a small life assurance, her energy and her courage alike
failed her. Now the mother and daughter virtually
changed places. Delicate in health and broken in spirit,
Mrs. Elliot came to rely wholly on the stronger, braver
spirit of her child; and Mary became the protector while
she should still have been the protected. At an age when
her young friends had no weightier cares than concerned
a becoming spring bonnet, or gloves of the proper shade,
Mary was, unaided, supporting her mother and educating
a delicate younger brother — unaided, for, though Mrs.
Elliot had two sisters, neither was able to be of much as-

sistance. One, Mrs. Alston, was herself in somewhat strait-
ened circumstances, and, with three daughters of her own
to educate, was living abroad. Miss Dwight, who lived
at home, and was constantly under the stern eye of her
father, dared make no movement to befriend the sister
whom she really loved and pitied, and would gladly
have assisted. Of the happiness which flows from an ap-
proving conscience, and the sense of duties well performed,
formed, Mary, of course, had much; but of the sweet,
confident reliance of the child upon the parent, of the
thousand nameless enjoyments which life offers to careless
youth, she knew nothing, save as she saw them in the lives
of others. Keenly, even passionately, alive to the beauty
and joy of existence, she saw her best years passing away
in an unequal contest with poverty. With all its draw-
backs, Mary's position was not, however, without some
advantages. In the quiet, fussy old town of her birth.
there was a good deal of agreeable and cultivated society,
in which she was always warmly welcomed, and had many
friends. A certain brilliancy of manner, a gay and graceful exterior, which covered at all times the wearing care
and anxiety of her life, and a great share of social tact
made her society, even with her manifold occupations, a
great deal sought in Windham.

It was about four in the afternoon when the girls returned. Lucy lingered on the doorstep to talk with Ben
Miller, who was just coming up the hill; and Mary went
in to Hannah, whom she found sewing in the sitting-
room.

"Well, Mary," questioned Hannah, " does it look natural
up at uncle Robert's?"

"O, yes; everything is just as I left it, except, indeed, your grandmother. I am sorry to see her looking so ill."

"Didn't Lucy come back with you?"

"Yes; I left her on the doorstep talking with Ben Miller. By the way, does Ben still hold his old fancy for her?"

"I believe so."

"And how is it with Lucy? If I remember rightly, we used often to be puzzled last summer to make her out."

"I am puzzled now, sometimes. Still, I don't think there is much room for doubt. I know she likes him, and her father and mother set everything by Ben. He *is* a right good fellow, very steady for his age, and worth some property — not near so much as Lucy will have, but enough to give a young man a good start in life."

"I do not believe the fact that Ben has property, or that her friends desire the match, will decide Lucy in his favor."

"No, perhaps not; but all these things have their influence. Uncle Robert and aunt Susan would feel dreadfully to have Lucy settle far away from them. For my part, I should be right glad, in the course of a year or two, to see Lucy and Ben married, and have little doubt but I shall. Lucy loves to tease Ben, and make him think she doesn't care more for him than for a dozen others; but you know, as well as I, that she will always *do* a little different from what she *feels*."

"In that, Hannah, she is like the rest of us. I believe we have the reputation of looking one way and thinking another. I don't know what would become of our sex but for that privilege."

"I can't say, Mary, that I consider it a privilege. For

my part, I like to have people act just as they feel. It
saves a great deal of fuss, and often a great deal of unhappiness."

"In that case we should lose all the delightful uncertainty,
which, in novels at least, makes half the charm of these
affairs. I foresee that we are to remain in that uncertainty,
for I doubt if thumb-screws would extort anything from
Lucy which she did not choose to tell."

"No; with all her talkativeness she is as close-mouthed
as any other Fraser about what she thinks her own affairs.
But, dear me! it is almost five this minute, and I must go
right about supper."

Hannah and Mary had both left the room when Lucy
came in and stood by the window, looking musingly out.
She had just parted from Ben Miller, who, though his
anxiety had been measurably allayed by the report of Heman and Lydia in the morning, could not be quite satisfied
till he had heard from Lucy's own lips of her entire recovery. Ben's heart was in his throat as she turned her
bright face towards him, and made room for him on the
doorstep beside her. Lucy must have been very much
pre-occupied not to observe the earnestness of Ben's demeanor, or to see the soft fire in his eyes. Quite unconsciously she stood, with eyes fixed upon the far-off purple
horizon, chatting in a lively way of the events of the previous evening; but when she turned, and for the first time
met his gaze, it troubled her. She returned it for an instant, a pained look gathering in her eyes. A moment
after, she dropped them quietly, and went on talking as
before.

Lucy had long known that Ben admired her, perhaps

liked her better than any of the girls; but at that moment she read for the first time all that was in the simple,
manly heart of her companion. She felt a choking sensation in her throat, and in a few minutes contrived to end
the interview. As she stood now, looking absently out into
the twilight, her heart was ill at ease. With all her ca-
price and girlish love of power, she yet shrank from giving
pain; and she knew that the feeling which she now for
the first time recognized in Ben could be productive of
nothing else. Bitterly she reproached herself for her
blindness and heedlessness; and she resolved that the fault
should not be hers if Ben further deceived himself. O, she
had been so wrong! She felt sure that she did not love
Ben; and, at the thought, far other eyes than his rose to
her memory, and Ben and his troubles slowly faded from
her mind, a crowd of pleasanter fancies floating through
her brain.

Fanshaw, returning from school, passed the window, and,
seeing her, looked up with a smile and a bow.

"Ah, truant," he said, coming in a moment after, "how
do you excuse yourself for being absent all day?"

"I had not thought to invent an excuse," she answered,
gayly. "And O, Mr. Fanshaw, I haven't a bit of a lesson
for to-night. What will you say to me?"

"I must forgive you this time, I suppose. But listen,
Lucy; if it happens again, I shall declare war against Miss
Elliot."

"Against Mary! Why?"

"It is her fault; she demands too much of your time.
I cannot patiently see our pleasant lessons broken up.
How long does Miss Elliot stay?"

" Five or six weeks, perhaps."

" O, Lucy, not so long as that!"

"Indeed, sir, and why not? She is my friend."

" Ah, well! one must submit; but we had such a cosy and pleasant time with only Hannah and the children! It was entirely to my taste; and I do not care to see a foreign element added to our society."

" But you will like Mary, I know. You must like her."

" If you say so, I will try."

Mary's voice from the stair-head summoned Lucy, and Fanshaw holding open the door, she ran lightly up to her friend.

CHAPTER VII.

The slight ripple which Miss Elliot's arrival caused in
the tranquil current of life at the Pages' quickly subsided,
and the stream flowed as before. Mary glided readily and
at once into its quiet course. Her overtasked energies
found the rest for which they longed. Worn and weary
with months of teaching, the peace and repose of her present life were inexpressibly refreshing. Happy to be again
with friends she loved, finding an unexpected pleasure in
Fanshaw's acquaintance, and with every hour regaining
some portion of her wasted strength, her days went swiftly by.

These were golden days to Lucy, too, embracing in
their round so much of the joy of existence — family ties,
friendship, love. In the warmth of this last and but half
acknowledged presence graces hitherto unseen were
blooming in her. Admiring friends said Lucy Fraser grew
prettier every day; and to Ben Miller's adoring eyes she
seemed more nearly allied to the angels than ever before.
Around her breathed an atmosphere of pure enjoyment;
and under some new and subtile influence her nature was
slowly and silently unfolding, as, leaf by leaf, the graceful,
dark-green sheath of the hyacinth uncloses, revealing at
last the perfect spike of fragrant flowers.

One quiet afternoon, when Mary had been a couple of

weeks at Hillsboro', the two girls sat in the chamber which they occupied together, busy with some sewing. The sun was sinking slowly. Now he rested his glowing disk on the hills of Edgehill, burnishing with gold their snowy summits, and pouring a flood of yellow down their rugged sides, marked with many a ravine and chasm. Mary dropped her work, threw open the window, and leaned out to inhale the mild winter air.

"Put down your work, Lucy," said she, "and come to the window."

Lucy obeyed the call, and stood with her arm round her friend's waist.

"How lovely it is!" said Mary. "See, far away on those hill-sides, what exquisite lights! and those shadows, revealing the most trifling undulations as distinctly as we see each other's faces! And there, miles away to the south, is a house we cannot see for the trees, but its windows are all ablaze like a watch-fire. Ah! now the sun is sinking, and the flame in the window grows crimson; and now, fainter and fainter, it is fast dying out. Now look where the sun has set; how the sky shades through burning orange and purest amber into rose-purple and pale-green!"

Lucy stood silent, her heart beating quickly as she gazed on the evening's gorgeous show. There were few who brought to the beautiful in nature so quick an eye or so loving a heart. She inhaled beauty as the air she breathed, and with just as little heed of the source of her pleasure. Her childish eyes had early been familiar with the noble scenery of Hillsboro', and her little feet with its wide forests and hill-sides; but, in all her wanderings, the happy child had never asked why her heart was so light, any more than why the sun shone. As she grew older it was the same. The world was lovely — life was a long delight. Of late she was aware of a new element in her enjoyment, when pleasure rose almost to pain.

"What are you thinking of?" asked Mary, noticing her rapt and speaking face.

"I was thinking how beautiful it all is to-night — how lovely Hillsboro' always is. I should be so sorry to go far away for any length of time! I cannot understand how people can leave pleasant homes, and go wandering off for years. It would make me wretched."

"Of course it would, my dear Contentment; and take my advice, and refuse every man who would take you more than five and twenty miles from home; or, better still, never leave home at all."

"Do you really advise me so?"

"Ah, well! I don't know. One thing is certain, however: there is no chance of your following such advice, if I give it."

"Perhaps I may; who knows?"

"Not if somebody I know can prevent it. Look in my eyes, Lucy," she added, taking the beautiful face in both her hands, and looking into the clear depths of the violet eyes. Lucy returned her gaze steadily for a moment, and then closed her eyes and turned away, a slight blush staining her cheek.

"Ah! you are not fair, Lucy! I talk my heart out to you; but no sooner do I catch a little glimpse of yours, than it is withdrawn."

"What nonsense you talk, Mary! One would suppose

I had some great secret. There! Hannah is calling us to supper; come!"

Tea was over, and the family were gathered in the sitting-room. A round, cherry-wood work-stand was drawn to a warm corner beside the fire, and on either side of it sat Captain Fraser and Mary Elliot, absorbed in the former's favorite game of piquet. The fire-light flickered over them, giving a deeper shade of bronze to the old man's massive features, as, with his eyes fixed on the cards, and one hand thoughtfully stroking his heavy beard, he contemplated the chances of the game. Mary, in a dress of brilliant hues, her black hair arranged in shining, satiny bands, sat leaning back in her chair, regarding her opponent with an air of triumphant satisfaction. The warfare at piquet had become a thing of almost daily recurrence between these two, for the captain spent a part of every day with his grandchildren, and Mary's idle hours were often given to his entertainment. It was seldom that her skill was equal to beating him; but she had now won several games, and was in a fair way of winning another; so she enjoyed her victory the more from its rarity. Lucy, on the other side of the fire, was bending over her desk, working hard at a difficult French exercise. Fanshaw sat by Hannah, half leaning on the arm of her rocking-chair, talking to her occasionally, and watching the others, his gaze resting longest, perhaps, on Mary's eloquent face.

There was silence for a few minutes, broken at last by Captain Fraser exclaiming, as he swept up the cards, —

"I give it up, Mary. You have had revenge enough for one night. Lucy, how much longer do you mean to pore over that lesson?"

"Only a few minutes, grandpa."

"You will spoil your eyes with all this studying."

Lucy went on with her lesson, and the conversation among the others became general. When the exercise was finished, Lucy folded her papers, shut up her desk, and went round and stood behind her grandfather's chair. They were talking about the significance of names.

"Names mean a great deal to me," said Mary. "Many have a distinct personality, quite independent of any association with persons who have borne them. Anne is always tall, and fair, and cold. Margaret is stately."

"What does Lucy suggest?" asked the owner of that sweet name, resting her chin on the top of her grandfather's head, and looking down at Mary.

"It suggests the torment of my life," growled the old man.

"Now, grandpa, I shall have to choke you a little for that," she answered, tightening her clasping arms about his neck. "But tell me, Mary; what does my name suggest?"

"Lucy — Lucy — why, a 'russet gown and apron blue,' to be sure."

"Or,

'A violet by a mossy stone,
    Half hidden from the eye;
A modest star, when only one
    Is shining in the sky,'"

prompted Fanshaw, glancing with a smile at Mary.

"Where did you get your name, Lucy?" asked the latter. "Who gave it you?"

"My mother, I suppose, in honor of some great aunt, or cousin ; I never asked."

"No," said the captain; "your mother had nothing to do with it. I named you myself, and for my first love."

"Why, grandfather Fraser! what do you mean? Grandma's name is Alice," exclaimed Lucy, with perfect seriousness.

"That is very true, and so is what I tell you. When I was sixteen, I fell desperately in love with Lucy Reide, aged twenty-three, and daughter of my old captain of that name. I thought the sun would never shine again, because she laughed at me when I told her of my love. It nearly broke my heart—indeed, I don't think I have quite got over it to this day; and I named you Lucy in the hope that you would resemble her; but you don't."

"She is inclined to be equally destructive, sir," observed Fanshaw.

"Grandpa, I am astonished that you ever cared for any one but grandma."

"My dear child, I was crossed in love eight several times after that, before I married your grandmother. It runs in the blood of the Frasers; so, look out, young lady!"

The others laughed, but Lucy was perfectly serious. Just then Jerry, Squire Fraser's "hired man," who had been to the "Centre," came in with letters and papers.

"Wal, cap'n, most ready to go?" he asked, as he took the chair Heman offered him.

"I will go directly, Jerry," said the captain, who was breaking the seal of a letter. As he tore off the envelope, Lucy caught his hand to see the post-mark.

"M-a-r—a little nearer, grandpa; I can't see distinctly — M - a - r — Marseilles. From whom is it, I wonder?"

"I can tell better when you allow me to read it."

He opened the letter, and Lucy, with the privileged freedom of long habit, leaned on his shoulder and read from the page with him. She was accustomed to read his letters, for she usually answered them all, the old man insisting that one of his fingers was getting stiff.

"What is it all about, grandpa?"

"Look here, little simpleton; cannot you turn that into English, with all your French lessons?"

"But it is such a crabbed hand! Please turn it over, so I can see the name — André — André Lascaux; and he is your friend, ever very devoted. Ah! it is from the dear, funny little captain, the grandfather of Julie, to whom I sent the comb and the ear-rings. Does he say she has received them?"

"Why, no, child; that could hardly be expected, as it is little more than a fortnight since they went. But he talks of the pleasant home he has with his children at Marseilles, and urges me to visit him. What do you say, Lucy? shall we go?"

"*I* go to France, grandpa? Why, I would not be hired, as Heman says, to cross the Atlantic."

"O, you silly goose!" exclaimed Mary. "I will go with you, Captain Fraser, and you will not have to hire me, either."

"Ah, Mary! I am afraid I am too old to go boxing about the world any more. They make such a baby of me that I doubt if anything would drive me from my chimney-corner now."

"I shall never let you go away again, grandpa. You belong to me now, and I cannot spare you; neither can I go roaming off with you."

"Mr. Fanshaw," said Mary, "have you ever seen so amusing a grandchild as this? She seems to think Captain Fraser was made for her exclusive benefit, and claims him over the heads of all other pretenders."

"It must be pleasant to be so claimed, Miss Elliot. I dare say younger men might be found not unwilling to bear it."

Lucy pouted a little, and her grandfather pinched her cheek as he rose, saying, "The young men must content themselves as best they can. Lucy promised me, years ago, to live an old maid for my sake; and I expect her to keep her word."

"And I will, grandpa."

"Very demurely spoken. Now, bring me my overcoat; there — that is right — now turn up the collar. Good night, dear. Good night, children, all; that may include Mary and Mr. Fanshaw. Now, Jerry, I am ready;" and, nodding kindly to those remaining, and followed to the door by Lucy and all the Pages, the old man took his leave.

"How happy she is!" said Mary, softly, when she and Fanshaw were alone. "Is it not refreshing to have known so bright and unshadowed a nature?"

"It is, indeed. The recollection of her will be to me like some of those exquisite May-days our memories of childhood hold. Excuse me, but a friendship between you two is a constant enigma to me."

"Indeed! and why so?"

"I can hardly tell; and yet Lucy is so different — as you said just now, so unshadowed — so completely a child. I would not be afraid to assert that you have no other friend who in the least resembles her."

"You are right; nor have I another so dear. There are many from whose society I enjoy more, but none whom I love so well. How that old man worships her! And her father, too! It will be a sorry day for them, when they give her up to a younger claimant."

"You think it down on the cards that Ben is to have her?"

"I suppose so, of course. The family all regard it much the same as settled."

"And you would be quite satisfied to see her given to our young friend?"

"Unhesitatingly, yes. I cordially like and respect Ben; and he would offer her the sphere in life she is best fitted by nature to fill."

"And that is — ?"

"The sphere her mother has filled before her — to be the wife of an honest, upright man, her wishes bounded by the pleasant round of duties and interests falling to her share as wife, mother, friend, and neighbor. Ben is a man who will grow in consequence in the community in which he lives; and with such a wife as Lucy at his fireside, I think he will be one to be envied. Do not you?"

"He will, indeed; but I must dissent from one thing you have said. You describe the sphere which Lucy is best fitted by *nature* to fill. I should have said, best fitted by *education*."

"I hardly see the force of your distinction."

"Lucy is, by nature, Ben's superior, and only made his equal by the accidents of circumstance. Had she been, in some respects, differently educated, she might have graced almost any sphere. As it is, I dare say she has never dreamed of any other than the one she will probably fill."

Here Lucy, coming back into the room, interrupted the conversation of the two friends, who were so confidently discussing and deciding upon her destiny.

CHAPTER VIII.

ONE cold, pale afternoon in January, Mary and Lucy were alone together in their chamber. Mary, with her hair unbound and streaming over the pillow, was lying upon the bed, her fingers between the closed leaves of a book, marking the place where the deepening twilight had arrested her reading. Her eyes were fixed absently on the distant hills, from which the cold sunset light was slowly fading. There was a droop to her usually firm lips, and an unwonted look of sadness in her dark eyes. Mary had been a month at Hillsboro', and all the days had slid so rapidly by, each bringing its certainty of quiet enjoyment, that she was almost surprised to know how much of the time allotted for her visit was already passed; and she contemplated, with an aversion even greater than she had expected, the approaching period of her departure. Rare, in her hard-working life, were these intervals of leisure; and she knew, when this one ended, it would be followed by months of toil and weariness to heart and brain. The prospect had never been less attractive; or, rather, it had never seemed more dreary and discouraging. Of course this was very weak and foolish. If she had been in the least heroic, or strong-minded, she would have "gloried in the conflict of life," and despised the joys which are said to enervate the soul. But, then, she wasn't heroic. She was a good girl, and she had done her duty bravely, setting her lips hard when she came to the disagreeable places, and carefully covering up whatever in her lot was most hard and grinding, in order that people need not pester her with compassion; but as for finding pleasure in her duty, she did not: she hated it. Her whole nature craved happiness, rest, and shelter, as the plant craves sunshine and fresh air; and, contemplating the bare, laborious years that lay before her, so empty of all that more fortunate lives contain, her heart would fail her sometimes, as it did to-night. She wished she had never come to Hillsboro'—never known the last four calm and happy weeks. Of what use were they? Had she staid with her mother, her thoughts would not have been turned from what was inevitable; but here nothing reminded her of labor or poverty; and every day was making the return more difficult.

But, after all, she had been very happy here; and was it not folly to waste in vain regrets the hours of enjoyment which might remain? She would enjoy while she could, and not dim present pleasure with the thought that it was passing. She roused herself, and turned to Lucy, who was bending forward to catch the last faint daylight.

"Dear Lucy," she said, "pray put away that work. You are ruining your eyes."

"Yes, Mary; it is this moment done; and isn't it pretty?" the other exclaimed, holding up her work—a frock of her own, round the low neck and short sleeves of which she had been setting a border of swan's down.

"It is charming, my dear, and so will you be when arrayed in it."

"I am glad you like it. But, Mary, do come and look out. I am afraid it looks like a storm for to-morrow."

The pale light of the setting sun, whose cold gleam had but partially enlivened the gray curtain of cloud, was slowly dying out. The day had been intensely cold, and now a piercing east wind was blowing, affording some foundation for Lucy's fears regarding the weather for to-morrow. The evening of the next day had been appointed for the ~~wedding~~ of a young friend of Lucy's, who lived at the ~~Corners, and~~ a large company were invited to be present at the ceremony. Lucy had looked forward to this occasion with a good deal of pleasure, which, of late, however, had been somewhat damped by reason of a long-given promise to Ben Miller that he should be her escort. But, despite this slight drawback, she anticipated the event with natural eagerness; and she now laid down her work, and hurried from the room to consult Hannah's greater wisdom on the subject of the weather.

As Mary looked out at the chill and forbidding sky, she felt some disposition to return to her sombre and desponding mood; but, resolute to throw it off, she moved about the room, putting various little things in their places, smoothed her hair, arranged her already perfectly-ordered drawers, — finding a relief in the most trifling occupation, — and finally went down to supper.

At the table she found only Hannah, the children, and Lucy. The master, Hannah explained, had gone to Deacon Sharpe's to tea.

"Yes; I remember he said at dinner he should go. I wonder if he enjoys these tea-drinkings as much as I did last summer. My scholars always knew as well as myself when I was invited out to tea. They knew instantly the two or three trifling additions to my toilet, which indicated one of these festive occasions in prospect. And then the children of the family where I was to go would wait till school was done, and trudge beside me, with their dinner baskets, along the quiet roads, now scampering after a squirrel on the fence, now picking a wild flower that grew beside the road, and bringing it shyly to me. Ah, how pleasant it all was, Hannah!"

"And how well you seem to remember Mary!"

"Remember it, my dear friend? It was the happiest summer of my life. Why should I not remember it? But, to come back to the present, Hannah, what is your opinion of the weather for to-morrow?"

"I guess it will be fair. It has looked cloudy for three or four nights, and cleared away again in the morning."

"I thought it threatened a storm. I hope you are the truer prophet, for Lucy here will cry her eyes out if she loses the chance to transfix somebody, with all the finery she has been at such pains to get ready. I assure you, Hannah, the effect of that blue silk and swans-down is quite irresistible. I half wish I were a man myself, that I might, with a show of propriety, go down on my knees — such is the effect of that gown."

"I wish you were a man, Mary."

"Why, my dear?"

"Why, then I should have an admirer just to my taste."

"I supposed you had that already, Lucy." ·

It was towards nine o'clock when Fanshaw returned. Mary sat sewing alone in the sitting-room. She looked up as he came in, but gravely, and without her usual lively greeting. He saw the change at once, and, as he drew off his overcoat, observed her face narrowly.

"No ill news from home, I hope, Miss Elliot," he said, motioning towards an open letter lying on the table.

"O, no; a very lively note from my brother, in which the only unwelcome allusion is to my some time leaving Hillsboro'. H———— had a pleasant evening?"

"Extremely so; and I have here something for you which I begged of Mrs. Sharpe;" and he opened a paper parcel, containing some sprigs of geranium and half a dozen large clove pinks, which had blossomed in a box beside the good woman's kitchen window.

Mary's old, charming smile flashed over her face at sight of the flowers.

"Beautiful!" she exclaimed, as she took them from his hand. "Thank you for the flowers, Mr. Fanshaw, but more for the pleasant memories they suggest. Ah, what lovely summer days in old gardens they bring back to me, with blossoming roses and white, sailing clouds! The eyes of old friends, too, look at me from among these blossoms," she added, gently, as she put them, half unconsciously, to her lips. In a moment she laid them on the table, and began gathering up her sewing materials.

Fanshaw took up the flowers, looked at them for a moment, and then touched them to his own lips, looking steadily at Mary the while. She met his glance for a second, and then turned away, angry at feeling herself growing crimson under his prolonged and earnest gaze. She gathered up her things somewhat hastily, took her flowers in silence, and left the room with a nervous haste, quite at variance with her usual self-possession.

CHAPTER IX.

THE next morning the sky wore a pall of dull, unbroken gray, through which the blue eyes scanning it so
closely could see no token of fine weather. The air was
intensely cold, with a strong north-east wind, not violent,
but steady, and telling plainly of the vast waste of ice and
snow over which it blew. Lucy took heart from Hannah's
assurance that it was too cold to snow, and finished her
preparations for the evening; but her hopes suffered an
eclipse when her grandfather came in towards noon, and
gave it as his opinion that they were in for something
more than a squall this time. She had such unbounded
faith in the captain's prognostics that her spirits sank to
zero; and when she followed him to the door, and saw
for herself that fine flakes of snow were already beginning
to fall in the angry way which often begins a storm, she
gave up all hope, and could have cried very easily just
then.

For an hour or two the increase in the storm was hardly
perceptible; but by three o'clock it had made some head-
way. The snow fell faster, and began to sift in sudden
showers from the eaves of sheds and out-houses. By
dark the wind had risen to a gale, and went howling
through the orchard, and round the buildings, and sweeping the snow in blinding clouds far down the hill-sides

and through the lonely valley. About four o'clock a sleigh drove to the door, and Ben Miller came in.

"Why, Ben! you don't think of going to the Centre to-night?" cried Lucy, as she came to meet him.

"No, indeed; but I had to get my horse out to carry Mrs. Perkins home, — she has been spending the day at our house, — so I thought I would just come in for a minute. Good evening, Miss Elliot."

"Good evening, Ben. A wild night — is it not?"

"It is dreadful: we haven't had anything like it this winter."

"Sit down, Ben," said Lucy. "Lydia, please take Heman's coat off that chair, and turn it round for Ben."

"No, Lucy, I can't stop; I shan't get home to-night if I do. The snow is drifting into the road very fast, and it will be hard keeping the track when the daylight is gone."

"Well," said Lucy, a little plaintively, "I am sorry it happens so, for I had set my heart on going; and I don't suppose they will postpone the wedding on our account — do you?"

"I am afraid they will not."

"Perhaps, Lucy," suggested Lydia, "some one else will have a wedding that you can go to; or you could get married yourself, you know."

"O, one's own wedding would be so serious, it would not be half so nice to go to as some one's else."

Ben did stay some time, for all he had declared that he could not sit down. He found Lucy so gentle and engaging that it was hard to tear himself away. He went at last, however; and Lucy watched him from the window as he drove away, his horse just discernible in the fast-

7

gathering darkness. When she could no longer hear the sound of his sleigh-bells, she brought a low stool and sat down by the fire, feeling very lonely and dispirited. Tea was over, and all the family were quiet and busy. Mary was lying on the settee across the room, and Fanshaw was occupied in his own apartment. Hannah, as usual, sat knitting, and her younger cousins, with a basket of butternuts on the stand between them, were busy reading. The crackling of the fire and the slow ticking of the tall clock were for some time the only sounds that broke the stillness of the room.

Without, the storm raged furiously. Lucy listened for a time to its tumult, and at last exclaimed, —

"Mary, isn't this awful? What a night for Emma's wedding!"

"It is a dreadful storm, but I rather enjoy it. These thick walls defy the weather."

"But think of any one on the road to-night!"

"No one in his senses would be abroad on such a night. It is just the time for a ghost story. I wish we had one."

"And I am glad we have not; that would be too much," answered Lucy, rising and walking about the room. She was restless and uneasy, and at length she went into the entry, unlatched the door, and looked out. The door flung open with a loud bang, and a cloud of snow swept in.

"O, Lucy, what did you open that door for?" cried Hannah. "Run, Heman, and help her shut it; she can never do it alone."

Heman ran to Lucy's aid; and she, as she shook the snow from her hair and dress, again exclaimed, "Isn't it frightful, Heman? Ben would never get home in the world."

"Nonsense! He is at home safe enough long before this. It is a rough night, though; and I'm glad I ain't out in it." He came back and shut up his book, and stood tossing into the fire the shells of the butternuts, watching them as they snapped and sparkled in the glowing coals. "I believe I'll go to bed," he said, stretching himself lazily. "This wind will put me to sleep in no time."

"Put you to sleep, indeed! I do believe it will drive me crazy."

"Come here, Lucy," said Hannah; "bring your cricket and sit down by me." And, as Heman lighted his candle and went off to bed, Lucy brought her stool, and, sitting down, laid her head in her cousin's lap. Hannah stroked the young head with a gentle, motherly hand for a few minutes, and then went on with her knitting.

They sat silent for a short time, and presently the door opened, and Fanshaw entered. He had a book in his hand, and said, as he came to the fire, —

"I have something here which I should like to read, if Miss Elliot is not too sleepy, and Miss Lucy too disappointed to listen."

"I wish you would do something for these girls, Mr. Fanshaw," said Hannah. "I believe the storm has given Lucy the fidgets — something new for her."

"Yes, do read, Mr. Fanshaw," said Lucy; and Mary's smiling eyes looked a similar request.

The charm of the pages soon failed to fix Lucy's attention; even the voice of the reader no longer filled her ear.

Between her and the glowing imagery of the author would come the blinding snow-clouds; and she listened with strained hearing to the voice of the storm. Fragments of wild stories and legends crowded to her memory; long-forgotten tales of shipwreck, violence, and murder — of ghost, banshee, and demon. The wind, shrieking through the leafless orchard boughs, sounded like the cry of some despairing victim, or, wailing in the great chimney seemed

" The fatal banshee's boding scream."

When the snow swept in clouds across the window-pane, she seemed to hear trailing garments, and in the adjoining rooms and passages light, ghostly footsteps. To her excited imagination, voices, sighs, and shrieks of demoniac laughter filled the night. As the evening wore on, her nervousness rose to a pitch almost unendurable; and when Fanshaw laid down his book, she sprang up and began walking about the room. Her cheeks were flushed, her eyes bright, and her whole manner betokened extreme excitement and restlessness.

Mary was the first to observe her unusual demeanor, and, rising, she went to her and took both her hands firmly in her own.

"Lucy, what spirit has possession of you to-night? I never saw you so excited and uneasy."

"I don't know, Mary. I think I must feel as our Dolly does when she says she feels as if some one were walking over her grave. It seems to me as if *something* were going to happen. I wish I were at home. I am afraid some one is sick there."

"What nonsense you are talking, child! Your grandfather was here at noon, and every one was well then. What puts such an idea into your head?"

"Nothing, perhaps; only this is just the time when something is sure to happen, when no doctor could reach them. Just listen to the storm, Mary. O, I wish grandpa were here."

"That is just like Lucy," cried Lydia, laughing; "she thinks grandpa can take care of her through everything. I can remember — and it was not so very long ago, either — when she used to get on his knee if it thundered."

Lucy blushed a little when they all laughed, but did not attempt to deny the charge.

"I think, Lucy," said Hannah, "the best thing you can do is to go to bed and forget all about it."

"It is of no use to go to bed, Hannah; I shall never go to sleep."

"Pshaw! yes, you will. You don't think of sitting up all night — do you?"

"No; but I cannot go up stairs. That chamber rocks like a cradle. Mary, won't you take Lydia up there with you, and let me sleep in the bedroom with Hannah?"

"Lucy, what a baby you are!" exclaimed Hannah, but in a tone which showed she had no idea of opposing her, baby or not. Lydia readily acceded to the proposed change, and she and Mary gayly departed together.

When the others were gone, Lucy assisted Hannah to secure the doors and windows, cover the fire, and make everything safe for the night; and then, held fast in her cousin's friendly arms, her beautiful head nestled close to that honest, kindly bosom, she shut her blue eyes, and soon her soft and regular breathing attested that the disappointments and anxieties of the day were forgotten.

Sleep had fallen on all, and deep stillness reigned throughout the house; but without the storm raged with, seemingly, increasing fury. The windows rattled in their frames; even the huge beams and timbers jarred; and occasionally, when a blast more violent smote the walls, the old house trembled to its foundations. Hannah, undisturbed by the wild fancies that had troubled her young cousin, listened quietly for a time to the elemental tumult, and then herself sank into deep and tranquil slumber.

The hours passed on. The clock had struck eleven, twelve, one, when Lucy's first light sleep was disturbed. She turned uneasily, and murmured in her dreams. Suddenly she sprang up broad awake, and looked wildly round her. She was aware of some sound, loud and sudden, apart from the roar of the storm, which had at once and effectually aroused her. She listened, but could hear nothing except the driving wind and snow. Startled and terrified, she awoke her cousin.

"Hannah! Hannah! do wake up! Did you hear that noise? and what was it?"

"Noise? I didn't hear any noise. What was it like?"

"I cannot tell. It was something loud and strange."

"It was the cat, most likely. But, Lucy dear," she added, taking the poor girl's trembling hand, "how nervous you are to-night! Lie still, child, and go to sleep."

"I cannot, Hannah. O, how glad I shall be when it is morning! There! that was the same noise!"

"Why, Lucy, that is only the shutter of the wood-house window. It has got unfastened in the wind."

"Do you think that is all, Hannah?"

"I know it is, dear. There it goes again."

"I am glad it is nothing more; but it did frighten me dreadfully."

Lying down, she was quite still for a few minutes, during which the offending shutter was several times blown open with a loud noise. Presently she again roused her cousin.

"Hannah, can't I get up and light a candle, and hook that shutter?"

"Of course you can if you wish to, Lucy; but I wouldn't get up in the cold."

"I don't mind the cold; but I cannot endure that noise;" and, springing quickly from the bed, she ran to the bureau, struck a match, and lighted her candle.

"You had better put on some clothes, Lucy, for it is very cold, and you will have to open the window."

Lucy pushed her feet into her slippers, threw on a part of her clothes, and pinned a small shawl over her shoulders. Passing through the sitting-room and kitchen, she found the draught in the back rooms so strong that it would extinguish her candle if she kept on; so she placed the light on a window-sill in the kitchen, while she went out in the dark to execute her design. She had some difficulty in this, for the snow blinded her, and the wind several times blew the shutter out of her hand. She succeeded at last, however, and, closing the doors carefully after her, returned to the kitchen, where she had left her candle. As she raised it from the window, she was again startled to hear a loud knocking at the end door. But this time she was wide awake, and, obeying her first impulse, — that of compassion for any human being exposed on such a night, — she sprang to the door. When she reached it, she involuntarily paused an instant, with her hand on the latch, and asked who was there. "For God's sake, open the door, and don't stop to ask questions!" answered a voice from without, evidently that of a man.

Lucy no longer hesitated; but her hands trembled so violently that she could scarcely draw the rusty bolt. It yielded at last, and she raised the latch. The wind flung the door forcibly back, extinguishing her candle and covering her with snow; and, in the darkness, she could scarcely discern the figure which, blind and staggering, reeled into the entry.

Hannah, meantime, had heard the disturbance at the door, and, having flung on her clothes, now appeared in the sitting-room, where there was a faint light from the covered fire. While Lucy exerted all her strength to close the door, Hannah hastened to light another candle and open the fire. As the light flashed through the room, she at once perceived that the person who advanced to the fireplace, and deposited the burden he carried upon the warm hearth, was an entire stranger. Kneeling beside the bundle, the man quickly unrolled from what seemed to be a horse-blanket, a child — a little boy, apparently eight or nine years old, whose tattered garments, and unstockinged feet protruding through his worn shoes, showed how poorly he was prepared to brave the horrors of such a night.

Hannah soon had a blazing fire, and then, while Lucy applied herself to restoring the almost frozen child, she procured a lantern, and gave the man directions for securing the comfort of his horse, which was still exposed to the fury of the storm. Then she prepared hot water and cordials, and, leaving the boy in Lucy's care, busied herself with concocting a steaming bowl of hot ginger tea for the elder traveller. By the time it was ready the man returned, and, taking off his overcoat, — for he was better protected than his little companion, — he seated himself by the glowing fire. He seemed stiff and dull with cold, and accepted almost in silence Hannah's revivifying draught, watching, meanwhile, the movements of Lucy, who, kneeling beside the boy, chafed his little brown, dirty hands in her own soft and warm ones, or urged him to taste the brandy she held to his lips. After a time these efforts had the effect of restoring the benumbed and frozen child to consciousness. Lucy raised him on her arm, and he looked about the room. The elder stranger smiled a little, and, stretching his feet towards the bright fire, said, with no great amount of parental feeling, Lucy thought, —

"Well, youngster, I am rather glad to see you open your eyes. I began to think we had parted company for this life."

The boy glanced, with bright, quick eyes, at the man, with something of the look which a favorite dog might have worn, but said nothing.

To Hannah's simple hospitality, curiosity respecting her guests was unthought of. On these quiet country roads, where public houses are few and far between, strangers come and go at the scattered farms as a matter of course, exciting little interest and no surprise. Belated wayfarers so often sought the shelter of her father's roof that their coming awakened no wonder or surmise.

When the boy had been induced to swallow numerous hot cordials, — each an infallible specific in such cases, — the settee was drawn in front of the fire, and, rolled in hot blankets, he was placed upon it, Hannah declaring that it would be the height of imprudence to take him away from the fire until much better. A whispered consultation then ensued between the cousins as to what should be done with the man. It was finally decided to give him a small bedroom over the wood-house, where the hired man usually slept; Hannah remarking, to end the conference,—

"I can't be at the trouble of making up another bed at this time of night; and that is perfectly comfortable — better than he is used to, I dare say. Besides, nobody knows who he is or where he comes from. Just as well to have him up there out of the way."

When the stranger had sufficiently warmed and refreshed himself, Hannah lighted him up the narrow back staircase, saying, as she pushed open the door and gave him the candle, —

"I hope you will find the bed all right. If you think there are not clothes enough, there are two more blankets on that chest; you can throw them on. This is all the bed we have in order to-night; so I hope you will excuse it."

The man expressed his entire satisfaction with the room and the bed, apparently only too glad to be safe from the storm, and not in the least inclined to be fastidious. Indeed, as everything about the room, though coarse, was scrupulously neat, and the thick blankets and ample pillows promised warmth and comfort, he could well afford to be satisfied.

Returning to the sitting-room, Hannah found Lucy watching the already sleeping child.

"Isn't it dreadful, Hannah," she whispered, "to think of this poor little thing exposed on such a night?"

"It is, sure enough. I believe I never saw a child so poorly clothed in winter. His father was better dressed, and, though he didn't seem very tender, he appeared to take pretty good care of his boy. But, Lucy, we *must* fix up the fire, and go to bed. It will be morning before we know it."

All Lucy's restlessness seemed to have vanished. No sooner was her head again on the pillow, than she was overtaken by sleep, which held her fast until a late hour of the morning.

CHAPTER X.

When Lucy opened her eyes in the morning, she saw that the storm still continued with unabated violence. Hannah was gone from her side, and the gray light gave her no idea of the hour; so, thinking it must be still early, she was just smoothing her pillow for another nap, when the clock in the adjoining room struck nine. When she had finished dressing, and was leaving the bedroom, she met Mary and Lydia, who, as lazy as herself, were just coming down stairs. They stood by the sitting-room fire, talking over the storm and the advent of the two strangers, till Hannah came to call them to breakfast. Lydia asked where Heman was.

"O, he and the master had their breakfast long ago, and are gone."

"Where is the use of going to school in such weather as this? There will be no scholars."

"Yes; some of the largest boys who live near will be there. They go as much for fun as anything; and the drifts are so hard they can almost walk over them."

"Where is that man who came in the night?"

"He has just come down, and is sitting by the kitchen fire with his little boy."

"What does he look like?" asked Mary.

"O, I don't know. I rather think he is a pedler, or

agent for something, — a book agent, likely enough. They come along quite often. He has a valise, and they generally carry one."

"And, as the storm continues, he must stay all day, I suppose."

"Hush, Mary. Lydia has left the door open, and I am afraid he will hear you. Come out directly — won't you?"

The morning meal at the Pages' was usually spread in the large, cheery kitchen, and thither the two friends presently proceeded. They found Hannah, Lydia, and the stranger already seated at the table. Mary bowed silently, and sat down by Lydia. Lucy bade the stranger a civil good morning, adding, —

"The storm, you see, sir, is as wild as ever."

"Wilder, I believe. I have just been blessing the great good fortune which has brought me to such a shelter."

It was the first time Mary had heard the voice of the stranger, and she looked up at him in surprise. The words were nothing; but the tones had instantly struck her trained ear, — clear, polished, and perfectly modulated, every syllable falling as if carved in ivory, yet with that complete absence of effort which belongs to the most perfect culture. He was talking busily now with Hannah, and she took advantage of the fact to scan him closely.

He was apparently about thirty, or a little less; a tall man, with magnificent chest and shoulders, and clean, shapely limbs, tapering to strong, white hands and handsome feet. His complexion had, perhaps, once been fair, and the red blood still showed warm through the brown with which wind and sun had overlaid it. The features were clear cut and bold; the lower part of the face cov-

ercd with a close, curling beard, of a warm dark-brown;
and hair of the same color clustered thickly about his temples. His eyes were large, and the color of a ripe chestnut, alert, keen, and penetrating, with a shifting expression,
which now was mirthful and mocking, and now grave
almost to melancholy. It was a face which, by careless
observers, would have been pronounced singularly frank
and open; but Mary was not a careless observer, and her
quick eye did not fail to discover in it traces of the habit
learned among men, — the habit that draws between the
interior man and the world the close veil of a reserve
which is not the less impenetrable because it is so fine as
to be nearly impalpable. For the rest, book agent or pedler he might now be; but in his conversation there were
observable certain turns of thought and language seldom
acquired but in the polite world; and in his frank, unstudied manners, was apparent not only the perfection of acquired polish, but that fine, nameless something which
almost to a certainty indicates good blood and gentle ante-
cedents.

Mary had been so occupied with the observations she
was making, that she paid little heed to what the others
were saying. Her attention was recalled by Hannah.

"Mary," she said, "will you please pass the sugar to
Mr. —— " She hesitated, a little confused.

"Stafford — allow me to prompt you," said the stranger,
turning to her with a smile. "The truth is," he continued,
"you made me feel so entirely at home, that I forgot I was
really a stranger."

A general laughing introduction followed, and they
began to get very well acquainted. Of course, the ex-

traordinary weather came in for its share of the discussion.

"Are such storms common among these hills?" the stranger asked, addressing Hannah.

"Not very common, so severe as this. We seldom pass a winter, though, without one bad, drifting storm. Did you find much difficulty in getting along before dark?"

"None whatever; and my horse kept the track very well for some time into the evening. I should have stopped, but really there was no place to go to. I drove for miles without passing a human habitation; and as I knew what was behind me, and nothing was to be gained by turning back, I kept on."

"What road were you travelling?"

"I came from a town called Kiffton. It is a railway terminus, and, they told me, distant thirty miles, or thereabouts, from Edgehill, whither I was bound."

"Then you must have come through the Notch. Of course you didn't pass any houses, for there are none. But after you passed the cross-roads, you came by several before you got to ours."

"I knew nothing of them, the darkness was so great; and although I shouted again and again, I could raise no one, the storm so drowned my voice. At last my horse refused to be driven another step; and so, rolling the cub there in the robes, and stowing him safely under the seat, I walked, and led my horse by the bridle, thinking I might, perhaps, see some sign of life, and knowing I could give it up, and lie down in the snow at one time as well as another. You look horrified, young lady; but danger and I have shaken hands too often to make such an alternative any

longer startling. Not that it was by any means an attractive one, however; for I will confess, that, with all my resignation, the sight of your candle, glimmering faintly
through the storm, was more welcome than I can tell. I
had not before seen the house, though so near it."

"How fortunate it was, Hannah, that I got up to hook
that noisy shutter!"

"Fortunate enough; for I don't believe, sir, your little
boy could have stood it much.longer."

"*My* little boy! I hope, Miss Page, you do not think
that little whelp belongs to me!"

"Why, I thought so, of course."

"Not on account of any personal resemblance, I trust,"
he exclaimed, with a merry glance at the child, who,
wrapped in a faded woollen shawl, sat in a small arm-chair
by the fire.

"Well, no; I won't say I did think of that; but you
had him with you, and I took it for granted he was your
child."

"Such is the reward of good nature! But this is the
way I came by him: Early yesterday afternoon, when I
was a few miles from Kiffton, I suddenly came upon that
little imp, standing with his bare ankles plunged in the
snow beside the road. He demanded, in good highway-
man fashion, a seat in my sleigh; and my compliance de-
noted a degree of weakness for which I blush. I ran the
risk of infection from every known disease, and some that
are unknown. He informed me that his mother had died
the week before, and that he had been sent to the poor-
house, from which he had just made his escape. As he gave
me no trouble whatever, I allowed him to come along. Of

course you will perceive that I could not have foreseen such a contingency as being mistaken for his father. If it had occurred to me, I presume I should have left him to his fate."

Mary laughed; but Lucy was shocked, and answered, with some degree of spirit, —

"I think there are worse impressions that might prevail."

"Hardly, young lady," he answered, glancing at her with a sudden sparkle of mischief in his eyes. "I can really conceive of nothing worse."

Mary here interrupted with some remark, and they began to talk of Edgehill, which the stranger had mentioned as his destination. He asked a question or two regarding the distance.

"Excuse me," said Mary; "I understood that you lived in Edgehill."

"O, no; I am an entire stranger. Do you know anything of the place or people?"

"Very little, indeed."

"Do you chance to know a family named Gore?"

"No — yet, on second thought, the name sounds familiar. Lucy, did I not see a gentleman of that name at your father's last summer?"

"Yes; Mr. John Gore. He comes there frequently."

"That is the person. Do you know his family?"

"He has no family; he has never married."

"Indeed! and he must be past the age when men are usually tempted to matrimony."

"I should think so; he is nearly as old as my grandfather. But he is a very pleasant man, and has a beautiful house."

8

"I am happy to hear it, since it is to that house I am bound; but the prospect of getting there does not look very flattering," the stranger said, as they rose from the table.

Hannah conducted her guest to the sitting-room, stirred the fire, and returned to the kitchen, where the girls still remained.

"Isn't he the strangest man you ever saw, Mary?" asked Lucy, when they were alone.

"He is rather odd, perhaps; but, Hannah, he is not a pedler, you may be sure."

"What do you think he is?"

"That is more than I could possibly guess. He is a gentleman, however."

"I never said he wasn't."

"I know — but we do not mean quite the same thing. You mean a gentleman-like person; and I mean — well — I mean a gentleman. But what is this?"

"It is the overcoat the man wore; all those things are his."

The coat was of shaggy but soft gray cloth, and had a full lining and collar of rich, dark fur. A heavy travelling shawl and sable cap lay beside it. Mary had noticed the dress of the stranger at breakfast — a uniform suit of gray, gracefully worn, though of coarse fabric, chosen plainly rather for warmth and comfort than with any regard to appearances.

"I wonder who he is," she said to Lucy. "Don't you?"

"I cannot say that I care particularly. I do not think I like him very well; do you, Mary?"

"Yes, rather."

"But didn't he strike you as a little — not exactly callous, or heartless, but rather unfeeling?"

"Not in anything he said or did, certainly."

"How could he make fun of that poor boy?"

"He had just done enough to prove himself not unfeeling towards the child. Understand me, though — I do not mean that he may or may not be all you say, and more; there is no judging on first acquaintance with people like him. We should be a long time, I suspect, in getting at his real sentiments, let them be good or bad. But I rather like him — he promises to be amusing." And Mary took up the basket of beans that were to be picked over for Saturday's baking, and went into the sitting-room, as she said, to be entertained by the stranger.

She found him sitting by the hearth, gazing, with a somewhat moody abstraction, into the fire. He rose as she entered, his face clearing instantly, placed a chair for her, and helped her to draw up the work-stand; then, as she placed her basket on it and began her work, he stood watching her very attentively for a few minutes. Presently he drew his own chair to the other side of the table, and took up a handful of the beans.

"It is hardly fair," he said, "that I should be the only idle one in the house this morning."

"I beg you will not let any idea of that kind induce you to offer me assistance."

"I will acknowledge that I have another motive. I am so heartily tired of myself just now, that any employment would be a relief."

"In that case I shall accept your help, and thereby serve two ends — confer a benefit, and oblige myself."

"That last clause contained the secret of a great deal of philanthropy."

"You think so?"

"Do not you?"

"I hardly know. I like to believe all things perfect until proved the reverse."

"Does the disposition arise from a trusting temper, or a fancy for pretty illusions?"

"From the last, probably. But what would the world be without what you term pretty illusions? Some always believe them, and the rest must pretend to."

"Certainly — we only differ in one respect; your pretence goes a little farther than mine. I say I believe, and thus discharge my duty to society; you say so, and try to convince yourself that it is true."

"According to your reasoning, I am not so consistent as yourself. But I am ready to admit it; I have a horror of a perfectly consistent person."

The stranger was quick enough to detect the slight shade of bitterness hidden under Mary's words, and he hastened to change the conversation.

The two younger girls remained to assist Hannah in the kitchen. As Mary, bearing her basket of beans, disappeared through the door, Hannah said, —

"Now, girls, if you will get the things ready for me to begin my baking, I will take this boy in hand."

"What do you mean to do with him?"

"I am going to have him in a tub of warm water for the first thing. Do you suppose I will have such a dirty child round my house all day, and then sleep in one of my beds come night?"

The boy, who had made a very hearty breakfast, watched Hannah in attentive silence as she produced a tub of warm water, crash towels, and soap. When all was ready, she introduced the little wanderer to their acquaintance, and, with strict injunctions to thoroughness and fidelity, left him to his ablutions, while she went in search of some clothes. By the time the bath was finished, she had ready a sometime outgrown shirt of Heman's, — it was too large for the child, and the sleeves hung bagging about the wrists, but it was snowy white, — and a pair of pantaloons, once the property of the same youth, made shorter by being rolled up around the ankles. Warm stockings, and a pair of shoes of Lydia's, which could only be kept on by scuffing his feet, and a blue cloth sack belonging to Lucy, completed his costume.

It has been said that the child was apparently eight or nine years of age. Judging from his size, he might have been; but his face showed him to be several years older — fourteen, at least. He had thin, sharp features, a sallow complexion, and small, bright eyes, intensely black. Hardship and ill-usage had dwarfed his figure, and his mind too, it seemed, for there appeared to be some mental want; it was hard to tell precisely what. The little vacant face told plainly enough in what a night of ignorance his brief years had been passed; yet there was in it a great deal of a kind of semi-human intelligence, a curious, precocious cunning, such as is often seen in the faces of small animals.

Lucy brought a comb, and tried to smooth his matted and tangled hair. It was a task of no slight difficulty; and credit was due the child that he bore the operation without flinching. Clearly, it was not often that gentle hands had performed that office for him. When it was finished, she took his small brown hand and led him to the sitting-room. On entering, he seemed quite overcome, for the first time in his life, perhaps, by something which, if not bashfulness, was the nearest approach to the feeling of which he was capable, and was possibly caused by the novelty of clean face and apparel. He held firmly to the little hand that led him, and drew Lucy's skirt about his person as if to shield himself from observation. As they came near the fire, Lucy gently drew her gown from his grasp, and laying her hands on his shoulders, turned him towards Mary, blushing herself a little under the steady gaze of the stranger.

"Look, Mary," she said, "and see if Hannah cannot work wonders."

"Miracles! Do you recognize your *protégé*, Mr. Stafford?"

"Not in the least; he has suffered a sea-change," replied the gentleman, turning round to look at him, his hand arrested in the act of throwing a handful of beans into Mary's basket. "But what is your name, youngster? I have never thought to ask before."

"Tate," answered the boy, looking straight in his questioner's face.

"Is that all the name you have?"

The boy nodded his head with a jerk, but did not move his eyes.

"What was your mother's name?"

"Never had no mother."

"Indeed! But you told me your mother died a week since."

" No, I didn't."

" Will you be so kind as to state what you did say? " the other continued, with an air of grave and ceremonious politeness.

" I said mammy was dead, but she warn't my mother."

" How do you know? "

" She said I's no child o' hern."

" Did she happen to mention whose child you were? "

" Al'ays said I's the devil's own."

" My dear child, she was probably correct. What do you mean to do with yourself? "

" Mean to stay with you."

" That resolve, formed on so short an acquaintance, is very flattering to my vanity; but, really, I do not deserve such a mark of esteem. I think I shall take you back to Kiflton."

" 'Twon't do no good; I never'll stay there," responded the imp, with a grin.

" Lucy," said Miss Elliot, as the gentleman paused in his questions and resumed his occupation, " don't you think we might find, among Hannah's stores, a jacket, or something of which we might make one? "

" I dare say we could; and if you are done with these, I will take them out to Hannah, and ask her about it."

" Yes; thanks to Mr. Stafford, they are all ready. I will go up stairs and get my work-basket while you are gone;" and, shaking the scattered beans from her little black silk apron, she left the room. Lucy lingered long enough to brush up the hearth, and find a picture-book for the boy, and then she too went out.

They presently returned, Mary bearing the implements

for sewing, and Lucy an armful of old clothes, from which their ingenuity was to fashion a jacket for the little outcast. Lucy also brought a number of newspapers, which she gave to the stranger, remarking, —

"Perhaps you would like to look at yesterday's papers, sir."

"Where did you get those, Lucy?" asked Mary, as the stranger took them, with thanks. "No one went to the post-office yesterday."

"No; grandpa left them here by mistake. How he will want them through this storm!"

"He will, indeed; and there is no one to play piquet with him. Do you think we could get up there this afternoon, if the storm abates?"

"It is plain, Mary, you know nothing of the drifts between here and there, or you would not ask such a question. This is Saturday, and I have no idea a sleigh will go over this hill before Monday afternoon."

"My dear young lady, are you serious?" asked the stranger, quickly, looking up from his paper.

"Perfectly serious. Perhaps by Monday morning they will clear a road that will be passable; but I doubt it."

"I hope, Mr. Stafford, your business admits of delay; for it is plain you must wait," said Mary. "As well resign yourself with what patience you can."

"It is not a matter in which my patience is so much concerned as that of my kind hostess."

"Then give yourself no further uneasiness, I entreat. There is no call for any."

The girls were already seated at their work, and busily plied the needle and scissors, while the stranger read his

papers, glancing up now and then to address or to admire
his companions, so attractive, yet so different. They were,
indeed, in striking contrast. Mary, in her plain print
morning-gown and black apron, a net of scarlet silk con-
fining the dark hair which, smooth as satin, marked her
pale cheek and slightly shaded her slender neck, looked
really elegant, in spite of the simplicity of her attire; while
Lucy, whose dress was much the same in outline, yet wanting in the grace and niceness of detail which distinguished
everything worn by her friend, had no air at all. She was
simply a neatly-dressed girl. She was so lovely that she
could well be forgiven her ignorance of some of the secrets
of the toilet; yet to the eyes now scanning the friends
over the margin of the "Colchester Inquirer," the beauty
stamped with the seal of fashion and society was more
really attractive than the fresh loveliness of the rustic
belle.

The short forenoon slipped rapidly away, and, as they
were seating themselves round the fire after dinner, the
stranger said, addressing himself to Hannah, —

"Is there no way in which you can make me either useful or agreeable? If I were to offer my services to the
young ladies, I fear they would not trust me with either
thimble or scissors."

"Girls," said Hannah, "how is it? Can't you find something for him to do?"

"Yes," answered Mary. "He may first hold this skein
of silk for me, and then, if the mood still holds, he may
read to us."

"With the greatest pleasure," taking the thread on his
handsome hands; "and, for the second clause, shall I give

you the contents of these?" motioning towards the news-papers.

"I think not. Lucy, where can we find a book? for we cannot let this opportunity pass unimproved."

"If the master were here," said Hannah, "he would find you something."

"But he is not here, and will not be for several hours. What are those books in the closet in our room, Lucy?"

"They are some old books that belonged to cousin William. I do not believe there is anything there we should like."

"Lydia might bring them down," said Hannah, "and you could look them over. Run, Lydia, and see what you can find."

Lydia, obeying, soon reappeared with about a dozen old volumes in her arms. There were several school-books, one or two volumes of sermons, a copy of "The Pleasures of Hope," a torn book of travels, and an old dog-eared volume without covers, which, on examination, proved to be the "Tales of the Crusaders."

"Ah, here is a treasure for a stormy day!" cried Mary, turning over the yellow leaves, and opening at "The Talisman." "Lucy, you must allow me to choose, if you have never read these. You never have? Then to-day you shall know Cœur de Lion and the matchless Saladin."

CHAPTER XI.

Mr. Stafford took the book, the little bustle of preparation subsided, and, leaning back in his easy, cushioned chair, beside the bright, warm blaze, he began to read. His voice was singularly rich and mellow, with great flexibility and compass. It gave to his commonest conversation something fascinating, and hinted what the charm of his tones might be when inspired by deeper feeling. His reading could hardly be otherwise than delightful; and his listeners soon became so absorbed as quite to forget surrounding scenes. As the brilliant pageant of kings, and knights, and armies, evoked by the hand of the great magician, defiled before them, the low farm-house walls expanded, and, stretching far away, disclosed those burning plains where Richard of the Lion Heart fought for the Holy Sepulchre. Groaning orchard boughs gave place to groves of stately palms; and, though the storm still raged without, they saw only the intense glow of the hot Syrian sun. The king, the soldan, and the knight lived and breathed before them.

Lucy listened with a deep and entire delight. The world of fictitious literature was new to her. In history, travels, and biography, she was very well read, those being the books from which it had been her habit to read for her grandfather's pleasure; but at the rich fount of poetry and romance her lips had drunk but sparingly. Hour after hour went by unheeded by her now, in her fascinated enjoyment of the book. Indeed, the whole party had become so absorbed that they took little note of the flight of time; and they were all surprised when, during a slight pause made by the reader, Hannah, looking up at the clock, exclaimed, —

"Bless my soul! it is almost five! — time for the master and Heman this minute. I declare, I got so interested I forgot about supper and everything else. Come, Lydia, come right along and help me."

Mr. Stafford laid down the book, and, rising, walked round the table to see what success the girls were having in their work.

"We make but indifferent progress," said Mary. "I am a poor tailor, and Lucy is a worse. Do you think this garment will, by any effort of the imagination, pass for a jacket?"

"Indeed, it wears a very promising look; and you may be sure the boy will not be fastidious."

"I should hope it may be right," said Lucy, "for I have pricked my fingers to the bone. Let me put it all away now, Mary: it is too dark to see."

"That is, you want a pretext to be idle. Well, so, in truth, do I; and we will lay it aside for the present."

Just then the sound of steps was heard in the entry, and the next moment the door opened and Fanshaw appeared. The girls rose and came forward to greet him. The stranger also advanced to the fire; and Mary mentioned the names of the gentlemen, by way of introduction. They bowed, each measuring the other with a rapid glance, as men do, and then they all stood for some time around the hearth, talking rather pleasantly. Lucy was the most silent. As she listened to the graceful flow of Mary's conversation, watched her as she turned from one to the other of her evidently admiring listeners, saw her perfect ease and self-possession, and marked her ready wit and lively play of fancy, she was more than ever convinced of her own inferiority. She would have given, at that moment, every worldly advantage which she possessed — and she well knew that these were many — for the charm of Mary's gay and graceful manner. She saw that the stranger turned always to Mary; and even Fanshaw was just then listening with an evident pleasure and admiration, which caused her a momentary uneasy pain. · By and by the conversation drifted far away from her. It was of people and things, and of events transpiring in the great world outside her own — that world which she had hitherto thought of and cared for so little, to which Mary, and Fanshaw, and the stranger, all belonged, but in which she had no part.

It was a pleasant and cheerful group which gathered around Hannah's evening fire when tea was over. As Mr. Stafford took down from the high mantel-piece the book he had been reading, he said, turning to Fanshaw, —

"You see what sort of 'Talisman' against *ennui* we have found this stormy day. You, I suppose, are no stranger to Sir Kenneth."

"No ; he was the first whom I knew of that train of gentle, perfect knights made famous by Sir Walter. I shall be glad to renew my acquaintance with him."

Hannah had taken Lucy's place at the work-table, and

the jacket, under her skilful hands, was coming on rapidly; while Lucy, on her favorite low seat by the fire, with her head leaned against Lydia's knee, gave herself up wholly to the pleasure of listening. Not a syllable escaped her, as chapter after chapter was begun and ended; and when, late in the evening, the story was finished, and the stranger laid down the book, she drew, unconsciously, a long, fluttering sigh, as if some pleasant spell were gently broken.

The reading ended, and the sewing laid aside, they all drew close about the fire, and Heman brought forward apples, a pitcher of cider, and a large basket of nuts. With these, and with much talk and laughter, they wore away an evening of such length as was seldom spent under that roof. Of all their enjoyment the stranger, so unexpectedly thrown among them, was the life and soul. There was a charm in his buoyant, infectious gayety — whatever might underlie it — which was irresistible. His humor was so genuine, his courtesy so sincere, he charmed all alike, from the oldest to the youngest. Though he seldom spoke of himself, and always in the most general and indefinite manner, it was evident that he had travelled much, and known men in all stations and in many lands. He had ever some pointed anecdote or bit of graphic description, some adventure or keen satiric comment, that made his conversation sparkle like a mosaic, but the effect of which is quite lost in any attempt to repeat it. For, in truth, it was not so much in the superior force or brilliancy of anything he said that the charm of his talk lay, as in the personal magnetism of the man, which affected all whom he came near. Add to this the singular grace of a manner which united the highest polish of society with an almost boyish naturalness, and it is not surprising that the dwellers in that lonely farm-house should feel themselves rather indebted to the storm which had driven him to find shelter among them. When Hannah conducted her guest to his room that night, it was not to the little apartment over the wood-house, but the best the house afforded, warmed and lighted, awaited him. So much had he won upon her regard, that her housekeeper's pride was mortified that, even under the stress of circumstances attending his first arrival, she had not better provided for his comfort; and it was with many apologies that the good soul now led the way up stairs.

CHAPTER XII.

THE next day dawned clear and bright. A cloudless blue overarched the scene so lately dark with storm. The sunlight was reflected with dazzling brilliancy from the new-fallen snow, which stretched, far as the eye could reach, a white, unbroken surface. Towards noon, Sunday though it was, the dwellers on the various roads began to appear with shovels and slow, ponderous oxen, to "break out" the track. Heman, with a commendable public spirit, brought out his broad-horned team, and joined his efforts to the rest. Fanshaw, and the stranger also, after watching the proceedings for a time from the windows, offered their services, which were cheerfully accepted. Fanshaw's student life here developed its effects. Unused to violent exertion of any kind, he soon fell behind the line of shovellers, while the stranger — white-handed, and apparently quite as unused to manual labor — held his own with the best, his shapely arms showing hard ridges of muscle, and his strong, deep chest never varying its regular rise and fall. Before a very long time, Fanshaw, quite exhausted, threw down his spade and retired to the house; but the stranger remained behind, his restless fancy caught for the time by the novel employment and the new companions. Resting for a moment on his spade, surrounded by the huge piles of snow, he was accosted by Deacon Sharpe, who stood wiping the perspiration from his shining bald head with a yellow silk handkerchief.

"Master give up rather easy."

"Rather — but he is used to work with his head, while we work with our hands."

"Sartinly. He keeps a fust-rate school. Know him well, I spose."

"Never saw him till yesterday. Should think he would, as you say, keep a good school."

"Wal, he doos — gives gineral satisfaction. I don't believe the deestrict has been better suited these ten year than with the two teachers I've chose, last summer and this winter."

"It requires a very judicious person to choose a school-master."

"Jest so; but I've hed, fust and last, considerable experience. Stoppin' long in these parts?"

"Only till I can get away. Delayed by the storm."

"O, travellin'. Got folks in this neighborhood?"

"No."

"Come on business, most likely."

"Not precisely."

"You'll find it pretty bad doin' for considerable of a spell now. Which road be you travellin'?"

"I hardly know yet; think I shall take the best, however."

"They'll any of 'em be bad enough for a while. Here, Ben Miller, fetch them oxen up this way," cried the deacon, in despair of getting anything out of his new acquaintance.

Mr. Stafford turned again to his spade, and worked long

9

and to the purpose, his strong limbs seeming to defy fatigue. The drifts on those hilly roads were hard and deep, and it was almost sunset before they had reached the limits of the district and the completion of their task. Then, resuming his coat, and swinging the shovel over his shoulder, he took his stand on one of the heavy runners of Heman's ox-sled, and rode slowly back to the farm. As they approached the house, he saw Mary and Lucy standing in the doorway, talking with a young man whose back was towards him. He turned at the sound of the approaching oxen, and revealed the pleasant face of Ben Miller. Stafford recognized him as one he had particularly noticed during the afternoon, and greeted him with a nod and a smile.

"We are come, young ladies," he said, taking off his cap and running his fingers through his damp curls, "to receive from you the praise due our exertions."

"We are prepared not only to praise but to reward you," said Mary; "and that is not always the meed of valor in these degenerate days."

"I should think not. You will convince me that Hillsboro' is really the paradise which Miss Lucy this morning declared it to be. Will it be altogether out of rule if I ask the nature of the reward?"

"You are bidden to a banquet. The good Hannah has prepared such a dinner as only she knows how to serve."

"Miss Page is an angel."

"Of course she is, and not an unappreciated one, either. But come; I suspect she is waiting for us. Ben, you must come too and dine with us."

Ben glanced at Lucy, to see if she seconded the invitation; but she was occupied, or seemed to be, with something Heman was telling her, and did not turn her head.

"No, I guess not to-night, Miss Elliot: it is getting late," he said, really wishing to stay, yet determined not to do so without encouragement from Lucy. But Mary, who supposed that, of course, nothing could give her friend so much pleasure as to have Ben remain, compelled her attention.

"Lucy," she said, "cannot you say something to induce Ben to stay to dinner?"

"What can I say that you have not thought of?" answered Lucy, sweetly. "I am sure Hannah will be very glad to have him."

Ben was dissatisfied. There was no lack of civility or kindness in Lucy's manner, but there was nothing more than these. He felt that it was a matter of real indifference to her whether he went or staid; and so he declined the invitation, bade them all good evening, and went down the hill with a sorrowful heart.

That evening, as Lucy was kneeling, with glowing cheeks, before the fire, busy emptying the contents of her corn-parcher into a basket at her side, Hannah, looking up suddenly, inquired, —

"Why didn't Ben Miller stop to dinner, Lucy?"

"I do not know," replied her cousin, putting back a long curl that had fallen over her face, but without looking up.

"Did you ask him?"

"Certainly; and so did Mary. He could not stay, I suppose. There, Lydia, isn't that beautiful?" she added, in the same breath, as she raised her basket, heaped high with snowy corn.

Hannah was observing her cousin narrowly, and sighed softly as she rose to her feet. Fanshaw and Mary exchanged quick, smiling glances. They thought her carelessness assumed; but Hannah, who could read her better, saw that it was real, and she sighed because it was confirmation of a suspicion which had begun to give her much anxiety.

The next day Mr. Stafford was induced, by the advice of both Fanshaw and Hannah, to postpone his departure until the afternoon, in the belief that even in that short space of time the roads might improve. As they sat at dinner, Hannah said, with her usual hearty hospitality, —

"I hope, Mr. Stafford, if you come back this way, you will not fail to call and see us."

"That is the very thing I would have asked permission to do, Miss Page. Believe me, I shall not soon forget all your kindness."

"Well, for the matter of that, we haven't done anything to speak of, or worth remembering long. But we shouldn't like to have you go by without giving us a call."

"How long shall you stay in Edgehill, Mr. Stafford?" asked Lydia, who, by the way, was become a great favorite with their new friend, and was his ardent admirer as well.

"That must depend. I hardly know, myself. A week — perhaps two."

"And what do you mean to do with Figaro?" — a name by which he had chosen to christen the little companion of his journey.

"O, take him back to the workhouse, where he belongs."

The child, who was sitting by, grinned, showing two white rows of small, even teeth. The stranger noticed his look of incredulity.

"You don't believe me, you little vagabond," he said, laughing; "but we shall see. Ah! some one has taken the road before me, it seems," he added, as a sleigh drove slowly up to the door.

"Why, it is Jerry!" cried Lucy, recognizing her father's horse and sleigh, as well as the "hired man" in the person of the driver. "I think, Mary, grandpa has grown desperate, and has sent for you and me to go up there. Well, Jerry," she continued, as the man entered, "does grandpa want me?"

"No, Miss Lucy; it is your ma sent for you this time."

"Is anything the matter, Jerry?" she asked, impressed by something in the manner of the messenger. "Is any one sick?"

"Your grandmother has had one of her bad spells."

"Is she very sick, Jerry?" asked Lucy, rising, with an anxious face.

"She was dreadful sick Saturday and part of yesterday. The squire has gone to Edgehill after a doctor to-day. Couldn't get there afore, you know."

"When was she taken, Jerry?" asked Hannah, who had also left the table.

"In the night, Friday, I believe; but they warn't much scairt about her till next morning."

"Did aunt Susan say anything about my going up?"

"Yes; she wanted you to come if you could; but Lucy was to come, anyhow."

Hannah and Lucy lost no time in making their preparations.   They bade a hasty good by to Mr. Stafford, whose
horse´ already stood harnessed at the door, and taking
their places in Jerry's sleigh, drove quickly away.

Arrived at Lucy's home, they found their grandmother
better than, from the man's account, they had been led
to expect, but still suffering very much.   The gentle old
lady smiled a pleased, though feeble, smile, as Lucy bent
over her, and seemed glad to see the bright young face
once more about her room.   The doctor arrived in the
course of the afternoon, and pronounced her out of immediate danger, but looked grave when her ultimate recovery
was mentioned.

To none — not even to her grandmother — did Lucy's
coming seem to give so much pleasure as to the captain.
He had consented to her leaving them, and had never
complained of her absence; but daily and hourly he had
missed his darling — missed her gay voice and presence
through the house, her companionship, and even her teasing and tyrannical ways.   Of late he had seen less of her
than in the early part of the winter.   First, the little evening calls were given up; then the Sunday visits grew
shorter and shorter, till they were nearly abandoned; and
now he seldom saw her unless he went down to the house.
Lucy was touched at the pleasure the old man manifested
in having her once more near him.   She saw how much
he had missed her, and how much he wanted her with
him, though he would not ask her to stay; and she resolved to remain at home, at least for a few days.   This
may seem a very trifling sacrifice; but it really needed
some effort of decision to resist the strong attractions

which drew her another way, and to devote herself to the happiness of two old people, who did not in the least require her presence beyond the pleasure that it gave them. When, towards evening, Hannah was preparing to go, she said to her young cousin, —

"Come, Lucy, we ought to hurry. It is getting dark, and you know how bad the road is."

"I think I will not go back to-night," replied Lucy, who had assumed her old place upon her grandfather's knee, beside the sitting-room fire.

"But you had better. You will only be late in the morning, if you stay."

"I am not going back in the morning, either."

"What new crotchet have you got in your head now, child?" asked Hannah, pausing in the act of tying on her hood to look at her cousin.

"To tell you the plain truth, Hannah, I have been gone from grandpa so long that he is getting perfectly unmanageable; and if I don't give him a day or two of discipline now, by the time school is done I shall be able to do nothing with him."

The old man did not reply, except to tighten his clasp upon the small hands he held; but Hannah asked, in some dismay, —

"And what do you suppose Mary and Lydia will say, when I get home without you?"

"I don't know. Tell them they must spare me a few days," she answered, laying her head caressingly against the old man's breast.

When Hannah was leaving, she followed to the doorsteps, and said, —

"I did mean to go back with you; but I think grandpa wants me badly, though he will not say so. I couldn't leave him if he did, you know. I shall stay the rest of the week. Tell Mary to come up and spend the day. Good night." And she tripped back into the house.

CHAPTER XIII.

IT must be confessed that Lucy found the days at home going by a little heavily. She could not prevent her thoughts from wandering away, across the snowy fields, to Hannah's snug sitting-room, and fancying what they were all doing — if they missed her at all, and who would probably miss her most. The week she had allotted for her stay was gone, and another nearly ended; but still, much as she wished to return, she could not bring herself to leave her grandfather. She could not fail to see how much pleasure she gave by remaining; so, with a well-assumed appearance of cheerfulness and content, she postponed her wishes to his. She waited upon her grandmother with the utmost sweetness and patience; read to and otherwise amused the old captain; and, to as great an extent as possible, filled her thoughts with the interests of home and its dear circle.

One evening Lucy had been flitting about the invalid's room, arranging various things with a dainty niceness of touch, and brightening, as the two old people thought, all that she came near. Her grandmother's eyes followed her with a fond observant glance; and, as the young girl left the room, she said to her husband, who was sitting beside her, —

"It appears to me, Thomas, that Lucy is altered lately. She seems different from what she was."

"In what way, my dear?"

"I can hardly tell. She was always the most affectionate child in the world; but she seems more thoughtful and
gentle now."

"Lucy is getting older, my dear; and it would be
strange ·if that handsome head-piece of hers didn't grow
a trifle steadier. She is a good girl, though — our Lucy;
and the man who gets her, one of these days, will be a
lucky fellow."

"And Ben's chance is as good as any one's, I suppose."

"Very likely: yes; I dare say it is; though, of all the
unaccountable pièces of machinery, a girl of eighteen is
the most difficult to reckon on. There was a time this
winter when I thought the French lessons, and the poetry
reading, and all that nonsense with the master, wouldn't
help Ben any; but I rather think the danger in that quarter is all over now."

"You think he has a fancy for Mary?"

"Unless some very good signs fail, that is the case. I
am quite willing such an arrangement should come about.
Mary is a capital girl, and deserves a first-rate husband;
but I think she could do worse."

Lucy came back into the room, and they said no more.

It was a day or two after this that Mary came up to
spend the afternoon with her friend. The two girls passed
the long, bright hours undisturbed in the sunny sitting-
room. Mrs. Fraser went in and out occasionally, without
interrupting the flow of their pleasant talk. Mary, in a
low rocking-chair by the window, .sewed industriously
while she chatted; and Lucy, on a footstool at her side,
sat idly snipping bits of paper with bright, dangerous-

looking scissors. It was a day destined to be long remembered by them both, though for the most widely differing reasons. Lucy was very happy, and Mary had
never been more engaging and affectionate; for a new
and yet unacknowledged happiness warmed her heart
towards all the world. What bright dreams they indulged! What pleasant next-summer plans they discussed! — destined, for one at least, to be as short-lived
as the sunshine of that brief winter day. How little could
they foresee the years that would have passed, the changes
that would be wrought, before they two would meet
again.

While they sat at the tea-table, Mrs. Fraser said something about Jerry's taking Mary home in the sleigh.

O, no, Mary insisted, that would not be at all necessary.
The walking was again very good; and, besides, Mr. Fanshaw had said he should come up to see them during the
evening, and she would not be obliged to return alone.

At this announcement Lucy felt her heart give a sudden bound; and her hand shook so that she spilled the tea
Dolly was at that moment handing her over her dress, and
was obliged to leave the table.

It was an hour later when Fanshaw raised the great
brass knocker on Squire Fraser's door, and its loud peal
sounded through the house. The two friends were standing, arm in arm, by the window, looking out at the still
winter moonlight, which, like a flood of silver, lay over
all the wide hill-side, and drew, with an exquisitely fine
tracery, the shadows of the elms standing motionless in
the night air. Lucy turned round with a heightened color,
and a shy, happy look in her eyes; but it would have

needed a very close observer to detect any change in Mary's composed though smiling face. A somewhat lingering pressure which her hand received from the visitor's might, however, have been set down as significant by any one who remembered that it was scarcely half a dozen · hours since they had met; but the circumstance was unnoticed by all.

Lucy enjoyed this evening intensely. She was gay and light-hearted as a bird. Mary, though seemingly very happy, was unusually quiet, saying little; but Fanshaw was charming. Lucy thought she had never seen him so animated, so full of life and spirit. And then he had been so glad to see her, had said they missed her so much, and expressed regret at losing their pleasant lessons; all of which was strictly truthful, but uttered merely as pleasant, though sincere, compliment, and forgotten as soon as spoken. By and by the captain came in, and they had a game of whist, in which Lucy and Fanshaw were badly beaten by Mary and the old gentleman.

When the rubber was ended, the captain returned to his own room, and Mrs. Fraser, bidding Fanshaw and Mary good night, went with him, as the invalid would require her attention for the remainder of the evening. Very soon after, Mary rose to go. Lucy begged her to wait a few minutes, while she went for something which she wished to send to Lydia. She was detained longer than she had expected, and it was some fifteen or twenty minutes that her guests were left alone.

As she came hurrying back, the words of apology on her lips, and her light, slippered feet making no sound on the soft carpet, she was suddenly arrested at the threshold by the sight disclosed through the half-open door. Fanshaw was standing with one elbow resting on the chimneypiece, and looking down with happy, tender eyes into the face of his companion, who stood beside him with her hand laid lightly on his arm. She had her face raised to his, and was speaking rapidly and with evident earnestness, for her usually pale cheek was flushed with a warm color. She paused a moment, as if for an answer, still looking up. He did not speak, but returned her gaze for a second, then, laying his arm across her shoulder, bent his head and pressed his lips to hers in a long, unresisted kiss.

Lucy turned from the door and walked back into the empty dining-room. She laid the things she held on the table, and rested her hand on a chair for support. Her breath came thick and hard, and her brain seemed to turn round. Rapidly her thoughts ran back over the past few weeks. Had she been blind? Things unregarded before, and slight in themselves, took weighty meaning; tones, looks, and words came back fraught with a fatal significance. Had she been living in a delusion? The very earth seemed crumbling beneath her feet.

In the first sharp agony of the moment everything was forgotten, even the presence of Fanshaw and Mary in the house. But when she remembered them, and what the emergency demanded of her, she made a vigorous effort to rally her scattered faculties, and partially succeeded. She passed her hand over her forehead, as if to dispel some oppressive weight, called up a dreary counterfeit of the smile she had so lately worn, and went back to the room she had left with a feeling as if she were suddenly frozen.

It was fortunate for Lucy that her guests were too much occupied with themselves, or with each other, to observe her narrowly, or they must have seen something unusual in the cold quiet of her manner. She was like one but half recovered from a stunning blow — bewildered and uncertain. She busied herself with getting Mary's things, warming her overshoes, and other little attentions, which kept her occupied till their departure. The leave-taking on Mary's part was warm and kind, on Lucy's a little quiet, but not otherwise unusual. When Fanshaw took her hand at parting, her assumed composure had nearly given way. But she was come of a resolute race, this soft and petted child; and, though her heart was ready to cry out in its anguish, the little hand did not tremble, and the dim light in the hall where they stood concealed whatever evidences of emotion her face may have worn. She spoke her good night steadily, and stood watching them as, arm in arm, they went slowly down the moonlit hill.

For a moment a hard, angry feeling arose in her breast against Mary — a feeling, however, which could not long find room in so loyal a heart as hers. How could Mary know the secret which she had hardly confessed to herself? That her weakness was not even guessed at by either of the two who had just left her was all the consolation she could find. Hour after hour she lay, in the silence of her chamber, gazing, with hot, tearless eyes, out into the white moonlight, and revolving in her mind what she had lately seen. She tried to think calmly, to comprehend what had really happened to her; but, poor child, her beautiful dream had been so suddenly shattered, the blow had fallen so heavily, that she was too much stunned to reason. At first she could comprehend nothing but the one simple fact of irreparable loss. She accepted that as something fixed and remediless. At length, however, there came the reflection that, if she had lost, some one else had won; and the bitterest ingredient in her cup of humiliation was that she realized only too well why she could have had no hope to rival Mary. She saw herself an ignorant, awkward, uncultivated country girl. And so profound was her sense of inferiority that all harsh and bitter feeling against her friend vanished after the first resentful moment. What possible chance, she thought, in her excessive self-depreciation, had there ever been that such a man as Fanshaw should feel for her anything more than a generous friendship? How she despised herself for what she called the blind vanity that had led her to misinterpret the evidences of such a feeling!

Her first impulse was to avoid both Mary and Fanshaw; but she was wise enough to reconsider it. It had been arranged that afternoon that she should go down to her cousin's the next day, and she resolved not to fail. With all her humiliation, pride was yet too strong to allow her to do anything which might reveal her wound to those who had inflicted it. She might die, — at that moment, poor child, she really believed that she should, — but, like the Indian who sees the stake prepared, she would never cry out.

CHAPTER XIV.

THE next day brought company from out of town, whose coming detained Lucy at home, and it was not till the evening of the second day that she found an opportunity to go out. As she was putting on her hood and shawl, her mother, who was sitting by, laid down her work, and said, after a short, thoughtful pause, —

"Perhaps it would be best, Lucy, if you should tell Hannah to write to her father very particularly how your grandmother is. If anything should happen while your uncle is away, he would never forgive us for not writing; and I think if he knew how she is, he would come home soon."

"Mother, you frighten me! Do you think grandma is going to die?"

"No, Lucy; I will not say that; but I feel very anxious, and I know the doctor does. But your uncle ought to know that we have some fears, though we still hope for the best."

"It relieves me to hear you say that, mother; I will tell Hannah to write. Good night — I do not think I shall come back till morning."

"No; better not. You look too tired for so long a walk. Kiss me before you go, my child. Good night."

Lucy walked down the hill slowly, and with bent head, unmindful of the clear, calm starlight, of the faintly-glowing east, brightening with the rising moon, and of the night wind, soft and sighing, which came like a whisper of approaching spring, from the beech-wood on the hill. She had walked more than half the distance when the sound of voices attracted her attention, and she perceived two figures advancing up the hill. In another moment she heard her own name called by Heman, and her heart beat violently as she thought who his companion might be. She soon saw her mistake. It was not Fanshaw, but Ben Miller, who accompanied her cousin, and she could hardly tell if she were more relieved or disappointed at the discovery.

"Were you going to our house?" she asked, as they came near.

"Yes," Heman answered; "Hannah sent me to ask your mother about the blue yarn; and Ben, here, undertook to come too, for the sake of keeping me company, which was very good of him — eh, Lucy?"

"You will find mother at home," Lucy replied, taking no notice of her cousin's clumsy raillery; and she was turning from them, when Ben informed Heman that he could go on alone, as he himself should see Lucy to her uncle's door. Though this arrangement was not entirely satisfactory to her, she had no excuse for objecting to it, and the two accordingly walked on together.

"Aren't you going to school any more, Lucy?" asked Ben, after they had proceeded some distance in silence, or exchanging only an occasional word.

"I presume so — by and by, when grandma gets a little better. But, Ben, I have hardly seen you since the storm. What a night that was! And I was so sorry and disappointed!"

10

"I was disappointed, too, Lucy," answered Ben; and he added, after a moment's pause, and in a lower tone, "Do you want to know why?"

"I am not very curious— There! Ben, did you see that lovely meteor?"

"No."

"It was the largest one I ever saw —a beautiful green, with a long train of light behind," she continued, rapidly, a little afraid of Ben's tone.

"Lucy, I wish you would listen to me, and not try to talk of something else."

"I will listen, if you will not talk nonsense."

"It is not nonsense, Lucy, all I have in my mind, and all I would say if I could. I haven't the ready tongue some have, and can't put my feelings in words as I wish."

"Then I wouldn't try, Ben; better let all go unsaid," Lucy answered, softly, and a little sadly.

"But I *must* speak," persisted her companion, with a sudden, warm energy; "and you must listen. It is not nonsense I am talking when I tell you, Lucy Fraser, that I love you better than everything on God's earth; and I haven't a hope or a wish in this world that I wouldn't give up this minute to hear you say you feel the same for me. There —it is all out now— what I have wanted for weeks and months to say. I have tried a long time, and in every way, to make you understand this; but whether I succeeded or not, I could never tell; and now I ask you plainly, Do you, can you, will you love me? Answer me something, Lucy. After all this miserable waiting, any answer is better than none."

"O, Ben! you do not know how unhappy you make me! I wish you would not speak so."

"Don't put off my question in that way; it is no kindness to me," entreated Ben, in a voice low and husky. "Only say that my love is not disagreeable to you — that some time, if not now, you may value it — some time, when you have thought more about it."

"I hoped, Ben, you would not force me to say what may seem unkind. I never thought you cared so much for me. I cannot love you as you love me. Hush! don't urge me — it can do no good; but O, forgive me if I ever gave you reason to think differently. I never meant it — I did not know. It hurts me, Ben, to say this," she added, with a choking voice; "but you had better understand me fully now, and begin to forget me as soon as you can."

"It is easy to *say* forget; do you think it will be easy to *do?* But won't you give me one last chance? Let me think you may change your mind. I will wait — a year — ten years — as long as you please."

"It is of no use, Ben. I shall never change my mind, and it would be wicked in me to give you any such hope. Indeed, dear Ben, I know my own mind, and I cannot deceive you. Here we are at uncle Page's," she added, pausing and holding out her hand, while the tears stood in her beautiful eyes. "Don't come in, but say good night here. And O, Ben, forgive me if I have said anything unkind. It was the farthest from my wish."

"I have nothing to forgive," he replied, tenderly pressing between his two strong palms the little hand she offered him, "and nothing to blame but my own foolishness. God bless you, Lucy — good night;" and he turned slowly away down the hill, while Lucy went quickly in, without once looking back.

Much to her annoyance, she found Hannah occupied with a visitor — a neighbor, who had brought her knitting-work, to spend the evening. No one else was present, and as soon as the first salutations were over, she inquired for Mary.

"Why, she has gone home. Didn't Heman tell you?"

"No, indeed. When did she go?"

"Yesterday. They went away about four o'clock in the afternoon."

"'They'?" Who went with her, and what made her leave so suddenly?"

"Her mother sent a man up from Windham for her. Her grandfather is dead; he died very suddenly, the man said, in a fit."

"What an awful providence!" ejaculated Mrs. Smiley, the neighbor, while Lucy remained too much shocked to speak. "I've heerd say, Hannah, that old Squire Dwight was a terrible hard old creetur. So he's dead at last. I wonder if he left a will."

"To tell the truth," answered Hannah, a little hesitatingly, "that was the first thing I thought of myself. It seems rather unfeeling to think of a man's money first; but he wasn't a man to be mourned for much. If there is no will, Mrs. Elliot will come in for her full share of the property, and Mary's fortune will be quite large. But I dare say there is a will. The old man always said there was."

"Did Mary leave any word for me?" asked Lucy.

"Yes; she wanted to see you again very much, but said she should expect you to come to Windham in the summer, as you promised. She meant to leave a note for you, but hadn't time to write it — said she would write soon, though."

"Ah, Lucy! is that you?" said a clear voice at the door, that made Lucy start. "I am glad to see you back again. We are losing our family rapidly."

"Yes, Mr. Fanshaw; Hannah tells me that Mary is gone — a disagreeable surprise."

"I hope you have come back to stay. Hannah and I shall be positively dismal if left to ourselves much longer."

"I am afraid I cannot stay this time," Lucy replied, with a very good imitation of her old bright smile.

"You are not intending to return to-night?"

"No."

"Then I shall see you again in the morning;" and he passed on to his own room.

Lucy sat down by the fire, paying little heed to the gossip of Mrs. Smiley, whose tongue and knitting-needles played a lively and continuous tune. Lydia had gone to spend the night with some young companion, and she was thus left quite to herself and the company of her own thoughts. She was distressed by her interview with Ben Miller, and reproached herself for much of her conduct towards him. His generous denial of any blame on her part did not wholly relieve her conscience. Then she thought of Mary's departure, and how much she regretted it; and the next moment she reproached herself that she did not regret it more.

Mrs. Smiley staid until quite late; and then Heman came, and they sat round the fire talking until Hannah ordered her brother off to bed.

"I am glad you came down to-night," Hannah said, when they were alone. "I have been real lonesome since Mary went away."

"You must be — and Lydia gone, too. And so Mary's grandfather is dead," she added, thoughtfully. "It is sad to think, Hannah, that nobody will really be sorry he is gone."

"It is his own fault that no one regrets him. But I have a good deal of curiosity about his will, though." And she continued, — rising and going to the clock, which she began to wind, with her face carefully turned from her cousin, — "Did it ever strike you, Lucy, that Mary and the master had more than just a fancy for each other?"

"I may have thought of it sometimes. Why?" replied Lucy, in as calm a voice as she could assume, glancing quickly at her companion, whose back was still towards her.

"Because Mary told me, the day before she left, that they were engaged. She said she meant to have told you the day she was at your house; but, somehow, she couldn't find a good chance. It seems she has taken the master on condition he will wait for her. She says she can't afford to marry now — they are both too poor. So, you see, the old man's will may make a good deal of difference to them. Are you surprised?"

At the first of these announcements, which Hannah delivered without once looking round, Lucy had caught her breath sharply through her white lips, and then remained perfectly quiet, though extremely pale. To Hannah's question she replied, in a voice so low and husky as to betray to her cousin the effort it cost her, —

"Not wholly — I have expected as much recently — no; I am not surprised."

Hannah had no heart to pursue the subject farther, and adroitly appeared to have her attention drawn to something else. During their preparations for bed, Lucy said little, but Hannah kept up a show of interest in a variety of topics, with sensitive delicacy striving not to see the too evident distress of the young girl.

They were to occupy the same bed, and after exchanging good nights, both lay for more than an hour in perfect silence. Lucy thought her companion sleeping, and a long, tremulous sigh escaped her lips. The next instant she felt Hannah's arms clasped closely about her, and her head pressed to that kind bosom. This silent, gentle sympathy, from one she loved so well, overthrew the last barrier raised by pride, and tears, restrained till then, and choking sobs, gave evidence of the anguish that wrung her heart.

"My poor lamb!" whispered Hannah, softly. It was all she said — it was all she ever said; but each fully understood the other.

After a time Lucy's wild sobs ceased; and though her tears still flowed, it was softly. But no sleep gave her temporary forgetfulness; and when her eyelids opened on the dull gray of early morning, the coming day seemed insupportable. A single day seemed a misery impossible to endure; and yet there flashed on her mind the thought that she was to endure years of days as hopeless. Poor child! she had not yet learned the sad yet blessed truth which Wallenstein expressed, when he said, —

> "Verschmerzen werd' ich diesen Schlag, das weiss ich,
> Denn was verschmerzte nicht der Mensch! Vom Höchsten
> Wie vom Gemeinsten lernt er sich entwöhnen,
> Denn ihn besiegen die gewalt'gen Stunden."

The joy and the sunshine of life were gone. That they could return never seemed to her possible. Nothing remained now but to endure while existence should last. To the violent outburst of feeling on the preceding evening had succeeded a dull, brooding calm, a kind of sullen apathy, more fatal than the most frantic grief.

Rising carefully, that she might not disturb her cousin, she dressed and passed noiselessly out of the house. With heavy footsteps, in the dim, early morning, she took her way homeward. Her pale cheeks and heavy eyes at once attracted the attention of her family. To their anxious inquiries she returned answer that her head ached, and she believed she had taken cold; and she was obliged to submit herself at once to her mother's anxious nursing. Mrs. Fraser thought she had not seemed well for a week, and insisted that she should go no more to her uncle's, but stay at home and be taken care of.

Lucy readily consented. She had no longer any wish or preference. Her days passed heavily enough. Her dreary forebodings were all true; life *was* the burden she had looked for it to be. She saw, with a passionate regret, that the past few months had made a return to her old careless, happy life impossible, even if she could outlive the present pain. And what had these months brought her in exchange? A few brief, bright weeks of illusive happiness, and a present and a future without hope!

This passive acceptance of her fate as something she might and should have foreseen, induced a dull, apathetic state of feeling from which nothing was able to rouse her. A violent and passionate sense of injury or injustice would have been far less dangerous. But for Mary and Fanshaw she had no bitter or resentful thought. Looking her sorrow steadily in the face, she saw — or believed she saw — that she had merely deceived herself. She had shut her eyes and allowed herself to dream a beautiful dream which had no foundation in reality. She could not see — and it was fortunate for her that she could not — how different might have been the result but for Mary's coming to Hillsboro'. At that time but little, but very little, was wanting to make Fanshaw her lover. He was not, however; he was only a rather warm admirer. Had nothing occurred to change the current of that feeling, it would possibly, and very probably, have deepened gradually into an earnest and lasting attachment. But Mary came, and in a week the fate of all three was decided. Fanshaw himself was no more aware of the truth of this than Lucy. He honestly believed that he now entertained for his lovely pupil the same feeling that he always had. It did vary but very little — yet that little was everything. Of the real state of Lucy's feeling neither he nor Mary had a guess. The general impression among her friends concerning Ben Miller had completely blinded them.

The state of extreme mental and physical depression into which Lucy had fallen would have caused great anxiety to her family, had it not seemed to them to be partly explained — as it was in a great measure thrust out of sight — by the increasing illness of her grandmother. Old Mrs. Fraser was rapidly failing; they could no longer deceive themselves. Lucy devoted herself assiduously to the invalid, glad to be employed in a service which demanded all her thoughts. She gave herself no rest by night or day; and the neighbors, as they saw her faded cheek and wasted form, said Lucy Fraser was killing herself taking care of her grandmother. When her father remonstrated with her, and begged her to take a little rest, she replied, with a passionate burst of tears, —

"It will not be long, father, that I can do anything for dear grandma. Don't deny me now."

And so they let her have her way.

CHAPTER XV.

MARY ELLIOT had been gone two weeks when there came a long letter from her to Lucy. In it she expressed regret at not having been able to see her friend again, and told, in happy words, of her engagement, adding that she should expect Lucy, if not disqualified before that time arrived, to act as her bridesmaid. She spoke briefly, though kindly, of her grandfather, but did not allude in any way to the disposition of his property; from which both Lucy and Hannah inferred that it was left, as the old man had always said it should be, to his elder daughters.

One morning, about three weeks after Mary's departure, as Hannah was at work in her kitchen, she heard a knock at the outer door. Hastily dusting the flour from her hands, and rolling down her sleeves, she went to open it, and was surprised to find standing on the doorstep the stranger who had sought the shelter of her roof on the night of the storm. The warm words of welcome that sprang to her lips were indorsed by the kindly smile in her eyes.

"Why, Mr. Stafford! I declare, you are the last person I expected. Walk in — do. I am right glad to see you."

"Many thanks. I could not resist the temptation, as I was passing, to look in upon you for a moment. Are you alone?"

"Yes, just now. My folks are at school. But sit down."

"I must not stay five minutes," he answered, standing, cap in hand, before the fire. Your little family, I presume, is much the same as when I saw you."

"It is some changed: we have lost two out of our number."

"Ah! And which two, pray?"

"Well, Miss Elliot has gone home. Her grandfather died, and they sent for her. And cousin Lucy is gone, too. Her folks are sick."

"A change indeed — so the day is changed when the sun sets. But you have still that agreeable schoolmaster?"

"Yes. He will stay a week or so longer. But do take off your overcoat, and stay to dinner."

"Impossible, my kind friend. I should be most happy to do so; but it is really impossible, as I have to go to Kiffton between this and one o'clock, to see a person who will arrive there in the train at that time."

"Have you been in Edgehill all the time since you were here?"

"Yes, except some brief excursions into the neighboring towns."

"What has become of that boy?"

"Good heavens! he sticks to me like a bur. He has made up his mind to abide with me; and I see no way but to submit."

"But what can you do with him, Mr. Stafford?"

"You might ask, what will he do with me? I plainly foresee that I shall be as wax in his hands. I can't get rid of him. I told him this morning that I should send the Kiffton overseers of the poor after him; and the rascal grinned in my face. He waits upon me like a slave, and obeys me like a dog in everything but this — he refuses to leave me. I dare say I shall end by liking the imp. He is a prime favorite with Mr. Gore."

" O, you are staying with Mr. Gore still ? "

" Yes ; and I find it, as your pretty cousin assured me, a delightful house. I have long known Mr. Gore by reputation, and we had exchanged a good many letters, first and last. I regret now that I should so long have delayed making the personal acquaintance of a man I so much admire."

Although Mr. Stafford declined sitting down, pleading great haste, he still remained some time, standing opposite Hannah at the fireplace, or taking, now and then, a quick turn up and down the room, restless not so much from nervousness as from an abundant fulness of life. It was not until after several attempts at leave-taking that he finally found himself on the doorstep. As he buttoned the fur collar of his coat more closely about his neck, and sprang into the sleigh, Hannah asked, —

" When shall you come back this way, Mr. Stafford ? "

" To-night, probably. I think I left a promise with my host to that effect."

" Can't you get back in time to stop and take tea with us ? I should be very glad to have you. The nights are fine, and you can drive to Edgehill after eight just as well as before."

" I should be only too happy to do so ; and, if I can get back in season, I certainly will. Having one of Mr. Gore's best horses, I may find it practicable. However, if I am not here by sharp six, do not wait for me."

"We'll see about that. But you will be here, I guess. It is a pleasant day to go to Kiffton, and the sleighing is better than I expected to see it again this winter. Now, be sure and come back;" and, as he turned his horse's head, and lifted his fur cap with a low bow, Hannah added to herself, —

"Strange what makes me like that man so much! I don't know the first thing about him; but when he is here I feel as if I had been acquainted with him all my life. I wonder why Mary didn't like him any better. But there, she was all taken up with somebody else. Well, if I am going to have company to tea, I had better be at work. I wish one of the girls was here to help entertain him. But then, he doesn't need much entertaining; he can look out for himself. I don't know but that is one reason why I like him."

Thus soliloquizing, Hannah went about the household work, which had been delayed by the time spent with her visitor. As they sat at dinner that day, she mentioned her guest of the morning, and the half promise with which he had left her.

"Well, upon my word," said Fanshaw, "that is pleasant. I, for one, shall be very glad to see him. I have seldom met a person who interested me more; and Lydia, here, will be charmed, no doubt. I believe he was a prime favorite with you, young lady."

"Yes; he is real splendid, Mr. Fanshaw. I think King James, in that poem of the Lady of the Lake you read to us one evening, must have looked just as he does."

"Hannah, do you hear that? Our Lydia is growing enthusiastic. I had no idea of the impression this gentleman was making — had you?"

" Lydia's fancies were always odd. She hasn't a great many, but they generally mean something when she takes one."

" I am not surprised at her present very romantic admiration. This Mr. Stafford, unless I greatly mistake, is accustomed to please your sex."

" What makes you think so ? "

" He was born for it. It is in his voice, his eyes, in everything he says and does. Nature has given him the gift of charm ; and it is his fault, not his misfortune, if he fails to please. What time will he be here ? "

" About six. Don't be late to tea."

Hannah was busy most of the afternoon with preparations for the reception of her expected guest ; and it was evidence of the high place he held in her regard, that she was at great pains in arranging her supper. The best china, in bright, old-fashioned colors, — part of her mother's wedding outfit, — graced the table. The best silver and the most cherished and snowy damask were brought out and arranged with scrupulous care. The number and variety of the viands also attested to the importance of the occasion, and would have tempted the most fastidious appetite. She regretted that she had not control of the parlor, but was in some measure reconciled to the deprivation by Lydia's assurance that " men folks didn't mind such things so much as women did."

When everything was ready, she seated herself by the window to await the appearance of Mr. Stafford. I wish I could show her to you exactly as she looked, sitting there in the gathering winter twilight. She was not handsome — our good Hannah ; but, in the midst of all that warmth and comfort evoked by her hands, she was a most attractive object. She looked, as she was, the fit presiding spirit of such a place. The kindly face, the neat gown of brown merino, the smooth hair and snowy linen collar, the strong, helpful hands, now folded placidly in her lap, the look of calm content, which was habitual on her face, — all were in perfect keeping with the well-ordered room, the warm fire, and with the atmosphere of peace and comfort which pervaded the apartment.

Soon " the children " arrived from school, and not long after, Fanshaw appeared. " What! not come yet?" he said as he entered. " I shall be more disappointed than I care to own, if he fails to keep his word."

" It is hardly six yet; and I shall look for him till half past," Hannah said.

Just then there was a sound of bells, and Lydia ran to the window.

" Here he is! " she cried. " No; it is only Deacon Sharpe. I hope he won't take it in his old head to come in here. There, he has gone by."

Another minute and bells were again heard. This time they did not pass, but came up to the east door, and stopped. Heman went to the door, and found Mr. Stafford just alighting. He came into the sitting-room, and, as Hannah met him, he exclaimed, triumphantly, —

" Let no enemy of mine assert, after this, that I am incapable of punctuality. Look at your clock."

" We will give you credit for being very prompt, though Lydia was confident you would not keep your promise."

" Miss Lydia, all men, in the eye of the law, are held innocent until proved guilty. I trust you will regard me in the same lenient fashion."

Fanshaw entered at this moment, and the greeting between the two gentlemen was very cordial — on Stafford's
part, gay. Indeed, he appeared to be in most exuberant
spirits. He seemed a man who at all times — partly from
habit, but more from natural temperament — could catch
the pleasure of the passing hour, fling himself into the
spirit of the moment, and identify himself with the feelings and the interests of those with whom chance might
place him. As they were sitting down to the table, he
said, turning, with a whimsical smile, to Mr. Fanshaw, —

"Are you a believer in the theory, which obtains quite
widely, that we mortals are impelled to the fulfilment of
certain ends by the influence of superior intelligences?"

"That 'there's a divinity that shapes our ends, rough-
hew them as we will'?"

"That is not the idea, precisely; but that some special,
kindly intelligence prompts us to certain acts or omissions,
which lead to important consequences, when a choice
seemed to lie with us, and we might naturally have acted
otherwise than we did."

"Something of the nature of guardian angels? Yes;
I believe I am half a convert to that theory of late."

"I am wholly a convert. Four weeks ago I sat in the
parlor of a public house in Kiffton. My guardian angel,
disguised as the bar-keeper, — and he was very well disguised, — brought in some choice cigars. Enjoying them,
I sat over the fire two good hours, which, if spent upon
the road, would have taken me to Edgehill before dark,
and lost me — all I am enjoying now."

"I suppose," said Lydia, "it must have been the same
spirit that jerked open our wood-house window that night,

11

and made cousin Lucy get up and strike a light to
fasten it."

"I have no doubt you are right, Miss Lydia. It is quite
apparent that the beneficent intelligence in question intended to bring me hither. What its ultimate design in
so doing could have been, who shall tell?"

They lingered long over the table, the changing humor
and gay fancies of their guest, Fanshaw's genially respon-
sive mood, and Lydia's lively sallies making the time pass
swiftly, and the evening was well advanced when they ad-
journed to the sitting-room.

"Come, Miss Lydia," said the visitor, drawing forward
the cherry-wood work-stand, and seating himself beside it
in a large arm-chair, "bring the backgammon-board: we
have time for a rubber before I must go."

"Why must you go to-night?" said Hannah. "Your
room is all ready for you, and you know we should be very
glad to have you stay."

"My dear friend, do not urge me. If you do, I fear I
shall consent in a mortifyingly short space of time."

"Then I shall keep urging."

"Please do stay, Mr. Stafford," said Lydia.

"You see, Mr. Fanshaw, to what my firmness is exposed.
I am in danger of yielding without a struggle."

"Yield gracefully, then, and let us decide for you. We
are quite capable of doing so — are we not, Hannah?"

There the matter rested. The talk, the laughter, and
the backgammon went on, and no one seemed to note that
the evening was passing rapidly away, until some remark
was caused by the sound of sleigh-bells without. They
were evidently approaching the house, for presently the

sound of runners was heard crunching on the snow-covered drive, and then the steps of a horse at the door.

" I wonder who that can be," said Hannah.

" Perhaps it's Jerry," suggested Heman; " he was going to the Centre to-night, and I guess he's got a letter from father."

" Those were not uncle Robert's bells; and, besides, they came down the hill. There, somebody is knocking. Take a candle, Heman, and go to the door."

Heman did as desired, and directly a man's voice was heard outside, asking some question, immediately after which came an inquiry for Mr. Stafford. Heman replied that he was there, and asked the questioner to walk in.

At the first sound of the stranger's voice, Mr. Stafford started visibly, and his countenance changed. He may or may not have lost a shade of his usual color; but a look difficult to define settled on his face. It was like the look of a man suddenly brought to bay — forced unexpectedly to meet something disagreeable or dangerous. A single troubled glance around, as if he would have escaped had escape been possible, and then his lips closed firmly, and his brows gathered into a look of fixed resolve.

The stranger who entered was a florid, pleasant-looking man of forty-five or fifty, handsomely and carefully dressed, and altogether of a very prepossessing appearance. Mr. Stafford, who had risen as he advanced, accepted his offered hand with a scarcely perceptible air of restraint. The salutations which passed between them were those of ordinary acquaintances — polite, but not familiar. When they were over, and the stranger — whom he introduced by the name of Lovell — turned, with a few courteous words, to Hannah, Mr. Stafford sank back in his chair, and, passing his hand over his now somewhat pale forehead, a deep breath escaped him. Something in the manner or greeting of the stranger seemed to afford him inexpressible relief; and nothing unusual in his appearance now remained, except that he was a shade more formal than with his friends of the farm-house. He continued very quiet, his hand resting on the backgammon board, and his fingers playing idly with the dice. When the stranger turned again to him, he said, civilly, —

"I am even more surprised, Mr. Lovell, to meet you in this remote region than to find myself here."

"You well may be. But the truth is, I had the ill fortune to fall heir, through the will of an uncle, to a tract of wild land some fifty miles from this. Thus far this legacy has been productive of nothing but trouble, but of that it has yielded a plentiful crop. This is the second journey I have made to look after it, and I think it will be the last — certainly the last in midwinter."

"You will never make an Arctic voyager, Mr. Lovell."

"Fortunately, I have no ambition leading me in that way. But excuse me for not before mentioning my reason for intruding upon you this evening. Being at Mr. Gore's to-day, he mentioned that you were staying with him; and it occurred to me that you could undoubtedly furnish me with some information on a matter of business in which I am interested. As I could obtain this much better in person than by letter, I have ventured to call, Mr. Gore having told me that I might possibly find you here."

"I shall be most happy, Mr. Lovell, to be of any service to you which lies in my power."

"Thank you." And the stranger proceeded to state his errand, which, having no bearing on this story, need not be repeated. They talked for half an hour, Mr. Lovell evidently getting all the information he desired. As the latter rose to go, he said, —

"Mr. Stafford, I am greatly indebted to you. How much longer do you remain in this far-away region?"

"I can hardly tell. Until I am tired of it, I presume."

"Knowing nothing of the resources of Edgehill, I can, of course, make no estimate as to how soon that is likely to be. Can I give you any news regarding our New York friends? We have a few in common, I believe."

"I am so much a stranger there of late, that they are, probably, very few. Can you tell me anything of the Lawtons?— the Grant Lawtons, I mean."

"Very little. They are to sail in a few weeks for France — a plan of old Mrs. Lawton's."

"Do you see Brainerd, ever?"

"Quite seldom. I have returned to bachelor habits, and see but few people. Mrs. Lovell went to Cuba some weeks since."

"Indeed! Did she go alone?"

"She was accompanied by our daughter, whose health has been delicate for some time. Mrs. Lovell thought her failing, and the doctors ordered her south. We hoped the voyage might benefit her. Excuse me, madam," he continued, turning to Hannah, "for intruding on your family so unseasonably, and allow me to wish you good night. — What shall I say I left you doing, Mr. Stafford?"

"I doubt if any one will take the trouble to ask," Stafford replied, rising and accompanying his guest a part of the way to the door.

"That is an excess of modesty, I am sure. No farther, I beg. Good evening."

"Good evening, Mr. Lovell."

When the stranger was gone, the game of backgammon was renewed; but now Lydia had it all her own way. Her antagonist seemed to have lost all his skill. He sat silent, his eyes bent moodily upon the board, throwing mechanically, but with his thoughts evidently far away. It seemed as if the coming of the stranger had diverted them from their pleasant channels into courses rough and dark. When the game was ended, he pushed the board away, and said, —

"Now, Heman, if you will let me have my horse, I shall be obliged to you."

"Why, Mr. Stafford! you promised to stay all night," cried Lydia, while Hannah also protested warmly against this decision.

"Do you wish to see this family in tears, Mr. Stafford?" said Fanshaw, laughing.

"My dear friends, you flatter me. But the truth is, I quite forgot a promise made to Mr. Gore to return to-night. I know, in your kindness, you will forgive me, and let me go."

"Why, if you must, you must, I suppose; but we shall expect you to come another time, and finish up this visit."

"You may be sure, Miss Page, I shall not fail to do so, if possible. Miss Lydia, I am forgiven — am I not?"

"I don't know about forgiving you. I don't like it one bit."

"It wrings my heart to think you are offended past forgiveness. I trust to time to soften your displeasure."

"We shall at least see you before you leave Edgehill?"

Hannah asked, as the sound of the sleigh was heard at the door.

"Certainly; I shall come to make my peace with your young sister. Good by. I shall not soon forget all I have enjoyed in your house. Miss Lydia, I postpone our reconciliation. Mr. Fanshaw, how soon do you leave?"

"One week after this, and I bid adieu to Hillsboro'."

"Then I may not see you again; let us shake hands to our future meeting. Again, farewell, all;" and he was gone.

As they came back into the sitting-room, after watching his departure from the door, Lydia exclaimed, a little ruefully, —

"I don't see why he need have gone to-night. Mary and Lucy both gone! and next week you will go! O, dear! I wish people could always stay together."

"That would be very pleasant, Lydia. But what do you think the gallant Fitz James would say if he could see your doleful face now?"

"I don't care what he would say. Good night. I am going to bed."

"Our friend did take rather a sudden departure; didn't it strike you so, Hannah?" asked Fanshaw, when they were alone.

"Yes; and, between you and me, that promise was got up for the occasion."

"I had some such idea myself. That Mr. Lovell seemed a very pleasant man; but I do not think his coming was, in all respects, a pleasure to Mr. Stafford."

"I thought so. Well, the children have left us early, seems to me. And so you are going next week?"

"Yes; and I hope you will believe me when I tell you that I shall be sincerely sorry to go. I shall retain a most grateful recollection of my stay here."

"O, I can readily believe that you will remember Hillsboro' pleasantly, and without feeling much flattered, either."

"Ah, you are unfair. I have other reasons than those to which you refer for grateful recollections of your home. But I will not keep you up to-night to listen to protestations. You look too tired to make that agreeable." And he, too, went.

CHAPTER XVI.

DURING the remaining days of Fanshaw's stay, he saw Lucy but twice — once on Sunday at meeting with her father, when he had no opportunity even for a word, and once the day before he left Hillsboro', when he went to call upon her. On this occasion she had been up all of the preceding night, and was lying down when he arrived. Mrs. Fraser received him, and, while waiting for Lucy's appearance, he could not refrain from commenting, with the anxiety of genuine friendship, on the pale and wearied look he had seen her wearing on Sunday. Her mother readily accounted for this by the young girl's unceasing care of her grandmother, and told, with fond maternal solicitude, of her constant watchings by the invalid's bed.

Lucy's hand may have trembled that day, as she stood in her own room, putting up the long braids of her hair; and her heart beat quickly as she caught the sound of a well-known voice in descending the stairs; but both were still as she entered the room to meet the visitor. Her greeting was marked only by extreme quiet, her mother sustaining the chief burden of the conversation. Fanshaw did not stay long, feeling that more than a brief call would be intrusive. On leaving, he bade Mrs. Fraser good by, and then, turning to Lucy, took her hand in both his own. Most sincerely he expressed his regret that the illness of one she loved should have interfered with their pursuit of studies which both had enjoyed so much, adding a hope that their pleasant friendship might not end there, but that a portion of her regard for Mary might be transferred to himself. Then, raising her little cold, white fingers to his lips, he bowed and was gone. Mrs. Fraser left the room at the same time, and Lucy, walking to the window, leaned her aching forehead against the cold pane, and watched his retreating figure till the gathering shadows of twilight received and hid him from her view. When he was gone, wholly gone from her sight, she sank down upon her knees beside the window, and a low, moaning cry of hopeless anguish escaped her lips.

The school was done, and Fanshaw was gone; and Hannah was now in daily expectation of her father's return. Old Mrs. Fraser, who, it was now quite evident, could live but a short time, seemed to have no wish ungratified except to see her son-in-law again; and Mr. Page had accordingly been sent for in all haste.

It was well, perhaps, for Lucy, that at this time her energies were taxed to the utmost, and her mind and heart filled with thoughts for others. From Mary she heard often, and learned all her hopes and plans. For the latter, the wheel of fortune had made a complete revolution. Almost the last act of her grandfather's life had been to order his daughter, Miss Dwight, to burn, in his presence, the will, made many years before, from whose provisions Mrs. Elliot and her children were excluded. It had been his intention to make a new testament, differing from this in some slight particulars; but death overtook him before that design was carried out. His wealth was shared equally among his three daughters, and Mary was now rich enough to marry when she pleased. Fanshaw had, as he expected, been admitted to the bar, and to a partnership with Mr. Burke, an old and prominent lawyer at Colchester. No reason existed for longer delaying their marriage, and the approaching month of June was appointed for the wedding. Lucy learned all this—we can scarcely say unmoved, but with no shock of feeling. She had endured the worst, and nothing further seemed of any moment to her.

Fanshaw had been gone two weeks, when, one afternoon, as Hannah and Lydia sat at their sewing, Mr. Stafford suddenly looked in upon them. To their eager inquiries he returned answer that he was just leaving Edgehill, was to sail in a week for Europe, but could not think of going without one word of farewell to his kind friends. He laughingly called Hannah's attention to the fact that the young barbarian, "Tate," *alias* "Figaro," was snugly ensconced in his sleigh at the door, that young person having expressed an intention of remaining with him indefinitely, and of accompanying him wherever he might go. The visitor chatted in a lively manner; seemed altogether in the gayest spirits; protested he must not stay, as he had not a moment to spare; yet lingered for an hour, and was only driven to leave-taking by a reasonable fear of being too late to catch the night train from Kiffton.

"Shall we ever see you again, Mr. Stafford?" asked Lydia, rather sadly.

"O, yes, Miss Lydia. I shall come back in a year and a day, as the fairy folk always do."

"I hope you will; but I'm dreadfully afraid you won't."

"What shall I say to convince you? What! tears in those bright eyes, and on my account! Dear child, you do me too much honor."

The words were light, but the tone was full of genuine feeling, and, taking her hand, he touched his lips lightly to the blushing cheek of the half-offended girl. Then, with a smile that was a little sad, he turned to Hannah, saying,—

"Half the pleasure of finding friends is dimmed by parting with them. Dear Miss Page, do not forget me; I shall always remember most warmly you and yours. Good by!" and he went.

Lydia watched him out of sight. "I don't care," she said, "if I did cry. I felt bad enough to. I wish we had never seen him — just to come and make us all like him so much, and then off to the ends of the earth; and there is the last! That is always the way with people I like. I can't keep one of them."

Poor Lydia seemed to think her case peculiar; but, fortunately for her, Mr. Page arrived that night, and in the delight of again seeing her father, any regrets for her new friend were quite driven out of her mind.

Old Mrs. Frazer seemed to have lingered only to see once more beside her this member of her family. Two days after Mr. Page's arrival, she closed her gentle eyes, and passed quietly from earth. She passed away clasping the hands of the two she loved best in life; and the last words upon her lips were a murmured charge to Lucy, confiding to her love and care the old man whom, after fifty years of companionship, she was leaving widowed and alone.

It was strange what a void her departure made through all the house. She had been so long a close invalid,

scarcely mingling at all in the family circle, and hers was
ever such a quiet, unobtrusive presence, it might have
seemed that its vanishing could make little difference. Yet
her very feebleness had made her the central object of
every one's thoughts and cares, and, when she was gone,
the whole house seemed empty; the occupation of all
seemed gone. For a time, at least, this was so. But, as
the weeks went by, and the waves of their daily life settled back into the old unruffled current, it began to be apparent that the grief for her loss was far from being felt
alike by all. Her children, kind and affectionate as they
were, and tenderly attached as they had been to their
mother, had yet their strongest ties in life elsewhere and
unbroken. For them there were hopes, and plans, and
enjoyments, in which the gentle old lady had no share.
But for the old man who mourned the partner of a lifetime, the fond watcher for his return after every period of
absence, the bride of his youth, the mother of his children,
the affectionate companion of his later years,— for him
there was no such solace. Each succeeding day seemed
to deepen his sense of loss. He would talk for hours with
Lucy of the departed, finding in the silent sympathy of her
mournful face his greatest comfort. Never had these two
been drawn so closely together as now, when united by
the bond of sorrow. On each had fallen the loss of what
had seemed to make the chief joy of existence. For one
was ended the happy reality of wedded love; for the other,
love's rosy morning dream.

At length the old man began to grow restless, and to
talk of going away for a time. At first his children paid
little heed to what he said, scarcely believing he could

seriously contemplate anything of the kind; but when he commenced to speak definitely of one more voyage, and to discuss plans for it, they became alarmed. Though they did not openly oppose him, they saw the necessity of taking some steps to alter his determination; and many and anxious were the family councils held to talk over this new difficulty.

One cold evening in the latter part of March, Lucy and her father were walking together down the hill towards the Pages'. There had been a long silence between them, which was broken by Mr. Fraser.

"Lucy, cannot you do something to get your grandfather's mind off the idea of going to sea? He seems bent upon it; but it will never answer."

"Of course it will not answer, father, for him to go to sea as he used to; but don't you think he might go away somewhere, and stay a while, and come back happier?"

"But where could he go, child?"

"O, I don't know! Couldn't he go and visit that French friend of his, and stay a few months?"

"Why, Lucy! your idea is as wild as his."

"No, father; I do not think it is wild. It takes but a few days to go to France now, and a steamer is as nice as a hotel. He would see new people and new things, and it would do him good."

"But it is a great way for an old man like him to go alone."

"He would not go alone, father; I should go with him."

"*You* go with him! Why, Lucy, you are crazy, or else you think I am. I could never consent to your leaving us for that length of time."

"Father, you would not refuse me! The last words dear grandma said, she made me promise never to leave grandpa. You will not make me break my promise!" cried the poor girl, her voice broken with sobs.

"Hush, child! Don't cry so, my little Lucy! I will consent to anything, if you will only look happier. Come, we will go and talk with Hannah about this; she always has a clear head."

Hannah was accordingly consulted, and, much to her uncle's surprise, she sided with Lucy. What were the arguments she used, both then and afterwards, privately and in family council, to convince Lucy's family of the wisdom of her plan, it is unnecessary to state; but, judging from the result, they were eminently forcible. The arrangement had commended itself to her mind at once. If change of occupation and of scene were likely to be of benefit to her grandfather, she believed they were even more desirable and necessary for Lucy. She had watched her young cousin with deep anxiety. The state of listless, apathetic melancholy, into which the latter was fast sinking, alarmed her. She felt that some means must be devised to rouse her from it; and what was more likely to prove effective than the change and excitement of travel, the sight of new scenes and faces, and the formation of new interests?

She carried the day at last. The plan finally decided upon met the approval of all parties. It was that Captain Fraser and Lucy should, about the middle of April, leave Hillsboro' for New York, travelling as slowly as they pleased. Thence, when all arrangements were completed, they were to sail for Havana, where the captain had many

Spanish and other friends. After remaining in Cuba as long as suited their pleasure, they were to proceed to France, spend a month or two with the old man's friends there, and return in the early autumn.

There were a few weeks of hurried preparation, and then all was ready. One misty April evening, when the warm earth sent up a smell of fresh coming life, and the pale stars shone faintly from the dusky heavens, Lucy Fraser stood on the front doorstep of her uncle's house. She had said good by to her uncle, to Lydia and Heman, and was now parting with Hannah. Her arms were clasped close about her cousin's neck as she whispered, —

"Good by, dear Hannah. Go often and see father and mother — will you not? I know they will be lonely; but I shall try and come back a better child, and think more of them and less of myself — more like you, dear Hannah."

There were tears in Hannah's kind gray eyes as she kissed the sweet lips of the young girl; but she answered only by a close embrace and a low "Good by," and Lucy darted away up the hill, and took her homeward way under the soft spring sky.

Early the next morning, as Hannah was opening the window of her chamber, she heard in the still, morning air the quick roll of wheels, and, bending out, she was just in time to catch a glimpse of her uncle Robert's carryall, driven rapidly past, and to see Lucy's handkerchief waving from the carriage in token of farewell.

CHAPTER XVII.

It was a fair morning in June, and from a heaven of cloudless blue the sun poured its full splendor over a landscape of tranquil beauty. With eyes that rested dreamily on the quiet scene before her, Hannah Page sat in the front door of her father's house. The drooping boughs of the butternut tree flung their cool shadows round, and screened her from the morning sun. All down the hill-side, and through the wide valley, the green and velvet fields slept in the warm and lazy light. Her eye took in the drowsy cattle ruminating in shady places, marked her father and his men at their labor in the fields, or, wandering far away, followed the yellow high road in its sinuous windings through the valley. In her ear sounded the ringing notes of an oriole, swinging on an orchard bough, and the delirious warble of a bobolink, as he reeled in the intoxication of his summer joy across the sloping clover field, while from distant pastures came the occasional tinkle of a cow-bell, mingling with the far-off shouts of children at their play. The frequent forest lines were rounded with masses of full, dark verdure, and over the rough faces of the Edgehill crags Summer had thrown her graceful veil, tenderly concealing their harsh outlines, and heightening every charm. All around was sweet and quiet. The green sward at her feet, starred with dandelions, still showed

12

sparkling drops of dew; the air was heavy with the fragrance of lilacs; close beside her the great green balls of the peonies were ready to burst into brilliant bloom, and along the roadside the pretty white clovers showed their heads.

Three years have passed since we last saw Hannah, leaving on her calm countenance scarcely a trace of their flight. In peaceful lives like hers, the lapse of years is marked mainly by the change in surrounding circumstances — they plough no deep furrows on the face. But, had Hannah been disposed to forget how time was passing, the appearance of the two young girls now approaching from up the hill might have refreshed her memory. In one of these it would not have been difficult to recognize Lydia Page, although three years' time had transformed her from a plain girl of fifteen to a very pretty one of eighteen. Her companion was a sweet-looking, blue-eyed maiden of about her own age — no other than our old acquaintance, Fanny Miller.

"Well, Lydia," said Hannah, as they drew near, "what did aunt Susan say?"

"She can't go to-day. Uncle Robert is gone to Edgehill with the only horse you can drive."

"When can she go?"

"Some day next week. But she said," continued Lydia, seating herself on the doorstep, "that she wanted to see you, and wished you'd go up this afternoon, if you could — wants your valuable advice about something, I believe. Come in, Fan; you are surely not going home now, right in the heat of the day."

"I must, Lydia. I ought to have gone two hours ago,

instead of up to Mrs. Fraser's with you. Shall you come down to-morrow?"

"Good gracious, Fanny! don't ask Lydia to go anywhere. She has got enough to do to keep her close at home all summer. If girls will get married they must take the consequences. I have advised her all along to put it off a couple of years."

"If you can't make her hear reason, why don't you say something to Ben?"

"He is no more open to conviction than she is. Have you been up to the house lately?"

"Mother and I rode up last week."

"How does your mother like it?"

"Very much, particularly the chambers; they are so high and airy. Hannah, who is that coming up the hill?"

"That is just what I am looking to see. Nobody I know."

"It must be; for, see, the lady is waving her handkerchief to you."

"So she is. Why, it is Mary Fanshaw, as sure as you are alive; and that is her husband with her."

The carriage which was approaching did indeed contain Ralph and Mary Fanshaw, and their child, a boy of something less than two years. In the graceful, fashionably-dressed lady alighting at the farm-house door, it is easy to recognize the Mary Elliot of former years, grown handsomer, if anything — beautiful with the reflection of new and ennobling experiences. In the person and appearance of Fanshaw, as he talks gayly with Hannah, is apparent less of the dreamy indolence that once characterized him, and more of the ambitious, hard-working man of business, who lays down the harness of life only when he returns to the circle of home.

"Fasten your horse to the hitching-post there, Mr. Fanshaw, and come right in; the men folks will be up soon and take care of him."

"Thank you, Hannah; but I cannot stop. I have to go to Edgehill to attend a justice court, and must be there by eleven o'clock. Mary will spend the day with you, and I shall come back for her to-night."

"I am glad you are going, Ralph; you talk all the time, and leave me no opportunity whatever."

"You see how it is, Hannah; when we are with you we both want your ear, and if we are ever in danger of quarrelling, it is on these occasions. Who was that pretty girl we met as we came up the hill?"

"That was Fanny Miller: don't you remember her?"

"I thought her face familiar. She looks like Ben. By the way, where is Lydia?"

"She has gone in with little Elliot."

"Yes, Ralph.; she disappeared at the first mention of the Millers. But allow me to remind you, sir, that if you are in a hurry to get to Edgehill, you had best drive on."

"Very good advice, Mrs. Fanshaw, which I shall proceed to act on at once. Tell Lydia I have a great deal to ask her when I come back. Good morning. Take care of the boy, Mary; don't let him break his neck while I am gone;" and with a smile and a nod he drove away.

Mary and Hannah turned into the entry, and the latter said, as she opened the parlor door, "Come in here, Mary; you must be tired and warm."

The room was deliciously cool, and sweet with the fra-

grance of lilacs, which, arranged in a quaint blue china
jar, nearly filled the fireplace. Mary threw off her bonnet,
and sat down in a large arm-chair.

"Ah! how quiet and pleasant it is here, and how unchanged everything looks! If it were not for little Elliot's voice in the other room, I could almost believe it to be
four years ago, and that I have just come from the old
school-house down the hill. And the thought of that summer brings me to the Frasers. How are they all at your
uncle's?"

"Very well indeed. There is nobody at home but uncle
and aunt, and the hired folks, you know."

"I suppose so. And when do your grandfather and
Lucy propose to come back?"

"Well, Mary, I don't know; I think sometimes they
never will."

"Hannah, what is the reason they have staid away so
long? They are fond of their home."

"Yes; but everything has conspired to keep them. At
the end of the first six months grandfather was not willing
to come, and their return was put off till the next spring.
Then they wrote that they were going to England for a
while, and should sail for home about midsummer. Next,
they took it in their heads to make a little tour in Scotland; and there Lucy got nearly drowned while out sailing
on a lake, as I told you, and was sick for some time in
consequence. It was during that sickness that she first
knew Mrs. Fleming, an American lady, who was kind as a
mother to her. She got well quite slowly, and the doctors said it would be very imprudent to take her back to
our cold climate in the autumn, and advised a winter in

the south of France or Spain. Mrs. Fleming was going to Spain to visit a brother who lives there, and they all went together."

"That brings it up to a year ago this spring, when you were at Colchester. What happened next?"

"Well, they kept writing that Lucy was quite well again, and that they were coming with the warm weather; and, just as we were expecting them every day, came a letter, saying that their return must be postponed indefinitely. You know that a great deal of their time has been spent with the Lascaux family, those friends of grandfather's. Before starting for home, they went to Marseilles to say good by; and there they found Mr. Maurice Lascaux, son of the old captain and father of all the young people Lucy is so fond of, on his death-bed. He died in a few days after, leaving his children to his father's care. The old man has been a cripple for several years, and the eldest child is a girl of nineteen."

"And I suppose that dear old grandfather of yours had to stay and take care of the poor souls."

"Exactly, Mary. Mr. Lascaux had been an East India merchant, and his affairs were, somehow, in a great snarl at the time of his sudden death. There was property enough if it was taken care of; but it was absolutely necessary that somebody should go to Calcutta, or Madras, or wherever it was, and attend to the settlement of the business, or the poor little orphans and the helpless old man would have little or nothing. So grandfather offered to go."

"So like him! But what became of Lucy meantime?"

"She went with him, of course. They are perfectly inseparable. They came back to Marseilles last April, and now they write they shall be off for home as soon as Julie Lascaux is married. We don't allow ourselves to expect them in the least, though the first of July is the time set for their coming."

" Do you imagine that Lucy will be a great deal changed, Hannah ? "

" O, she will be altered, of course — in some respects a good deal, perhaps. You have never seen that picture of her taken just before she went to India ? "

" No ; is it like her ? "

" I suppose it must be. She wrote that the Flemings and Lascaux, and all her friends, thought it perfect. It was painted in Paris by a great artist ; so of course it is good. There is just the head and neck ; the shoulders fade away into a sort of cloud. It is a beautiful picture, though hardly our Lucy. But, the same or changed, grandfather is just as proud of her as ever. In his last letter he said there was a young French lawyer, who, if he could plead his own cause as well as he did other people's, would make trouble for the folks on the hill. I don't know but it would kill uncle Robert if Lucy should marry a foreigner."

" You thought a year ago there was a chance of her marrying Mrs. Fleming's son."

" Horace Fleming ? O, yes ; I did think so, and do now, sometimes. Should like that better than the Frenchman."

" And we all thought she liked Ben Miller, and would marry him."

" Yes, I know we did ; but we were mistaken, you see ; and I think Ben is much better mated with Lydia than with Lucy."

" Perhaps so ; but I know so little of Lucy of late that

I can scarcely judge. We have never corresponded since she left home."

"How does that happen?"

"Partly through negligence, but more, probably, through preoccupation on both sides. I have frequently wished to write, but would not know her address at the time, and that was the end. But when is Lydia to be married?"

"In October, if Ben gets his house ready, and she gets her sewing done. She has her wedding dress in the house now; shall I show it to you?"

"By all means."

Hannah rose and went into the bedroom adjoining the parlor, whence she soon reappeared, bringing a parcel carefully wrapped in tissue paper. Sitting down beside Mary, she unrolled to her admiring eyes yards of India muslin, of cloud-like delicacy, and enriched with exquisite embroidery.

"Beautiful! Where did she get it, Hannah?"

"That is the best part of it, Mary. It was a present; and, as you can never guess from whom, I may as well tell you. Don't you remember that winter you were here, there was a man staid with us two or three days through a storm?"

"Certainly; I remember him perfectly. His name was Stafford. Ralph liked him very much, and often speaks of him. Did he give this to Lydia?"

"Yes."

"Then you have seen him again?"

"No; this was sent from a Boston express office; but the note that came with it was dated at Paris, a month or six weeks before. Lydia has the note somewhere; she will show it to you. In speaking of the muslin, he said he knew nothing of feminine apparel until it was worn, and he had depended upon a lady, acknowledged to have faultless taste, to select for him, otherwise he should expect to make some fatal mistake. It was a very pretty note — sounded just like him. And isn't the dress pretty, too?"

"It is, indeed; and are you aware that it is quite expensive?"

"I thought it might be. I don't know much about such things. You see Lydia has had it nearly two years. She didn't make it up at first, because she was growing still; and at last she concluded to keep it to be married in."

"It will make a beautiful bridal dress, and Lydia will look charmingly in it. It was an odd idea, his sending it."

"Perhaps it was; but he seemed to take a great fancy to Lydia. We like to laugh at Ben about him. But he doesn't trouble himself much about her fancies."

"He has no reason, I presume. But if I were a man, I should not want my wife or sweetheart to admire such a person too much."

"Why, Mary! don't you think he was a good man?"

"O, I dare say. I did not mean anything to the contrary. But he was one of those singularly fascinating men against whom ordinary persons would find it difficult to compete. Bless me! Lydia is calling us to dinner; and there come your father and Heman."

CHAPTER XVIII.

THE day passed very pleasantly to Mary; yet there was one whom she missed constantly. So intimately associated was Lucy Fraser with all her memories of Hillsboro' that she felt her absence everywhere; and again and again she expressed her impatience at the latter's long delay, and her eager desire to look once more upon the face of the dear wanderer. As they sat together, towards the close of the afternoon, Hannah proposed to walk up to her uncle's; but Mary declined.

"No, Hannah; I cannot think of going to the house, to find neither Lucy nor your grandfather."

"You would scarcely miss them through a short call. It always seems to me, when I go there, that they must be about somewhere. Grandfather's cane stands in its old place in the entry; and on the rack is a straw hat of Lucy's, as if she had hung it there an hour ago. Everything is just as she left it; her books lie about with the leaves turned down where she read them last; her chamber, even her work-box, are undisturbed."

"Yet I prefer to wait till July and see herself. Who could have dreamed, when we were last together, and she planned so gayly to visit me, of all that would come and go before we met again? I remember that her father cut five from the six weeks we had allotted for that visit, because, he said, he could not spare her so long. Ah! how pretty she was that day, and how full of bright young life! Hannah, do you know that I almost dread to see Lucy?"

"Dread to see her! Why so?"

"I can hardly tell; yet it seems to me that she will be entirely changed — that I shall have lost my friend. Lucy was a strange girl; I sometimes think we none of us knew her as she really was."

"Perhaps not; but still, I think I knew her pretty well, and I will venture to say that you will not find the change so great as you fear."

"I sincerely hope you know best. Look! there comes Ralph down the hill this minute; and I wonder who is with him. Why, it is Singleton Burke! Where could he have found him?"

Both Mary and Hannah went to the door as Fanshaw drove up.

"Ah, Ralph, you are early. Hannah, you have not forgotten our friend, Mr. Burke?" said Mary, as a dignified-looking gentleman, a little older than Fanshaw, approached the doorstep.

"Certainly not; and I am very glad to see him again. Come in, Mr. Burke."

"Thank you, Miss Page," answered the gentleman addressed, following her into the parlor. "I am expecting my horse along every moment. I left him for my boy to drive down, while, for the sake of a companion, I took a seat with Fanshaw."

Singleton Burke was the son of Fanshaw's old friend and partner, Mr. Burke of Colchester. Still comparatively

young in years, his talents, his dignity of character, and
doubtless, too, his worldly success, had given him a kind
of prominence not usually achieved by men of his age.
Though unmarried, he maintained an establishment of his
own, occupying a fine old house left him by a bachelor
uncle.   Between this person and the Fanshaws there existed a strong friendship.   He was a reserved man, in general, had few intimates, and went little into mixed society;
but he was a constant and familiar visitor at their house,
where Hannah had often met him.

Mr. Burke's horse did not arrive as expected, and, supper being announced, he accepted an invitation to join the
family at their meal.

"Now, really, Hannah, this is very pleasant," said Fanshaw, as they sat round the table.   "Do you know, I think
I shall never wear off the feeling I have of coming home
whenever I come back to Hillsboro'?"

"I am sure I hope you never may, Mr. Fanshaw.   This
is one of your homes," Hannah said, while Burke turned to
Mary, with a smile.

"There are many delightful associations connected, in
your husband's mind, with this place, I believe, Mrs. Fanshaw."

"O, you must not attempt to make me responsible for
any nonsense Ralph may have talked to you about Hillsboro'.   One thing, however, I feel it my duty to impress
upon you: this is a very dangerous place for unwary
bachelors."

"You would have me take warning from Ralph's un-
timely fate?   But I trust you exaggerate the danger.   How
is it, Miss Page?   You should know."

" Perhaps I am not a good judge, Mr. Burke. We have a good many pretty girls in Hillsboro'; and we think a man would be hard to suit who could not please himself here."

" And if at any time you should desire it, you shall have the benefit of our personal influence," said Mary.

" Indeed, you are very kind. I will not fail to claim your assistance, should it become necessary," answered the gentleman, greatly amused, Mary thought, at an idea so preposterous in his case.

" You are very confident, Singleton," said Fanshaw, laughing; " but a man never knows when he is in danger of that kind; so look out, old fellow."

Mr. Burke's horse arrived while they were at table; Fanshaw's was brought round soon after, and the guests took their departure. When they were gone, Hannah said to her sister, —

" Now, Lydia, if you will see to putting away the things, and, when the milk comes in, look after Becky a little, just to make sure she takes care of it properly, I will go up to aunt Susan's a little while. I dare say she is wondering why I haven't been before."

" Very well; but you had better hurry off. It is almost sundown now."

Hannah tied on her gingham sun-bonnet, and took her way up the hill towards her uncle's. The evening was beautiful, as the day had been. Far as the eye could reach, the fields and forests were clothed with the intense green of early summer, here deepened into blue shadows, there burnished with the slant golden sunshine. The far mountains, where the sun was setting, were veiled in purple

haze. A few small clouds, like flecks of gold, floated above
the sun ; but for these the sky was cloudless. The air was
sweet with countless flowers, and filled with the evening
songs of birds. Swarms of insects danced up and down
in the yellow light, and night-hawks wheeled in great
circles overhead, or swooped down on their prey with that
dull whirr of wings peculiar to their tribe. She met bare-
footed boys, who whistled as they went, driving home
sleek, sweet-breathed cows; or, now and then, a neighbor
passed her, jogging slowly home from the Centre, or, perhaps, from Colchester, behind a fat, lazy mare, at whose
side ambled a frisky, long-legged colt.

The sun was just disappearing as Hannah stepped upon
the broad granite door-stone in front of her uncle's house.
The drooping elms that shadowed the little lawn were
clothed with luxuriant foliage, and the graceful Persian
lilacs were in profuse bloom. A trumpet honeysuckle clam-
bered up one side of the green trellis over the door, and
the dark, shining leaves of the Virginia creeper covered
the other, while clustering roses and syringas gave promise
of future blossom and fragrance. Hannah paused a moment to look back over the scene, before she pushed open
the Venetian summer doors and entered. She found her
aunt in the kitchen, superintending the labors of two stout
young women.

"Is that you, Hannah ? " she said, as her niece appeared.
"I had about given you up."

"I suppose so; but we had company, and I couldn't get
away before."

"Well, I am glad to have you come now. We will go
up stairs," continued the elder lady, leading the way up

the broad staircase. "I want to show you the new curtains in Lucy's chamber while we are talking."

The curtains were exhibited and admired, and Lucy's coming discussed in the doubting, half-despairing manner in which they had come to think of that possible event; and then followed a long consultation on some important family question. Hannah was the person to whom appeal was always made in every time of perplexity, her unfailing sense and shrewdness being fully appreciated among her relatives. At length, when they had exhausted the topic under consideration, Mrs. Fraser rose, and, carefully closing the blinds, said, —

"There; we must shut the room up again for a week or two. I have kept it just as the dear child left it, and all is ready now, except some tassels for her little book-shelves. Desire Sharpe went to the Centre this afternoon, and said she would get them for me. I am looking for her every minute now; and I do hope she will bring me a letter, too."

"There is somebody coming up to the door now, aunt; I guess it is the deacon," said Hannah, looking through the blinds.

"Yes; that looks like the deacon's horse. We will go down. Be careful how you step. Mary Jane has been putting down the stair carpet to-day, and I believe she has left it a little loose there."

There were no lamps lighted yet, and the faint twilight revealed a woman standing in the entry, while the tall figure of a man filled the doorway.

"Good evening, Desire. I hope you have brought me a letter. Pray, walk in, Deacon Sharpe," Mrs. Fraser said, advancing. But she was startled by a sweet, familiar voice, exclaiming, —

"Mother! dear, dear mother! don't you know me?"

The next moment she held her long-lost daughter in her arms, and Hannah, sober Hannah, was crying on her grandfather's neck.

CHAPTER XIX.

WHAT a change the return of the two wanderers made in the old home! To Lucy's father and mother it was happiness enough to realize her presence, to see her filling again the old familiar places, and to hear her gay voice waking once more the echoes of the still house. They marked her strong, lithe figure, noted the hues of health upon her cheek, caught the sunshine of her smile, and looking in her fond and happy eyes, said, "She is the same — she is our own dear Lucy come back to us again." The neighbors and her young companions said, "She has grown older, and a little steadier, to be sure; but she has the same pretty way with her she always had." Lydia saw her cousin, and pronounced her more adorable than ever. Ben Miller, when the tones of her voice first struck his ear, experienced something of the old-remembered thrill. It was transient, however. It may be that simple Ben was quicker of perception than some of those around him; at least, it is certain that when Lucy laid her little soft hand in his, so large and brown, and spoke a few sweet words of greeting and cordial congratulation, he smiled a little faintly at the folly which had once led him to believe he could win *her* for his wife, and turned to Lydia with entire content.

Day by day, as Lucy became again familiar with home life, and fell, by degrees, into its quiet routine, Hannah

13

watched her with observant eyes, waiting patiently for a
fuller comprehension of the change which she, at least,
could see in her young cousin. This change it is difficult
to define; indeed, it was not so much a change as a matter
of growth to which different circumstances had .contrib-
uted. The hard experience of her early grief had not been
without its benefit. The knowledge of the emotion from
which that grief had sprung left its influence long after
both the love and the sorrow that followed it were things
of the past. As the trouble of her spirit subsided, new energies were born in her; as the mists of sorrow were dissipated, her vision became clearer. After a time, serenity
returned to her, and, by degrees, amid new lands and
scenes, all the old elastic joyousness of spirit, but tempered now by a sweet thoughtfulness. The depths of her
nature had been stirred, not exhausted; and she was half
surprised, at times, to recognize in herself a capacity for
pure and high emotion of which her youth had but dimly
hinted. Existence had come to have a fulness of beauty
and meaning of which those early girlish years had no con-
ception. Outwardly, she had exchanged her old careless,
unstudied grace for natural and high-bred ease. She was
not fashionable, for her life had not run in the grooves of
fashion. The free and careless existence she had led with
her grandfather had given her a serene self-possession, while,
at the same time, it had preserved from the pumice-stone
of conventional society all that was fresh, piquant, and original in her character. Her beauty was more conspicuous
even than formerly, and heightened by a rare, enchanting
grace, now gay, now tender, which pervaded look, smile,
speech, and gesture, and seemed more an emanation from

within than any acquired art of society. In many other
respects, too, she seemed changed merely by a purely harmonious development. Her old girlish daintiness and
fondness for finery had grown into a love of elegance and
refinement in all the appointments of her life. Her taste
in dress was marvellous, and was very freely indulged.
She liked rich, soft fabrics, harmonious tints, and full, flowing folds. Everything she wore, too, seemed to take a
kind of individuality from her way of wearing it, and to
become, in some manner, a part of herself.

Captain Fraser found the return to old scenes sad, but
no longer unendurably so. Time and absence had done
for him, in softening his grief, what his children had hoped
for; and now, firm in health, vigorous in mind, and active
as many a boy, he came back to spend the evening of his
days among the scenes and faces dearest to him.

One morning, about two weeks after Lucy's return, she
was standing in the door of one of the great barns, watching her father, who, on his knees at her feet, was busy with
hammer and nails, mending some one of the farming-tools.
The door looked northward, up the sunny, orchard-crowned
slope. The morning breeze stole in, fluttering her light
drapery, lifting the hair from her temples, and stirring
lightly the last year's hay that overflowed the deep mows.
She made a charming picture as she stood framed in the
great square setting of the door, with her straw hat on
her arm, and her old favorite, Carlo, lying stretched at
his length on the floor at her side. Lucy and her dog
had been together most of the morning, revisiting long-
deserted but unforgotten haunts; and for the last half hour
they had been exploring the barn. Probably Carlo was

fatigued with his unusual exertions, for he breathed hard as he lay with his black muzzle resting on his outstretched paws, watching, through one sleepy, half-shut eye, the flies that danced up and down in the sunshine before him. If one ventured too near — quick — there was a snap, a flash of white teeth, and the silly thing's days were ended.

"Do you know what time it is, Lucy?" asked Mr. Fraser, looking up, after a time.

"I have left my watch up stairs, but the clock in the kitchen has just struck ten."

"Then I shall have time to go to the ridge and back before dinner. Jerry says there is a piece of wall that needs looking after. Are you going with me?"

"Certainly; we are going — are we not, Carlo?"

The dog looked up in his mistress's face, and thumped his tail on the floor two or three times in token of assent.

"Do you remember how far it is, Lucy? The sun is pretty warm this morning."

Lucy laughed as she answered, "I am sure, father, I could outwalk you. When we were at Mr. Lester's, we used often to visit a friend of his, an English lady, who lived six or seven miles from us. Horace and I always walked. Mrs. Fleming would always ride upon a mule, and so would Juan, Mr. Lester's servant, who usually went with us."

"But that was winter weather; and though winter in Granada and in Hillsboro' are not quite the same, still it makes a difference. But speaking of winters, Lucy, I fancy I should really like ours best."

"Perhaps so. I think, however, that I like our climate, as we are obliged to like many of our friends, in spite of its faults."

"Have you ever seen anything, in any foreign country, prettier than Hillsboro' in June?"

"Never; and therefore I am silent about Hillsboro' in January. I wonder why grandpa is so late."

"Where is your grandfather?"

"He went to the Centre with Lydia, who had a trifle of shopping to do."

"We don't see much of Lydia these days."

"Not as much as we might like; but a wedding is not an every-day affair, and demands time."

"That is true enough; and this is, happily, one of the weddings in which all parties seem to be suited. Do you know, Lucy, we used to think before you went away, that Ben had a fancy for you?"

"Ben is altogether too sensible to prefer me to Lydia; it is only such silly old fellows as you and grandpa who do that."

As she spoke, the captain came into the barn, and, seating himself on the threshold beside his grandchild, pulled off his wide Panama hat, and began fanning his hot face.

"Confound your temperate climate, Bob!" he said; "I believe that piece of road between here and the Centre is the hottest stretch I ever went over. Commend me to the tropics for comfort."

Lucy laid her hand on the gray head, and drew it against her, as she said, "Did you bring me anything, grandpa?"

"Ah, Lucy! you are just as much of a tease, and quite as much of a baby, as when you used to climb in a chair to hunt my pockets for sugar candy. Come in the house, and brush my hair, and read this paper to me, while I make some lemon punch."

"Presently; I am going now to the ridge with father."

"Not in this broiling sun, child! You will get a sunstroke, and tan your face the color of old mahogany."

"Then I shall look all the more like you, old sea-dog that you are! Don't you remember that it was you, not I, who in Madras grumbled at the heat? But my letters, grandpa, — did you bring me any?"

The old man put a letter into her hand, and presently strolled back to the house. Lucy broke the seal, and ran her eye over its contents. It was from Mary Fanshaw, announcing the day on which she might be expected in Hillsboro'. One of Lucy's first acts, when rested from the fatigue of her journey, had been to write to her friend, claiming this visit. Several letters had been exchanged, and Mary now wrote that she might be expected on the following day. Her reason, she added, for naming so early a day was, that her husband, who would himself bring her to Hillsboro', was about to leave home for an absence of several weeks.

Lucy remained very quiet for some time after reading her letter, and a shadow seemed to have fallen on her face. The prospect of so soon meeting Fanshaw and Mary could not fail to awaken many recollections. The time was long past when it could cost her a pang. The old love and the old sorrow were gone, faded utterly out of her life; but the remembrance of them remained; and she could not contemplate with entire indifference a meeting with the man she had so deeply loved. She remained silent, quite absorbed in her own thoughts, until her father, having finished his work, recalled her attention.

"Well, Lucy, I am ready now if you are."

"O, yes; we were going to the ridge. But, father, if you please, I think I will not go this morning."

"Very well, dear; perhaps it is a little warm for you. Just take these nails along with you to the kitchen, and tell Dolly to take care of them."

Lucy lingered a moment, watching her father as he took his way over the sunny fields, and then, with a deep breath, turned to the house, followed by Carlo, who walked with drooping tail and ears.

CHAPTER XX.

MARY and Fanshaw arrived next day. Lucy was in her grandfather's room, helping him to arrange a fine collection of coins, of which he was very proud, and she did not know of their coming till Dolly was sent to call her. As she came down the stairs, there met her in the entry a pretty, dark-eyed child, whom she knew at once from his resemblance to Mary. She stooped and gazed tenderly into his soft eyes, while a mist came over her own, as she pressed a kiss on his sweet, baby lips. The next moment she found herself in the parlor, with Mary's arms around her neck, and her disengaged hand clasped in Fanshaw's.

When the first confused moments were over, and Lucy had time for thought, she was surprised at herself, at the calmness of her own emotions in this meeting, which, in spite of herself, she had somewhat dreaded. She had never so fully realized how entirely the old had given place to the new in herself as now, when renewing her intercourse with these two friends who had exerted so strong an influence upon her life, and in recognizing their wholly altered relations towards her. Could Lucy have now met Ralph Fanshaw, as free in fancy as when she first knew him, it is not venturing too much to assert that no sentiment warmer than pleasant friendship would have been possible in her; and yet Mary, a woman far more brilliant than herself, loved her husband with a fond and proud devotion. As Lucy looked from one to the other of her friends, her thoughts reverted to her own full, abundant life;. and the last faint shadow cast by those early days, if one yet existed, vanished forever.

With friends who met after so long a severance, there was, of course, much to be said, innumerable questions to be asked and answered. As in the old days, it was Mary who was the chief speaker. She talked, and Lucy listened. The one had grown no more communicative than of old, and the other loved as well her friend's gentle sympathy. Fanshaw had but a few hours in which to renew his acquaintance with his quondam pupil, as he was to return to Colchester that night, and to commence on the morrow a business tour in the West. For some time he had sat watching, in the intervals of his talk with the old captain, the animated encounter of the two friends; and at length, seating himself on a low seat between them, he said, —

"As I look at you, Lucy, I find it difficult to believe that it is really the same girl to whom I taught algebra and French verbs three or four years ago."

"I am very sorry that you should have trouble in recognizing her," replied Lucy, with a sweet smile; "for I assure you that in all essentials she is quite the same."

"I do not find Lucy changed," said Mary. "She is far less altered than Miles, who is just her age."

"By the way, Mary, I have not yet asked you of Miles. Where is he?"

"He is with mother just now; he left us only a day or two since. He said he should take the occasion of my visit to drive up to Hillsboro' for a few hours some day."

"That, though very pleasant, will not by any means satisfy me. I shall write to him to come up for a week."

"You know nothing of what you are bringing upon yourself, my dear, when you ask that boy into your house. I would as soon have a bomb-shell."

"Why will you persist, Mary," remonstrated Fanshaw, "in calling your brother a boy, in such disregard of his feelings?"

"I know Miles is fond of thinking himself a man, and the Colchester girls regard him, I believe, in the same light. But he has some boyish habits still, in spite of his twenty years and that dainty little moustache, of which he is so vain."

"You know, Lucy, that Miles was always a source of great anxiety to Mary; he is more so now than formerly. Then she had only such trifles as his health to give her uneasiness; now she has graver reason for alarm."

"Indeed, Mr. Fanshaw! Am I indiscreet in asking what it can be?"

"Her chief source of apprehension at present is a sister-in-law."

"What preposterous nonsense you talk, Ralph!"

"It is perfectly true what I say. She is in mortal terror of every girl Miles speaks to or looks at."

"He will be perfectly safe if he comes to Hillsboro'," answered Lucy, laughing. "Lydia has her wedding gown in the house; and I think I am not rash when I promise for Hannah."

"You are as bad as Ralph, Lucy; but you don't give your own *parole d'honneur*."

"I will, my dear, if you think it necessary."

Here little Elliot made his appearance at the door, and Lucy, going to the child, lifted him in her arms, and carried him out under the elms, whither the captain had betaken himself. Mary watched from the window the graceful figure of her friend.

"The same dear Lucy, unaltered," she said to her husband, who was now alone with her in the room.

" Completely changed," he answered, smiling.

" Ralph, how can you think so ? "

" Mary, how can you think otherwise ? "

" I own she is changed outwardly. That was to be expected."

" The change is something deeper than mere externals ; and I wonder that you, who are usually so much clearer sighted than myself, do not see it. You have known Lucy longer ; still I must think that I knew her better, understood better the springs of her character. Yet how blind we both were ! We gave her to Ben Miller, and thought we had done a very judicious thing. Compare them now !"

" Ralph," exclaimed Mary, suddenly, in a low voice, glancing, as she spoke, furtively through the window, — " Ralph, I have a splendid idea."

" Well, what is it ? " he asked, turning his eye from the group under the trees to his wife's eager face.

She did not answer for a moment, but stood leaning with crossed arms on the carved back of a large chair ; then, as he bent towards her, she said a few rapid words, in a low voice, in his ear. He smiled at first, then laughed outright, and called her a little goose for her pains.

When, towards evening, Fanshaw was preparing to leave, Mary said, —

"I find, on opening my trunk, that I have forgotten several things which I shall need very much. Give me your pencil, and I will write a list, and Nora can make up the parcel."

"My dear Mary, I shall leave home at daylight to-morrow morning, and really cannot attend to sending it."

"Tell Nora to give it to Burke; he will see to it. I know there will be plenty of opportunities to send it, and it will oblige me very much."

Fanshaw promised; the last adieus were spoken; he sprang to his place, and drove away. Mary brushed her hand over her eyes, laughed away a little disposition she felt to look rueful, and followed Mrs. Fraser into the parlor. They were presently joined by the captain and his son, while Lucy sat down before a large, old-fashioned mahogany secretary that stood in the entry. This piece of furniture, being heavy and cumbrous, had been banished successively from every room in the house; but here it had made a stand. The wide and ample entrance-hall seemed just fitted to receive it. Its dark, polished sides and carved ornaments made no mean appearance here; and a high-backed chair of the same material and ancient date, cushioned with dusky red leather, stood always before it. Opening the leaves, and drawing out pens and paper, Lucy began to write, occasionally joining in the conversation going on in the parlor. By and by Mary came and stood beside her.

"What are you doing, Lucy?"

"Writing letters for Jerry to post in the morning. That one is to Miles. O! it is sealed; you cannot see what is in it."

"Have you really written to him to come up for a week?"

"Just that."

"It is kind of you, and he will be delighted."

"Have you written to Mr. Dutton, Lucy, as I asked you?"

"Yes, father; here is the letter. I will read it to you;" and she proceeded to read a letter to a farmer in a neighboring town, relative to some fat oxen which the latter had for sale. Being entirely satisfactory, it was sealed and laid aside.

"Did you write to Cheeseman the other day, Lucy, about the 'Flying Cloud'?" asked her grandfather.

"I sent a letter on Monday, sir; and it is quite time, I think, that you had a return."

"You seem to be general business agent for the family, Lucy."

"I am; and, should you chance to desire it, I could give you information about stocks, railway shares, agricultural matters, or shipping interests," Lucy answered, as she closed her desk, and went to say good night to those in the parlor.

‧CHAPTER XXI.

THE cool mornings, the sultry noons, and quiet, lovely evenings, followed in quick succession. Mary and Lucy were, hour by hour, weaving up the torn web of their friendship, and growing daily better known and more attached to each other. Mary had been several days at Hillsboro', when they sat one morning by the open door of the front entry. All that side of the house was in shadow, and the air deliciously cool and fragrant. They had brought their work-baskets, and sewed as they talked, while Elliot with his toys played on the floor beside them. They made a pretty group — Mary in a becoming white wrapper, and Lucy in a delicate morning dress of chintz-colored cambric, from the folds of which her little slippered feet peeped daintily. An open note lay on the floor with its envelope, as if just read and flung there.

"It is very provoking," Mary said, "that Miles cannot come to Hillsboro' this week. I wish Stratton Kingsbury had kept away. I do not like him for a friend for Miles; and detaining him just now interferes with our plans very much."

"To be sure, we had depended on him to drive us to Edgehill on Monday; but my grandfather will enjoy going."

"I had intended to have Captain Fraser to myself. I particularly dislike dividing a gentleman with one or two other ladies."

"Lucy, dear, will you come here for a minute?" called her mother from the adjoining room.

Lucy laid down her work, and went to see what was wanted of her. Mary sewed a few minutes, looked out through the door at the hay-makers, just beginning the hay-harvest, played with the boy a moment, and finally picked up Miles's note, and began, for the third time, to read it over. While she was thus occupied, a carriage stopped before the door. Looking up, she saw a gentleman alighting from it, and quickly recognized Singleton Burke. Hastily disengaging her dress from Elliot's clinging hands, she rose to meet him.

"Mr. Burke, this is a pleasure! I am really delighted to see you."

"Thank you, Mrs. Fanshaw. I never question your sincerity. I have no need, looking in your face, to inquire of your health."

"No; this air of Hillsboro' is the sworn enemy of pale cheeks. But come into the parlor, and let me call Mrs. Fraser and my friend Lucy."

"First suffer me to speak of my errand. This package was given me several days since to forward to you. I have had no opportunity of so doing until now, but trust I have caused you no inconvenience by the delay."

"All apology should come from me, Mr. Burke, for giving you so much trouble."

"It has given me only the pleasure of this call. Ah! what a noble country!" he added, as Mary threw open the blind and gave him a seat near the window. "If the people are equal to their scenery, I no longer wonder that you and Ralph rave about Hillsboro'."

"You must judge for yourself, Mr. Burke. Excuse me while I call Mrs. Fraser."

She left the room as she spoke, returning, after a short absence, accompanied by her hostess, and, a few minutes later, Lucy entered.

Mary was sensitive about the friends she loved; and on this occasion she was particularly desirous that Lucy should make a favorable impression. She watched Burke narrowly, pleased to mark his surprise in the slight dilatation of his calm gray eyes, and his admiration in their slightly softened expression. She had the more satisfaction in this as she knew that he did not greatly admire the majority of young ladies he was accustomed to meet in society; and, looking at Lucy, she thought she had never seen her more animated and charming.

Mr. Burke's call was considerably prolonged, his own enjoyment and the hospitality of his entertainers quite precluding the thought of how time was passing. By and by a neat-looking girl brought in a tray on which were arranged cake, napkins, and glasses containing Mrs. Fraser's delicious currant wine; and Lucy gracefully presided over the distribution of the refreshment.

"Did you tell me, Mrs. Fanshaw, that you are looking for Miles?" Mr. Burke asked, in the course of conversation.

"Yes; and we are thoroughly vexed that he does not come to-day. We wanted him to take us to Edgehill on Monday. There is to be a political mass-meeting, as they call it; and the famous Mr. H—— is to speak."

"Mrs. Fanshaw is interested in politics, Miss Fraser; pray, are you?"

"Not very deeply," answered Lucy, smiling. "But people who live as we do avail themselves of everything that offers variety."

"I think you will be interested in H——. Business will take me to Edgehill on Monday, and I shall endeavor to hear him."

"O, then we shall meet you," said Mary; "or, better still, come this way, and be one of our party."

"Thank you, Mrs. Fanshaw," began the gentleman.

"Do come, Mr. Burke; it will be pleasanter for you all," added Mrs. Fraser, cordially, while Lucy's smiling eyes seemed to await an assent, which was soon given. It was at length arranged that Burke should dine with them on Monday, and accompany them to Edgehill in the afternoon; and then, seeing no reasonable excuse for longer delay, the gentleman took his leave.

14

CHAPTER XXII.

MONDAY arrived, and with it, punctual to his appointment, appeared Mr. Burke. The dinner, or, rather, luncheon, was served at an early hour; and as soon as it was over, the horses were brought round. Burke, who drove a single horse, in an easy, smooth-rolling phaeton, had secured Lucy as his companion; while the captain handed Mary to a seat in a light, open wagon, to which were harnessed a finely-matched pair of spirited young bays.

"I think, father," remarked Mr. Fraser, "that you would have been wiser to take the carryall. Mary's bonnet would have been safer in case of a shower."

"There is not the least danger of a shower, Mr. Fraser," Mary answered. "See, what a lovely sky! And I like the feeling of being out of doors one has in these open wagons."

The day was charming,. the roads excellent, and the country smiling in the fulness of summer beauty. Along their way the fields of grass were yielding to the swinging scythe, and a sweet smell of new hay filled the air. There was a fresh west wind, that bent in rolling waves the standing grass, and turned up the white linings of the maple leaves. Shadows from sailing clouds traversed the hill-sides or darkened the valleys; and, now and then, from a distant field came the music of a scythe-stone on the ringing blade, as a white-sleeved haymaker, pausing in his work, sharpened the dulled edge.

Captain Fraser was in advance, and drove rapidly, his strong, young horses seeming to feel the exhilaration of the day as well as the old gentleman and his companion. After the first mile or two, Mr. Burke gave up trying to keep pace with him, and, checking his horse, soon fell far behind. That the drive was a pleasant one, both to himself and to Lucy, may be inferred, perhaps, from the fact that each was secretly surprised, on reaching Edgehill, after something more than an hour and a half had passed, that they should have accomplished the distance in so short a time. It was eight miles from Mr. Fraser's house to Edgehill.

"Have you any idea," said Lucy, as they rose over the crest of the last hill, "how far in advance my grandfather and Mary are?"

"My last sight of them was some time ago. They have driven like the wind; but we shall probably find them at the hotel." Consulting his watch, he continued, "We have still some minutes to spare, Miss Fraser, before the hour for this meeting. Would you like to alight and rest, or shall we drive through the village?"

"I am not tired, and should prefer the drive."

The village of Edgehill stands upon a broad, natural terrace, facing the south-east. Behind, the cliffs rise almost perpendicularly, frowning down sternly on the little town at their base; while in front, the hill, though still wild and rugged, falls away less precipitously. The table on which the village is built is perfectly level, and varies from thirty rods to half a mile in width. The road runs through the middle, and descends at last into a wild ravine, where, along the banks of a full and rapid stream, are clustered several factories, which make the chief business of the place. The dwellings are' scattered in picturesque groups along the plain; a hotel, a pretty wooden church, and a school-house, occupying a central position.

Towards the farther end of the town, where the plateau is widest, standing on a broad artificial terrace of its own, might be seen a square, old-fashioned mansion, built of brick, with quoins and balustrades of gray stone, and clusters of massive chimneys rising among the tangled growth that covered the face of the cliff. The grounds — which, in that position, could not, of course, be very extensive — were enclosed by an ancient buckthorn hedge, and kept with the most perfect care. Scattered horse-chestnuts, singly and in groups, broke the emerald surface of the lawn; and here and there a locust tree shed a shower of bloom and fragrance around. A stone table and seat stood in one sheltered corner; and from the great stone vases on either side the gateway drooped sprays of brilliant flowers.

As Lucy and her companion drove slowly past, they observed a gentleman walking meditatively up and down in the shade before the house, while a grave-looking hound paced, with dignified step, at his side. This gentleman was Mr. Gore, to whom allusion has already been more than once made. He was apparently about sixty years of age, tall, slender, and noticeably graceful in figure, with a thin, handsome face and silvery hair. Rich, agreeable, and well connected, it was thought a noteworthy thing in that section, that Mr. Gore had reached the age just mentioned a bachelor; but for what reasons he had done so was his own secret. He lived alone but for the servants of his establishment, dispensing elegant bachelor hospitalities, and giving himself to the various claims on the attention of a man of wealth and leisure. In his more youthful days he had travelled extensively, and mingled a great deal in society; but of late years his life had been rather quiet.

"This is a pleasant place we are passing," said Burke, as he turned his horse's head to retrace the way they had come. "Do you know Mr. Gore?"

"I can hardly say I do. He frequently comes to my father's; but it is now several years since I saw him. I have been told that this used to be a very gay house."

"It looks anything but that to-day. But I have seen nothing of our friends yet. We will drive on to the hotel, and try and find them."

He quickened his horse's pace, and they soon reached the hotel. Here, in answer to their inquiries, they learned that the captain and Mary, after waiting for them some time, had walked out, leaving word that they might be found in the neighborhood of the grove where the speaking was to take place. Lucy and her companion left their carriage, and walked up the shady village street to the place indicated. Here a striking scene was presented.

It was the summer preceding an important presidential election, and an exciting canvass had already commenced. Mass meetings were being held in many places, and eloquent and effective speakers from the large towns were procured to advocate the principles and set forth the policy of the respective parties. Among such speakers, few possessed in a more eminent degree the requisites of an effec-

tive "stump" orator than Mr. H——. Let no one imagine
that these requisites are either few or slight. To command the attention, convince the judgment, and move the
feelings of the class of men who make up the audience at
a New England mass meeting, requires, in large measure,
those capabilities of clear statement, logical deduction, and
forcible and earnest utterance, which are the chief ele-
ments in the highest oratory. If to these be superadded
the graces of scholarship and the charm of wit and humor,
their effect is neither unappreciated nor undervalued.
Woe betide the luckless wight who, mistaking the homely
sense of the men who make up such an assemblage, under-
takes to *talk down* to them. Swift are they to detect the
impertinence, and pitiless to punish it with well-merited
contempt.

The spot selected for the meeting was a small grove,
lying just back of the village green, between it and the
cliff. Its trees were the natural growth of oak and maple
which had once covered the plateau, and above whose
shining, dark-green foliage a few tall pines, relics of a still
more ancient growth, lifted their heads in sombre, decaying grandeur. Here, under the flickering shade, a wooden
platform had been erected, from which, as they drew near,
Mr. H—— was already addressing the crowd below. On
the platform, just behind the speaker, were seated several
of the more prominent citizens of Edgehill belonging to
Mr. H——'s political party, and a few gentlemen from the
neighboring towns. The Colchester brass band occupied
one side of the platform, making a very pretty show in
their gray and scarlet uniforms. They had been very
useful, too, in keeping the crowd from growing impatient .

during the hour they had been compelled to wait for the speaker.

The audience, numbering some twelve hundred persons, perhaps, was composed chiefly of men, rough-handed, stoop-shouldered, hard-headed farmers from the country round. Quite a number of ladies were also present, some on foot, and some sitting in carriages; while perched in the branches of the trees were numerous boys, who, secure in their leafy "coigns of vantage," kept up a low buzz of talk among themselves, and made their presence constantly manifest by scattering a shower of peanut-shells on the heads of the crowd below.

The press was so great as to prevent Lucy and her companion from getting near the platform; so, leaning on a garden paling, they fell into pleasant, low-toned talk, quite careless of the throng and of the great interests uppermost with it, save when their attention was recalled by an occasional burst of applause, or a murmur of laughter sweeping over the crowd like a breeze across a wood.

As the afternoon wore away, and a slight movement on the outskirts of the throng indicated that the speaker was drawing to a close, Lucy began to look a little anxiously among the various groups for her grandfather. She was about to suggest making an attempt to find him, when the massive head and shoulders of the old man rose above a group of ladies not far off. At the same moment several gentlemen approached from an opposite direction, one of whom Lucy at once recognized as Mr. Gore. He also recognized Mr. Burke, and, bowing slightly to his companions, allowed them to pass on, while he drew near our friends. After the usual exchange of salutations, Mr. Burke turned to Lucy, and formally presented the elder gentleman. Mr. Gore was an old man, and his head was white, but he had still a quick eye for beauty; and as he bowed over the little hand she gave him, there was in his manner a delightful blending of the condescending suavity which age accords to youth with the deferential gallantry which was the man's natural tribute to her sex and beauty. Lucy received him with a quiet, unconscious grace, the farthest from timidity, and than which nothing could be more unlike her former shy reserve.

Leaving Lucy in Mr. Gore's charge, Burke went in search of the captain and Mary, with whom he soon returned. Mr. Gore and the captain, between whom there was an acquaintance of long standing, were mutually pleased at this accidental meeting; and the former coined many phrases of elaborate compliment for Mary, whose family were well known to him.

The crowd was now rapidly dispersing, and they began to speak of returning to the public house, where they had left their horses. Mr. Gore at once interposed a protest, urging the whole party to accompany him home, and partake of a "bachelor's dinner," postponing their drive to Hillsboro' until the evening. As there was really no valid reason for declining so agreeable an invitation, it was so arranged. Lucy accepted the offered arm of Mr. Gore, and Burke walked by her side, while Mary and the captain followed a few steps behind.

It was not a long walk to the pleasant old house under the horse-chestnut trees. As they were entering the hall door, Mr. Gore gathered for Lucy two glowing king roses, one in full bloom and the other just bursting. She received them with a quick smile of pleasure; and when the housekeeper conducted herself and Mary up stairs that they might arrange their dresses, she placed the flowers in her beautiful hair. As they moved about the chamber, opening closed shutters, and admitting the bright sunlight, they seemed to wake slumbering echoes in the dim old house — echoes of a gay and stately life that had died out of it long ago.

Mary had finished her toilet first, and gone out into the upper hall, where, presently, she called her friend to come to her. Lucy found her standing before one of the numerous pictures — apparently family portraits — which were panelled in the wall. It represented a lady, and, though the colors on the canvas were fading, it had clearly been meant for one in the bloom of youth. She wore a close-fitting riding-habit of ancient fashion, and was looking over her shoulder at the beholder. On the raised white hand of the lady was perched a bird of brilliant plumage, whose head was also turned, its eyes looking in the same direction as her own. There was something in the form of the face and in the features which strikingly resembled Lucy, and in the drooping, rich, dark-chestnut hair glowed a red rose, like the one Lucy now wore. As I have said, the resemblance in form and coloring was noticeable; but the expression was wholly different. And, as Lucy gazed, the soft bloom, the sweet, enchanting smile, took the character of a mask, and seemed to cover something — what, she could not tell — something half seen, uncertain, and intangible. It almost seemed as if the expression of the picture changed like that of a living face, at one moment perplexing the beholder with a half revelation, which vanished in the next, leaving a vague feeling of sadness, which seemed caught from its haunting eyes.

The girls stood before the picture for some time, wondering if it were a portrait, or the creation of some artist's fancy, and quite reluctantly turned away at last, and went down to the drawing-room, where the gentlemen were awaiting them. Lucy crossed the room to her grandfather, while Mary turned to their host.

"We have been admiring one of the pictures, Mr. Gore, which hang in your upper hall, — that of a lady with a bird upon her hand, — and wondering if it could be a portrait."

"It is, indeed, the portrait of one Mistress Anne Wycombe, a daughter of our family, who was a famous beauty in the old colonial days. Did the picture interest you?"

"It did, exceedingly, partly from its beauty, partly from an indescribable expression which it wears, but, most of all, from its strong resemblance to Miss Fraser. Look at her now!"

As Mary spoke, a bright gleam of sunshine, falling through the opening in the curtains, shone full upon Lucy's head. Her face was turned, and she was looking over her shoulder at her grandfather and Mr. Burke, while Mr. Gore's rose, with its shining leaves, drooped low behind her ear.

"Wonderful! It is Mistress Anne herself!" exclaimed the gentleman, in a low voice. "Yet," he added, after a moment's pause, "one thing is wanting; and, Mrs. Fanshaw, if you love your friend, you will not wish to see the resemblance completed."

"She was very lovely, if the canvas speaks the truth."

"Yes," he replied, still looking abstractedly at Lucy; "but there is a shadow on her face. They say she died of a broken heart. However," he added, smiling, "people do not believe in that nowadays; and perhaps the disease has been exterminated. Mrs. Fanshaw, do you play? I see they have opened the piano. I was sure you did; will you not favor us?"

While they lingered about the piano, dinner was announced; and Mr. Gore, giving his arm to Mary, led the way to the dining-room. The dinner was perfect, the hospitality of their host at once graceful and sincere, his guests in the humor to enjoy everything — it could hardly fail to be a pleasant party.

They were still sitting over the dessert, when an exclamation of surprise and anxiety from Mary drew the attention of the whole company to a great change which had taken place in the aspect of the day. Dark clouds had arisen, obscuring the sun, and, at intervals, distant thunder echoed among the hills. Some uneasiness began to be felt about their return, for, though it still wanted some time to sunset, it was already growing quite dark. Mr. Gore insisted on the whole party staying all night; but this Mary was unwilling to do, on account of her child. After taking a survey of the heavens from the lawn, their host gave it as his opinion that they should have no rain; the clouds, he thought, were not rising from the right quarter; and it was determined that the captain and Mary should go at once in Burke's phaeton, which offered sure protection from the weather, while Lucy and Mr. Burke could wait until the shower was over, or the danger of one past, and come on in the wagon.

Accordingly Mr. Gore despatched a servant to the hotel
for the horses, and Mary rapidly making her preparations
for the return drive, she and the captain were soon on
their way home. After they were gone, the others, finding the air in-doors close and oppressive, paced slowly up
and down a grassy walk at one extremity of the terrace.
The walk was bordered upon one side by the thick hedge,
and on the other by young locust trees, whose light leaves
rustled mysteriously in the evening wind, while over all
were the stately, spreading branches of the great horse-
chestnuts. The gentlemen were in animated conversation,
while Lucy, wrapped in the cape Burke had carefully
folded about her shoulders, walked between them, leaning
on Mr. Gore's arm. She had fallen into complete silence,
and was occupied with watching the dense volumes of
cloud that rolled darkly up from behind the cliff, and listening to the fitful sighing of the wind as it mingled with
the hoarse roar of the river in the ravine below. The
whole scene filled her with a quiet but keen excitement.
The wild face of the sky, the great solemn trees that shadowed their path, the dark, still house, and the murmurous
gloom of the great cliff that hung close above them, impressed vividly her imagination. All around, low voices
seemed calling to her, and her thoughts were borne far
away on the wild evening wind.

"I fear we are fatiguing you with this long walk, Miss
Fraser. We will go in," said Mr. Gore, at length.

"On the contrary, I have enjoyed it very much. Mr.
Burke, what do you think of the prospect of returning to
Hillsboro' to-night?"

"My dear young lady," interrupted their host, "let me

answer for him. The evening is still too doubtful to admit of driving eight miles in an open wagon."

"Do you really think so? Look! the stars are shining overhead, and the clouds must be thinning in the west, for there is a faint brightness on those distant hills."

Lucy was right. The clouds, after long threatening, were breaking away. There seemed no longer any reason for delay, and Mr. Gore with regret saw his guests depart. But by the time they had cleared the village and the near hills, and were well out on the open road, they perceived a low, ominous-looking cloud rising rapidly behind them. Mr. Burke checked his horse.

"What shall we do?" he asked. "Return, or drive on and try and outrun the cloud?"

"What do you advise, Mr. Burke?"

"It is your advice I wish. But I think the cloud will scatter, as the last did. Even if it should rain, I believe these horses capable of taking us home before the shower can overtake us."

"Drive on, then, by all means," replied Lucy.

Obedient to her instructions, he slackened his rein, and the fiery young animals sprang forward. A light touch with the whip, a low whistle, and the fine creatures seemed to know what was expected of them, and, with level necks, put forth their utmost speed. It was a wild, exciting drive. The night had again grown black, but was illuminated at intervals by vivid flashes of lightning, and the flying hoofs of the horses struck sparks of fire from the stony road. The thunder rolled sullenly, and the wind came in sudden gusts. The occupants of the little wagon exchanged but an occasional sentence. Lucy felt no fear in the gathering storm, but rather a degree of exhilaration in watching its wild approach. Of her companion, I suspect, she thought but very little. Burke was nearly silent. He was deeply anxious for his lovely charge; for himself, he could have driven on all night, so she was at his side, and her sweet voice assured him, at intervals, of her welfare, and of her perfect confidence in and reliance upon himself.

They had accomplished six out of the eight miles of their way, when the cloud so long threatening seemed to burst above their heads. Down leaped the rain, and in an instant they were drenched. It was like driving under the sheet of a waterfall. Burke had wrapped his heavy shawl about Lucy, but it required all the strength of his arm to confine it in place against the wild wind that was blowing. The horses knew the road even better than their driver; so one cause of danger was removed. Neither could give much account of the remainder of their drive. Lucy only remembered that, as she hid her dazzled eyes from the blinding glare of the lightning, Burke's clear voice, a little shaken from its usual grave calm, sounded through the uproar and confusion in words of assurance and concern.

Very soon they were at home; and Lucy, drenched and cold, but laughing at her father's face of alarm, was lifted by him from the wagon, and carried into the house. A scene of confusion followed. Miles Elliot had arrived in their absence. There were hurried greetings, exclamations, laughter, running up and down stairs, and opening and shutting of doors. In the midst of it all, Lucy was ordered off to her own room, where her mother and Mary relieved her of her wet clothes, and forced her, under protest, into bed. Mr. Burke, who felt obliged to return to

Colchester that night, was furnished with dry apparel, and, the storm having somewhat abated, took his leave, assuring Mrs. Fraser, with his usual somewhat formal courtesy, that he should feel deeply anxious for her daughter, and should avail himself of the earliest opportunity to inquire after her health.

When he was gone, Mrs. Fraser went up to Lucy's room, and Miles and Mary turned into the parlor.

"Well, Miles, what do you think of Lucy?"

"I can hardly say I have seen her yet; but as nearly as I could determine from under her dripping bonnet, she has not grown plain. But, Mary, isn't Singleton Burke — well — a little — a little soft, perhaps, on Lucy?"

"Did you think so, Miles?"

"I did, certainly."

"You are probably mistaken. Burke is not a soft-hearted boy, like you — in love with every girl he sees."

"That only proves that he will have the disease hard when he does take it. Now, I am convalescent in a few days, and sound in a week; but when a man like Burke so far forgets himself as to let his eyes tell the story his did to-night, in looking after her as she turned round on the stairs — why, things look desperate. She was handsome enough, to be sure, to call a man's heart into his eyes. Poor old fellow! I am sorry for him."

"What is the ground of your compassion?"

"O, unless she is changed from the girl I knew, she will lead him a chase! Serve him right, too, for delaying till his time of life to fall in love. Come, Mary; I want to see little Elliot."

CHAPTER XXIII.

LUCY suffered no ill consequences from the wetting she
had got, and was quite ready next day to enter into all
plans for the general amusement. Mr. Burke, according to
his promise, came soon to assure himself of her welfare.
It was noticeable how often, about this time, business happened to call the latter gentleman in the direction of Hillsboro'; and as he never, on these occasions, failed to look
in upon his friends at the Frasers', they consequently saw
a good deal of him. Mr. Fanshaw was still detained by
the affairs which had called him to the West; and Mary
was thus enabled still further to prolong her visit. Miles
went and came between Colchester and the farms, staying
a day or two first in one place and then in the other, and
making himself very useful and agreeable.

Early one warm afternoon, a day or two after the meeting at Edgehill, Hannah and Lydia Page were together in
their own pleasant sitting-room. Hannah's needle flew in
and out of the long seam of a sheet she was sewing, while
Lydia was quite absorbed in the completion of a bit of embroidery destined to adorn some article of her bridal apparel.
The painted shades of the windows were drawn down to exclude the hot sunshine, but the doors of both entries were
open, admitting a draught of soft south wind. Both sisters
were occupied with their own thoughts, and the silence in

the room was broken only by the slow ticking of the clock and the drowsy buzzing of the house-flies.

So absorbed were they that neither had perceived any sound of footsteps without, till Lydia's attention was attracted by a shadow darkening the doorway, and, looking up, she saw a gentleman standing on the threshold. He wore a summer suit of white linen, and stood with one hand raised upon the casing of the door, while the other, holding his hat, rested lightly on his hip. Lydia regarded him for a moment in surprised silence. The intruder returned her gaze, also without speaking, but with a questioning look in his smiling brown eyes.

In an instant Lydia sprang up, a flush of pleasure overspreading her face as she exclaimed, —

"It is — it really is — Mr. Stafford! O, you said you would come back in a year and a day."

"And I have kept my word so badly, Miss Lydia," answered the gentleman, warmly clasping her extended hand, "that you had some difficulty in recognizing your old friend. Dear Miss Page," he continued, as Hannah came eagerly forward to welcome him, "I hope you, too, will not find me so changed."

"I should have known you anywhere," Hannah replied.

"And you, kindest of friends, are little altered. But your young sister here — three years have wrought a transformation in her, and of the happiest kind ; " and he looked with undisguised admiration at the young girl, whose flushed cheeks and sparkling eyes evinced at once her pleasure at seeing him again, and the agreeable consciousness of her own heightened beauty.

"And where have you been all these years, Mr. Staf-

15

ford?" she asked, when, their first excitement a little over,
he was seated between them, seeming to slide at once and
naturally into his old place in their regard.

"Wandering up and down the earth, Miss Lydia, a leaf
driven by the wind. When I left Hillsboro', three years
and more ago, it was to proceed to England, whither some
business called me. I remained for more than a year in
Europe, and then joined some friends who were going to
South America. I returned to this country last winter,
and since then have been more than usually occupied by
business affairs; so that this is my first pleasure excursion.
I came to Edgehill on a short visit, arriving only last night,
and you were my first thought after receiving the kind
greetings of my cousin John."

"Your cousin, Mr. Stafford! Is Mr. Gore a relative of
yours?"

"Certainly; the nearest, almost the only, relative I have
in this country. He was first cousin to my father, his
mother being a Stafford. I thought I had mentioned our
relationship before."

"No; we thought he was a person you had business
with."

"And so he was — poor man! He was appointed my
guardian, or, rather, joint guardian with another gentleman; and he has had trouble enough with my belongings,
though I never saw him until that winter when I first met
you."

"How long had you been standing in the doorway when
I saw you?"

"Only a moment. Will you believe me, dear friends, I
half resolved, as I drew near your house, to drive on, and

not risk the chances of a disappointment here. I was afraid of change — of forgetfulness. I dreaded to dispel the happy recollection I retained of our brief acquaintance. I think I remember everything connected with my stay here. What has become of that charming young friend of yours — Miss Elliot?"

"She is not Miss Elliot now," Hannah replied ; "she is married."

"Of course she is ; and I dare wager whatever you please that the handsome schoolmaster is the fortunate man."

"Ah! you used your eyes those stormy days. Yes, Mary is Mrs. Fanshaw now."

"And your pretty cousin — where is she ?"

"She is at home."

"Do you mean me to understand that she is still single?"

"Yes."

"What are the young men of this town thinking of, to allow so much beauty to go unappropriated? They cannot be greatly alive to their own interests."

"I don't know how that is. But Lucy is at home this afternoon. If you would like to walk up there, I know she would be glad to see you."

"I will go, with pleasure."

"Did I tell you that Mary Fanshaw is there on a visit?"

"Indeed you did not. I shall be charmed to renew my acquaintance with her. Shall we meet Mr. Fanshaw, also?"

"No; he is away in the West, and she is staying with Lucy."

"I see it was my fortunate star which brought me hither

to-day. So many old friends at once; it is an unlooked-
for pleasure."

Hannah summoned a boy, who was at work in the garden, to put Mr. Stafford's horse in the stable; and presently
she and their guest set out together, Lydia exacting from
them a promise to be sure and return to tea.

"Which way?" asked Stafford, as they crossed the
greensward between the door-stone and the road.

"This. I forgot that you had never been at uncle Robert's."

"You remember my knowledge of Hillsboro' was limited
to your house. Up this hill? This is the way I came.
Which of the many pleasant farms I passed is the one?"

"Neither. Uncle Robert lives on that road going up
the hill to the north. But, Mr. Stafford, did you notice, as
you came down, a new house, about half a mile from here,
among some pretty trees?"

"On the right, coming from Edgehill?"

"Yes. Well, that is where Lydia is going to live in
October."

"A—h! Then there is a young gentleman in this case.
I half hinted to your sister, while you were out, my suspicion that there must be; but the little hypocrite denied it."

"It is true, however; and we are all much pleased with
the connection."

"It gives me sincere pleasure to hear you say so. I have
always cherished a strong regard for your frank, warm-
hearted sister; and no one will more cordially congratulate
her on her prospects of happiness. Who is the young
man?"

"It is Ben Miller, son of Major Miller, a neighbor of ours just below here."

"Ben Miller. That name sounds familiar. Is he a handsome fellow, with blue eyes and fine shoulders?"

"Ben *has* blue eyes, and we think him good-looking. But where have you seen him?"

"I shovelled snow beside him for several hours after that eventful storm which you remember."

"Mr. Stafford, I have not thought, until this minute, to inquire what ever became of that boy you picked up that dreadful night."

"What — Figaro? He is one of my chief retainers, and is invaluable to me."

"How did you happen to keep him?"

"I kept him at first because he insisted upon staying; there was no getting rid of him; and I keep him now because I really could not well live without him."

"I did not think he knew enough to be useful."

"He is extremely useful. There is scarcely anything he cannot do, from cooking an omelet, or making a bed, to loading my pistols and grooming my horse. Nature seems to have been a little niggardly to him in the matter of brains; and yet he has a wonderful quickness in some things. He never fails to detect the slightest shade of meaning in the orders I give him. My face and voice seem to be the book he has undertaken to study, and he has well mastered the lesson."

"You must be attached to him."

"It is impossible not to give some portion of regard to one who so blindly believes in us. Perhaps it is just because his faith is so unquestioning that I like him."

"What is his name?"

"He has none. I called him Figaro for the whim of it, and the appellation has stuck to him. I made inquiries at Kiffton, but nobody knew anything about him. The old woman who kept him either did not or pretended not to know. You see I am home, friends, and country to the boy."

"And religion, too, I suppose."

"I doubt if the little scamp has much religion. He speaks the truth *to me;* he does not swear, for he is not talkative; he need not steal, for I give him everything he wants. Beyond that I will not undertake to speak."

They were now approaching Mr. Fraser's house, and Stafford paused in surprise to look around over the wide and varied prospect. "This is a fine place," he said, as he followed Hannah up the walk under the drooping elms. "Has your uncle a large family?".

"Lucy is the only child. It seems very still here. I hope they have not gone away."

The house did, indeed, wear a somewhat deserted look. The blinds, even to the summer doors, were closed; no sign of life was anywhere visible, and perfect silence reigned about the premises. The long branches of the elms drooped languidly in the hot sunshine, and the white roses blossoming everywhere looked faint in the heat. Hannah threw open the Venetian doors, and they stepped into the hall.

"There must be some one round," she said. "Just walk in here, Mr. Stafford, and I will see if I can't find them."

She ushered him into the cool, dim parlor, and left him there while she went in quest of some of the family. As his eyes became accustomed to the dim light, Stafford had leisure to look about him, and observe the room in which he found himself. It was a large apartment, running across the entire end of the house, and filled with handsome, old-fashioned furniture. A rich, soft carpet muffled the sound of his footfall; vases of flowers stood here and there, filling the air with fragrance; while scattered all about the room were articles rare and curious, collected by the captain in his many voyages.

These, however, received but a passing glance, for the attention of the gentleman had been riveted, almost from the moment of his entrance, by a picture which hung upon the wall. It was the portrait of Lucy, which had been sent from Paris to her parents about a year before. Stafford stood entranced before what he conceived to be some ideal head, not detecting, not even dreaming of any resemblance between it and the lovely young girl who had opened to him a door of shelter on that wild, stormy night, so long ago. About the sweet mouth hovered the faint dawn of a smile, and the brow, shaded by flowing hair, had an almost child-like purity; but in the deep-blue, level-looking eyes slept a world of steadfast purpose, and in the sweet curve of the red lips was the tenderness, not of a child, but of a woman.

As Stafford stood earnestly contemplating the picture, and vainly endeavoring to determine what dim memory it recalled, he was roused by a light step near, and the soft rustle of a lady's dress; and turning, he beheld, radiant with warm, youthful life, the counterpart of the picture. He heard Hannah pronounce the name of Lucy Fraser, a sweet voice uttered some graceful words of welcome, and fingers like rose-leaves rested for a moment in his own.

He stammered and was confused. For one of the few times in his life he lost his self-possession. In place of the pretty, bashful girl he remembered and expected, there met him this peerless creature, whose graceful equanimity, fortunately, went far in restoring his own.

Motioning her visitor to a chair near herself, Lucy pushed open the blinds of one of the front windows, which lay in the shadow of the trees, and, seating herself, she placed the little work-basket she carried on the table before her. Leaning back in her chair, with one arm resting on the low window-sill, and fingers playing idly with the leaves of the creepers that looked in, she turned to Stafford, with renewed assurances of her pleasure in this unexpected meeting. As she sat with the broken light which fell through the trees playing over her figure, a soft color in her cheek, and a smile of pleasure on her lips, Hannah contemplated her with a feeling of secret satisfaction. She had observed with how much more animation Stafford had spoken of seeing Mary than he had evinced at the prospect of renewing his acquaintance with Lucy, and she indulged in a slight feeling of triumph at his evident surprise and admiration. She had seen, before returning to the parlor, that Lucy wore one of her most becoming gowns — a rose-colored muslin of cloud-like delicacy. The thin folds, edged with narrow lace, were closed at the throat with a spray of green leaves, and the large, open sleeves, falling back, displayed her round, tapering arms.

" Hillsboro', Mr. Stafford, gives you a different welcome from that extended to you three or four years ago."

" Different, and yet the same. The warmth of hospitality made a summer only less delightful than this. But it is very beautiful here now. We were admiring, as we came up, the magnificent reach of country from this hill-side. It is quite unsurpassed in its way."

"Every man, woman, and child in Hillsboro' fondly thinks it unsurpassed in every way — do they not, Hannah? But the whole country is, indeed, looking more beautifully than I ever saw it before. Perhaps the season is propitious."

"Perhaps, Lucy," said Hannah, "you have been gone so long that you had forgotten how it did look. My cousin, Mr. Stafford, is almost as much a stranger here as you are."

"Indeed, Miss Fraser, have you been long away?"

"Something over three years. I went to Europe with my grandfather in the spring after you were here, and we have led a kind of vagabond life ever since."

"Vagabondizing is not to your taste, I infer."

"O, yes, it is; I am almost ashamed, under this respectable roof, to confess how much so. I used to think of my father and mother, and the dear old house on the hill, and shed a tear or two now and then; but I staid away."

"Did you weary that you came at last?"

"No. My father threatened to come after us, bring me home, and shut my grandfather up in a lunatic asylum; so, to save him a voyage to India, we came."

"To India?"

"O, yes. My grandfather was compelled to go to Madras, and I went with him, unwilling to lose the possible chance of riding in a howdah, or seeing live tigers in real jungles."

"And were you gratified?"

"In the first, yes, to my heart's content. But for the other, I returned as ignorant as I went. I fear I shall never see a tiger hunt."

"The show hunts are very tame affairs, and anything else very terrible. I carry two rows of white, stinging scars in my arm here near the shoulder, as the principal result of my experience in that direction."

"Why, Mr. Stafford, how did you get them?" exclaimed Hannah, in a tone of horror, while Lucy's eyes dilated.

"From two rows of sharp, terrible teeth, set in the jaws of a royal Bengal tiger — a more intimate acquaintance with such a character than was really pleasant, and one which I naturally embraced the first opportunity of ending. But pardon me for mentioning an incident so unpleasant. I would sooner listen to your Indian experiences, which I trust were more agreeable."

Lucy and her guest glided off into the current of pleasant chat about countries familiar to them both, and Hannah listened, quietly interested. The call had extended to a considerable length, and the latter was beginning to think of Lydia and supper, when steps were heard outside, and presently Miles's voice, singing snatches of a serenade. Attracted by their voices, he came and leaned on the window where Lucy was sitting. Looking from the bright sunlight into the shaded room, he did not perceive the presence of a stranger, as he threw into Lucy's lap a magnificent nosegay of roses of different varieties.

"There, Mistress Lucy," he said; "I met the most fervent of your admirers mooning along the road below here. He gave me these, with directions to bring them to the 'queen rose in the rosebud garden of girls,' and so

forth, and to tell her that he should do himself the honor
to follow his flowers in the course of an hour or two."

"What do you mean, Miles? and where did you get
these?" said Lucy, putting the flowers, quite unconsciously,
to her lips, to inhale their fragrance.

"I mean precisely what I have said; and I am wondering now if Burke will meet as sweet a reception as his
flowers."

"What a simpleton you are, Miles!" said Lucy, laughing, but blushing a little.

"That is gratitude!" exclaimed Miles, with a stage air.
"Here I bring another man's flowers for him, say all his
pretty things,—Burke wouldn't do as much for me,—
and get myself called a simpleton for my pains!"

He turned away from the window, and the next moment passed the open parlor door, and seated himself by
Lucy's desk in the entry.

Stafford, meanwhile, had been regarding with no very favorable eyes this handsome youth, whose careless assurance
of manner, and evidently familiar footing in the house, he
found, somehow, strangely distasteful. He caught himself
wondering who the fellow could be. He knew that Lucy
had no brother, and he might be almost anything else.
And there was another fellow too, it seemed, who had the
assurance to send flowers and familiar messages to this
perfect creature — confound his impudence! And the
next moment the gentleman was laughing secretly at his
own absurdity in being jealous of a woman whom half an
hour before he had cared nothing about.

Their conversation was now interrupted by the sound
of wheels, and Mary and the captain, who had been out

for a drive, entered the room. Stafford met from the former
the same warm reception accorded him by his other
friends. She assured him, with the most winning cordi-
ality, of her pleasure in again meeting him, answered his
inquiries for her husband, and presented her handsome
boy to his notice. The captain, too, tendered the hospitalities of the house with a bluff but not ungraceful hearti-
ness.

"I think, young gentleman," he said, "that I remember
your father as a young man. He used to come to Edgehill in those days. He was afterwards Bishop Stafford, if I
am not mistaken."

"My father was Bishop Stafford; but he died before I
can remember."

"So he did, to be sure. He was a gay young man then,
according to our puritanical notions of a parson. Though
you have his figure, you do not look like him in the face.
Bless me! how time does fly! It is fifty years and more
since I came home from Canton, a wild young fellow. He
was staying with the Gores that summer, and a gay one
we made of it."

"My cousin John was not master then."

"O, no. He was a lad at school — the only son; but
there was a houseful of girl cousins, and other gay young
folks. I courted and married my wife — Heaven rest her
sweet soul — in the four months I was at home."

"I am fortunate in awakening recollections so pleasant.
It is an auspicious beginning to a new acquaintance."

"I believe you. Well, come and see us, Mr. Stafford.
How long do you stay in Edgehill?"

Now, the gentleman addressed had, an hour or two before, intended to leave his cousin's the next morning; yet he answered promptly, " I shall remain for some time, probably; perhaps for several weeks."

" Then come often and see us. You will always bo welcome — to the old man for your father's sake, to these young folks, I know, for your own."

"I appreciate your kindness, sir," Stafford replied, warmly grasping the captain's proffered hand, " and I shall not fail to avail myself of it. But now Miss Page is growing impatient, and I am compelled to take my leave ;" and making his adieus to the others, he allowed Hannah to hasten him away.

CHAPTER XXIV.

WYCOMBE STAFFORD, the father of the personage who
figures in this story, was a descendant of one of the few
families among us which have retained in their possession,
ever since the first settlement of this country, an amount
of wealth sufficient to secure them an enviable social position. Sprung of an ancient English family, claiming gen-
erations of honorable gentlemen as ancestors, good tories
before the Independence and mild conservatives after, they
had always maintained their dignity at home, and a share
of consequence abroad. In the passage of time the family
had been gradually narrowing, until, some forty years before the present date, Wycombe Stafford and John Gore
were all that remained, on this side the Atlantic, of the
ancient stock. The former had been destined by his
friends for the church, and his quiet, scholarly tastes led
him to find that life congenial. While still very young,
he took orders. With fair talents and more culture, with
wealth, influence, charming manners, and a dignified presence, the road to preferment was easy to him, and the ascent rapid. The prosperous years passed swiftly, thinning
slightly the fine hair about the white temples of the bishop,
but leaving the youthful fire of his eye undimmed. I have
my own reasons for thinking that he was not insensible to
feminine charms; but it is certain that at the age of forty he

was still a bachelor. It was during a summer spent in England, and while paying a visit to some friends in the country, that he met and loved Georgiana Ross, the beautiful daughter of the neighboring rector. Gay, admired, and only nineteen, she gave her heart to the handsome American clergyman; and before the leaves fell in autumn he received from the hands of her father his lovely bride. When they fell again, in a foreign land, and far from the home of her youth, they covered her new-made grave; while her stricken husband sat in his lonely home, his ears pierced with the complaining cry of the infant that had cost the life of its mother.

For two years he bore with outward calmness his heavy bereavement, and at the end of that time a fever, terminating fatally, left the poor child doubly orphaned. The boy, who bore the united names of his parents, being called George Wycombe Stafford, was left by the will of his father to the joint guardianship of Mr. Gore and of Captain Ross, his mother's brother, an officer in the British army. The property which Mrs. Stafford held in her own right was left to the management of the latter, while the former was to assume the care of the child's American inheritance — much the larger of the two.

The boy's early years were passed in England, under the roof of his grandfather. Bright, high-spirited, and engaging, he managed to have his own way with nearly every one. His guardian was usually absent, and the old rector could never bear to cross a wish of the child whose beautiful brown eyes were so like those of his own lost darling. Naturally he grew up wilful and undisciplined; but, possessing an affectionate and loyal nature, with a strong

innate sense of justice and right, they could not wholly
spoil him. Agreeably to the provisions of his father's will,
he received his education at Harvard, afterwards went
through the form of studying law, and was admitted to
the bar in New York. But the possession of wealth enough
to satisfy his not extravagant tastes had possibly been
among the causes of his not pursuing his profession with
any great degree of ardor. With a man whose sense of
enjoyment was more keen than his ambition, this could
hardly fail to be the case. Entering the world with every
social and personal advantage, with youth, wealth, good
family, and the most perfect health, life beckoned him gayly
on. Everywhere society received with smiles her favorite.
Sometimes in America, sometimes in Europe, roaming the
broad world over wherever pleasure or adventure called,
years went over his head. How they left their impress,
what of good and what of evil was their fruit, how the
man fulfilled the generous promise of the boy, this story
must be allowed to tell.

Two weeks before the appearance of Stafford at Hillsboro', he had sat one morning at breakfast with his friend
and law partner, Francis Brainerd, Esq., at the latter's
bachelor home in New York. The two had been cronies
in college, and the friendship between them had since remained unbroken — deepening, indeed, with the lapse of
years, notwithstanding the extreme diversity of their characters. Brainerd, a grave, practical man of business, with
quiet and rather scholarly tastes, might have been thought
to have little in common with a brilliant worldling like
Stafford, the spoiled darling of society. But, then, such
anomalies are occurring every day; and, indeed, usually

they are, as in this case, anomalies only upon the surface. The law partnership between them had, it must be acknowledged, been merely nominal, at least until recently. Stafford had seldom troubled himself much with the business of the firm. But when, a few months before, he had returned from his journey to South America, it was to announce that he was tired of idling, and to enter with energy and ardor into the pursuit of his profession.

On the morning referred to, the two friends were occupied in the discussion of plans for the future. Brainerd, who found himself compelled by the exigencies of business to go to Calcutta, was endeavoring to persuade Stafford to accompany him. The latter had already visited India at a time when his uncle, Captain Ross, was serving in that country, and was half inclined to accede to his friend's request. He was withheld by a consciousness that to leave his present life of useful activity, and return to his old wandering habits, was not in reality the most judicious thing for him to do.

While they were yet discussing the question, a letter was brought in for Mr. Stafford. It was from Captain — now Colonel — Ross, and in it the uncle endeavored to impress upon his nephew the necessity for a change in his mode of life. He begged him to be *something*, either an American or an Englishman, outright — anything rather than the nondescript character he had so long sustained. He reminded him of the duties he owed to society, referred to his old and honorable name, which seemed likely to end with him, hinted discreetly at a choice among the fair countrywomen of his mother as a proper means of perpetuating it, and closed with some matters of business,

16

which he thought earnestly demanded the personal super-
vision of his nephew. This last part of the letter settled
the India question at once; and Brainerd saw with disappointment that he would be compelled to make the journey
alone. Two weeks would intervene before Stafford proposed to sail for England. The first was occupied with
seeing Brainerd off, and with other engagements in New
York; and some days of the second he determined to employ in a short visit to his cousin at Edgehill. He went;
he met his old friends at Hillsboro'; and the lovely face
of Lucy Fraser, and the soft music of her voice, proved a
spell more potent than the demands of lawyers, or the
sales of property in England. He despatched a letter to
his uncle, bidding the latter act for him, as his affairs would
detain him some time longer in America, and then gave
himself completely to the enjoyment of this new fancy.
It was a peculiarity of his that he brought to the pursuit
of whims all the ardor and persistency which other men
give to the graver ends of life — to the struggle for wealth,
fame, or power. Was he pursuing a whim now? He had
known many lovely women; their smiles had been lavished
on him almost from boyhood; nevertheless, no deep and
serious attachment had ever been among his experiences.

CHAPTER XXV.

SOME time passed, during which Burke's visits increased in frequency, and Stafford found occasion to be at Hillsboro' more than once. They had never met, however, though each often heard of the other; and each had gathered some idea of the other's footing in the house. Burke heard of the pleasant stranger, storm-bound among them years ago; and Stafford needed only the frequent allusions to their Colchester friend to perceive the probable magnet which drew him to Hillsboro'.

It was near the close of a pleasant afternoon about this time that Lucy was sitting before the open desk in the entry. Some half-written sheets lying before her showed the occupation in which she had been interrupted; but now she was leaning back, her head resting just below the wreath of carved lilies that finished the chair-back. Beside the desk, and facing the young lady of the house, sat Mr. Burke, and, in his arm-chair by the door, the captain was busy with his evening papers. Mary's voice was heard singing to her child up stairs, and Miles lay on the grass under the trees. Lucy had been very gay during the gentleman's call; but just now she sat in a listening attitude, trying to catch the chorus of a hay-maker's song that floated up from the valley below. The slant sunlight streamed into the room, and brightened, like a halo, the beautiful,

reclining head; and her companion was regarding her with
an expression which would have been quite unmistakable,
if it had been observed.

She had not yet looked up, when the sound of a strange
voice outside caught her ear. Some one was talking with
Miles; and the next moment the figure of Stafford broke
the sunshine in the doorway. Lucy recognized the new-
comer with some animation, as, with a courteous word to
her grandfather, he advanced to where she sat. She greeted him gayly, giving him her hand, and pushing her cat,
which had grown old and lazy, from the chair near, to give
him a seat at her side. Lucy briefly introduced the gentlemen, who bowed to each other with something more than
the usual *empressement*. But the two men had not raised
their heads from that profound obeisance before the mind
of each had arrived at certain conclusions. There was hos-
tility behind the mask of politeness, and keen scrutiny in
the glance with which each surveyed the other. A pang
of angry jealousy shot through the heart of Singleton
Burke, as he marked his handsome, smiling rival, — for as
such he instinctively recognized him, — and Stafford saw,
with extreme dissatisfaction, the evidently high place this
grave and dignified gentleman held in the good graces of
the young lady and her family.

The cat, which had been so unceremoniously dislodged,
stretched himself lazily, looked at the chair and its new
occupant, and then, turning his sleepy eyes upon his young
mistress, gave a light spring and curled himself in her lap.
Burke smiled.

"I see, Miss Fraser," he said, "your cat evinces the natural jealousy of an old friend at seeing a stranger promoted
to a place he had thought his own."

"Rather the readiness of a skilful general in retrieving a lost advantage," remarked Stafford, in the same strain. "Ah, Mrs. Fanshaw, I am glad to find you still here," he added, as Mary just then glided down the stairs.

She returned his greeting graciously, and then took a seat by Burke, to whom she chiefly devoted her attention, leaving Stafford quite to Lucy, while the captain called Miles in to play piquet with him. Conversation flowed smoothly on, sometimes general, sometimes divided into separate channels. Burke's politeness was severely taxed to be properly attentive to his kind neighbor. Ordinarily he enjoyed Mary's sparkling chat — all the more, perhaps, that he had no fund of small talk himself; but now he could not help keeping a listening ear for the low and marvellously sweet voice which, across the tall desk, discoursed to Lucy of the commonest things, but in a tone whose rich modulations were more expressive than most men's words. Once he darted a look of keen inquiry at Lucy's face, and drew a breath of relief as he noted its perfect serenity, and the easy, courteous smile with which she listened or replied to her companion.

"Have you been told of our pleasant plan for to-morrow, Mr. Stafford?" she said, at length.

"Not yet. Pray is not this something of yours which has fallen to the floor?"

"Ah, yes; my handkerchief. Thank you for returning it."

"This a handkerchief! It looks like a mist-wreath."

"It is a handkerchief, and considered, by competent judges, to be very beautiful. Mrs. Fanshaw will tell you so," answered Lucy, laughing, as she spread the gossamer thing on the desk before her.

"What is that I am called on to testify to?" asked Mary, coming forward, while Burke also leaned towards the desk.

"To the beauty of my handkerchief, which Mr. Stafford's uneducated eye failed to detect."

"Elegant!" exclaimed Mary, in a genuine burst of feminine admiration. "What exquisite embroidery, and what lace!"

"Yes, Mary, that lace is of fabulous value — real Spanish point. But I see you do not detect in the thing what to me is its chief beauty."

"I see nothing peculiar, beyond the embroidery and the lace. Do you, Mr. Stafford?"

"Nothing, unless it be this delicate flower-scent," raising it to his face. "What do you find, Mr. Burke?" reaching it to that gentleman.

"I am dull," answered Burke, dropping the pretty trifle as if it had burned his fingers. "I see nothing different from all handkerchiefs."

"It does differ entirely from all and every handkerchief."

"Has it a magic power, like that given by the Moor to his wife?" asked Stafford.

"Not precisely; yet it came from the land of the Moors. It was given me under the shadow of the Alhambra."

"You pique our curiosity, Miss Fraser," Stafford said, taking the handkerchief again in his hands and turning it from side to side, examining it carefully. In an instant he looked up, with a smile.

"You have found the secret?" asked Mary.

He pointed with his finger to the four corners of the bit

of linen, where, wrought with exquisite delicacy, and hidden in the sprays of flowers and ferns which ornamented it, appeared the four letters that formed the musical name of its owner, distinct when known to be there, but quite escaping the careless eye.

"It is a pretty fancy," said Mary, as Stafford laid the handkerchief gently down; and Lucy, with a sudden blush, for which she could hardly have accounted, began to speak of something else.

"I think I was telling you about our fishing-party, Mr. Stafford."

"Yes. Where do you go, and when?"

"To Long Pond, to-morrow. Miles was to have sent you a note to-day; but he, careless boy, forgot it, and promised to go to Edgehill this evening. The party will consist, besides ourselves, of cousin Hannah, Lydia, Ben Miller, and his sister Fanny. May we reckon upon you also?"

"With the greatest pleasure on my part. At what hour?"

"At nine. Miles will give you all particulars."

Miles looked up suddenly from his cards. "I beg pardon, Lucy," he said; "I quite forgot, until this moment, another commission with which you charged me, when I went to Colchester. I have carried this "— handing her a small parcel—"in my pocket since yesterday. I hope it is not ruined."

"I presume not," answered Lucy, laughing; "as it is only some riding-gloves I ordered from Barker's."

"What in the world, child, possessed you to send for riding-gloves, when the only saddle-horse on the premises is lame?"

"In the natural course of events, grandpa, that horse must recover from his accident."

"It is an event you are likely to have in prospect some time yet."

"Yes; but we are to go to Major Miller's one day this week, and I mean to use my best generalship to get from him an offer of his pretty gray."

"Have you no fear of a strange animal?" asked Stafford.

"None, whatever; if he will carry a saddle, it is all I ask."

"Then allow me the pleasure of furnishing you with a horse until your own has got over his lameness. It is a beautiful creature which Mr. Gore has just purchased; and I am sure he would be delighted if you would consent to ride him."

"Indeed, you are very kind, Mr. Stafford; but I hardly like — I fear Mr. Gore might —" Lucy hesitated, but her sparkling eyes told with how much pleasure she regarded the proposition. Mr. Stafford did not wait for her objections.

"Believe me, I speak with a full knowledge of my cousin John. The horse was bought with reference to a young lady who is to visit him in the autumn, but is standing idle in the stable now. Do not hesitate, I entreat."

"Since you are so kind, then, I accept. The truth is, I have not been in the saddle since my return home; and I am getting childishly eager to enjoy the pleasure of a good gallop once more."

Burke, impatient and uncomfortable at what seemed to him Lucy's open show of preference for this new admirer, here rose to go. But his time was coming. Lucy, who was talking with Stafford, looked up as he approached her, and said, with a smile not to be resisted, —

"O, not yet, Mr. Burke. I have been practising that song you liked the other day, and when the light grows dim and pleasant in the parlor I will sing it to you."

Burke's face flushed with surprise and pleasure. "How shall I thank you?" he began.

"By staying, if you please," answered Lucy, sweetly.

The sunset brightness was fading slowly; even near objects were growing indistinct in the twilight, and on the sward before the door the moon flung faint shadows of the elms, when Lucy, rising, led the way to the parlor. Within the room the light was faint and uncertain, and her white figure moving about was the only object discernible. Stafford remained standing in the doorway, while Burke leaned on the piano at the singer's side.

Lucy's voice was not powerful, but it was clear and sweet, and had a wonderfully tender and sympathetic quality. The song she had chosen was an old, old ballad, simple and plaintive, a story of love, and constancy, and death. The music — low, sweet, and slightly monotonous — suited well with the theme, and with the rich, tender tones of the singer's voice, and its effect was heightened by the plaintive notes of a whippoorwill, which, hidden in the green shadows of the orchard, breathed out its sorrowful complaint upon the evening air. Stafford loved music passionately; and his taste was cultivated by familiarity with the finest productions of its masters, and the renderings of its highest artists; but seldom had its power so touched his heart as now. He stood leaning against the doorway, the soft, odorous gloom of the room, the shadowy figures, the broken, trembling shadows cast by the moonshine, the murmur of the summer night-wind, and the melting pathos of the singer's voice, with that answering echo from the mournful bird without, all combining to produce a sense of exquisite delight, which thrilled him through and through.

When the last note died away on the stillness of the room, he drew a long, deep breath, like one released from some soft spell. Burke spoke his thanks in a few simple, well-chosen words; but something in Stafford's heart refused to express itself in the compliments usually so ready upon his lips. In a very few moments after, he took his leave.

CHAPTER XXVI.

THE weather next morning proved entirely propitious — gray, with thin clouds, a southwest wind, and not too warm. Half an hour before the appointed time, most of the pleasure party were assembled at Mr. Fraser's. It consisted of the captain, his daughter-in-law, and all the younger members of the family, Hannah, Heman, and Lydia Page, Ben Miller, and his sister Fanny. The conveyances provided were Squire Fraser's carryall, over which the captain was to preside; Ben's one-horse buggy — at Lydia's service, of course; and a similar vehicle belonging to Heman. It wanted but a few minutes to nine, but neither Stafford nor Burke had yet made his appearance.

"Now," said the captain, coming out on the doorstep, spy-glass in hand, "I can see nothing along the road of those young fellows. It wants a quarter to nine; I shall wait twenty minutes for them, and no more. Teach them to be prompt. Here are the cattle; now, how shall we bestow ourselves?"

"It is all arranged, grandpa," said Lucy; "I am going with Heman; Ben and Lydia must not be separated, of course; the carryall will accommodate the rest of you. We are going directly, and shall expect to meet you at Ephraim Green's. We shall drive fast, as the morning is cool. Good by. We are off."

"Stop a minute. Here comes a boy on horseback. I think it is a messenger."

It proved to be the bearer of a note from Burke, in which the writer expressed his regret that an unforeseen but unavoidable engagement would prevent his making one of the party.

"I am sorry to lose him," said Lucy; "but we cannot afford to miss our day's pleasure on his account. Come, Heman;" and, just touching her cousin's offered hand, she sprang lightly into the buggy, and they drove away.

They were scarcely gone, when the captain, who had been reconnoitring the road, announced that Stafford was coming.

"I knew he would be here in season," Hannah said, straining her eyes to catch a sight of the approaching carriage.

"He will have sharp work to get here before the clock strikes," answered the old man.

"He will come well up to it, sir, if he keeps that pace," said Miles, suddenly coming out of a brisk flirtation with Fanny Miller.

But a very few moments elapsed before Stafford's light phaeton whirled up to the door, and that gentleman, springing out, exclaimed, —

"My dear friends, I hope you will pardon me if I have kept you waiting."

"The clock is just striking; you are punctual to a minute," replied the captain.

"I am very glad to hear it. It is better than I expected, as I was detained this morning by some unexpected arrivals. Good morning, Mrs. Fraser;" and he greeted each one of the party, looking around meanwhile with a secret uneasiness at seeing nothing of Lucy or of Burke. "I do not see your friend, Mr. Burke, Mrs. Fanshaw; are we not to have his company to-day?"

"I am sorry to say we are not. Lucy had a note from him this morning. He is detained by a stupid meeting of trustees."

"And Miss Fraser?"

"O, she was off some time since with her cousin, Heman Page. Just the weather for us — is it not?"

"Perfect. Mrs. Fraser, I hope you will do me the favor to take a seat in my phaeton. You will find it more comfortable than the carryall."

"Mr. Stafford is right, Susan," said the captain. "Fan and Mary are younger, and can bear crowding."

The two gentlemen assisted Mrs. Fraser to a seat in the phaeton, and the rest of the party, with much laughter and confusion, bestowed themselves in the carryall. The shawls and overcoats were stowed away, the hampers securely buckled on, and off they drove, the captain leading the way.

The distance to Long Pond was some dozen or fifteen miles; and the road by which it was reached, after continuing northward for some time, turned to the east, leaving the hilly district of Edgehill and Hillsboro' for a region not less interesting, but of softer outlines. They passed no villages, but all along their way smiled green and fertile farms. Winding among these, through still woods and by half-hidden watercourses, they came at length in sight of the pond. Still and calm it lay in the embrace of the wide landscape, reflecting on its smooth surface

every shade of the soft gray canopy of cloud bending over
it, and showing in its clear depths every rock and tree,
green field and swelling knoll along its shores. In the
more immediate neighborhood of the pond the country
was but thinly peopled; and the farm of Ephraim Green,
lying near the head of the lake, was nearly a mile from
any neighbor. A winding road, skirting the edge of the
pond, led to the house — a large, weather-colored, wooden
edifice, facing down the green slope to the pebbly edge of
the water.

As the last detachment of the fishing party came round
a curve in the road, and drew up in front of the house, its
proprietor was engaged in sharpening an axe on a screech-
ing grindstone under an apple tree. His eldest son, Caleb
Green, together with Ben and Heman, was busy about a
pretty sail-boat, that swung at anchor a little way out from
shore. Lucy and her cousin appeared from within as the
carriages stopped, and Mr. Green laid down his axe and
approached the side of the carryall.

"Wal, I declare, Cap'n Fraser! You hain't got too old
to go a pleasurin' yet. These all your grandchildren?"

"How are you, Ephraim? All my grandchildren! Good
Lord! I hope not. You have got three or four of our
young folks here — haven't you?"

"Yes; I s'pose they belong to you. There's one gal I
knew for Robert Fraser's darter the minute I clapped eyes
on her. Walk right in, ladies; we'll see to your things.
Show 'em into the settin'-room, Sally" — this to a freckle-
faced girl who appeared at the door.

While the ladies were ushered into the house by Sally,
to shake out their dresses, smooth their hair, and make all

final arrangements for a day on the water, Stafford and Miles attended to the conveying of the well-filled boxes, baskets, fishing-tackle, and so forth, to the beach. The room into which Sally conducted the ladies was a large, uncarpeted, unpapered apartment, the sitting-room of the family. It was scrupulously clean, but had a chilly, uninviting aspect, from the scant furniture and staring, whitewashed walls. In an arm-chair by the window sat an ancient dame, the mother of Ephraim, who viewed the party curiously through her iron-bowed spectacles, and put innumerable questions to Captain Fraser about the excursion, the party, and his relationship to every member of it.

Stafford presently appeared with the announcement that the boat was ready; and he gave his arm to Mrs. Fraser, while the others followed to the beach. The water being too shallow to allow of the sail-boat coming near the shore, the party were to be transported to it in a small row-boat, which was now drawn up on the sand. Ben Miller, with a brisk, white-headed boy to assist him, had the management of the smaller craft, while Heman, with Caleb Green, a young man of twenty, was already on board the sailboat.

Mrs. Fraser, Mary, Hannah, and Fanny Miller were to go first. They were quickly handed in, and Miles sprang after them.

"Quick, Stafford! you will be too late," he cried, as the boy, almost knee-deep in water, was pushing the boat off the sand.

"I will wait and go with Captain Fraser; you are full enough without me;" and, sitting down on the log where the old gentleman was resting himself and enjoying a cigar, he watched the little boat as the strong arms of the young men rowed it out into the deep water, where, rocking idly, the "Juliana" lay at anchor. Lucy and Lydia, arm-in-arm, walked up and down the beach until the boat returned.

"A little more up on the sand, Miller; the young ladies will wet their feet. There, that will do. Miss Lydia, now for it. — Miss Fraser, allow me;" and the girls were transferred from the beach to the little, shell-like craft. The captain and Stafford followed, and the latter, taking an oar, assisted Ben.

"Who is commander of this expedition, Ben?" asked Lucy, as they shot from the shore.

"Caleb Green, of course. He manages his own vessel."

"Is he a competent officer?"

"Yes; he has kept a boat on this pond ever since he was a dozen years old."

"You see, Ben," said the captain, "Lucy got a ducking once by going sailing with a crew of ninnies, and it cost her the only fit of sickness she ever had."

"Are you afraid, Lucy?"

"O, no, Ben. But I remember how I felt when I went under water the last time, sure that I should never see home or the faces of friends again. It was not a pleasant sensation, and I have no desire to experience it twice."

"*I* should be afraid if *I* had been through all that," said her cousin.

"I am not afraid, Lydia; I have only learned to be cautious. I like to know whom I am trusting, and how far I may. When we have suffered once from a too ready confidence, we do not forget the lesson."

She was looking away over the gray expanse of water as she spoke, and did not see the long, keen look with which Stafford searched her face. Just then the boat touched the side of the Juliana, and in the bustle of transfer the subject was forgotten.

The anchor was lifted, the sails spread, and a light wind bore them smoothly over the pond. The thin veil of clouds remained unbroken; the day was warm, but not sultry. Dropping their anchor near the middle of the pond, where, according to Caleb, fish abounded, the business of the expedition fairly began. Hannah, Heman, their grandfather, and Mrs. Fraser fished. It was what they had come for. The others made fishing a pretext for entertainment of a different kind. Miles found quite constant employment in baiting Fanny Miller's hook — which hook, by the way, caught but two fish during the day. The rest of the party, gathered in the stern of the boat, held their lines, and now and then drew in a fish; but the presence of a strong counter interest in the minds of two or three of them prevented the occupation from becoming an absorbing one.

Mary watched Stafford and Lucy narrowly. She had seen from the first the gentleman's admiration of her beautiful friend, and observed with some dissatisfaction his increasing attentions. For a notable plan had lately taken form in Mary's brain. She thought of a great, lonely house, near her own, at Colchester, and pictured to herself Lucy enlivening and adorning it with her presence. She pleased herself with imagining all she would enjoy in having Lucy so near her; and she saw with delight that, so far as Burke was concerned, everything went as she wished. He was as deeply enamoured a man as she could

17

desire to see. But there all her satisfaction ended. Just
as she had begun to congratulate herself that he had made
a favorable impression, and to believe that by perseverance the hoped-for result might be effected, this dangerously agreeable stranger had stepped upon the scene. She
could not help seeing that in some respects the rivals were
unequally matched. Burke, with all the advantages of his
recognized position, his commanding talents and honorable
character, yet lacked the personal qualifications which
would make such advantages available. Indeed, with a
girl so little calculating, so wholly unworldly, as Lucy, the
question of comparative eligibility between two suitors
was likely to be settled, should it call for settlement, on
principles of her own. If she had been in the least degree
in love with Burke, if the interest she felt in him had had
even a shade of tenderness in it, not the most fascinating
of mortals could have had power to rival him. But, being
completely heart-whole, she was ready to be entertained
by whomsoever could make himself most agreeable. Burke
did not shine in conversation. He could argue a knotty
question closely, or discourse with dignity, and even with
eloquence, upon matters of which he had been led to think
much; but his intellect had no rapid play. He lacked the
abandon, the mental *laisser-aller*, which allows the mind to
glance lightly from point to point. He wanted the sense
of humor, also, without which there is apt to be a certain
clumsiness in the movements of the most superior intellect; and he had a too sensitive *amour propre* to be able
ever quite to forget himself and the impression he might
be producing. Stafford, on the contrary, with a less commanding mental ability, yet had those traits of temper and

disposition which the other lacked — a quick sense of humor, fine taste, a mind rapid as lightning in its play, and, above all, a perfect sweetness and amiability of temper, and a genuine, almost boyish, unconsciousness. A vainer man than Burke he might be, — Mary thought him so, and I am inclined to think she was right, — yet his vanity was without self-assertion, and its chief outward manifestation was seen in his desire to give pleasure to all around him. The hundred little nameless graces and courtesies which displayed themselves in his manner were therefore as much the natural outgrowth of kindliness and good taste as of mere vanity. Burke held all these in contempt, as in some degree unworthy the dignity of a man of character.

When she looked at Lucy, Mary was completely at fault. She could not understand her friend's serene unconsciousness and sweet impartiality. Was she cold? Was she so dull as not to perceive that both these men were in love with her? or was she engrossed with thoughts of one absent? In all these suppositions Mary was wide of the mark. Lucy herself gave the key to her conduct when she said, a few pages back, that she was cautious. The lesson of her early experience had been deeply learned. Ardent and impulsive as she was by nature, will now held feeling in check. She would not too easily give herself permission to love again. It might be, however, that in this very self-control and power of repression lay a source of pain deeper than the old child-like unconsciousness. The carefully guarded heart, once surrendered, might not be so easily recalled.

Lucy had grown tired of sport, and, throwing aside her

line, leaned languidly against a coil of rope. Mary and Stafford were eagerly playing a huge pickerel upon the hook of the former.

"Safe, at last, Mr. Stafford; draw him in," cried Mary, a little disconcerted by the struggles of her prize, as Stafford flung him into the bottom of the boat.

"There, Mrs. Fanshaw; I think our side can afford to take a holiday until Captain Fraser's detachment can equal that."

"Lucy seems to be taking one already. Are you tired, my dear?"

"No; but I believe I don't like fishing; and if it is not agreeable, why should I do it?"

"Didn't you come to fish?" asked Lydia.

"By no means: I came for the fine weather, the people, and the sail."

"I," said Lydia, "came for all those, but with an eye for the fish at the same time. We have enough for dinner, now. When shall we land, Ben?"

"In an hour or so."

"Where?"

"Down below here about a mile, at a place called the Table Rock."

"If Mr. Burke had only come with us, now!" said Lucy. "He said there was a story about the Table Rock; and he could have told it."

"Mr. Burke is unfortunate in losing so fine a day on the water."

"Yes; and when I left home this morning, you, too, were given up."

"I nearly failed of my time. But on reaching home

last night, I found company at my cousin's; and it was only by pleading important business that I made my escape. Mrs. Sandoval exacted from me a promise to return as soon as I had disposed of it."

"Is it Mrs. Lawrence Sandoval you are speaking of?" asked Mary.

"The same."

"Are her daughters with her?"

"One daughter, whom I think she called Laura."

"Laura Sandoval at Edgehill!" exclaimed Lucy, turning to look over her shoulder. "I have heard so much of her! Is she not very beautiful, Mr. Stafford?"

"If so, I did not observe it. Is she reputed a beauty?"

"I have heard that she is very lovely."

"You awaken my curiosity. I shall observe Miss Sandoval more closely. Never having heard of her before, I remember only a tired, rather languid young lady, not so interesting as her mamma, whom I met at breakfast this morning."

"You must have been very much preoccupied," said Mary, dryly."

"Possibly. But the advent of visitors was not an agreeable surprise. The quiet of my cousin's dim old house, with its overhanging cliff and shadowy trees, was delightful. Put in a party of half a dozen fashionable men and women, and — pshaw! it is just like any other house."

"Lucy, you will lose the rings from your fingers, trailing them in the water so."

"I wear but this one, Mary, and it fits closely; but I should be loath to lose it."

"Why has it so great a value? Is it a *gage d'amour?*"

"Nothing of the kind. Look at the legend;" and, drawing off the ring, she laughingly laid it in Mary's hand.

"'E. L. to her friend. Dec. 12, 185-,'" read Mary, aloud. "What do E. and L. stand for, my dear?"

"The initials of a friend of mine, whom I hope you will some day know."

"Who is she?"

"Mrs. Henry Lovell, of New York."

"I never heard of her before."

"No. I knew her first at Havana, and afterwards in Germany. We were at the same hotel, and she was very kind to grandpa during a short illness. When I first met her, she had just lost her only child, a very beautiful daughter. There were, I suspect, some peculiarly painful circumstances connected with her death, though I do not know what; and, indeed, my impression comes mainly from surmise. She is the saddest person that I ever knew. She seldom mentions her daughter, but broods over her loss continually."

"Is she still in Europe?"

"She was when I last heard from her. — Mr. Stafford, will you assist me?" Lucy added, turning suddenly to that gentleman, and holding up her line, which, in her neglect, had become entangled with his own.

He was sitting with his elbow leaning on the side of the boat, and, in a sort of nervous, impatient way, was whipping the water with a willow bough. Lucy scarcely noticed at the time, though she remembered afterwards, that his face was darkened by a heavy frown, and a stern, rather defiant expression showed itself in the firmly-drawn lines of his mouth. So absorbed was he in his own reflections that he did not hear Lucy's request; and she was obliged to repeat it before she caught his attention.

The boat was now got under way, and, with a light wind, they went smoothly down the pond, past the still, green shores, and round a little headland to a cove, where they came to anchor under some steep, shelving rocks. The Juliana was soon emptied of her passengers and cargo, and energetic preparations were made for dinner. A little way from the landing rose a large gray rock, its perpendicular sides washed by the water, and its flat, even surface justifying its appellation of "Table Rock." This was the immemorial dining-place of all fishing parties on the pond; and here their repast was to be spread.

Fires were lighted on the shore, and the freshly-caught fish soon sent up an appetizing savor. At the end of half an hour, Captain Fraser, using his hand as a speaking trumpet, summoned the stragglers with a call that was taken up in long echoes by all the surrounding hill-sides. A day on the water is a good sharpener of the appetite; and nobody was at all tardy in answering to the call. Mrs. Fraser, being the oldest lady present, was assigned the best seat, — a Hingham bucket turned upside down, — and the others bestowed themselves on various stones and boxes, without much regard to the graceful or the picturesque.

Gypsy dinners, when the party is at all a desirable one, are apt to be very pleasant, but they are also very much alike; and I cannot stop to describe this one. It was considerably prolonged, but it was over at last, and the company scattered in various directions to seek such amusement as they liked. Hannah and Lucy wandered away

together up the steep, rocky hill. They found a few wild
flowers, but presently grew tired of picking them, and sat
down in a little cleft among the rocks. It was a pleasant
nook, overhung with wild roses and tangled vines, and
within sound of the mingled voices that came up to them
from the shore. The captain's breezy tones rose conspicuous among all. Lucy listened for the sound of his voice,
and an expression of deep tenderness softened her beautiful face.

"Dear grandfather," she exclaimed, "how he is enjoying this day! As much a boy as the youngest of them.
O, Hannah," she continued, in a low voice, "I can never
tell you how much that old man's love was to me, in that
time, long ago, when — when I was not so happy as I am
now. I shall never forget that voyage to Cuba — those
long nights passed upon the deck of the vessel, clasped in
his arms, and watching the still heavens, while silently our
hearts seemed to hold communion. He was so kind — so
tender! Even then, while the deepest sorrow of his life
was fresh upon him, he had no chiding for the selfish, way-
ward child, who forgot all but her own light griefs. It
was his patient smile that first taught me the lesson of self-
forgetfulness."

"You were always thoughtful of others, Lucy."

"When too happy to think of myself, perhaps I was;
but then I was a different creature. That was a hard time
to bear, Hannah; but I have come to look upon it as the
most fortunate of my life. — Some one is coming," she added hastily, sweeping away a tear that had stolen to her
cheek, and affecting to busy herself with the cluster of late
wild roses she had found lingering in the rocks above.

The next moment Stafford appeared round a projecting rock near by. At the first glance he saw by the misty softness in Hannah's eyes, and the slight quiver of Lucy's lip, that he had interrupted a conversation of more than common interest.

"I beg pardon," he said; "but Mrs. Fanshaw sent me to find Miss Page."

Hannah rose and moved away, and Stafford was also about to withdraw, when Lucy, looking up from her flowers, motioned him to the seat her cousin had just left, saying, with a smile that was very sweet, albeit a little forced and faint, —

"It is scarcely fair to take Hannah away, and refuse to stay yourself. See, I will give you this as a bribe."

"Thank you; but I waited only for permission to remain," he answered, as he took the rose she offered. There was something in the low tone of the reply that made Lucy half regret the flattering invitation she had given. Perhaps he detected the feeling, for the next instant he spoke in a tone which, though equally low, seemed softened only by respect for her apparent mood.

"To how light a touch will our deepest buried memories sometimes vibrate! At sight of these late-fading roses I go back step by step through the years, and see a boy asleep under a hedge, with a cluster of fresh-blown wild roses clasped in his unconscious hand. To gain them he had braved fatigue and danger, as well as anger and punishment by venturing on forbidden ground. The gardens of his home were bright with a varied profusion of roses; but his eyes coveted the forbidden flowers — forbidden because the cliff where they grew was dangerous.

At last he possessed them; and I do not remember that he enjoyed them the less for the thought of the punishment that was to follow his disobedience. Poor boy! That act of wilful rebellion against established law and authority has had many a parallel in his life."

"Perhaps the parallels would have been fewer if the punishment had been heavier," answered Lucy, mischievously.

"Possibly. And yet I hardly know. When I see some wild and turbulent child subdued by the sweet voice of a mother, I know what influence was wanting to my own life. Had my beautiful mother lived, I think her son might have been more worthy of her. But look! O, inauspicious omen! The flower you gave me has scattered its petals in my hand. Must I keep this poor reminder of beauty and fragrance wasted, or may I rely on your bounty to replace it?"

His manner had changed from quiet earnestness to a tone of half-serious, half-playful gallantry; and Lucy answered, with a shake of the head, and something of her old gay perversity, —

"No; it cannot be. Mine, too, have fallen, except these two buds, which I shall carry home. They will blossom in water, and I shall want them for my hair. But do you see, Mr. Stafford, how these thin clouds are breaking along the west? We shall have fine moonlight for our drive home. Ah! already the sun is bursting through. See what a flood of splendor streams over the water below us."

Like molten gold the pond now stretched away before them, its waves rippling with low murmurs at their feet. The wind lifted Lucy's long curls, and stirred the wild vines that drooped above her head. She had risen from her seat, and stood looking down on the brightening expanse of water, quite forgetful, for the moment, of her companion, whose admiring glance was fixed upon her animated face. He stooped to gather up the gloves, veil, and other articles which had fallen from her lap as she rose, and at that moment Mary appeared before them.

" Come, laggards," she said ; "everybody is ready to embark, and the captain has sent me to you with a peremptory summons."

"O, Mary! Must we go so soon ? This is the most beautiful hour of the day."

" It will be a beautiful hour of the night if we do not go soon."

" It will be charming to go home by moonlight."

" But not so charming to arrive at midnight. Think of my motherless child at home ! "

" I have no more to say, Mary. You always crush me with that boy of yours. We must go, Mr. Stafford. Thank you for restoring my property. I am apt to leave such tokens of myself scattered about."

They walked on somewhat quickly towards the shore. They had gone but a few yards when Lucy stopped, and seemed searching for something. She shook her dress, examined the articles she held in her hand, hesitated, and then said, —

" I must go back; I have lost my handkerchief."

" O, Lucy, do not stop for a handkerchief. See, they are all in the boat, and are calling us."

" I must, Mary. It is that one I was showing you last night; and it was a gift from Mr. Lester. I should not like to lose it."

"We will go back, then, of course; but you were a foolish child to bring it on an excursion like this."

"I know that; but I caught it up hastily this morning, without observing what I took."

Stafford and Mary went back with her, and together they prosecuted the search for the missing handkerchief. It was in vain, however. The pretty trifle was nowhere to be found; and Lucy was obliged at last to resign the hope of recovering it, and to beg her friends to give themselves no further trouble.

"You must have lost it higher up the hill, Lucy."

"I am sure I had it while I sat here with Hannah."

"Then it must have been blown away."

"I dare say it was. But we will waste no more time. Come."

As they went swiftly down the hill, Lucy looked back, and said to Stafford, who was assisting Mary, —

"You compared my handkerchief to poor Desdemona's. Do you think I shall get smothered for my carelessness?"

"You can best judge whether your friend is enough like Othello to make such a dismal fate probable."

"The resemblance is not great — bless his kind gray head! But how impatient my grandfather is growing! I must hasten on and appease him."

The whole party were soon embarked. Lucy appeared to have been quite successful in appeasing the wrath of the impatient captain. He was in a very mild and placable frame of mind; and the two sat together in the stern of the boat, the young girl leaning lightly against the old man's shoulder. They glided on over the smooth water, the sunset brightness fading from the shores, and the Table Rock growing more and more indistinct as it receded behind them.

Lucy remained quite silent for a time; but at length she broke into a low, monotonous Spanish song. It was one which she had caught from the muleteers of the mountains during her sojourn with the Lesters. The words were simple and mournful, and the air wild and plaintive in the extreme. Lucy had often heard its melancholy refrain coming down some mountain defile, as one by one the train of mules crept round a point in the high, winding path; and she loved the song for its association with scenes among which she had enjoyed so much. She had sung two stanzas, and was beginning the third, when a full, mellow tenor glided into the strain. Lucy turned to look at the singer. It was Stafford. Clear, sweet, and liquid, the united voices blended in the most perfect accord. As the song continued, there seemed to have stolen into it with the added voice a subtle thread of meaning, to which Lucy's unconsciously vibrated. The languid entreaty of the tenor awoke an answering chord of tenderness, of which probably her ear was unaware. With eyes fixed dreamily on the lessening shore they had left, and her thoughts wandering far away, she sat motionless, while the song floated over the still lake — a song which for centuries has been known to the wild sierras, now waking for the first time, doubtless, the softened echoes of that New England forest.

When the last note died trembling away into silence, Lucy raised her head suddenly and looked at Stafford. He was leaning against the side of the boat, and was looking at her, though, to judge from the absent expression of his eyes, not thinking of her. She felt like one just aroused from a pleasant, indistinct dream, and languidly drooped her head once more on the strong, kind shoulder of her grandfather.

A substantial supper awaited the party on their arrival at Ephraim Green's; and as soon as it was despatched the horses were brought up. The ladies assumed the warm shawls they had provided for the evening drive, and reported themselves "all ready" on the green before the door. Lucy was the last.

"Where are mother and Mary?" she asked, not seeing either of them.

"Gone," said Hannah.

"How, pray; and why?"

"O, Mary was getting fidgety about Elliot; so she and Miles took Heman's wagon, as they could drive faster with Black Bess than in the carryall. Grandfather and your mother went with them in Mr. Stafford's carriage. He insisted on their taking it, it is so much easier for aunt Susan, you know."

Lucy made no answer, and the party proceeded to take their places. Stafford handed Lucy to the front seat of the carryall, and turning to Heman, who approached at the moment, said, "With your permission, I should like to drive this team."

"All right," answered Heman, taking his place on the middle seat. "I can make myself very useful here in holding Fanny in."

Stafford took the reins from the boy who held them, and sprang to Lucy's side. The freshened horses obeyed his signal, and they were soon rolling along the smooth road towards Hillsboro'. Fanny Miller and Heman kept up a lively interchange of good-humored railleries. Hannah, a little tired with the unusual nature of the day's exertions, leaned back in her corner of the carriage, silent and uncompanionable. Lucy, too, seemed little disposed to talk; but, nestled in her warm shawl, she sat watching the flying objects along the roadside, and listening to the music of the low voice that murmured in her ear.

As for Stafford, he sat by her side with a demeanor outwardly calm, and only a shade more serious and thoughtful than usual; but his eye seldom wandered from the lovely face which the tender moonlight revealed to him ; and the thrill of that delicious song, across whose slender thread of melody her soul had for one moment answered his, was yet vibrating in his memory. In this hour of exquisite happiness every harassing doubt was forgotten. Every mistake of the past, every cloud in the future, vanished before the enchanting present.

Rapidly the long miles were accomplished; and before any of the party had thought of it, Carlo's loud barking announced their approach to home. As the carryall drew up before the door, Stafford threw down the reins ; but before he could alight, Mr. Fraser, who was waiting for them, had lifted his daughter from the carriage.

While his horse, which the captain had driven, was being made ready, Stafford stood in the doorway with Lucy and Miles, and the subject of the projected ride was again brought up. Mr. Gore had expressed his pleasure that Miss Fraser should wish to ride his horse, and it was entirely at her disposal. Stafford suggested the next day for their first trial; but Lucy objected, — she should be too tired, — and at length fixed the day after, mentioning an hour towards evening, when it would be cool. It was so arranged ; and the gentleman presently took his leave, carrying with him the light of a most enchanting smile as he went.

CHAPTER XXVII.

Burke came next day to hear about the fishing-party, express his regrets, and propose a pleasant plan of his own. He had heard Miss Fraser express a desire to visit "Indian Head," a famous locality in a neighboring town, having historical associations of much interest. It lay at a point somewhat nearer to Colchester than to Hillsboro', though in a different direction. Burke's proposition was, that the Fraser party, including Mary and Miles, should drive over next day to the place in question, where he himself would meet them; and after examining at their leisure the various points of interest, they should all return with him to his house in Colchester, and dine.

Mary caught eagerly at this plan; but Lucy, remembering her engagement with Stafford, expressed a fear that they might not return in season for her to keep it.

"You could easily postpone your ride for one day, Lucy. I dare say it would make no difference to Mr. Stafford."

"I have already postponed it once for my own convenience; I should not like to do so again."

"Well, then, perhaps we could go to Indian Head a day later, if Mr. Burke does not object."

"I object, if Burke does not," interrupted Miles; "for that throws me out. You forget that to-morrow is my last

18

day here. Why not double up the two arrangements into one?"

"Why not, indeed?" replied Burke; and he added, with what Miles afterwards declared to be a fearful sacrifice of truth to politeness, "If you can induce Mr. Stafford to make one of our party, it will give me great pleasure to see him at my house."

"Even then, Lucy, you will have to give up the ride. So many miles on horseback would hardly be a pleasure."

"My dear, you have no idea what a horsewoman I am."

"I know that you have travelled three years with Captain Fraser, to whom a horse is only less beautiful than a ship."

"That is true; and often, for weeks, we actually lived in the saddle. He will tell you that I am not easily fatigued."

After a good deal more discussion, it was finally settled in accordance with Miles's suggestion. Lucy agreed to acquaint Stafford with the change of programme, which would oblige him to report himself at an earlier hour than that first fixed upon; and Burke took his leave, considerably disappointed at the unexpected shape his plan had assumed, but more in love than ever.

Mr. Stafford was loitering with Miss Sandoval in the locust walk at Mr. Gore's when Lucy's note was brought to him. He was in the act of clasping upon the beautiful arm of his companion a bracelet which had been carelessly dropped, when a servant approached and offered the pretty white messenger. Miss Sandoval took it in her disengaged hand, and, glancing at the superscription in Lucy's clear, delicate characters, said, gayly, still keeping possession of the note, —

"A lady's hand! Ah, Mr. Stafford, you must positively tell me from whom this comes before I give it to you."

"I am as ignorant as yourself, Miss Sandoval, not having seen it."

"Doubtless you could make a shrewd guess."

"How should I, when I don't know a lady in Edgehill?"

"Is that so?"

"Really so — this was a wilderness until you came."

"I am a little doubtful of you. This middle initial looks like familiar acquaintance. But I take compassion on your impatience. Now tell me where you went yesterday."

"Dare I believe that you missed me?" he answered, as he received the note. But, instead of opening it, he deposited it in the breast pocket of his coat.

When Miss Sandoval, a handsome and accomplished woman of six or seven and twenty, had first arrived in Edgehill, she experienced a feeling of agreeable disappointment. She had come to please her parents, who were old and valued friends of Mr. Gore; but she anticipated a dull time. To find domesticated there a man so agreeable as Mr. Stafford, and one of whom she had heard enough to be aware that he was also in a high degree eligible as a *parti*, was a very pleasant surprise; and she mentally congratulated herself on having a clear field, and the game all to herself. Miss Sandoval was not, perhaps, more calculating than the majority of her sex; but still, after eight years of brilliant bellehood, she saw the propriety of establishing a position different from the very enviable one she had so long held; and it certainly did occur to her, as, on the evening of her first arrival, she politely listened to Mr.

Gore while he spoke of his guest and relative, that this un-
desired visit might prove a providence after all.

The evening was warm, almost oppressively so. The
captain had moved his arm-chair out under the trees, and
sat there enjoying his evening cigar. Lucy came and
stood beside him, leaning on his shoulder. The sky all
day had been brilliantly clear; but now there was a soft
indistinctness in the atmosphere, an almost impalpable
haze — the mere ghost of a haze, Lucy said. A breathless
hush rested upon nature, and, as Lucy stood silently gazing,
there floated to her ear, from far down the valley, the faint
sound of an evening bell. She knew it to be swinging in
the white belfry of the little church at the Centre.

"Didn't I hear you and Miles talking of some excursion
for to-morrow?" asked her grandfather.

"We have one in prospect."

"You may as well give it up. It will rain before sun-
rise."

"Why, grandpa! there is not a cloud to be seen."

"Not yet, it is true; but this pretty haze you admire so
much will roll itself into clouds soon enough. The glass
has been low all day; and I can hear very plainly the nine
o'clock bell at the Centre, showing that what wind there is
must be south-east."

"Do you think yourself an infallible prophet, Captain
Fraser?"

"You will find I am a true one this time. There — that
cigar has gone out, and I won't light another. Kiss me
good night, child, and I'll go to bed."

The captain was right. The first sound that saluted

Lucy's ears, on awaking next morning, was the continuous patter of the rain-drops on the leaves without. She rose and went to the window, where an unpromising prospect was revealed. The sky dripped rain incessantly, and thick mist hid even the near hills. Lucy surveyed the wet landscape with rather a rueful expression, and proceeded about her dressing with a decided twinge of disappointment. She had anticipated the excursion very pleasantly; the arrangements were quite to her mind, and she was a little fearful that, if once broken up, they might not be made so perfectly again. However, she quickly banished the slight cloud from her face, put on her most becoming morning dress, and went down to prepare her grandfather's invariable cup of chocolate, which could never be made just right by any hands but hers.

A wet day in a lively country house, with newspapers, books, music, and plenty of people, does not drag so wearily after all. This one passed quickly, and evening came on, but still with no appearance of better weather. After the lamps were lighted, but before the family were fairly settled to their evening occupations, Miles proposed to Lucy a game of shuttlecock.

"Dear Miles! I haven't touched a battledoor for years, — not since that first summer you were here with Mary."

"Neither have I; but I saw your old battledoors this morning, when we were rummaging in the attic. Shall I bring them?"

"Where can we play?"

"In the upper hall — just the place — wide and high." And up stairs he sprang after the battledoors.

The game began. Mary, leading Elliot, came up to

watch the players. Lucy entered into the sport with girlish gayety, and the contest was growing very spirited, when the tramp of a horse's feet was heard, and presently a knock from the great brass knocker on the front door resounded through the house.

"There!" cried Miles, laughing. "That is just my luck. My very last evening at Hillsboro', and I thought, thanks to the rain, I should have you to myself; but here comes some one of your many swains to spoil our last delicious *tête-à-tête*. Let us see who it is," he added, looking down over the banisters. "By my soul, it is Stafford!"

Lucy's eye followed that of her companion, and saw Stafford just giving his overcoat to Dolly. The parlor was lighted, but empty, for Mrs. Fraser had had a fire made in the dining-room, and her husband and the captain were established before its cheerful blaze. Battledoor in hand, Lucy went down the stairs to greet the guest, who, on learning the way in which they were amusing themselves, instantly challenged her to a renewal of the game. She consented, and they returned together to the upper hall.

At a small table, at the extreme end of the hall, Mary sat reading a newspaper, with Elliot playing at her feet. She looked up, as they approached, to give the visitor a smiling welcome, and then resumed her paper. Miles took himself off to the room where the elders of the family were assembled.

The game grew animated. Lucy enjoyed it, and played with the graceful *abandon* of a child. Her round, lithe figure was thrown into postures of free, unconscious grace, and the quick exercise gave a warm flush to her cheeks. The gown she wore, of rich, dark-purple silk, heightened the effect of her brilliant complexion. Her white arms, from which the large sleeves occasionally fell back, were without ornament; but nestled in her hair was the lovely wild rose she had brought a bud from Long Pond.

They played a long time, for Lucy was not disposed easily to own herself beaten. She was strong and deep-breathed too, this unconventional young lady, and wholly unacquainted with faintings and palpitations. But she soon found that Stafford, to whom fatigue was almost a thing unknown, was a very different adversary from Miles, and in the end she was compelled to throw down the battledoor and own herself vanquished.

"Rest here," said Stafford, leading her to the seat arranged in the one large window that lighted the upper hall. Lucy very willingly sank down upon the cushions, while Stafford walked across to where Mary was sitting, exchanged a few words with her, tossed little Elliot, laughing and crowing, into the air, and presently returned to the window.

"I received your note, Miss Fraser; and my reason for not reporting myself at the hour you appointed is, of course, obvious. I hope this rain is not finally to prevent the excursion."

"I hope not, also, though we have been obliged to re-write our programme since we saw you." And she acquainted him with Mr. Burke's proposition.

"And has this rain spoiled so very perfect a plan?"

"I should be sorry to think so. Mr. Burke has kindly written to say that the invitation holds for the first fine day. Miles still insists that he must leave us to-morrow; but we are strongly urging him to give us another day, and I think I see signs of yielding in him. If you can tell us now what the weather promises to be—"

"No signs of clearing were visible when I came in. Listen, how it pours!"

"Let us take a look at it," said Lucy. "Will you open the window? There! the air is refreshing. I like these summer storms; the sound of the rain-drops pattering on the trees is pleasant music to me. I always have an impulse to rush out and feel them on my head."

"But are you quite prudent to expose yourself to this damp wind, after such brisk exercise?"

"Perhaps not; we will close the window presently; but first, do you see—here, lean this way—far up on the hillside, those two lights that with their sharp rays pierce the darkness?"

"Yes; I see them. What are they?"

"Those lights have burned there nightly for forty years. Winter and summer, through storm and fair weather, never for a night have they failed to shed their brightness across the valley. Scores of times, when a child, have I kept my mother or her maids waiting, as they brought me up to bed, to peer from this window at old Nancy's lights; and I love to watch them now."

"Who, then, is old Nancy?" he asked, putting down the window; "and what is the object of her lights?"

"I will tell you the story; it has always seemed a touching one to me. Forty years ago Nancy Cline was a pretty young girl of twenty. Being pretty, she naturally had lovers—at least, she had one. I have forgotten his name, if I ever knew it; nor can I tell you positively what he was like. It is fair to suppose, however, that he was hand-

some, and manly, and true, for Nancy loved him with a
devotion which, after the lapse of all these years, is yet
undiminished. Are you listening?"

"With interest."

"One fatal winter night there raged among these hills a
wild storm of wind and snow. It was fearfully cold, and
the fierce wind blew the snow in blinding clouds, heaping
the road with drifts. In the midst of it all, Nancy's lover
set out to visit his lady. Confused in the darkness, with
nothing by which to direct his steps, he lost his way, and,
wandering blindly, sank down chilled, and perished in the
snow. When the cold, lifeless body was brought to Nancy, the shock was so terrible that her reason gave way.
For a time, I have been told, she was wild and raving;
but, under the tender care of her friends, the character of
her madness changed. She became quiet and gentle, and
has remained so ever since. She now lives with a brother,
who is very fond of her, and humors all her whims, of
which the chief one is to keep those two lights always
burning in the night-time. As soon as the first shades of
evening fall, she grows restless and uneasy, talks to herself
of some one wandering in the valley who will be lost if she
fails to light her lamps; and in the care of trimming and
tending them she grows calm again.—I see that my story
has interested you," she added, turning her eyes on his,
which were fixed upon the dark hill-side, where Nancy's
lamps were burning brightly.

"It has, indeed," he answered. "But I am thinking of
a snow storm not so long ago, when a lamp, placed by another hand in a window, saved a benighted traveller from
a fate as sad."

His voice, earnest and a little husky, thrilled slightly the heart of his companion; but she was not disposed to encourage a lapse into sentiment; so she answered, smiling, —

"O, not so sad! for no poor Nancy waited to go mad for your sake."

"Sadder for that very reason."

"Unprecedented selfishness! If you stood face to face with death, would the prospect be any less dreadful for the conviction that some poor heart would break for your loss?"

"I cannot imagine so improbable a case. But did you not promise me that wild rose when you should have worn it in your hair?"

"Never. What a memory is yours!"

"You are quite sure?"

"Perfectly."

"But you will give it to me?"

"I had not intended so to dispose of it."

Now, Stafford had begged that rose once before. He attached some whimsical significance to it, and he was resolved that Lucy should give it to him; but he bided his time. Just then little Elliot, who had been playing about the hall, and growing wilder as the hour grew later, came running to Lucy, and flung his little arms upon her lap. She stooped to caress him, and the child, taking one of her long curls in his pretty hand, laughed as he drew out its shining length. Presently his attention was caught by the rose in her braids, and, with one of those quick impulses of mischief common to children, he snatched the flower, and ran away to his mother. Lucy sprang after and cap-tured him, when a laughing struggle ensued. Failing to unclasp the pretty pink fingers that so resolutely held the flower, she lifted him in her arms and returned to the window, alternately pleading and bribing. Stafford stood by laughing at her unsuccessful attempts to move the little inexorable.

Mary now came forward to claim her offending child, declaring that his bed-time was already long past. The boy demurred at first; but, knowing by experience that resistance was useless, he sought to prolong the ceremony of leave-taking. With one dimpled arm round Lucy's neck, he made mischievous feints of kissing her. At last he put his lips to hers, then teased to kiss her on her eyes. His mother here interposed; but, to gain another moment, still clinging fast to Lucy, he leaned towards Stafford, and entreated quite irresistibly for a good-night kiss from him. The gentleman bent his handsome head to the child's face, and in so doing, brought his cheek so near to Lucy's that he could feel her soft breath warm upon it. A sudden strong impulse flamed for an instant in his eyes; the next he stood erect, though with a deep color flushing his face, and Lucy was giving the child to his mother. As she did so, she turned to Stafford and proposed that they should go down to the parlor. They were descending the stairs, Lucy a step or two in advance, when Elliot, breaking from his mother, ran towards them, and threw the rose over the banisters. They both looked up, and Stafford caught the flower.

"May I keep it?"

"Certainly; it is Elliot's gift now."

He felt himself baffled. The prize was in his hand, yet he had lost the game.

When, an hour later, Stafford took his leave, the rain had ceased, and the clouds were breaking overhead. The wind was blowing freshly from the west, and the next day promised to be fair. After turning the corner into the Edgehill road, he could for some distance command a view of the window where were the two lights, the beacon fires fed by the undying love of poor Nancy Cline. As he drove slowly along, his gaze became fixed thoughtfully upon this one distinct point in the landscape. Like most men of vivid imagination, he had a slight tendency to superstitious feeling, which would occasionally assert itself in spite of reason and education. Those gleaming lamps, piercing far down through the gloom, had suddenly taken a deep significance to him. They identified themselves, in some vague way, with certain doubtful issues in his mind; and he found encouragement for some wild hopes he had begun to cherish in the thought of their steady, unfailing brightness.

As he gazed, it seemed to him, all at once, that the rays grew unsteady and flickering. Suddenly they flared up wildly, and the next instant died in utter darkness.

Stafford checked his horse so abruptly as almost to throw the animal upon his haunches, and, leaning forward, tried to discern, through the gloom, the lights which, a moment before, had been so distinctly visible. Determined not to be deceived, he turned his horse's head, and drove back some rods to a point where he knew they had been plainly visible, in order to convince himself that no intervening object hid them from his view. But all was darkness. The lights were gone out!

For one moment the conviction struck a sort of chill

through his heart, as if he saw in the fact some omen of
evil. The next, he uttered an impatient exclamation at
his own folly in giving himself so much trouble because a
lamp in a farm-house window was extinguished; and,
wheeling his horse with sharp, firm hand, once more in
the direction of Edgehill, he drove home with a rapidity
which might almost leave troublesome thoughts behind.

CHAPTER XXVIII.

LUCY had just taken her place at the breakfast-table next morning, when Miles, who had been visiting the stables, came in with the announcement that Stafford's boy, Figaro, had arrived with the horses.

"It was a good idea, sending them over thus early," Miles added, "as now they will be fresh when you want them; and it is a good stretch to Indian Head. Mr. Gore's horse, which you are to ride, is a beautiful chestnut, black-maned, small-eared, limbed like a ballet-dancer. Stafford's horse is a powerful bay, full of blood and speed. That brown imp, Figaro, says his master brought him from England. I almost wish I had a mount: I would try a race with you."

"Leaving me to drive myself and enjoy my own society," said Mary, laughing. "I hardly know," she added, "whether to be most jealous of Lucy or the horse."

"I do not seriously propose to desert you so basely," Miles replied. "But is not Mrs. Fraser going with us?"

"She is unable to leave home to-day. I am to matronize this party."

"And Captain Fraser?"

"Has business at Kiffton, not postponable. You see the squireless condition to which your sister would have been reduced if you had persisted in leaving us this morning."

"I begin to appreciate my own consequence; and I expect to be treated to-day with the most distinguished consideration. Does anybody know the road to this Indian place?"

Just then Dolly announced that a neighbor wished to see Mrs. Fraser. Death had come suddenly into a house not far away, and some office of neighborly service was wanted of the Frasers. Lucy, too, went out to inquire into the particulars, and make herself of use, and did not return.

Punctual to the hour appointed, Mr. Stafford drove to the door. The saddled horses were standing ready, and Miles was just handing his sister to the carriage which had been provided for them. Lucy came forth arrayed in the close-fitting, dark-blue habit which so well became her, and the pretty black hat, with long-feather drooping to her shoulder. She was in high spirits, exhilarated by the fine weather, and the prospect of enjoying her favorite exercise. I think, too, that the young lady had a certain amount of pleasure in the consciousness that she appeared remarkably well on horseback. She managed her horse with perfect fearlessness and skill, and rode with a free, unstudied grace, as far removed from timidity as from jockeyish boldness.

It was one of those delicious days which follow summer rain, when the sky takes a darker, intenser blue, when the fresh wind rolls in billows over the standing grain, and troops of white, sailing clouds chequer the landscape with alternations of sunshine and shadow. Stafford and Lucy had finished their first dashing gallop, in which they had left the carriage containing their companions a mile or two behind, and were now riding slowly through a dense wood, where the freshness of yesterday's rain yet lingered, and the air was fragrant with the odor of rank-growing ferns. Lucy, who had been silent for some minutes, looked suddenly up at her companion, and said, —

"Do you remember the story I told you last night of Nancy Cline and her lamps?"

"Certainly."

"To-day there is a sequel to the tale."

"They *did* go out, then!" exclaimed Stafford, in a tone of some excitement.

"They did, indeed. How did you know it?"

"I saw them. As I drove home from your house, the direction of the road enabled me to watch the lights for some distance. I was gazing very intently at them, — for some strange interest seemed to attract my eyes to them, — when I observed their rays flicker and grow unsteady. Suddenly they shot up a wild, brilliant light, and in an instant died in darkness. Do you know the reason?"

"Yes. Another light than theirs went out just then. Old Nancy died last night with the flame of the lamps she had tended so long."

"Tell me how it was."

"She died suddenly, while sitting with the family. In the confusion, doors and windows were thrown open, and a draught of air extinguished the lamps. It was, of course, a purely accidental coincidence, but none the less fit and touching."

Lucy's companion, whose face was turned slightly away from her, did not reply immediately; and when he did, it

was with a question which seemed to have little rele-
vancy.

"Do you believe in omens, Miss Fraser?"

"In some omens, certainly: when the clouds gather, I
look for rain."

"That is simply one of the signs of nature, and not an
omen. But did you never on some trifling chance stake
the realization of a hope, the success of an endeavor, and
say to yourself, if it falls thus, fortune sits with me; or
thus, and failure is mine?"

"Very possibly I may have, though my success or failure
are alike forgotten now. Why do you ask?"

"Twice within the week the fates have written failure
against me in their book. I await the third trial."

"May better success attend you." She laughed lightly
as she said it.

"Do *you* wish me that?"

The sudden, suppressed vehemence of his tone, the flashing, eager look that leaped out of his eyes, warned Lucy
that they were coming on dangerous ground.

"See!" she broke in; "we have talked ourselves out of
the wood, and here we are at the beginning of this long,
level reach. It is a good place for a brisk canter. But
stay — whom have we here?"

This exclamation was called forth by the appearance of
an open barouche, which just then came round a curve of
the road directly in front of them. Lucy immediately recognized the equipage of Mr. Gore; and that gentleman
himself was one of two who occupied the front seat. On
the back seat were an elderly lady and a young one,
whom she correctly surmised to be Mrs. Sandoval and her

19

daughter. As the carriage passed them, Lucy bowed, with
a smile like sunshine, in answer to Mr. Gore's stately salu-
tation, and Stafford bent low his uncovered head to the
ladies.

"The nature of Mr. Stafford's frequent urgent business
is explained," said Miss Sandoval, rather dryly, as the equestrians swept out of sight. "Pray, who is that lady, Mr.
Gore?"

"That was Miss Fraser, a charming young friend of
mine, whom I hope to give you an opportunity of meet-
ihg."

"From Colchester?"

"No. Her father's house is just above here, on the hill
we passed a while ago."

"O! one of these farmers!"

Miss Sandoval was displeased. She was surprised, also,
to learn that there was some one in this remote region
whose attractions outweighed her own. Besides, she had
made up her mind to some day ride that very horse on
which she saw Lucy mounted, and had been told, with
many expressions of regret, that it was lent. Miss Sandoval, however, fell into a very common error — that of undervaluing an adversary she did not know; and she resolved to put a speedy end to this defection, believing that
her powers of raillery could hardly fail to rid her of any
rival this rural region was likely to furnish.

"Miss Sandoval, I presume," said Lucy, as the carriage
disappeared. "It is a handsome face," she added, honestly,
though without any enthusiasm.

"She is handsome — very, though far less beautiful than
her mother. Mrs. Sandoval has one of those plain faces

which yet are full of a beauty that defies time; a beauty, indeed, which ripens with age. We never see it in the faces of the very young."

"Such beauty, for instance, as my cousin Hannah's?"

"Just that. Hannah's face is really lovely to me. I doubt if even you, who value her so truly, can understand the sense of perfect enjoyment, the deep and entire content, with which I each time found myself under her roof, during that eventful winter when I first met you. I am by nature domestic in my tastes and feelings, — you smile, but it is so, — and in the serene atmosphere of that family circle I was at once as much at home as some long-absent wanderer welcomed back to his own roof. I was received by Hannah to her hearth, and afterwards to her friendship, with such generous trust and confidence, that in parting with her after our brief acquaintance I felt like leaving an old friend. She has ever since held much the same place in my regard which other men keep for the dear elder sisters and kind maiden aunts. Why has she never married?"

"She was to have been married many years ago. I can just remember the young man to whom she was promised. Poor fellow! he died of a fever a few days before that appointed for the wedding; and every one thought that Hannah would die, too. But she lived, — people do live through so much, — and came back again to a healthy, cheerful place in the world. The only change discernible in her is, that she is, if possible, more of an angel than ever. See! we are coming to the river."

They were, indeed, close upon it — a broad and rapid stream, flowing between bold and wooded shores. The road

ran sometimes near the bank, giving pleasant glimpses of the
birches and young pines that leaned over the brink; sometimes swept away from it, leaving space between for farm-
houses and cultivated fields. The great bluff known as
Indian Head already appeared in view, and a moment
later the fertile plain at its foot, where a rude shaft of dark-
gray stone, surmounted by a Latin cross, marks the scene
of one of those terrible and bloody tragedies so common
in the early history of New England.

Lucy and Stafford had been riding slowly in order to
allow Miles and Mary to overtake them. Now, however,
the carriage wheels sounded close behind; and as the riders
rose over the crest of the last hill, and had the wide plain
before them, they both yielded to the same impulse, and,
gathering up the reins, which had been allowed to drop
loosely on the horses' necks, they dashed forward at the
topmost speed of the spirited animals on which they were
mounted.

Burke, meantime, accompanied by Mrs. Rodney, a married sister of his own, who lived at Colchester, was awaiting the arrival of the Hillsboro' party. Mrs. Rodney was
older than her brother, and wholly unlike him, being a cordial, bustling, rather fussy little body, fond of managing,
and as talkative as he was taciturn. She was extremely
fond and proud of her brother; and the most ardent wish
of her heart was to see him happily married, though she
had never yet been able to find a woman who seemed to
her really worthy of him. She had sufficient penetration
to perceive that it was no common attraction which was
drawing Burke so constantly to Hillsboro'. The Frasers
were well known throughout the county, especially the

captain; and gossip had not failed to circulate some ru-
mors of the beautiful grandchild who was sure to be his
heiress. When, therefore, her brother had told her of this
little party, and asked her assistance in doing the honors
to his guests, she had been at no loss to guess on whose
account the excursion was planned. But in jumping at
her own conclusions in this matter, good Mrs. Rodney
made one very natural mistake. Her brother being in her
eyes the most exalted of human beings, it did not occur
to her that any young lady whom he might distinguish by
his preference could be insensible to the honor. She had
often felt anxious lest his choice should fall on some one
whom she could not wholly approve; but that, when he
did choose, there could be any question of the success of
his suit, had hardly entered into her mind as possible. She
was quick enough to detect the evidences of his strong
interest when he spoke to her of Lucy Fraser; and, thinking she understood the whole affair perfectly, she was prepared to welcome the latter as a prospective sister-in-law.
She even anticipated with much pleasure the thought of
introducing Miss Fraser to the home over which she was to
preside, and to examine which she did not doubt was the
real object of this excursion.

Burke and his sister had alighted from their carriage,
the horse was fastened in the shade of the trees, and the
two, leaning against the pedestal of the monument, watched
the approach of the party. As the two equestrians swept
over the plain, and came at a swift gallop along the winding lane which, skirting a cornfield, led to where they
were standing, Mrs. Rodney uttered an exclamation of
surprise.

"I never saw so graceful and fearless a rider. And what a pace they are keeping! Singleton, is that young Mr. Elliot with her?"

"No; Miles is in the carriage behind. That is a Mr. Stafford, a chance acquaintance of the Frasers, and attached to the party by accident merely. I asked him because I could not civilly avoid it."

Mr. Stafford was a person of no interest to Mrs. Rodney; she had eyes only for the beautiful girl who rode beside him, and whom her brother at that moment stepped forward to assist in alighting. Unluckily for him, his foot became entangled in a tuft of rank-growing weeds; and, though he did not fall, the momentary delay gave Stafford time to spring from his saddle, and, releasing Lucy's foot from the stirrup, to receive her in his arms as she descended. Burke could have struck him for thus forestalling himself; but he was compelled to cover his chagrin under the mask of politeness, and his embarrassment by the ceremony of introduction.

Mrs. Rodney greeted Lucy with a degree of *empressement* which slightly surprised while it gratified that young lady.

"I am delighted to know you, my dear," she whispered, kissing Lucy's cheek. "Singleton has prepared me to love you at first sight, and I am sure we shall get on charmingly."

"I do not doubt it, my dear madam," replied the unconscious Lucy, with a smile which Mrs. Rodney thought wonderfully sweet. She had spoken the truth when she said that she was ready to be charmed with her brother's choice.

The others were now alighting; and, the greetings being over, they prepared for a walk to explore the various points of picturesque or historic interest in the neighborhood. Lucy gathered up the long skirt of her habit, and put her arm through that of Miles; Stafford offered his to Mary; Mrs. Rodney attached herself to Lucy's side, and Burke was left to lead the way.

"This way," he said, indicating an opening in the close-lying forest.

Stafford scanned the path pointed out, his observant eye noting at a glance the character of the soil.

"Could we not find a path higher up the hill?" he said. "I am inclined to think there is water here: the ladies will wet their feet."

Now, there was no particular reason why Burke should take offence at these words; but he chose to consider them an imputation upon his judgment, and he was annoyed to see that Lucy slightly hesitated.

"You have not confidence in my guidance, then?" he said, in a tone in which injured pride was plainly percep-tible.

"I have confidence in these boots," answered Lucy, laughing, as she held out one little foot, encased in the neat leather boot she wore for the stirrup.

"Come, then," Burke replied; and they plunged into the tangled path. For a short distance they proceeded very favorably; but the way lay through a hollow where the soil, loose and porous, was filled like a sponge with yesterday's rain. The whole party, following close upon each other, talking and laughing, and rather heedless of their steps, were suddenly and very disagreeably recalled

to a sense of their position by finding themselves sinking
in something very like a bog. The gentlemen — thanks
to high, thick boots — escaped unharmed. Lucy, quick
of eye and foot, made two light springs, just touching
the yielding tufts of moss, and landed safe on *terra firma ;*
Mary, before her feet had time to sink in the treacherous
sponge, was caught in Stafford's strong arms, and lifted
over dry-shod ; but Mrs. Rodney was less fortunate. She
felt the loose soil yielding under her feet, and, quite irresolute what to do, stood still, and continued to sink, uttering
a little cry of perplexity and distress. Stafford, having
deposited Mary in a place of safety, turned back to Mrs.
Rodney's assistance, and quickly extricated her from her
disagreeable position.

To be planted ankle deep in black forest mud is not an
agreeable experience for any lady; and as Mrs. Rodney
ruefully contemplated the spectacle of her lately trim boots
and spotless stockings, she may be excused if a slight feeling of vexation disturbed the serenity of her spirit.

"Really, Singleton," she said, " I think you might have
ascertained what sort of a place this was before you led us
into it so confidently."

"I am very sorry, Eliza," replied poor Burke, humbly.
"I have often been here, but never found it wet before."

" We all forgot how recent the rain had been," said
Mary, anxious to smooth away the ruffled feeling. " But
Mrs. Rodney cannot remain in her present plight. I think
in some one of these farm-houses she might find the means
of repairing damages."

As this was entirely the most judicious proposal which
could be made, Mrs. Rodney acceded to it; and, Stafford

and Miles both offering their services as escort, she accepted the arm of the latter, and set off across the fields to a farm-house not far away.

The rest of the party proceeded in their walk, choosing by common but tacit consent a path where Stafford had at first suggested, somewhat higher up the slope of the hill. Lucy and Mary both exerted themselves to dissipate the somewhat unpleasant mood which had come over their entertainer, and Stafford seconded them to the best of his ability. The latter was in the most excellent humor with himself and every one. He had enjoyed his ride with the zest of health and strength, and Lucy's sweet companionship more keenly than she guessed. His high spirits overflowed in gay and amusing talk, and in a hundred ready courtesies to all around him. Mary, who looked upon him with much disfavor, as one whose influence upon her own cherished plans she dreaded, could not escape to-day the infection of his sunny temper. As for Burke, she was thoroughly out of patience with him. He was conscious of having made himself slightly absurd, and the thought wounded his self-love so keenly that he could not dismiss the sense of mortification, nor could he hide the irritation which he felt. He really resented the presence of Stafford as something which had been forced upon him against his will; and, though too truly a gentleman to be capable of rudeness to a guest of his own, he was not able to banish from his manner towards Stafford a certain constraint and coldness which the latter was too penetrating not to understand. Mary felt sure that he understood it, and that on several occasions it required the exercise of considerable self-control not to disturb the harmony of the

party by any betrayal of his resentment. She saw, too,
that Lucy, despite the serene unconsciousness of her manner, was really noting every act, look, and tone of these
two pretenders to her favor, and shrewdly making her own
estimate of the temper of each. The folly of Burke in allowing himself to present so disadvantageous a contrast
to his rival provoked Mary, as it threatened the success of
her cherished hopes.

Mrs. Rodney and Miles did not return until the party
had nearly finished their walk; and by this time the appe-
tites of all began to suggest thoughts of dinner. They
had exhausted most of the points of interest in the neighborhood; at least, they had walked over the ground; but
I do not feel prepared to say that they had greatly enjoyed
their explorations. Certainly, when Burke proposed an
immediate adjournment to Colchester and dinner, the idea
was received with favor, and all turned their steps towards
the spot where they had left the horses.

Stafford, accompanied by Mary, was the first to reach
the place. He handed her to her seat in Miles's carriage,
and then busied himself with examining Lucy's saddle-
girth, and rebuckling her stirrup. He was thus employed
when Lucy came up, leaning on Burke's arm.

"All ready," he said, passing the bridle to his other hand
as she came near. Lucy withdrew her hand from her companion's arm, and was just reaching it to Stafford, when
Burke interposed.

"You are my guest to-day," he said; "it is my privilege
to assist you."

He did not offer to take the bridle from Stafford's hand,
thus leaving the office of the groom to the latter, while he

bent himself to receive Lucy's foot in his palm. Stafford's eye flashed for an instant, but he said nothing. Lucy perceived his displeasure, and hesitated, feeling — what Burke, to do him justice, never thought of — the discourtesy of thus thrusting aside one to whom she was indebted for the horse she rode. Stafford saw her color change, and, only half understanding, believed that she was embarrassed by his presence, while she preferred the attendance of his rival.

His face cleared as suddenly as it had clouded, and he stood quietly by, while Burke lifted Lucy to her seat and arranged her stirrup and habit; then he said, with a tone and manner full of cordial courtesy, —

"If you can induce Mrs. Rodney to accept me as her companion, I need not deprive Miss Fraser of the attendance of her host. My horse is entirely at her service and yours."

"You are extremely kind," answered Burke, surprised, yet pleased, at an offer which implied so much. "I thank you; but I cannot think of taking your horse from you."

"You have no choice where a lady's wishes are concerned," answered Stafford, gayly, though a pang of mortal jealousy pierced him as he caught a sudden flash in Lucy's eye, and interpreted it as a sign of pleasure at this change. Before Burke could offer any further remonstrance, he had bowed to them both, and walked away to acquaint Mrs. Rodney with the altered arrangement.

To that lady it seemed the most natural thing in the world. She took it for granted that Stafford was aware of the understanding between her brother and Miss Fraser, and felt a friendly desire to forward their wishes. She

thought he had shown a very proper degree of consideration for them, and grew extremely friendly with him at
once. She was quite unaware of revealing any family secrets; but, being of an expansive and talkative turn, and
her mind being full of her brother and his love affairs, she
naturally talked *close to* the theme uppermost with her.
Consequently, they had not accomplished half the distance
to Colchester before Stafford was fully in possession of her
view of the state of affairs between her brother and Lucy.
It could hardly be expected that he should guess how very
slight were the grounds on which she had based her conclusions; and he sat beside her, rather silent, listening politely
to her flow of talk, and striving hard to reconcile Lucy's unfailing impartiality of manner between himself and Burke
with so developed a preference for his rival. He had not
succeeded in adjusting the matter when their arrival at
Burke's house in Colchester interrupted the train of his
reflections.

It is doubtful if Burke had enjoyed his ride so much as
he might have expected. Lucy was not disposed to let
him fall into the mistake which Stafford had made; and
her manner towards him, though perfectly kind and
friendly, was yet marked by a delicate shade of reserve
which was new, and which he did not know whether to
interpret favorably or unfavorably to his hopes. But,
slight as was the barrier which she threw between them,
he could not get over it; and when he assisted her to alight
before his own door, he was as much in doubt regarding
her sentiments for himself as he had ever been, and quite
uncertain whether he had enjoyed more than the semblance
of a triumph.

But at least he had got back his self-control, and was prepared to play the part of host with dignity and propriety; and the whole party, as they gathered around the dinner-table, seemed as cordial and harmonious as if no opposing interests had place among them.

After dinner, the ladies withdrew, under the guidance of Mrs. Rodney, to private apartments, where they could take some rest, preparatory to another long ride back to Hillsboro'; and the gentlemen smoked their cigars in the garden. Burke exerted himself to do the honors of his house agreeably to Stafford; and, the latter responding frankly to his advances, conversation grew animated, and Burke was surprised to find himself yielding, as he had seen others do, to the charm of a manner which he had always chosen to consider artificial and false. When the ladies rejoined them, tea was served in the garden, and immediately afterwards orders were given to have the horses brought up.

It now wanted but a few minutes of sunset. Miles had called Lucy away to another part of the garden, and presently the sound of their laughter drew the attention of the others in their direction. Looking round, they saw Lucy standing, with her hat in her hand, the skirt of her blue habit gathered over her arm, and the sunshine brightening her lovely hair, watching Miles, who was apparently pelting some object with flowers from a handful which she held. The others moved down to the spot.

"What are you doing?" asked Mary.

"O, Miles made a boastful assertion just now, and I am forcing him to disprove his words."

"How?"

"He declared that, in throwing these flowers, he could, twice out of three times, lodge a cluster in the hands of that stone nymph yonder. He failed ignominiously."

"Why, I do believe I could do that myself," exclaimed Mary, catching up a handful of the flowers, and throwing one after another, with a good deal of energy. The first fell short of its mark by some yards; at the second trial she overshot her aim by about the same distance. The third attempt, though a failure, came nearer to success, for it struck the poor nymph full in the face. Disgusted with her ill success, and amiably desirous to see some one else fail, she selected three of the blossoms, and, bringing them to Stafford, invited him to try his luck.

Laughing, he took the flowers, confident, from long experience, in the accuracy of his eye and the steadiness of his hand. With a careless movement he flung the first; it fell lightly on the upraised hand of the statue, and rested there. In his next effort he was less fortunate; the two flowers, becoming entangled, were flung together as one; and, the added weight marring his nice calculation of distance, they barely touched the hand, and fell to the ground. Turning to Lucy, he begged another flower for his third trial. As she gave it, she said, in a low voice, and with a somewhat mischievous smile, —

"This shall be your third omen. Lodge the flower, you win; if it falls, you lose all."

He sent a quick look into her laughing eyes, while a sudden, strong color flushed his face.

"Will you guarantee success?"

"I am not fate."

"Come, Mr. Stafford," said Mrs. Rodney, "we are waiting to see you fail."

"The audience is getting impatient," said Mary.

Stafford silently took the flower from Lucy's hand, and threw it after the others. It touched the fingers of the statue, wavered a moment, and fell to the ground.

"Failed, by all the saints!" cried Miles, springing up from the grass, where he had flung himself. Stafford turned to Lucy.

"Do you believe in omens now?" she asked, laughing.

"Not in the least; I have lost all faith," he answered, forcing a laugh; but Lucy saw, with surprise, that he had grown slightly pale. She had not supposed it was a matter to which he attached any importance.

Miles called upon Burke to try his fortune; but the announcement that all was ready for their departure here interrupted them. Burke gave his arm to Miss Fraser; Stafford paused to make his adieus to Mrs. Rodney, and managed to prolong them until their host had placed Lucy upon her horse. He then mounted his own, the bay again ranged up by the side of the chestnut; and, with a bow and a word of farewell, the two riders swept through the gateway, and, followed by Mary and her brother, took their way rapidly homeward.

They rode for some distance in perfect silence. The day had been productive of numerous annoyances to Lucy; and, though she had maintained outwardly her usual gayety, it had, for some hours past, been with a good deal of effort that she did so. The various disagreeable occurrences which have been narrated had seemed to excite little attention from her; but not one of them had escaped her; and they had jarred painfully upon her feelings. She resented Burke's conduct, as showing a want of delicate consideration for herself; and, though she could not resent, she was deeply annoyed by the construction which Stafford had put upon her embarrassment, and which had led him to yield his claims to her supposed wishes. In addition to this, she had, during their absence from the gentlemen that afternoon, been constantly in the society of Mrs. Rodney, and she had not failed to detect the delusion under which that lady was laboring. Mrs. Rodney had, however, made no remark sufficiently definite to enable Lucy to undeceive her; and so she had necessarily been left undisturbed in her mistaken impression. It was all very absurd, and Lucy could have laughed at it heartily, only — only, somehow it pained and wounded her. She had promised herself a great deal of pleasure from this excursion; but, on the whole, it had disappointed her. She felt sad and dispirited; and, as she rode slowly along by her companion's side, she congratulated herself that the deepening twilight hid from him the tears which, in spite of her efforts, would keep swelling in her eyes. He was not long in perceiving her unusual mood, and respected it for some time by silence.

The daylight died wholly away, and the starry splendor of the summer night assumed its place. The dewy and fragrant air was cool and refreshing, after the heat of the day, and the stillness and repose of nature soothed and calmed the perturbed spirit of the young girl. She roused herself at length, breathed a quivering long-drawn sigh, and seemed to fling off some weight. Then, for the first time, Stafford spoke — quietly, gravely, only in some slight reference to the beauty of the night. But the tones of his voice were full of a tender and respectful sympathy that was very grateful to her; and talking on in a grave, earnest way, not of any personal theme, but of things which yet touch the deeper consciousness of all, he drew her, little by little, out of her sorrowful mood, and back to the cheerful mastery of herself. They rode slowly, yet they did not find the way long to Hillsboro'. The carriage containing their companions had passed them soon after the start, and was miles in advance; but they hardly thought of the distance. When they reached home, coming up the grassy slope at a slow walk, the feet of their horses made so little sound on the soft turf that no one in the house heard their approach, and the squire failed to be ready to receive his daughter. Stafford alighted and came to her side. She released her foot from the stirrup and leaned forward, placing her hands upon his shoulders for her usual light spring. But it chanced that a fold of her habit had become entangled about the saddle, and she would have fallen had not Stafford received her in his arms.

For one moment he held her there — for one wild, delirious moment, remembered often in the bitterness of after years with a thrill of passionate triumph; he strained her to his breast with a vehemence almost violent; he felt the beating of her heart against his own.

One instant only. Then, gently releasing her, he murmured a husky, almost inaudible good night, and was gone, leaving Lucy a little in doubt whether to be angry, or to believe that brief embrace had been only the result of an accident.

20

CHAPTER XXIX.

MILES bade farewell at an early hour the next morning. It was his final departure for that summer, as he was to set out in a few days on a long-projected journey to Rio Janeiro. The same day's mail brought to Mary a letter from her husband, fixing the time of his arrival, and to Mrs. Fraser a note from Mr. Gore, inviting them all to a small evening party at his house. A comparison of the two showed that Fanshaw might be expected on the day following that on which they were invited to Edgehill.

The intervening days passed very quietly. Mr. Burke called twice, and promised to meet them on Thursday at Mr. Gore's. Stafford came one morning, but found the younger ladies out. He lingered some time, talking with Mrs. Fraser, but the morning wore on without bringing them, and he was forced at last to take his leave.

Thursday came duly round. On the evening of that day, as Lucy and her friend stood before the mirror in a chamber of Mr. Gore's house, reviewing their careful toilets, there came a knock at the door. Mrs. Fraser and the captain had already descended to the drawing-room; and Lucy, supposing her father had come for them, opened the door. She found, instead, a servant belonging to the house.

The girl offered a magnificent bouquet of scarlet flowers, saying, "Mr. Stafford sends his compliments to Mrs.

Fanshaw, and would she do him the honor to accept these flowers?"

Lucy took them, and turned back into the room.

"See, Mary, what Mr. Stafford has sent you! What splendid cardinals! Isn't it early for them?"

"For me, from Mr. Stafford! You must be mistaken, Lucy; they were meant for you."

"I am not Mrs. Fanshaw, my dear. Don't be modest. I should need no urging to accept a bouquet like that."

"I do not need any urging; but it struck me as odd, his sending it to me. I do not see your hair ornaments, Lucy. I think they must have been left out of the box."

"It is no matter. Here is a very pretty substitute."

Lucy pointed, as she spoke, to a vase on the table, which was full of the fragrant and delicate blossoms of the sweet pea. Selecting some of the finest, she added a few glossy, dark leaves of an evergreen plant, and arranged them gracefully among her heavy braids of hair. This *coiffure* was perfectly becoming, and harmonized well with her dress, which was of white, simple in style and fashion, but of rich and elegant materials. Other ornaments she wore none.

The bouquet of cardinals, which Mary carried in her hand as they went down stairs, had really been intended for Lucy. The girl whom Stafford had made his messenger had somehow confounded in her mind the names of Fraser and Fanshaw, and hence they had missed their destination — a circumstance trifling in itself, but pregnant of consequences.

When Mr. Fraser, escorting his daughter and Mary, entered the drawing-room, where Mr. Gore received his guests, Stafford, who was standing talking before a sofa occupied by Miss Sandoval and another lady, turned to look at the group. Mary was hidden from his view by the tall figure of Mr. Fraser. His eye rested at once upon the delicate blossoms in Lucy's hair, — not his brilliant cardinals, — and then his glance ran quickly over the rest of her figure. One little gloved hand rested on her father's arm, and the other, drooping at her side, held a fan of white ostrich feathers, but nothing else. Stafford looked on while Mr. Gore, with even more than his usual warmth, welcomed this last arrival, and then he resumed his chat with Miss Sandoval.

The latter had noticed the entrance of our party, and, recognizing in Lucy the lady she had seen riding with Stafford, observed, with some surprise, the air of perfect high-bred grace which heightened the effect of her rare beauty. She began to think that perhaps she might have been a little hasty in undervaluing the attractions of this possible rival. Such a country girl as this might easily be dangerous.

Mary was presently carried off into another room, where she was seized upon by an old gentleman from Colchester, and fastened down to the card-table. Lucy, after exchanging some elaborate compliments with Mr. Gore, withdrew slightly apart, and, still leaning on her father's arm, stood to survey the different groups about her. Most of those present were strangers to her. The circle of her acquaintance, previous to her long absence, had, of course, been limited; and her return was too recent to allow of its yet being largely increased. They were soon joined by Burke, who presented a friend of his, Mr. Halstead. Standing under the brilliant light of the chandelier, in graceful and animated conversation, Lucy became the centre of many curious and admiring eyes. A lady sitting on the sofa beside Miss Sandoval drew Stafford's attention, and asked if he knew the young lady in white to whom Mr. Halstead was talking. Stafford turned slowly, and looked in the direction indicated. At that instant Lucy perceived him for the first time, and bowed with a charming smile of recognition. His bow in return was as bland as her own, though he could not help a slight feeling of angry resentment as he noticed the profuse display of pale pink blossoms in her hair, and thought of his own rejected offering. She might, at least, he thought, have appeared without flowers. Before he could answer the lady's question, she was carried off to join the dancers, and Stafford sank upon the sofa at Miss Sandoval's side, and, stimulated by his anger towards Lucy, flirted with that lady with a spirit and devotion quite noticeable.

Lucy, wholly unconscious of offence, was enjoying herself extremely. Transferred from her father's arm to Burke's, she sauntered through the rooms, made several new and revived some old acquaintances, looked over Mary at the card-table, and finally, at Mr. Gore's request, seated herself at the piano. Stafford started slightly as the first clear notes of her voice sounded through the room, and listened intently. Miss Sandoval, with her many artificialities, had a genuine love of music, and she now remained silent, a delighted listener. When the song ceased, there was quite a deep circle around the piano, which did not break up until a movement was made to the dancing-room. The carpet in one of the great parlors had been covered with smoothly-stretched Holland for that purpose, and some unseen musicians stationed on the veranda just now commenced a beautiful waltz. Lucy's hand was solicited by Miles's friend, Stratton Kingsbury, with whom she had a slight acquaintance; and very soon Stafford and Miss Sandoval glided into the revolving circle.

After a time Lucy and her partner withdrew a little from the dancers, and stood by a window watching the others. Stafford and Miss Sandoval swept slowly by. They were talking in low tones as they floated round the circle, and he was looking down into her handsome, up-raised eyes, and, conscious that Lucy was observing him, had thrown into his own an expression of absorbed admiration. Lucy observed them with a little thoughtful smile, and said to herself, as she intimated to her partner her desire to rejoin the dancers, "It is a thousand pities he will never be anything but a pleasant flirt!" She tried to think there was no touch of pain, only a little tinge of friendly regret at her heart as she said it.

The dancing ceased after a time, and Miss Sandoval being asked to sing, Stafford was left to himself. He crossed the room to where Lucy, with Burke, Kingsbury, and one or two ladies, was standing. Some polite phrases of greeting were exchanged, and Lucy said,—

"We were very sorry, Mr. Stafford, to have been out when you called yesterday. Mrs. Fanshaw particularly regretted it, for she leaves us to-morrow."

"Indeed! That is sudden—is it not?"

"Rather; Mr. Fanshaw returns on that day. Miles, too, is gone. I beg you will not entirely desert us, for you see we shall be quite alone. Mr. Kingsbury, I will look at that picture now." And she moved away, leaving Stafford astounded at what he called her consummate coolness. He addressed himself to the others until the music called a quadrille, and the ladies were claimed by partners.

He stood for some minutes moodily watching the figure, when a sudden thought occurred to him; and, with a half-repressed exclamation, he turned and passed quickly into the hall. There meeting Figaro, he sent him for the servant who had carried the flowers to Lucy.

"Jane," he said, as the girl appeared, "did you deliver the flowers just as I directed?"

"Yes, sir; I did."

"You are sure there was no mistake?"

"O, no, sir! there could be no mistake, for I gave them into the lady's own hand."

"Very well, Jane; you are a good girl; you may go."

Stafford turned and stepped out upon the veranda. To his surprise, he found that it was raining heavily. He felt sullen and out of humor—did not want to go back into the house, and would have liked nothing better than a furious ride under this black, dripping sky. He was roused by hearing the voices of two gentlemen, who appeared for a moment at an open window.

"Who was that lovely girl in white you just danced with?"

"O, that was the beautiful Miss Fraser, of Hillsboro'."

"Is she the one Singleton Burke is going to marry?"

"That is what they say; and his attentions to-night certainly look like it. Here comes Helen — I want to introduce you."

They moved away, and Stafford was alone again. Presently he thought of Mary, and remembering that Luey had said she was to return home the next day, resolved to seek for her. With this intention he had just entered the rooms, when he was met by Mr. Gore, who desired to present him to some ladies, hinting, at the same time, a wish that he should be particularly civil to them. For the next half hour, therefore, he gave himself, with great assiduity, to the entertainment of these friends of his cousin's, caring nothing about them, and wishing them in Egypt all the time. Having at last seen them to their carriage, he was about to resume his search for Mary, when he was claimed by Miss Sandoval, who required some trifling service at his hands. She overwhelmed him with a flood of talk. She had just been introduced, by Mr. Gore, to that lovely Miss Fraser — was never so charmed in her life — such grace, such beauty, and such perfect manners! It was lucky she was engaged, or certainly all the women would be sure to hate her! And what an agreeable man was that Mr. Burke! And so she talked on, obliging her companion to listen and reply, until she chose to seek a new topic. He had no mind to go near Lucy, although she sat at so little distance that the sound of her sweet, low voice frequently reached his ear; but he did desire to speak a word of farewell to Mary; and he waited, hoping she might come to seek her friend. Some time passed — the groups about him shifted and changed, but she did not appear; and, looking round, he saw that Lucy, too, was gone.

A moment after, fortune favoring him, he made his escape from Miss Sandoval. He hurried through the rooms, in which the throng was thinning fast, but could nowhere find the object of his search. Meeting Stratton Kingsbury, he asked if he had seen Mrs. Fanshaw.

"Yes; I saw her and Miss Fraser taking leave some time since. I think they have gone."

Disappointed and out of patience, Stafford was crossing the hall, when he saw Captain Fraser just handing Mary into a carriage that stood at the gate. At the same moment Lucy, ready shawled for her departure, came down the stairs. It was raining heavily, and Stafford, taking an umbrella from the servant who stood waiting on the steps, escorted her down the dripping walk, and handed her to a seat beside her grandfather. Mary leaned eagerly forward from beyond Mrs. Fraser, and reached him her hand.

"Why, Mr. Stafford! I have hardly seen you to-night. Where have you kept yourself?"

"The fates have been in it, I think, Mrs. Fanshaw. I have been seeking you in vain for the last hour. I began to fear I should lose the opportunity of bidding you farewell."

"And I was afraid," answered Mary, "that I should not be able to thank you for the beautiful flowers you so kindly sent me. You see I have them still." And she held up the luckless cardinals.

Mary wondered a little at the sudden flush that reddened the cheek of the gentleman, but he did not venture to look either at her or at Lucy. He made some polite reply, and, seeing them all ready, bowed, and closed the carriage door. They drove away into the rain and darkness, and he walked back into the hall with a clouded and troubled face.

When the guests were all gone, he sat a long time in his

own room, enveloped in clouds of smoke, thinking over the events of the evening. He looked composed enough, but, in truth, his mind was in commotion. He was in a rage with himself for the folly he had been guilty of in allowing his resentment to betray him into a course which might prove the ruin of his hopes. What must Lucy think of him? An idiot — a born idiot — would have known better than to make such an exhibition of coxcombry. That he should have dared, too, so to misinterpret Lucy's simple dignity of character! He might have known there was some mistake, or, at least, that she had good reason for what she did. He could not tell whether she had most reason to be angry or disgusted with his conduct. She was not likely — thank Heaven for that! — to guess the deliberate impertinence of which he had been guilty; but what impression of his general sincerity was she likely to receive from his exaggerated devotion to Miss Sandoval, and his marked neglect of herself. He could have strangled himself for his unutterable folly.

Then, too, the report of her engagement to Burke — could it be true? The thought maddened him. He did not believe in the rumor fully; but how much foundation it might have in truth he dreaded to think. He remembered many occasions when he had been impressed with the different footing held by himself and Burke. Sometimes — though these occasions were rare — he had believed his own to be the best. Even now, he thought, — the old elastic spirit rising again, — even now, give him but a fair field, and he would win her yet. Win her! If she had begun but in the least to care for him, the man did not live to whom he would resign her.

An hour later he lay stretched under the curtains of green damask, sleeping soundly. One arm was thrown over his head in a boyish attitude, and a slight smile curved his handsome lips, while the counterpane, flung back, revealed the regular rise and fall of his deep chest, the even breath telling of the quiet, unbroken slumber of vigorous, healthful manhood.

CHAPTER XXX.

For an hour after Mary's departure Lucy felt half inclined to be lonely and discontented. As she walked about
the house, and picked up, here and there, little traces of a
childish presence, or in Mary's chamber contemplated the
litter and confusion of recent packing, she was sorely
tempted to be a little dismal. But she soon thought better of it, and went busily to work instead, dusting the parlors, rearranging her drawers and closets, helping her
mother to make cake, and moving about the house with
everywhere that quiet, effective touch which some women
seem to have as a gift of nature, and which is so magical
in harmonizing and composing everything they come near.
In the course of the morning she took a long walk over the
fields, to carry a luncheon to her father. As she felt the
fresh air on her cheek, and saw Carlo bounding by her
side, she fell a thinking of the time when, with the dog for
her only companion, she had spent whole days among the
hills, a happy child, who wondered why her eyes would
often fill with tears when she was so glad ; and, in recollections of that dear life long ago, she forgot the discontent of the morning.

In the afternoon an old lady, talkative and gossiping,
came to pay her mother a visit; and, not before having
seen Lucy since her return, she had a great many ques-

tions to ask relative to her sojourn in foreign lands, and a vast amount of local news and gossip to communicate. Lucy gave herself to the old woman's entertainment with exemplary sweetness and patience. She answered all her questions ; she took a deep interest in each member of her numerous family; she played and sang to her ; she *earned*, in short, the flattering opinion which the old woman afterwards expressed, that "Lucy Fraser was just as pretty-spoken as ever she was; furrin parts hadn't hurt her a mite."

But still Lucy could not help feeling a little weary, and she found herself wondering, as she looked along the yellow high-road towards Edgehill, if Stafford would take it in his head to drive over to Hillsboro' that evening.

He did not come, however ; and the second day passed much· the same, no visitor appearing to break the unaccustomed monotony. But in the evening came Burke, who brought a new book, a very affectionate message from Mrs. Rodney, and an evident desire to make himself particularly agreeable. Lucy was glad to see him, but she was not sorry when he went. He embarrassed her. Ordinarily she had found no difficulty in getting on with Singleton Burke, — of whom, by the way, the majority of young ladies stood slightly in awe. His grave and rather stately manners had never that effect upon her, not because she had any especial claims to superiority, but because she was too free from egotism herself to be annoyed at it in others. I think Lucy had a good deal of pride ; but of that sensitive self-esteem which takes offence at the same quality in others, she had none. She was very catholic in her sympathies, and tolerant of all sorts of characters. But to-day her friend's presence seemed to embarrass her. For the first time she felt the suitor in his manner. She was glad when he went, and she was not sorry to hear him say that business would call him for two or three weeks to a distant part of the state.

Those two or three weeks slipped away almost imperceptibly. Stafford came and went between Hillsboro' and Edgehill almost daily. At Hannah's house he was a constant guest. At the Frasers' his visits were more uncertain. Sometimes he but just looked in upon the family; at others he would linger for hours. His manner towards Lucy had undergone a change. In her presence there constantly beset him a reserve which was almost timidity, and which was in singular contrast to the natural frank gallantry of his bearing towards all women. In truth, the recollection of his folly on the night of Mr. Gore's party haunted him constantly, and checked every impulse to reveal to her by his manner the feelings with which she inspired him. How could he expect her to put any faith in such revelations? Had he not himself taught her to believe them false and worthless? Day after day he lingered, fascinated, by Lucy's side, at one moment buoyed up by the hope that she returned his love, in the next convinced of her complete indifference, and half resolved to fly and torment himself no more for a woman as unreachable as a star.

And Lucy? Lucy thought she had settled definitely in her own mind what their intercourse amounted to — a pleasant, worldly friendship; no more, and no less. He cared no more for her than for any other attractive woman; and he was to her merely an agreeable companion. That

he was a *very* agreeable one she did not think of concealing from herself. He *suited* her to the very core of her
consciousness. She had seen many men more original, of
more commanding intellectual powers, wiser scholars, of a
deeper, though scarcely of a more elegant, culture, of a
loftier purpose, of a more consistent life. Those, no doubt,
were nobler natures; but this one harmonized with her
own. So, having settled the status between them, having
made it perfectly plain that there was no possible danger
of her being in love with this man, she gave herself permission to enjoy to the utmost a companionship so congenial.

Several days had passed, during which Stafford had not
appeared at Hillsboro', and Lucy was beginning to wonder
a little at the reason. It was Sunday morning, and she
was in her own room preparing for church. Her father
and mother had set out early for the Centre, where they
were in the habit of attending; but she had preferred for
to-day the simple service at the old school-house.

It was a still, hot day, in that brief period of the perfect
summer when nature seems to pause, as if loath to lay the
hand of change upon a world so beautiful. A dimness
seemed to have crept over the intense blue of the sky,
which was lined, here and there, by long, white, faintly-
pencilled clouds. The hay fields lay shorn and smooth;
the waving, golden grain already invited the reapers. The
grasshoppers made shrill music in the warm, dry grass; and
softly, from down the valley, came the faint sound of church
bells.

Moving slowly about in the softened light of the chamber, Lucy finished her preparations, smoothed the cool

muslin, and tied the plain straw bonnet, and, taking her parasol, went down to join her grandfather. She heard him, as she descended the stairs, in conversation with some one in the parlor, and recognized the voice as Stafford's. She met him with unaffected pleasure. The occasional sense of loneliness which had come over her during the past few days, made his presence doubly welcome, and gave a warmth to her reception of him which she had not before shown. He felt it, and his spirits rose at once. Perhaps he deceived himself slightly as to the significance of Lucy's manner. She had, as I have said, enjoyed his society, and from the first had received his attentions with pleasure, believing them merely the sincere tribute to attractions of which she did not affect to be unconscious. But she had seen the same show of deep devotion offered to Miss Sandoval, and knew, or thought she did, that the very next handsome woman would supersede them both. It was this conviction of his indifference which gave her manner a perfect freedom from restraint.

Stafford asked for Mrs. Fraser.

" She has gone with my father to attend church at the Centre."

" Have you no church nearer ? "

" No; but we have a service at the school-house, and I am going there. Will you come, too ? "

" With pleasure."

" Mind, I promise you nothing in the way of oratory or argument. I go because it is the habit of our family, and I like the Sunday church-going feeling. But our poor old minister is remarkable for but one thing: the drowsy influence of his discourses is really surprising. The old ladies keep themselves awake with fennel and caraway, and the younger ones — but I will not expose their devices. Are you ready, grandpa? Mr. Stafford is going with us."

Slowly along the grassy road-side, on that sweet Sunday morning, walked Lucy with her two companions. They talked together in low tones, with accents suited to the calm serenity of the hour. Many persons passed them, walking more rapidly towards the place of worship; and many were the eyes which followed them with kindly looks for the captain and his grandchild, and curious glances for the handsome stranger who accompanied them.

As they entered the low, red school-house, something in the groups around the door, or in the circumstances of their walk, recalled to Lucy's mind an autumn morning long ago, when she, with Fanshaw and Hannah, had come to this same place. O, how far away seemed that time now! Sitting down between her grandfather and Stafford, she began to turn softly the leaves of a hymn-book, and her eyes rested abstractedly upon its pages while her mind was busy with that old time. There was no bitterness in the recollection. The Lucy Fraser of those days — the eager, restless girl, whose heart yielded itself so readily to the first delusive dream of love, was a being so unlike herself as to awaken much the same feeling of compassionate remembrance she would have felt for another person. She was even conscious, as her thoughts reverted to the events of the past month, of a sense of thankfulness that, out of that old pain and bitterness, she had gathered an experience that had since served her well. Her own too ready confidence was not likely again to betray her.

The hymn was sung, the prayer was ended, and the ser-

mon fairly begun, but still Lucy remained wrapped in her
reverie. Stafford, sitting close beside her, watched attentively the little hand that fluttered over the hymn-book
leaves. He had often taken it when offered in greeting;
but now he longed inexpressibly to clasp it in his own, to
hold it a close prisoner. The hand was just as beautiful
and tempting as years ago, when it had been such a delight
to Ben Miller, or when Fanshaw had made little excuses
for taking it. From the hand his eyes wandered to the
face, which seemed lovelier than ever in the pensive softness of her present mood. Her abstraction was so deep,
that she remained quite unconscious of his intent gaze.
Suddenly he looked up, and met the keen, searching eyes
of Hannah Page fixed upon him. Her glance held his
own. For several minutes did the gray and the brown
eyes confront each other, the first with searching inquiry,
the other with resolute assertion. Presently Lucy looked
up, drew a soft breath, closed the book she held, and turned
her attention to the sermon. Stafford, too, made a feint
of listening, looking seriously straight at the preacher during the remainder of the service.

As they were going out at the close of the service, Hannah met them, and urged them all to go to her house; but
Lucy declined on plea of being housekeeper for that day,
and they proceeded homeward.

After Lucy had presided at the pleasant luncheon, which
in New England country houses is the Sunday substitute
for a formal dinner, the captain offered his guest a cigar,
and the two gentlemen betook themselves to the shade of
the elms before the house, to smoke and chat. Lucy closed
the Venetian doors of the hall, and, taking the leathern

arm-chair before her favorite desk, occupied herself with writing letters.

An hour or more passed. The gentlemen had finished their cigars and strayed to another lounging-place, the captain luring Stafford from one to another of the various points of interest about the farm. They were a well-assorted pair of companions, despite the wide difference in their characters. Indeed, they had many points of resemblance, after all. There was a certain simplicity and directness of thought, a half-boyish naturalness about them both, which neither the seventy-five years of the one nor the artificial associations of the other had been able to overcome. They were both originally of that class of strong, manly men who love animals and are gentle to women and children, whose vices, if they have them, are the vices of the hot blood, not of the perverted intellect. They were alike, too, in that both of them had always lived in the world as belonging to the whole of it; there was no provincial narrowness in the ideas of either. And so, mutually pleased, they talked on of farm-life and sea-life, of politics and travel, of sport and adventure, and whatever came uppermost. After a time, Lucy heard their voices at the end door, and went to open it. She had a wide straw hat upon her head and a book in her hand.

"Where now, Lucy?" asked her grandfather.

"Up in the orchard: I think it must be cooler there. Won't you two come along?"

"I suppose we may as well. Come, Mr. Stafford; there is cool shade under the apple trees."

The day had become intensely warm. There was not a breath of air stirring, and hazy, hot-looking clouds half

obscured the sun. Lucy led the way past the house and
round to the orchard gate. Stafford opened it, and the
three made their way up the slope to Lucy's favorite rest.
She found a seat on the bent trunk of an old apple tree,
and the captain and Stafford stretched themselves on the
grass at her feet.

"Now, Lucy," said the former, "produce your sermon
book. Read us out a homily; and it will be as well as if
we had gone to church."

"It is not a sermon book," answered Lucy, glancing
down at the volume, which had fallen at her side, "but
something which you like — 'Elia.' Mr. Stafford, do you
think this heat has left you sufficient energy to read a page
or two?"

"I think I might manage it," said Stafford, laughing, as
he picked up the book. "Elia is a lazy kind of fellow,
and all the better for such weather as this. But I think
you have made a mistake," he added, opening the volume.

"What have you there, then? Not Elia?"

"It is Tasso — the 'Jerusalem Delivered.'"

"It is all the same to me, if you do not care. In this
weather one must be extremely brilliant to know one book
from another."

"A good exchange, I call it. Tasso before a dozen
Lambs for me," said the captain, lazily striking a match on
his boot to light a fresh cigar. "You won't mind this,
Lucy? It is out of doors, and you know you like smoke.
Now, Tasso is a poet with what I call the genuine fire in
him. Worth a hundred of your Longfellows, and Tenny-
sons, and other pindling modern fellows. No robust life
in a ship-load of their rhymes."

"You talk so because you are such an old Ostrogoth, grandpa; you can't appreciate the spirit of modern poetry."

"Humph! Well, I'm tolerably content with my barbarism. It does not matter so much while I have your ladyship to do the refinements. Shakespeare and the musical glasses, you know."

"Please read, Mr. Stafford," said Lucy, not condescending to notice her grandfather's aspersion.

He opened the book.

"This page, I perceive, has the original and the English versions side by side. Which will you have?"

"Give us the English, if it is all the same," decided the captain. "My Italian is of the kind that sailors know. It serves me well enough to gossip and compare sea-yarns with the ship-masters of Genoa and Leghorn; but when it comes to poetry, there are some deficiencies apparent."

"And you, Miss Fraser?"

"O, I am almost as bad," she answered, laughing. "I can pick out a canto, by taking time; but my comprehension is slow. Read the English, unless you come to something good which is lost in translation."

"Where shall I begin?"

"Almost anywhere. This hot, dry day suits equally well with any of those Syrian pictures."

She smiled a little absently as she spoke. Her thoughts were wandering backward to a different time and scene. She leaned back a little languidly against the rough trunk of the apple tree, her broad hat shading her forehead from the sun, that occasionally flickered through the leaves. One hand played caressingly with the thick gray locks of her grandfather, who, half sitting, half reclining on the grass beside her, leaned his head against her lap, and occasionally blew a thin cloud from his cigar. Her eyes, as she listened, were fixed dreamily upon the dim, smoky landscape that showed between the branches of the trees. Stafford settled himself in such a position that, by lifting his eyes, he could watch the changes of her expressive face, and in a low, flexible, perfectly-modulated voice, began to read.

The flowing verse made a music of its own that mingled pleasantly with the soft rustle of the leaves, and the occasional sharp, ringing song of a locust in the hot grass. Scarcely any other sound broke the stillness. The captain listened enjoyingly for a while; but at length the drowsy air, the lulling murmur of the reader's voice, and the soothing motion of Lucy's hand, insensibly had their effect, and he dropped away into the land of dreams. As for Lucy, she listened, but her attention was only half given to the poet's theme. She followed, indeed, the march of Godfrey's host, as their horses' hoofs rang up the steep ascent that led to the holy city; she heard the silver plash of fountains, and caught the perfume of enchanted flowers from Armida's wondrous garden; all the brilliant pageantry of the poem moved, indeed, before her mental vision; but always, along with these dazzling pictures, she seemed to see another and widely-different scene — a low-walled farm-house room, with a bright fire blazing on the hearth, a fierce wintry storm raging out of doors, and herself, a dreaming girl, seated on a low stool by the fire, listening entranced to the same voice which now sounded in her ear, and catching her first glimpse of the world of poetry and romance. It was a repetition of the

experience of the morning — a sharp suggestion of the
contrast between her past and present self, and between
the hopes and dreams of that old time and those of to-
day. How little she had then imagined that their chance
guest of a night would ever come to be anything to her!
But then — he was nothing to her, of course. The reflection was driven back rather sharply the instant it arose in
her mind.

Insensibly the hours slipped away. A shadow crept
over the sky, and the hot, breathless air grew hotter and
closer. The clouds, which earlier had seemed only a soft
haze, deepened and gathered till they lay in dense masses
through the north and west, hiding the sun. But the
reader and his now single listener remained unconscious
of the change. Occasionally a sudden gust of wind
breathed like a quick, impatient sigh through the leaves
above them, and then all was still again.

The gathering gloom forced Lucy's attention at length.
She threw a glance at the heavens, then, leaning over her
grandfather, drew his watch from his pocket.

"Mr. Stafford," she exclaimed, while the captain, roused
by her movement, started up, "have you any idea what
time it is?"

"Not the slightest."

"It is near six — the primitive hour at which my mother
has her Sunday tea."

"I had no idea it was so late. Captain Fraser, what do
these clouds promise to bring us?"

"Thunder, lightning, and rain."

"Immediately?"

"I should say not at once. But suppose we return to

the house. I have a fancy that a dish of tea would agree-ably take the taste of Miss Lucy's *al fresco* poetics out of my mouth."

"Little you have known of them — sound asleep ever since we sat down here! Come, Mr. Stafford, we will go and see what my mother has to offer us."

Mr. and Mrs. Fraser had returned during their absence, and the latter was waiting for them in the doorway.

"I heard that you were here," she said, giving her hand kindly to Stafford. "I have been worrying for the last half hour lest the shower should overtake you all."

"We had lost all recollection of the time. I, for one, was quite shocked to learn how late it was, and to what an unconscionable length my call had extended."

"Pray do not think of it: we are the gainers. And you see it is impossible for you to go now. This shower would certainly overtake you before you were half way to Edge-hill. Then our tea is waiting, and we cannot allow you to slight our hospitality."

Stafford was too willing to be persuaded to make much resistance, and he followed his kind hostess to the supper-room.

The clouds, meantime, rose steadily, growing darker and more ominous; and by the time tea was over, the storm was close at hand. Gathered about the door, they watched its swift approach. The clouds, spreading, had already passed the zenith. The stillness was death-like; every leaf and blade of grass was motionless. The air felt heavy and close. A sudden twilight, deep and unnatural, had descended, its gloom occasionally broken by a broad glare of lightning, which was followed by the long roll of distant thunder. Momentarily the thunder grew heavier, and the flashes more blinding.

Suddenly a sharp, jagged line of fire leaped from the bosom of the cloud, followed by a short, deafening crash, and in the silence that followed they could hear the rising wind. The distant trees began to bend; and in the next instant it swept through the orchard, and bowed the tall elms before the house.

"Come in, Lucy. The rain will be here directly," said her father.

She came in reluctantly, the first harbingers of the coming flood glittering on her hair. Mr. Fraser closed the door, and he had scarcely done so, when the rain struck it in sheets.

They went into the parlor, and Lucy seated herself at the piano. She had still enough of her old childish nervousness in the presence of a wild storm to contrive that her grandfather should have a place near her. Stafford and Mrs. Fraser sat together on a sofa, and Mr. Fraser slowly paced up and down the room.

The noise of the storm outside precluded general conversation, and, as the thunder crashed louder and louder, even occasional remark was silenced. The liquid notes evoked by Lucy's fingers were half lost amid the tumult, but still she played on; and soon the listeners heard her voice rising sweet and clear in one of those grand old sacred melodies so beloved of all devotional hearts. Indistinctly at first, and often inaudible, as the thunder shook the house, but calm and steady, gaining as the storm rolled away, at length, unfaltering and triumphant, it swelled above all dissonance and confusion.

After a time the force of the tempest spent itself, the thunder muttered farther and farther in the distance, and the rain ceased. It was growing late, and Stafford again rose to take his leave. As he resolutely declined to stay the night, his horse was sent for. While awaiting its arrival, he stood talking with his host and hostess. The captain had walked down the path under the elms, and stood contemplating the aspects of the night. Lucy gathered her flowing muslin skirts over her arm, and stole down the walk to his side. She stood silent for a few moments, enjoying the freshness and stillness.

"How sweet and calm it is now!" she said, softly. Glancing up into the old man's face, she met his eyes fixed upon her with a searching, half-anxious look. "What is it, grandpa?" she asked, with her old childish directness of sympathy. "Does anything trouble you?" .

The old man laid his large brown hand over the little white ones that clasped his arm.

"Yes, dear," he said; "I am half afraid somebody is going to forget the promises she has always made to stay with her old sailor grandfather."

A quick flush rose to Lucy's face, but it was gone in a moment.

"There is no sort of danger," she said, gayly.

"I'm not so sure of that. All this riding and driving, and sending of flowers, and books, and music, — I don't like it."

"Mere gallantry, grandpa."

"Don't tell me. I know when a young man's eyes speak things that his lips don't dare to, and what it means when the brushing of a girl's dress makes him turn red and pale like any simpleton."

Lucy did not answer quite so promptly this time; she waited to still a little quiver, strangely like joy, that she feared would betray itself in her voice. When she did speak, it was gravely, and with an honest, steady look into her grandfather's eyes.

"You are mistaken, really. Young men nowadays are not so honest and straightforward as you, and a great deal goes for very little with them."

"It may be; but in certain respects we are all alike; and a man in love is the same thing the world over, and for all time."

Lucy made no reply, for at this moment Jerry appeared with Stafford's horse; and that gentleman, having finished his adieus to those within, advanced towards the spot where they were standing. He spoke a few words of farewell, the captain responding heartily, and Lucy, for the first time towards him, a little shyly. He felt the change in her manner, and hope grew warm at his heart. It was with inexpressible unwillingness that he prepared to depart. Even after he had taken his seat in the phaeton, and the reins were in his hand, he lingered, exchanging a few last words, and watching Lucy as she leaned against the tall figure of her grandfather. The rain had wholly ceased, and through the broken clouds the moon looked out. The lightning still glimmered at intervals along the southern horizon, and a cool wind was rising from the west. It sighed in the branches of the trees, lifted the one long ring of hair on Lucy's neck, and fluttered her airy summer draperies. He thought she made a lovely picture, standing there in the cool darkness.

That was the memory of her he was to carry for long

years. It was the picture he took with him down into the gloom of the valley of the shadow of death.

The last lingering adieu was spoken, and he turned his horse's head. But more than once, as he drove away, he leaned from the carriage to look back at the two shadowy figures standing relieved against the lamp-light that shone under the dripping boughs.

CHAPTER XXXI.

The next day brought an unexpected arrival. Lucy was busy in the upper hall, when, hearing the sound of wheels, she looked from the window, — that window from which she had watched, with Stafford, the gleam of old Nancy's lights, — and saw a carriage draw up under the shadow of the elms. It was occupied by a number of ladies and gentlemen, none of whom she could see distinctly through the close branches; but the sound of their gay voices came up to where she stood. She hastily completed what she was doing, smoothed the folds of her fresh morning wrapper, and went down. The carriage had driven away, a small portmanteau stood in the hall, and in the parlor she found her mother welcoming a single guest. Lucy uttered a little cry of pleasure as she recognized her former travelling companion, Mrs. Lovell.

"My dear Mrs. Lovell! This is indeed a pleasant surprise. To what happy chance do I owe it?"

"To a whim of mine, of course, that being the cause of most of my movements," replied the new-comer, with a charming smile. "Mr. Lovell had business which brought him to the vicinity of Kiffton for a few days; and as I knew it was not far from you, I resolved, at the last moment, when it was quite too late to think of writing, to come too. At the hotel in Kiffton I found a party of friends from Philadelphia. They had arranged an excursion for to-day to some place in this neighborhood; and, as they offered to bring me along, I accepted the chance of finding you, and came."

"How very glad I am that you did! But I think you look tired. Pray rest here by the window, — this lounge is comfortable, — and I will sit by you and ask questions."

As they talked on, and the first flush of interest and excitement faded from the cheek of her friend, Lucy was struck by the air of languor and fragility which showed itself in her appearance. She lay on a sofa, while Lucy, on a low stool beside her, sat talking in quiet, happy tones, and smoothing, with her gentle fingers, the luxuriant hair that drooped over the forehead of her friend. She noticed that the white temples were thin and hollow, and all the color in her face concentrated itself in the feverish brightness of her lips.

In Lucy's eyes Mrs. Lovell was the most beautiful of living women; and she was, indeed, singularly lovely. In age she was about twenty-eight. Her figure had been full and round, and yet retained its graceful contours. Her small, elegant head was poised on a neck white and graceful as a swan's. Her complexion was dazzlingly fair, with delicate, almost infantile features, full, ripe lips, and pearly teeth. Her hair was of the richest auburn, and her eyes, shaded by silken lashes, were large, dark, and full of passionate fire. It was the face of one born for gayety and enjoyment; but now its expression was one of settled melancholy and discontent. So profound was this air of sadness, that it pervaded all she said and did, gave a languid grace to her movements, breathed in her slow, sweet smile, and spoke in the soft accents of her voice. The friendship between her and Lucy had been the result rather of accident and circumstances than of any strong sympathy or affinity between them. Mrs. Lovell was the only child of wealthy parents — a beauty spoiled and flattered from her cradle. She had married, at seventeen, a man of more than double her age, who worshipped her, and spoiled and flattered her as her parents had done. Her life had been spent in an atmosphere at once superficial and artificial, and her ideas and tastes were formed and matured under such influences. The result was better than could have been expected. She was warm-hearted, capricious, wilful, and passionate; capable of generosity, but equally capable of selfishness; the creature of her impulses, whatever they chanced to be. She and Lucy had met in a foreign land, when each felt isolated and lonely, and when Lucy was half distracted by the sudden illness of her grandfather. Mrs. Lovell's kind heart prompted her to many friendly offices, which won the young girl's liveliest gratitude; and, in return, her beauty and sweet, innocent nature warmly attracted the elder lady. The latter had then just lost her only child, and she seemed to lavish on Lucy some measure of the affection which had belonged to the dead little one. Thus a friendship, which could not be called intimacy, had begun and continued between them.

Several days of Mrs. Lovell's visit passed very quietly. Fewer guests than usual came to interrupt them; even Stafford was unseen for some days, having gone with his host — the Sandovals had long since left Edgehill — on an excursion which Mr. Gore had been planning ever since his cousin's arrival. Burke, too, was still away; and with the

exception of one day, when they dined at Colchester with
the Fanshaws, they saw no one. The genial influences of
the house seemed to have the most favorable effect upon
the saddened spirits of Mrs. Lovell; and she really made
an unusual effort to repay the kindness of her entertainers
with an appearance of enjoyment. All the pleasures at
their command were drawn on for her amusement. They
rode, drove, and walked; they had music, and books, and
fancy-work, and Captain Fraser's stories. Mrs. Lovell, as
I have said, seemed grateful for all their efforts in her be-
half; yet it could be seen that she was accustomed to take
the homage of those about her as a matter of course.
Lucy, much as she admired and warmly as she loved her
beautiful friend, did sometimes find herself questioning
whether such protracted abandonment to sorrow were not
a form of self-indulgence scarcely consistent with one's
duty to others, and wondering whether Mr. Lovell, whose
adoring affection for his wife she well knew, was quite
satisfied with the position assigned him — whether, after
all, her friend, in forgetting the living in her sorrow for
the dead, had not missed the best cure which sorrow
can find.

Mrs. Lovell had arrived on Monday for a week's stay.
It was now Friday, and she had received a note from her
husband, saying that he would be in Hillsboro' Sunday
evening, and that they must leave early Monday morning.
It was afternoon, and she and Lucy were in the parlor
together. The latter was at the piano, which stood at the
end of the room farthest from the door. She had been
playing for some time such soft, sweet airs as drop into
the heart and bring tears into the eyes. Mrs. Lovell

reclined near by upon a sofa, her beautiful head supported by her hand, listening with closed eyes to the music.

There came a knock at the front door, and Dolly was heard admitting some one; but Lucy played on, while Mrs. Lovell neither changed her position nor opened her eyes. Presently the parlor door opened, and Lucy, turning on the music-stool, recognized Stafford. Her eyes expressed her pleasure, and a slight blush tinged her cheek. She rose, but he was the first to speak, coming to meet her with some remark upon his long absence.

At the sound of his voice, Mrs. Lovell started from her recumbent posture, and sat, pale and with hands convulsively clasped, and her eyes riveted upon his face. As he took Lucy's offered hand, bowing low over it, a faint cry broke from her lips, and, pronouncing his name in a tone of stifled anguish, she sank back in a swoon.

Stafford and Lucy both sprang to her side, and the latter, raising her head upon her arm, pointed, without speaking, to a cologne vase that stood on the table. Stafford brought it, and deluged her handkerchief, and she bathed the still face before her. A long sigh was the first evidence of returning consciousness; then the white lids began to quiver, and Lucy motioned to Stafford to stand back out of sight. He obeyed, and she leaned over her friend, and asked, as the latter opened her eyes, —

"Do you feel better now?"

"Yes, Lucy; but what is it? Did some one come in?"

She raised herself as she spoke, and looked about the room. Lucy rose also, and stood irresolute. Mrs. Lovell turned from her, and her eyes met Stafford's. He was very pale, and there was a stern, hard look about his lips.

22

He came a step towards her with some confused inquiry. She looked at him for a moment without speaking; but there were volumes of reproachful tenderness in the eyes she raised to his face. "Have you no other word for me?" she cried, at last, dropping her head upon the arm of the sofa, and bursting into tears.

Lucy made a movement towards the door, but Stafford detained her.

"Do not leave the room, Miss Fraser," he said. "I am the one who should go."

"I think, indeed, you should," she answered, coldly.

He bowed and turned: his hand was on the door, when Mrs. Lovell sprang to her feet, and, crossing the room hastily, stood before him. She laid her hand on his arm, and, raising her beautiful tearful eyes to his face, exclaimed, —

"Stafford, do not kill me! You have broken my heart; but do not kill me with your coldness!"

As she spoke her head fell upon his breast. Supporting her trembling form with his arm, he led her back to the sofa. "Emma — Mrs. Lovell, for God's sake compose yourself!" he exclaimed, as Lucy, going quickly out, closed the door, and left them alone.

She was pale, and felt cold and stunned. In the entry she met Hannah Page, who had entered by the side door.

"Do not go in there," she said. "Mother is in her own room, I think. Excuse me; I have to go up stairs."

Hannah looked after her cousin as she went slowly up to her own chamber. She was astonished at the face Lucy had turned towards her, it was so hard, and cold, and white. She walked into the sitting-room, and sat down by the window to wait for her aunt. Stafford's horse and

carriage stood at the foot of the walk, and Figaro, sitting
within, held the reins. The boy was humming a lively
tune; the soft cushions and the bright sunshine made him
happy. Hannah waited what seemed to her a long time,
and then Stafford came out of the parlor. She caught one
glimpse of his face as he sprang into the carriage; it was
pale as Lucy's had been. He took the reins from the half-
frightened boy, turned his horse with a sharp, quick whirl,
and drove rapidly down the hill. Hannah could see the
road for some distance, and observed the furious pace at
which he went. She waited a little longer in the hope of
seeing some one. After a while Lucy came down, but went
at once into the parlor. At length Hannah managed to
find one of the domestics, and, learning that her aunt was
gone out, gave up her errand for that time, and went home.
But the circumstances she had witnessed did not pass from
her memory.

When Lucy reëntered the parlor, she found Mrs. Lovell
lying on the sofa, her face buried in her hands, while her
frame shook with frequent sobs. Lucy drew near, and laid
her hand lightly upon her friend's head. The figure was
motionless for a moment, and then the sobs broke forth
afresh. Lucy let the tempest of her grief have its way,
and sat silently beside her, holding her hand. By degrees
she became calmer, and at length, raising her head and
laying it on Lucy's shoulder, she said, —

"Dear Lucy, pity me, for my heart is broken."

"Courage! the deepest wound will heal," replied Lucy,
pressing her hand.

"No; this will never heal. It bleeds always, and will
until I die. O, Lucy, that man has been the cause of the

intensest happiness, the sharpest agony, of my life. He won all the love of my poor, weak heart, and then flung it away as you might a yesterday's flower, leaving me the broken creature that you see. You wonder I do not hate him. I have no choice — I *must* love him and forgive him. It kills me to see him, and yet I have but one thought — when shall I see him again?"

"My poor friend, you will see him no more."

"I shall — I must — he will come to-morrow."

"But remember, dearest Mrs. Lovell; consider your husband, your friends."

"I have considered all that. In my life everything has been considered before my happiness. Think what it has offered! Married, when a child, to a man I did not love — ignorant even of what love was; then left to my own guidance. With no one to counsel me, with none of your strength of character, dear Lucy, what wonder that my heart went before I was aware? O, I struggled against the madness — the infatuation. But my weakness was quickly punished. When he knew his power over me, then he left me. When my heart was all his, he did not care for it. O, those were dreadful days. Then my child, my Alice, was taken from me. She was my only comfort. I have shed scalding tears over her innocent sleep, while I prayed Heaven that she might die rather than live for wretchedness such as mine. O, Lucy, my mad prayer was answered! I lost her — my darling!"

The poor woman paused in her torrent of incoherent words, checked by her tears. Lucy tried to soothe, to comfort her — reason was out of the question. At last she persuaded her to go to her chamber, and, sitting by her side as she lay on the bed, bathed her hot, throbbing temples, and at length had the satisfaction of seeing her sink into a deep sleep. Then, carefully closing the blinds to exclude the light, she withdrew from the room, and sought her own.

She sat down wearily, as if exhausted, her hands lying nerveless in her lap. A long time she sat nearly motionless, gazing out over the sunny fields. What she thought of it is difficult to tell, — probably not very clearly of anything. She had been inexpressibly shocked at the discovery of her friend's fatal weakness; but that was really little to the revelation which had come to her concerning Stafford. She saw now how large a place he held in her regard, now that he could hold it no longer. Of all lessons, the one hardest for her loyal nature to learn was the lesson of distrust. With the "believing heart" would go from her half the happiness of life. For Mrs. Lovell she had no feeling but compassion. She saw her in the light of a deeply injured woman. For the paltry gratification of his vanity, a mere wanton delight in conquest, he had struck a death-blow at the happiness of a woman he professed to love. She grew hot and angry as she thought of it.

Presently Mrs. Lovell's words about seeing him again recurred to her mind; and though she did not believe he would attempt such a thing, her resolution was quickly taken. She rose, and, going to the little desk which stood on her table, sat down by it, and wrote with a firm and rapid hand. She made no reference to the circumstances which had occurred, or to her own feelings or opinions in the matter, but merely expressed a hope that Mr. Stafford would see the manifest propriety of absenting himself from Hillsboro' for the present. She wrote briefly and formally, in a tone which was cold, indeed, but expressed no anger or displeasure, and without one superfluous word. She closed her note at once, without giving herself any time to change her mind, and, carrying it down stairs, despatched a boy with it to Edgehill. She then returned to the apartment of her friend, whom she found suffering from headache and nervous prostration.

That night and all the next day Mrs. Lovell kept her chamber. She wanted Lucy near her constantly; but the subject uppermost in the minds of both was not again referred to.

As the next day wore on, Lucy could perceive that a feverish hope or expectation took possession of her friend. She listened for every sound, and watched from the window the approach of every person to the house. Lucy could guess her feeling, and knew that it would be disappointed. No Stafford appeared. The day passed quietly, as it had begun; and on the following, towards evening, Mr. Lovell arrived. Mrs. Lovell was in the parlor to receive him, gentle and graceful as usual; and when Mrs. Fraser spoke of her recent illness, she smiled at his concern, and assured him that it was nothing serious — the effect of fatigue merely.

During the remainder of her stay she maintained the same apparent serenity. Lucy looked on astonished. She could not comprehend how one so evidently capable of self-control should so fail in its exercise when it seemed most called for. But the strain put upon her own feelings was intense, and she was glad when the hour of departure came.

Standing on the doorstep, she waved a last adieu to her friend with a sensation of inexpressible relief.

But when the carriage disappeared, she went back into the house with a far more dreary sense of loneliness than she had felt, weeks before, when Mary left her. Now, something more than a friend was gone — something which could not be replaced.

CHAPTER XXXII.

RATHER fortunately for Lucy, the next day brought a swarm of visitors, city cousins of Mrs. Fraser's, come to taste the pleasant hospitalities of the farm. They staid for a week; and the necessity of making an effort for others' entertainment withheld her thoughts from settling upon the painful revelation which had been made to her.

Thus occupied, it was several days before she saw any of her uncle's family. But when the guests were gone, she put on her hat and walked down the hill. She found Lydia full of matter. The most important of all frocks was in process of completion, and Lucy's taste and judgment had to be taken on any number of points in relation to it. Lucy gave various hints and suggestions, aided in arranging the flowing folds of delicate muslin, and admired the effect to her cousin's complete satisfaction. It was natural enough that the discussion of the dress should suggest the thought of its giver; but Lucy could not help a slight nervous shock at the sound of his name. Hannah was used to reading her cousin's face, and saw a slight change pass over it as Lydia asked, —

"Have you seen Mr. Stafford lately?"

"Not very recently."

"When was he at your house last?"

"Some time last week; Friday, I believe."

"He hasn't been here for more than a week; and yesterday father was at Edgehill and saw Mr. Gore. Father was asking about Mr. Stafford, and Mr. Gore said he left his house last Saturday morning for New York, and seemed surprised that we didn't know of it, for he said he was down here the day before. Did he speak of going away while he was at your house?"

"Not before me: but I saw him only a few moments."

"It is strange he did not call to say good by to us," said Hannah, looking sharply at her cousin, who had spoken in an even, quiet tone, but whose face had lost a shade of color. "Mr. Gore said," she continued, "that he had a letter from him yesterday. He was just ready to start for India, where his friend, Mr. Brainerd, has gone. I think he might have called a moment to say good by. It seems strange he should not."

"He may not have intended leaving when he was here," suggested Lucy, indifferently, and immediately began to speak of something else.

So Stafford was gone — was probably out of the country ere this. Gone to find in the pursuit of new pleasures and adventures a ready forgetfulness of whatever was disagreeable in the sudden termination of his Edgehill sojourn. As Lucy thought of the past summer, of all its gayety and enjoyment, so suddenly and painfully ended, she felt sad and unhappy. She had come back so glad and hopeful, she had begun the old home life so joyously; and how quickly it had brought disappointment and sorrow! Her trust had been misplaced, her faith shaken. She would not admit fully her position. She resolutely looked at her relations with Stafford in the light of friendship only. No warmer feeling, she said again and again, had entered into her heart. But for all that, in closing the chapter of this summer's life, in seeing it, with all its hopes, and plans, and pleasures, glide into the irrecoverable past, she was conscious of a great void in her life. She did not allow herself to look into it; indeed, she resolutely thought of something else, and strove to fill it with an active interest in everything around her. And if, sometimes, in the midst of her many avocations, she was conscious of an uneasy pain, — a dull longing for something dreamed of, but not found, — she stilled the hunger as best she could with the dry husks of philosophy. Of course, life could not be all a summer's day. Why should she expect to be an exception to the general rule? It was only another childish illusion gone. Did she not know already that in this world people could not afford credulously to cherish illusions? But then, after all, it would be pleasant if they could.

CHAPTER XXXIII.

SUMMER was gone, and autumn was trailing his imperial garments over the hill-sides. The flowers were dying, and the low wind sighed through the faded gardens and rustled the scattered leaves. From the elms about the house had vanished the flashing oriole, and in the woods the veery's evening song was hushed. In the houses now wood fires crackled cheerfully in the fireplaces where for months had stood great vases filled with flowers and evergreens; and the shortening, darkening days drew all life to its domestic centres.

On one of the serenest days of the mellow October there was a cheerful wedding party at Mr. Page's. All the Frasers were there, of course, and a great throng of Ben's kindred, and Fanshaw and Mary from Colchester. Lucy resisted the importunities of these latter friends to return home with them after the festivities were over. The idea of Colchester was strangely distasteful to her — why, she could hardly have told. When strongly urged, she pleaded unwillingness to leave her parents at present. She was going, by and by, to Philadelphia with the captain, to visit her friends, the Flemings; and two lengthened absences, she said, would not be fair to those at home. Besides, she was tired, and needed rest.

Mary had never known her friend to be tired before;

but she saw that Lucy did look worn and pale. However, though compelled to relinquish for the present the prosecution of her plans for the latter's future, she congratulated herself that the only man who could prove in any way a dangerous rival to Burke was far away, and apparently forgotten.

So Lucy staid quietly at home for some time longer yet. It was not till after Thanksgiving time, when the winter had fairly set in, that she and her grandfather departed on their projected visit. They had proposed to be absent a few weeks only; but their stay was continually prolonged; and when at last the captain insisted that he must be gone, their friends brought forward so many reasons why Lucy should remain longer, that she yielded to persuasion, and allowed her grandfather to return home without her.

Lucy had never seen much of the fashionable life of cities. Its novelty diverted her; and in the brilliant social circle, in which she speedily became the object of much admiration, there was always something to interest and turn her thoughts from herself. For the first time in her life she felt the thirst for excitement and change. A strange restlessness possessed her, and drove her from one scene of gayety to another with little cessation. She wrote home that she was very happy, and she told herself, over and over again, that it was so. It was new for her to need to give herself such assurances.

The weeks lengthened into months, and still she lingered with the Flemings, averse to face the monotony and the frequent solitude of Hillsboro'. But at length the home circle grew impatient and imperative; and in one of the late days of February she finally took leave of her friends, and turned her face northward. Horace Fleming accompanied her as far as New York, but was prevented by business from making the whole journey. He even attended her a few miles beyond the city, to a station where he could catch a return train, and then left her to proceed on her journey alone.

She felt lonely and uncomfortable for a little while, but soon became interested in the pages of a book which Horace had given her to beguile the way. Thus occupied, she did not observe the persons entering or leaving the car, until she was roused by hearing her own name pronounced by some one quite near. She looked up hastily, and recognized Mr. Lovell. She greeted him with surprise and pleasure; and, as he took the vacant seat at her side, she hastened to inquire for his wife. His face grew grave at once.

Mrs. Lovell's health, he said, had for some time seemed to be breaking, and physicians gave very discouraging reports. She had taken a violent cold about Christmas time, which had settled upon her lungs, and been attended by severe hemorrhage, and he dreaded the worst results.

Lucy was deeply shocked and pained at this report; and the profound dejection with which Mr. Lovell spoke of his wife moved her compassion. She had always hitherto found him a reserved and somewhat formal man, and she was unprepared for the evidences of deep and strong feeling which made themselves apparent as he told of his anxieties and fears. She tried to think that he must have overrated the danger. At the end of an hour he rose to leave the car; and as she pressed his hand at parting, she expressed with earnestness and sincerity her sympathy, and her hope that the future would prove better than his fears. He could only look the gratitude he felt, not trusting his voice with words.

It was long before Lucy could return to her book. Her mind was filled with thoughts awakened by the recent interview, and many things came back to her which it had been the labor of the last few months to forget. Her heart ached for Mr. Lovell in his present anxiety, and for the grief which, notwithstanding her encouraging words, she felt sure was coming fast upon him. For Mrs. Lovell she knew that life had been a failure, and that death would be welcome. Of Stafford she would not think. As in families there are nearly always subjects of which it is forbidden to speak, so in every human heart there lie memories, not dead, but buried, covered out of sight, never spoken of or looked at. Stafford to Lucy had become one of these. She could not at once, by an effort of her will, forget him; so, in the darkest and remotest recess of her consciousness she put the memory, and trusted to time to do the rest.

The remainder of her journey was accomplished without incident. At Kiffton she was met by her grandfather; and in his eager, boisterous welcome, and flood of home news and talk, the recent painful impression was somewhat dissipated.

CHAPTER XXXIV.

THE spring was cold, and late, and disagreeable, as only a New England spring can be. What with the raw east winds and the muddy roads, out-door life had few attractions, and Lucy went but little abroad. Only occasionally she found her way to Hannah's always cheerful fireside, or to the pretty new house over the hill, where Lydia's matronly graces were daily more and more unfolding. But the larger portion of her time was passed at home, where she was, in truth, the centre of every one's happiness, the object of a kind of idolatry that would surely have spoiled a nature less simple and true.

About the middle of April, while yet the winds were raw and the sun showed little power in rousing the growing year from its sleep, Fanshaw came to Hillsboro', armed with authority from Mary to bring Lucy with him to Colchester in the face of all opposition. With some little difficulty he won the family consent to a few weeks' absence, and bore his prize away in triumph.

Lucy had not allowed herself to feel really depressed by the dulness of Hillsboro' after her winter gayeties; but she was surprised to find what an agreeable relief was afforded by the more varied life with her Colchester friends. Mary had that happy art of society which is born with some women, and which would enable them to make a hovel

attractive as long as they reigned in it. It is not, therefore, surprising that her house was one of the most eagerly
sought by whatever was desirable in the large town of
Colchester. Lucy found herself in the midst of a circle
which, if less fashionable and brilliant, was not less cultivated or intelligent than that in which she had mingled at
Mrs. Fleming's. Naturally she saw a good deal of Burke,
who was now Fanshaw's partner, and who had always
been a constant visitor at the house. She met him with a
great deal of pleasure, taking up the thread of her friendship with him apparently just where it had dropped last
year. With Burke, if it was not the same, it was because he
was more in love than ever. He fairly haunted the house,
often dropping in in the morning, on his way to the office,
with some transparently trivial pretence of an errand; and
the evening was sure to bring him. He brought books,
and read aloud to the friends as they sat at their needle-
work, or music, which Lucy sang to him in the soft spring
twilights, while he held his breath to hear; and he was
often their escort when they went out. Lucy had always
liked him, and this pleasant intercourse was daily strength-
ening her regard. Her feelings towards him were really
approaching that state when, if no disturbance occurred,
they might readily crystallize into a positive form — might
grow and gather into a steady and true affection. But
such was certainly not, as yet, their nature.

Mary watched the progress of their intimacy with attentive eyes. Still, however much she desired a connection
between these two friends, she would not manage to bring
it about. She gave them every opportunity to advance
their own interest, but carefully abstained from the most

thankless of all friendly offices — match-making. She was
fully in Burke's confidence, for he had opened his heart to
her, and she had assured him of her strong faith in his ultimate success, if he had patience and perseverance. He
must not seek to hurry matters. She believed Lucy to be
too contented with her present situation, too happy in her
home after long absence from it, to be easily induced to
leave it. But she assured him, to her best belief, that he
had no rival. Upon this point Mary spoke quite confidently. There had never been but one, she said, whom
she had feared; and now she was quite convinced that
Lucy had never cared for him. With time and patience,
she was sure all would go well.

Burke resolved to be governed by this advice; but in
a moment of indiscretion, when returning one evening
from a small party, walking with Lucy slowly down the
moonlit street, he forgot Mary and her cautions, and ventured to press the suit which lay so near his heart. As
Mary had predicted, Lucy shrank from the subject. It was
one she did not wish to hear about. He could hardly feel
his offer rejected, for he had not been allowed to make
one. She neither refused nor encouraged; she only
silenced him. There was nothing in her words to lead
him to hope she would ever listen to him; yet there was
nothing to exclude that hope. He had not gained a single
step in advance; but, on the other hand, he did not feel
that he had lost anything. It was plainly not on any
ground of personal objection to himself that Lucy had
silenced his avowal, but from a repugnance to the whole
subject involved. He stood, then, precisely where he did
before, unless he might indulge the hope that the con-

23

sciousness of his sentiments established in Lucy's mind
might, as the thought grew familiar to her, work for him a
favorable change. When, in bidding him good night at
the door, she gave him her hand with all her accustomed
cordial frankness, he felt sure that he had, at least, not
offended, and left with a still hopeful spirit. Mary had
been right so far; might she not also be correct in the rest
of her encouraging prediction?

Mary was alone in her parlor when Lucy entered, and
she immediately handed to her friend several letters which
had arrived during her absence. Lucy put them in her
belt, and stood holding her bonnet by the strings, and
talking over the little incidents of the party at which she
had been. Presently Fanshaw came in; and soon after she
bade them both good night, and went up to her own room.
She drew back the curtain, and, sitting down by the window, through which poured a flood of mellow moonlight,
she remained for some time, looking dreamily out into the
still garden below. She was thinking of Burke — kindly,
pleasantly, yet with a shade of regret. She wished he had
not spoken the words she had just heard. She would have
liked far better that their friendship should flow on in the
same quiet channel which had thus far held it. She was
quite content with things as they were; and she had come
to feel a sort of dread of the approach of life's more tumultu-
ous and absorbing emotions.

At length she remembered her letters, and, lighting her
lamp, she closed the curtains, and sat down to read them.
One was from Horace Fleming, gay and lively as usual,
and soon disposed of. The next bore her father's superscription; and, as she took it up, she wondered a little at

its unusual bulk. On breaking the seal, she found only a few lines from her father, and a heavy enclosure directed to herself at Hillsboro', and bearing the New York postmark. Opening this, she was shocked to find a short note from Mr. Lovell, announcing his wife's death, and informing her that the letter accompanying his was written by Mrs. Lovell a week or two before her departure, and given to him with the injunction to forward it to Lucy after her funeral. Mr. Lovell recounted in few words to Lucy the circumstances attending his wife's last hours, and spoke of her with the settled grief of a broken-hearted man.

After she had finished reading this letter, Lucy waited some minutes before she could summon courage to take up the other; and her usually steady hand trembled as she tore off the envelope. It was long — too long to be given in full here. After speaking of her situation, of the near approach of death, and of her willingness to meet it, Mrs. Lovell alluded to her husband, and spoke with grateful feeling of his affectionate devotion, and with regret that in the years of their married life she had so little appreciated his kind and noble heart. She dwelt more briefly, but with earnestness, on the affection she had always felt for Lucy, and added, —

"I come now, dear Lucy, to my object in writing this letter. Looking back, as I now do, from the threshold of another world upon my past life, many things appear to me in a different light from that in which I once viewed them. Seeing this myself, I wish to know them righted, also, in your dear eyes. It is with the deepest pain that I refer to my visit to Hillsboro', and recall to your memory the unhappy events which then took place. It is from the

apprehension that in the resentful agony of that time I
may have given impressions and uttered words which, in
calmer moments, I should have wished unspoken and
known to be unjust. I cannot endure to think you unjust
to him or to me. The deep love which, in spite of all my
struggles, still lives in my heart, and must so long as it
beats, compels me, with a tender jealousy for its object, to
defend him against the mad, vehement accusations which
I made in my bitter anger. I can now see how much, in
all my unhappiness, I have myself alone to blame. I ac-
cused him to you of wanton cruelty — of intentional trifling. I now believe him to have been, from the outset,
thoughtless only; and O, Lucy, it is with a pang which
even now I cannot repress, that I admit the truth — he
never loved me as I loved him. The emotion, with him,
was transient only; with me, it was life-long. I cannot
blame him. I should have been the first to see the danger.
In my blindness I would not see that our positions were
so different. What to me was life and breath, must be
brief and passing with him, and end as lightly as it began.
For this was the result. When I saw him again, his short-
lived fancy was dead; and, secure in your indifference, I
may add, another and a stronger love had supplanted it.
Even if I had not read it in his face, whose every change I
knew, his own lips confessed it to me. Yes, Lucy; the
heart I had thought my own was all, all yours. What I
suffered I can never tell you. There had been a pleasure —
selfish, I admit, but still a pleasure — in believing him as
unhappy as myself; but when I learned that I was forgotten, when I plainly saw that all the past had left no ripple
on the surface of his life, then, instead of gratitude that

he was spared what I suffered, I felt only burning anger; and I believe if I had not seen so plainly that you entertained for him no feeling beyond that of friendship, my anger would have included you. But, as it was, your words fell like balm on my poor wounded heart. What little strength I have gained since then, I feel I owe to you."

There was more of the letter, but it is not necessary to repeat it here. Lucy read it steadily to the end; and, when it was finished, she sat for a long time lost in deep thought. Sorrow at the loss of her friend was overborne by the knowledge how welcome had been the summons which called her. She had lacked the wisdom — or the will — to govern her life, and so it had made shipwreck. But she was gone — let her mistakes sleep with her. Lucy's general impression of the whole unhappy affair referred to was unchanged. The letter, it is true, freed Stafford from the accusation of deliberate treachery; but it left him charged with a levity and reckless indifference to the feelings of others almost equally culpable. It proved, at least, however, the reality of the sentiment he had seemed to cherish for herself. Lucy was astonished at the thrill of pleasure which awoke in her at the assurance that this man, whom she was even now condemning, had indeed loved her. Surely it mattered nothing to her what his feeling had been. She put the thought away quickly — hid it out of sight.

It was late when she sought her pillow, and then sleep refused to come to her. Hour after hour she lay with strained, wide-open eyes, revolving in her mind all the tangled skein of events, all the conflicting thoughts and

feelings re-awakened by this letter; and it was not until
the morning was bright in the sky that she fell into her
first unquiet slumber. When, at a late hour next morning,
Mary, surprised at her friend's non-appearance, came into
Lucy's chamber, she found her sleeping; but her face was
pale, and her eyelids swollen, and there was an expression
of pain on her face which alarmed Mary.

As she bent over her, Lucy awoke, and, in answer to her
anxious inquiries, replied that she had slept ill, and com-
municated the sad intelligence her letters had contained.
Mary was full of sympathy and concern; and Lucy's pale-
ness and her clouded spirits for some days were readily
enough attributed to grief for the loss of her dead friend.

In the course of the ensuing week she returned to Hillsboro'.

CHAPTER XXXV.

I pass over an interval of several months. The summer had come and gone with no incident of importance. The Flemings had made a long visit to Hillsboro', and Burke still came and went at frequent intervals, sometimes with a hopeful heart, sometimes despondent.

The autumn was now fast fading. It was a day late in November, about the season when this story opened five years before. The sky was thickly overcast. The day was warm, unseasonably so, close and oppressive, in spite of a strong southerly wind, which had been blowing since morning. Indeed, this wind rather increased than diminished the sense of suffocation; it came hot, like the blast of a furnace.

A dreary, ominous day it seemed to Lucy Fraser. The air, to her fancy, was full of foreboding and dread: The dull, leaden sky, the rushing wind, filled her with vague, undefined fears. All day long her mind had been haunted by such fancies — a sense of *something* coming — coming — coming. She fought against the feeling; she called it absurd; but she could not shake it off. She sat by the parlor window that looked up into the orchard, and tried to sew. She was, except for the domestics, alone in the house. Her father and mother had left the day previous on a visit to some relatives in a distant part of the

state, and the captain was at Colchester. Lucy wished
them all at home, that she might know them safe. The
next moment she smiled at her own uneasiness, and tried
to think of the work with which she was occupying her
hands. Soon, finding it impossible to fix her thoughts
upon that, she threw it aside, and went to the piano. Before she was aware, she found herself playing a funeral
march. She precipitately left the instrument, and turned
over the books on the table.

Nothing there pleased her, and she went up to her own
room to find something more to her taste. From the upper shelf of her little book-case she took a volume at ran-
dom and opened it. It was the "Jerusalem Delivered,"
and between its leaves lay the bit of honeysuckle with
which Stafford had marked the place on that Sunday afternoon, so long ago, when he had read to her from its pages.
She had never opened the book from that day to this.
Now she flung it violently from her on the floor, and left
the chamber.

The loneliness of the house grew at last insupportable;
and she put on her shawl and bonnet, determined to spend
the remainder of the day with Lydia. Leaving word with
Dolly where she might be found, in case any one came,
she closed the hall door behind her, and set out for her
cousin's house.

As Lucy walked along over the dead, rustling leaves that
strewed the road-side, her lithe young figure breasting
firmly the strong wind, she formed the one brilliant point
of life and color in all the wide, dull landscape. She wore
a gown of dark, rich silk, which was blown in heavy folds
about her. Her shawl was of the gay-colored plaid she

was so fond of wearing, and her plain straw bonnet was brightened with a profusion of dark-blue ribbons. There was a warm, clearly-defined color in her cheek, and her eyes were bright with the spirit which opposed itself so unyieldingly to the wild wind.

The neat, white-painted house, with its dormer windows and smart green blinds, was soon reached. Passing through the little front yard, where Lydia's flower borders were now stripped of their summer glories, she laid her hand on the door, and, to her disappointment, found it locked. To her repeated knockings no answer was returned; and on inquiring of a tow-headed boy at work in the garden, she learned that the mistress of the house had gone to spend the rest of the day at her father's. At first Lucy thought she would go there, too; but, recollecting that Hannah had a tea-drinking of some neighbors that day, she changed her mind. She stood irresolute for some minutes, hardly knowing whither to direct her steps. The idea of going home was wholly distasteful. She looked up and down the road, and across the brown fields. The only signs of life she could see were some cattle on the remote hill-side, and a solitary horse and wagon approaching along the Edgehill road. Still uncertain, a crow, winging its lazy flight over some distant woods, caught her eye, and decided her.

"I will go to Beech Hill," she said, aloud. "It is years since I have been there; and this wind will be grand among the trees."

Acting upon this impulse, she left her place upon the doorstep and turned in the direction of Beech Hill. Her way took her for some distance along the high road over

which she had just passed, then, turning to the left, led
away over the farms. Walking rather slowly now, plunged
in deep thought, she paid no attention to the wagon which
was rapidly approaching her from behind. It would have
passed her unnoticed, but, just as it came opposite her in
the road, the driver checked his horse and turned to address her. She saw that he was a stranger, and the dasher
of his wagon, covered with fresh and various-hued mud,
showed that he had come some distance. He was a pleasant-looking man, not very young, and having the air which,
for want of a better term, we call "distinguished." So
much Lucy's observant eye took in at a glance, as, lifting
his hat, with a respectful bow, he asked, —

"Can you direct me, madam, to the house of a Mr. Page,
who lives, I think, in this neighborhood?"

"You are very near it now, sir; the first house over the
brow of the hill. It stands to the left."

"Thank you."

The stranger's eyes were scanning her face with a singularly earnest scrutiny, which yet had in it nothing of
rudeness. He seemed almost on the point of speaking again,
but checked himself, bowed once more, loosened his rein,
and drove on.

Lucy looked after him, wondering a little who he could
be, and what was his errand at her uncle's. Where had
she seen that face before? *Had* she ever seen it? It was
not recognition, nor simply inquiry, which had looked at
her out of those grave eyes; but what was it? She could
not tell; but more than once, as she pursued her walk, her
mind reverted to the stranger, the look with which he had
regarded her, and his possible errand. She grew, at last,

annoyed with herself for recurring so often to the matter, and wondered if her life had grown so barren of incident that the chance meeting with a stranger on the highway should have power to disturb her fancy for hours after.

She spent most of the afternoon upon the windy hill, among the beeches. For a time she succeeded in thrusting her sombre thoughts from her; but it was only that they might return with renewed force at a later period. She had grown tired of wandering through the wood, and weary of contending with the cloud of thick-coming and gloomy fancies that assailed her. She came to a spot where a broad gray rock, near the edge of the forest, marked the scene of many a childish rendezvous; and, sinking down upon the stone, and leaning her head upon her arm, surrendered herself to the tide of mournful and despondent emotions that was sweeping over her. The wind hissed in the withered grass and herbage, and roared in the branches of the great trees above her head. It whirled the dead leaves about her, and wildly fluttered her own dress; but she paid little heed to anything.

She sat a long, long time; and it was only when she saw the twilight approaching that she remembered it was time to return. She rose with an effort, shivering a little, though hardly with cold, and, with a listless, languid step, and an air of sad abstraction, took her way towards home.

It was nearly dark when she reached the house. She walked for some minutes up and down under the elms before the door, unable to bring herself to enter, so lonely and silent seemed the great empty rooms. But this could not last; and suddenly, with an impatient comment on her unusual nervousness, she turned and went quickly up the steps and into the hall.

At the foot of the staircase she was met by Dolly, who held a small package wrapped carefully in white paper. Heman Page, the girl said, had left it an hour before, with the message that Hannah was busy, but would come up to her in the evening. Lucy took the parcel carelessly, and to the girl's announcement that tea was waiting, replied that she wanted no supper then, she would wait till Hannah came, and went wearily up to her own room.

For some minutes she moved slowly about, putting away her bonnet and shawl, and endeavoring to occupy herself with something. After a time she took from the table, where, on first entering, she had laid it, the package Dolly had given her. A languid curiosity prompted her to sit down by the window and examine its contents, which there was still sufficient light in the room for her to do without difficulty. Tearing off the outer wrapper, she found two smaller packages, carefully sealed, with what seemed an explanation of their contents written on the outside. The handwriting was strange to her, but perfectly legible.

On the first package was written, —

"Articles belonging to George Wycombe Stafford, to be forwarded to Francis Brainerd, Esq., Calcutta;" and on the other, "Leaves from the note-book of Edward Lynch, containing certain instructions and dying wishes of George Stafford, also to be forwarded to Francis Brainerd."

As Lucy read these words, an icy chill crept over her; the blood slowly receded from her face, and seemed to freeze about her heart. With a quiet that was dreadful to see, she proceeded to break the seal and draw forth the enclosure. In the awful sense of oppression and cold ter-

rof of what was to come that was upon her, it did not
occur to her to wonder how this package should have come
to her, or through whose agency. There it was in her
hands; she felt the dreadful reality of it; but of whence
it came she never thought. She had no feeling of surprise or inquiry, only a strange sense of fulfilment. 'She
seemed to know the meaning now of the weight of foreboding which had hung upon her all day.

The first paper she opened was a written statement of
how the other came into the hands of the writer, was addressed, as were the envelopes, to Francis Brainerd, Esq.,
and had been prepared in case the writer should fail of a
personal interview. It was signed, "Edward Lynch," with
an address somewhere in England; and it told, in short,
cruelly terse and intelligible sentences, how the writer,
travelling in that part of Central Asia which lies to the
northward of the Himalayas, being on his return into the
Punjaub from an excursion through the passes of those
mountains, had come upon an American traveller named
Stafford. The latter had been wounded by the accidental
discharge of a gun in the hands of one of his servants, and
was lying at the point of death. The writer remained
with him until he died, taking from his lips his last wishes,
and some instructions which were contained in the leaves
of the note-book accompanying this communication.

That was nearly all; and as Lucy finished its perusal,
she laid the paper down, and mechanically took up the
others. They remained with ragged edges, just as a hasty
hand had torn them from the note-book. There were
numerous instructions written in pencil, and she read them
all carefully from beginning to end. After directions how

to find Brainerd, or to communicate with him, followed
requests of various kinds, which he begged the latter, for
the sake of their long friendship, to see executed. Some
messages to Colonel Ross, partly relating to property and
partly of affection, followed; and then was added, —

"Tell Frank to go to Hillsboro' and give the handkerchief to Lucy. Tell her that I never blamed her. It was
my hard fate only that honor forbade me to clear myself
in her eyes. Tell him to be kind to Figaro for my sake."

Here it broke off suddenly; and Lucy, with the same
cold calmness, proceeded to open the second enclosure. It
contained a faded wild rose and her own handkerchief, lost
on the day of their excursion to Long Pond.

There it lay — the delicate, gossamer thing — so suggestive of gay, airy dresses, of drawing-rooms, lights, and
perfumes. She brought herself at last to touch it. Good
God! there was a stain of blood upon it. She gazed at it
with eyes dilating with horror. Terrible pictures rose to
her mind — pictures of a lonely death-scene in the far wilderness, beneath the shadow of the awful mountains, where,
unsoothed by affection, unsustained by friendship, that
brave, gay spirit had breathed itself away. The room
which had lately seemed so empty was now filled with
ghosts — dreadful phantoms of past days, of dead hopes
and joys. They crowded upon her with hard, accusing
faces. Their pitiless eyes seemed to demand of her atone-
ment for some wrong. The agony of her feelings was
growing insupportable. She felt her senses leaving her,
and attempted to rise. The room grew dark; she caught
at the table to steady herself, reeled, and sank insensible
upon the floor.

Her swoon was like death. How long it lasted she never knew. It must have been long, however, for when consciousness did return, the chamber was perfectly dark, and she could hear the rain as the wind dashed it against the windows. She could not at first remember what had happened. She felt weak and cold, and tried to rise; but her heavy limbs refused to do their office, and she sank back upon the floor, only half conscious of place and season, but with a dull, leaden weight of misery upon heart and brain. After a time she became aware of a step approaching up the stairs; the handle of the door turned, and Hannah Page entered with a lamp in her hand.

CHAPTER XXXVI.

HANNAH PAGE had a tea-party of the neighbors that afternoon, and had sent for her younger sister to assist her in the dispensation of her hospitalities. Half a dozen good ladies, most of them elderly matrons, were gathered in the old sunny sitting-room; and there was a cheerful click of knitting-needles, and a pleasant confusion of voices. It was about three o'clock when an animated discussion of certain additions which Deacon Sharpe was making to his house was interrupted by a knock at the front door.

"There, Lydia," said Hannah, "somebody is knocking, and my work is just where I can't well lay it down. Won't you go and see who it is?"

Lydia, in compliance with this request, rose and proceeded to the door. She closed the inner door behind her as she passed into the entry; but still those in the room could distinguish the tones of an unfamiliar voice inquiring if Mr. Page lived there. Lydia replied in the affirmative, and was proceeding to say that her father was at his work, and that she would call him, when the stranger announced that his business was with Miss Hannah Page, and asked if he could see her.

"Certainly," replied Lydia. "If you will walk in, I will speak to her."

They heard her open the parlor door, and then a sound

of moving chairs and opening shutters, and presently she reappeared.

"Who is it, Lydia?" asked Hannah.

"Nobody I ever saw before," replied her sister. "He wants to see you."

"Did he say what for?"

"Not a word."

A buzz of half-suppressed curiosity ran round the group of women. Mrs. Smiley murmured, "How strange!" in the ear of her next neighbor; Mrs. Perkins nodded her head and looked very wise, as if she could guess a great deal more than people chose to tell. Hannah quietly excused herself, laid down her work, and left the room to ascertain the stranger's business.

When she entered the parlor he was standing by a window, looking out. He turned and bowed.

"My name is Brainerd, madam; Francis Brainerd. You may have heard it from a dear friend of mine and yours, Mr. Stafford."

"Yes, indeed; a great many times," replied Hannah, warmly, extending her hand. "You seem almost like an old acquaintance. Pray sit down. When did you come from India?"

"I am arrived but a few weeks. I perceive that the sad intelligence of which I am the bearer has not reached you before me."

He hesitated a moment. Hannah's quick eye searched his face; and she asked, in a changed voice, "Has anything happened to our friend?"

"The worst, Miss Page."

"Is he dead?"

24

His lips parted as if he would speak, but his voice was choked; he only pointed silently to the crape upon his hat. Neither spoke for some minutes. At length Hannah asked, in a voice tremulous with grief,—

"When did it happen?"

"It is now six months since."

"Were you with him?"

"No; he died among strangers."

"Not in Calcutta, then?"

"No; a thousand miles from there, at a little native village in the wild mountain region which separates India from Central Asia."

"What sent him there? and what was the cause of his death?"

"Your last question I can answer at once. He was shot. A rifle went off in the clumsy hands of a Hindoo servant, and the ball entered his lungs. But for the answer to your first question, it is what I have come to ask your aid in finding."

"My aid, sir! How can I help you?"

"If you cannot, I fear none can. It is this which has brought me here to-day. But, in order that you should understand my perplexity, I must go back some time. In going into the particulars of my friend's private history, I should not, even if necessity did not compel me, feel any hesitation, knowing the high place you held in his regard, —yes, in his affection. I know the circumstances of your first acquaintance and after friendship, and how strong was the attachment which he felt for your family, and especially for yourself."

Hannah's tears were falling fast, but she remained silent. Mr. Brainerd resumed, after a temporary pause:—

"In the spring before poor George's last visit to Edgehill, the question was raised between us of his accompanying me to India. I wished him very much to go; but he
objected, — mainly, I think, from a feeling that he had
already spent many years in aimless wandering about the
earth, and that it was time for him to settle down to some
useful employment. He was still uncertain, however, when
news from England decided his course for him. His uncle,
Colonel Ross, wrote that it was highly desirable, indeed
necessary for the settlement of some property in England,
that he should go thither at once. I was leaving then in
a few days. I knew that he went down to Edgehill for a
short visit before the steamer in which he meant to go was
to sail. I also knew that the business I have mentioned
required his *immediate* presence in England, and a stay
there of nearly, if not quite, a year. Judge, then, of my
surprise on receiving letters, after my arrival in Calcutta,
which showed him loitering through all the summer in
Edgehill. Weeks grew to months, and still he staid. I
could gather from his letters no hint of what detained him;
he assigned half a score of reasons, not one of which, I
knew, would have had power to hold him there for a day.
At length, suddenly, without the slightest intimation of his
intention, he appeared to me one morning in Calcutta. To
my astonishment, I learned that he had not been in England at all; he actually appeared to have forgotten that he
had thought of going there. It did not take me long to
discover that an entire change had been wrought in my
friend; but my utmost efforts failed to learn its cause. He
was moody — at times even sullen. At one moment he
shunned all society, and the next he eagerly sought what-

ever seemed to promise excitement. He soon had a host
of friends among the English and American residents, who
make up a very gay and hospitable society, and his company was much in request. But often, after having been
the life of some party, excursion, or adventure, I have
known him retire to his own room, which was near mine,
and spend the entire night in pacing restlessly up and
down,—he, whose sleep, all his life, had been sweet, and
sound, and healthy as a school-boy's!

"This continued some time. Business kept me a close
prisoner in the city; but I found that he had grown intensely weary of it, and only remained to be near me.
Suddenly he announced his resolution to occupy the remaining period of my detention there with an expedition
into the Punjaub, and perhaps through the passes of the
Himalayas into Thibet. It was a hazardous excursion, at
the best, and I opposed it strongly, begging him to stay
with me. But the restless fever had taken him, and I was
unable to shake his resolution. His preparations were
very rapidly made. He was to be accompanied by Figaro
and a native servant—a very insufficient retinue, as I then
represented to him; but he could see no necessity for anything further. The evening before his departure he dined
with me in company with one or two other gentlemen. I
never saw him more brilliant. He was the life and soul of
the party, and my guests went away delighted with my
friend. He remained after the others were gone, talking
on indifferent topics for half an hour. When he rose to
go, he shook my hand with an unforced gayety, which was
more like himself than anything I had seen in him since
his arrival. In going out, he looked back from the door,

as if there were something he was half inclined to say; but, without speaking, he came hastily back to where I was sitting, laid his hand upon my shoulder, and, stooping, kissed me on the forehead, and left me. I never saw him again."

Mr. Brainerd and Hannah were silent for a few minutes, and then the latter asked, —

"How did you learn of his death?"

"Through strangers. I heard from him several times; but when all intelligence ceased, I did not at first feel any apprehension, as I knew he proposed to extend his journey beyond the mountains, into a region with which there was none but chance communication. I had begun, however, to feel somewhat anxious at his protracted silence, when, one evening, there called on me a gentleman who announced himself as Mr. Lynch, an Englishman. He informed me of Stafford's death, and said he was with him at the time. Lynch, with some other travellers, was returning from an expedition similar to that which Stafford had undertaken, and, in the wild, unfrequented region of Western Thibet, at a little Tartar village lying some hundred miles to the north of the mountain city of Leh, they found our poor friend. He was lying upon the ground, his strength already nearly exhausted, his life fast bleeding away. His servants were too much frightened to afford any assistance, even if assistance could have been of any avail. Lynch learned who he was, and promised to see me and his uncle, Colonel Ross. He took from his lips his last wishes, and a few instructions how to see them carried out. Here are the leaves of the note-book in which he wrote them as they were uttered. He brought me this ring, which you may remember, and his watch for his uncle, with other tokens of which I will speak presently. Lynch staid with him until he died, but could no longer, as his party were impatient to move on. He brought back with him to Calcutta the Hindoo servant Stafford had engaged. Figaro refused to leave the body of his master. When they tried to compel him, he showed the dreadful rage of a wild animal. Lynch described him as positively dangerous; and so they were obliged to leave him, crouching, nearly senseless himself, at poor George's side. The natives had seemed friendly and kind, and Lynch gave them money — it was all he could do — in exchange for a promise to bury the body and take care of Figaro. O, Miss Page, I have no words to tell you of my grief, when I think of him — so beloved, so fitted to give and receive happiness. You, who have known and loved him, may judge in some degree what his loss is to me — my friend of so many years."

Hannah's tears prevented a reply. In a few minutes Mr. Brainerd proceeded : —

"I now come to the point where I hope to have your assistance. Here are the leaves of Lynch's note-book," — he laid a parcel on the table, — "and here the instructions. I have religiously complied with every one until this;" and he pointed to the one which referred to Lucy. "Here I have no clew to what he means. It is in the hope that you may aid me to find one, that I have come to you to-day."

Hannah bent over the papers for a moment, and then said, "I know nothing of any handkerchief. Where is it?"

He took from the envelope Lucy's handkerchief, and

laid it before her. She reached out her hand for it with a cry of surprise, but shuddered and drew back at sight of the stains it bore.

"Did he have that?" she asked, in a husky voice.

"It was in the inner breast pocket of his coat, wrapped in several folds of paper. He had not strength himself to draw it out, but could only indicate the place to Lynch, who took it at his request. Did you ever see it before? Do you know to whom it belonged?"

"I know it well; but it explains nothing to me."

"Who, then, is Lucy, and where does she live? What was her connection with Stafford, and what broke it off?"

"Part of your questions I can answer. Lucy Fraser is my cousin; she lives not far from here. There never was anything which could be called a connection between her and Mr. Stafford. Lucy is very beautiful, and people used to say he was in love with her. He was always coming to her father's that summer, and I must confess that, at the time, I thought so myself."

"Is Miss Fraser a lovely girl, with dark-blue, level-looking eyes, firm, sweet lips, and cheeks like a sea-shell?"

"That is a fair description of my cousin. Where have you seen her?"

"I passed a lady half a mile above here, and asked of her a direction. Looking into her face then, I felt a sort of conviction that if, as I suspected, poor George had given away that noble heart of his into a woman's keeping, it was to her he had surrendered it. What possessed me of the idea I cannot tell; but I had it. She has one of those faces which are a fate to men."

He resumed, after a moment: —

"I have learned from you, Miss Page, more, perhaps, than I could have expected — enough to enable me to do all that is required. Still, I had hoped to discover more. From the tenor of this message, it would seem there was something wrong. Have you any suspicion why your cousin refused Mr. Stafford?"

"I cannot positively say that she never refused him; but I am quite persuaded in my own mind that he never proposed to her."

"You complicate the affair, when I looked to you to make it clear. Here is my reason for thinking there must have been some connection which the lady, for reasons of her own, had broken off. In examining the papers of my friend, as I was obliged to do, I discovered these two notes; a faded rose was folded with them. There is an interval of several weeks between them. They are dated at Hillsboro', but the signatures had been carefully torn away. Do you recognize the hand?"

"Yes; it is Lucy's."

"I presumed so. This one, bearing date early in July, is a graceful, lively affair, and concerns some party of pleasure. It shows a pleasant, friendly, not too intimate acquaintance. But this, written on the tenth of September, is very different. Read it, and you will see how cold is the tone of it; how haughtily, and with what frigid politeness, she expresses a hope that he will see, as clearly as herself, the propriety of absenting himself from Hillsboro'. Now, what had occurred between the writing of these two?"

"I cannot tell you — I know nothing."

"My motive in seeking to get to the bottom of this is

not curiosity. By comparing this second note with the message sent through Lynch, it is evident there must have been some misunderstanding, something which could not be explained. My hope was, that I might discover its nature, and, from my intimate knowledge of the character and life of my friend, be able to dispel any shadow, however slight, that might rest on his memory. That hope I must forego. And now, Miss Page, will you do me a great kindness? Will you put these papers and the handkerchief into the hands of your cousin, and tell her whence they came?"

"O, Mr. Brainerd, don't ask me to do that! I cannot."

"But consider. I will believe that she must at one time have cherished a feeling at least kind and friendly, if not tender, for one who loved her so well. Even if she did not know of his love or return it, the proofs of its undying strength, coming in such form as this, must be full of pain to her. It will soften the blow to have her learn the truth from you."

"You are right, I admit. It is a hard thing to do; but I consent, for Lucy's sake. Have you seen Mr. Gore?"

"No. I went to Edgehill; but he is, unfortunately, absent in Washington. I am compelled to return immediately to New York, but hope to arrange a meeting with him soon."

He now rose to go; but Hannah urged him to stay and take some refreshment before proceeding on his journey. He thanked her warmly, but declined. The day was wearing away, and he had a long drive before him to reach Kiffton and the railway. He was drawing on his gloves, when Hannah, who had been sadly looking over the papers on the table, took up one of the notes in Lucy's handwriting.

"Strange!" she said, thoughtfully. "This note is dated the tenth of September, and must have been written on the very day that Mr. Stafford was last at my uncle's. I remember it because it was my birthday, and Lucy and a lady who was visiting her were to take tea with me, and they did not come, because Mrs. Lovell was taken sick."

"Mrs. Lovell, did you say?" exclaimed Brainerd, turning round sharply.

"Yes; she was a lady Lucy knew in Europe, and she spent a week with her at that time. Did you know her?"

"Good Heavens! You have unconsciously given me the clew to everything. Did I know Mrs. Lovell? I certainly did; and I knew her for a blind, selfish woman, who ruined her own happiness, and ended, it would seem, by ruining George Stafford's as well."

"What do you mean, Mr. Brainerd?"

"I will explain," he replied, re-seating himself, "if you will be good enough to tell me everything which you can remember of that last visit of Stafford's at your uncle's."

Hannah complied, relating with careful minuteness all the events of that day which had come under her own observation. Mr. Brainerd listened attentively, but nearly in silence, putting only now and then a question as to Stafford's position and habits of intimacy with the family.

"I understand it all now," he said, when Hannah had finished; "all the misunderstanding, and the perhaps natural misrepresentation. I can see, too, how poor George, with his exalted chivalry where a woman was concerned, and his fine sense of honor, felt himself compelled to accept the position into which he was thrust, rather than compromise a woman who never had any consideration for him — or, indeed, for herself."

"Do you think it was Mrs. Lovell who worked mischief between him and Lucy?"

"I do, certainly — with no malicious intention, but driven by the headlong folly which characterized everything she ever did. But I will tell you all about it, and you shall judge where the greatest blame should lie. During the autumn previous to the winter in which Stafford first came to Edgehill, he went with me to Vermont, to the house of my uncle. There was a gay party of visitors in the house, and, among them, Mrs. Lovell. Stafford had never seen her before, but I had known her all her life. Though very beautiful, and almost universally admired, she had, I confess, never been a favorite of mine. I had always thought her to be well-meaning enough, but vain, shallow, and passionate — plenty of fire, but no force. She had heard of Stafford, and before he arrived — this I know positively, from the ladies of my uncle's family — had boasted that she would do what it was said no woman had yet done — bring him to her feet. Accordingly, when they met, she brought the whole battery of her fascinations — and you know that they were many — to bear upon him. She meant to enslave *him;* she never reckoned on being caught herself. But I think from the very first she was fascinated by our friend. You knew him; you must remember the rare charm of his manner, inspired

by a spirit of chivalrous gallantry towards all women.
Then, too, his fine person was not likely to go for nothing
with one like Mrs. Lovell. She was an exacting woman,
demanding of her many admirers the most absorbing devotion. Stafford only followed the current of the crowd.
She was beautiful, and he admired her; she honored him
with her evident preference, and he acknowledged it by a
perhaps too assiduous attention. That was all. Thus it
continued through the fortnight we were together in the
country, and for a short time after we all met in New
York.

"Now, all this is not in accordance with your ideas of
life and its proprieties. I am not going to defend it; but
pray remember, there is a wide difference — in favor of
which I will not undertake to say — between your world
and theirs. Education makes men and women, you know.
After a time it began to strike me that Mrs. Lovell was
becoming more interested in her new acquaintance than
might be well for her. I hinted as much to Stafford; and,
though he treated my suggestion as perfectly groundless,
I saw that it had an effect. He did not abruptly withdraw from the intimacy, out of regard to her sensitive
vanity; but he allowed himself often to be kept away
from her by others. I believe that at first she thought
this the result of accident, for, as he retreated, she pursued. He attached himself, at length, quite exclusively to
other ladies; and then a violent exhibition of jealousy, in
perfect keeping with her character, put an end to all
doubt, if any had remained. He went out of town, absenting himself for several weeks, solely, as I could well
guess, to give her time to recover her senses. But imme-

diately on his return, it chanced that he met Mrs. Lovell
at a dinner-party. Exactly what passed I do not know;
but she extracted from him a promise to meet her the next
evening at some place to which they were both invited.
He broke the promise, — I think he never meant to keep
it, — and staid quietly at home. He was living in my
house at the time, or I should never have known these
circumstances. You must understand that I live alone,
having neither wife, mother, nor sister, and Stafford and
myself were the only persons in the house except the servants. Well, this evening of which I speak was nearly
spent, when a lady came to the house in a hackney coach.
She was closely veiled, and inquired for Stafford. My
man replied that Mr. Stafford was writing in his own
room, and had given orders not to be disturbed. She demanded, however, to be shown to him at once; and the
servant, without further parley, did as he was told. I was
sitting with Stafford in his room when she entered, and,
raising her veil, revealed the agitated, tear-stained features
of Mrs. Lovell. She had not seen him at the place she
appointed, and had heard a rumor that he was leaving
town the next morning, and in her desperation she had
come to him.

"Of what passed at that interview I, of course, know
nothing, — I escaped from the room as soon as she entered
it, — but from my knowledge of the characters of both, it
is not difficult to surmise its general tenor. What was
likely to be the bearing of such a man towards a beautiful
woman, whose only offence was loving him too well, and
who had braved everything to fling herself into his arms?
If he soothed her trouble with softer words or more tender

tones than his ordinary feeling for her would dictate, I
cannot think it strange, nor can I condemn him as insin-
cere. To win her to a more reasonable frame of mind,
and to save her from the consequences of her folly, was
unquestionably his aim; and that was what he did. She
remained some time, and then left, escorted by him to her
carriage. I believe the occurrence never got wind. The
servant who admitted did not know her; and I think I
was the only person who had any knowledge of it. The
next morning Stafford left New York, and set out to visit
his cousin, Mr. Gore, at Edgehill. He gave me no reason
for this sudden movement; but I did not need to be a
wizard to guess his motive in burying himself in a remote
country district at that severe season."

"Then it was directly after these events that we first
knew him?"

"Yes; and probably, but for what I have told you, you
never would have known him. He saw that prudence and
honor lay only in flight, and he came here."

Hannah was silent. Her thoughts had flashed back to
that first winter, and she was recalling many little traits
of manner and temper in the stranger which had seemed
contradictory then, but which were intelligible enough
now. It was easy to see whence had come the occasional
cloud of gloom which would gather over the natural gayety of his spirits. She remembered that evening when
Mr. Lovell had called at the house to ask a simple business question of Stafford, the peculiar demeanor of the
latter when he recognized the visitor's voice, and the unaccountable emotion he had betrayed. She could understand how, with his knowledge of Mrs. Lovell, he might

well believe there was no folly of which she was incapable, and no exposure her recklessness might not have brought on. Mr. Brainerd proceeded : —

"About that time Mrs. Lovell's little girl showed symptoms of illness, and the physician ordered her to Cuba. I am quite sure they never met again until this occasion of which you speak. And now you see the difficulty of Stafford's position. How could he say, 'I never loved this woman — I never even pretended to. It was my misfortune to be so irresistible that she adored me, while I had not a crumb to give her in return'? To think such a thing, even, makes a man feel like a coxcomb; to say it, he must be one."

"All this astonishes me, Mr. Brainerd. I remember liking Mrs. Lovell very much."

"And naturally, for she was a very lovely woman, after all. Much that was amiss in her was attributable to the faults of education. She was amiable and affectionate, but wholly undisciplined. She followed the wild lead of any impulse with no thought of whither it would carry her; and she owed it to the generosity and good sense of the man whose happiness she managed to ruin, that she retained what is of most value to a woman — that she lived and died with no stain upon her name. I would never have spoken of this, had not justice to the memory of our friend forbidden me to remain silent. And now, I must ask of you to set the facts of the case before your cousin. Both are dead, it is true, and passed beyond our censure ; but even now, it seems to me, the truth should be known, and the blame be apportioned between them as it belongs."

Mr. Brainerd again rose and prepared to depart. He thanked Hannah gratefully for the sympathy and assistance she had afforded him, received her renewed promise to make all needed explanations to Lucy, and then, shaking her hand warmly, took his leave.

CHAPTER XXXVII.

HANNAH returned to her guests, whose curiosity was greatly stimulated by the length of the stranger's stay. Briefly she explained who he was, and the sad intelligence he had brought, reserving, of course, all reference to Lucy. Lydia wept bitterly at the recital, and at the thought of that lonely death-scene. Ben, coming in and finding his wife in tears, anxiously inquired the reason; and Lydia told him, with her head upon his shoulder, and her voice tremulous with feeling. Hannah was thankful that the poignancy of her young sister's grief had the effect to distract general attention from herself; and she went about the duties which hospitality demanded of her with such steadiness as she could command. She had gathered the papers again into a parcel, and when Heman arrived she sent them by him to Lucy; for she had a strange dread of being herself the bearer of the first announcement to her cousin. Had she been aware, however, of the effect the news would produce, she would never have done this. But Lucy's placid exterior had deceived her.

It was eight o'clock, and raining heavily, when, the rest of the guests having gone, Ben brought his horse to the door, to take Lydia home. Hannah begged him first to carry herself up to her uncle's. They remonstrated with her for wishing to go that night; but she was so urgent that she carried her point.

25

When they reached Mr. Fraser's door, she sprang out quickly, and bidding Ben and Lydia a hurried good night, hastened into the house. To Dolly's exclamations of astonishment at seeing her, she replied by an inquiry for her cousin. The girl answered that Lucy was in her chamber, not having been down to supper.

"Is anything the matter with her?" asked Hannah, proceeding to divest herself of her dripping cloak and hood.

Dolly did not know. She had noticed all day that Lucy did not seem well — not just like herself. She had taken a long walk that afternoon, and had gone right up stairs after coming in. Dolly had been intending to go up and see if she wanted anything, but had been so busy helping Mary Jane with the ironing that it had slipped her mind.

Hannah took a lamp and ascended to her cousin's room. Her knock, once or twice repeated, eliciting no answer, she opened the door and entered. Lifting the light above her head, she peered into the gloom, and at length descried the object of her search, half sitting, half crouching upon the floor, and gazing at her with a dazed and bewildered expression. Hannah went hastily forward, and dropping on her knees, raised the poor head in her arms, and pressed the pale face close to her breast — just as once before she had held it when a strong wave of agony swept over the young heart. Then the form of the young girl had been shaken by a storm of sobs, and scalding tears had been wrung from her. Now the heavy lids drooped over dry, hot eyes, and a kind of stupor seemed to benumb all her senses.

Hannah was alarmed, and made efforts to rouse her cousin

from this condition, but with little success. With gentle force she induced her to lie down upon the bed, and then proceeded to remove her dress, and to administer such restoratives as she had at hand. But her alarm increased as she found that her measures had but little effect. It was only at intervals that Lucy seemed conscious of anything around her. She lay in a condition that was neither sleeping nor waking, her fixed, wide-open eyes alternating between wildness and vacancy. Convulsive shudders shook her frame; her temples throbbed; her flesh was burning hot even while she shivered like one in an ague fit. As the hours wore on the fever increased; her state of dull stupor gave place to excitement, and before morning she was raving in delirium.

Hannah never left her. Soon after midnight she became so anxious that she roused Jerry from his slumbers and sent him to the Centre to summon the doctor whom the family were accustomed to call in their slight ailments. He came at once, but seemed puzzled by the condition of the patient. Quite early next day Heman came to learn the cause of his sister's prolonged absence from home, and she immediately despatched him to Kiffton, that being the nearest point whence a telegraphic message could be sent to her uncle and aunt, while she hurried Ben off to Colchester, to bring thence the captain and a skilful physician.

The Colchester doctor arrived towards evening, and looked very grave as he listened to the report given by Hannah and the rural practitioner first summoned. Lucy's situation, indeed, warranted some alarm. Whether the seeds of illness had already been lingering about her, and the nervous excitement and shock she had undergone had only served to quicken them into activity, or whether she had taken cold by sitting so long in the damp woods that afternoon, I cannot say; but she was evidently in the grasp of a high and dangerous fever. And for days and weeks they hung over her, watching almost hopelessly, while her features grew wasted and shrunken, and her sweet lips parched and dry; while over her soft blue eyes passed alternately the lurid brightness of delirium and the dulness of a lethargy even more dreadful.

In her wanderings she seldom raved violently; but from the muttered words which escaped her it was evident that she had gone back in imagination to the winter when we first knew her, and that she fancied herself once more with Hannah, Mary, and Fanshaw, in her uncle's house. She lived over again all the incidents of that memorable snow storm, calling to Hannah's mind much which the latter had forgotten, and seeming always to be harassed by anxiety for some one wandering and perishing in the snow. She never mentioned Stafford, but seemed in some way to confound her own identity with that of Nancy Cline, fancying that it was herself who had the task to keep the beacon lamps forever burning.

Hannah alone, of all the kind nurses around Lucy's bed, guessed the significance of these broken wanderings. She had found, that first night, upon the table the handkerchief and the scattered papers; and, gathering them all up, she hid them away in one of Lucy's drawers, and turned the key upon their dreadful story. In the stronger excitement of Lucy's danger, her friends naturally lost, for the time, all thought of the news which Brainerd had brought; and as for connecting that news in any way with her illness, there was no one save Hannah possessing sufficient knowledge to so link them together.

Hannah established a willing substitute in her place at home, and she herself scarcely left the chamber in which the gentle girl, the light and joy of so many hearts, lay battling for her life. Long, very long, the combat lasted. Many times it seemed to those around that hope was wholly gone. But youth and the vigorous constitution of the Frasers triumphed at last. One still, sharp autumn morning, when the sun was shining clear, and the hoar frost lay white and sparkling over all the hill-sides, Lucy awoke from a sleep which had lasted a night and a day, and looked around with a conscious, recognizing smile; weak indeed, — so weak it seemed as if a breath might fan away the feeble spark of life, — but with reason in her eyes, and the fire of fever no longer burning in her veins.

Old Captain Fraser, who had not shed one tear in all the two dreadful weeks through which his darling's life had hung trembling in the balance, broke down now, and sobbed so wildly that Hannah was compelled to draw him from the room.

Lucy's recovery was not rapid. Her feet had strayed very near the entrance to the dark valley, and it almost seemed as if the chill shadows projected thence still rested upon her. It was a long time before she was able to rise from her bed; and the new year had begun before she was strong enough to be carried down stairs in her father's arms. But the tender care, the warm atmosphere of affection that surrounded her, could not but have their effect. Little by little her cheeks resumed their roundness, and her eyes their tender light; and, if her smile was rarer, it was sweeter, too, than ever before.

Hannah watched her cousin with anxious eyes, understanding as no one else could the sorrow that had fallen upon her. Once before she had seen how Lucy had struggled with and overcome a great grief; but she knew, by some intuitive comprehension of the heart of her cousin, that this blow had struck home far more deeply, and that the wound would never so wholly heal as that had done. She carefully avoided all mention of Stafford, waiting until Lucy should choose to interrogate her. The time came at last, as she had expected that it would. It was one mild evening in the early part of February. The cousins were sitting together in Lucy's room, Hannah knitting by the fire, and Lucy, in an arm-chair by the window, looking out into the fading, orange-colored west. She did not turn her face to look at her companion, but it was in a tolerably steady tone that she said, —

"I found those papers to-day, Hannah, in the drawer where you so kindly laid them. I know that they reached me through you. Will you tell me how you came by them, and what you know of *him?*"

Hannah sent a searching, anxious look at her cousin. The latter's face was carefully turned from view, but Hannah knew, by the steady poise of her head, that she might safely speak. She began at the beginning, and related the circumstances of Brainerd's visit, repeated all that he had told her of Stafford's death and last requests, described his anxiety to learn what had driven the latter from Hillsboro', and finally told how Mrs. Lovell's name had been mentioned, and faithfully repeated the account Brainerd had given of his friend's connection with her. Throughout the whole recital Lucy never turned her head, or spoke; only once or twice a low, sharp, shuddering sigh which broke from her revealed the constraint she was putting upon her feelings. When it was ended she rose up. Her face was very pale, but she did not tremble. Passing by the chair where her cousin sat, she stooped and kissed her cheek, and then, without speaking, went quickly out.

The subject was never renewed between them; but Hannah had no need of words to show her all that was in her cousin's heart. None but she knew — perhaps the captain may have partly guessed — why, though the fever was gone, and no vestige of disease remained, yet the surprised physician found in his patient a strange want of recuperative vitality. Her cheeks remained pale, and her form shadowy, and her step about the house was languid and slow. They thought the severity of the New England winter was injuring her, and talked of a milder climate; but she resisted the idea, and Hannah sided with her in her opposition. Once before Hannah had urged absence and change of scene; but she believed these would have no efficacy now. This new grief might be conquered, but it was not to be dissipated. She was right; but her heart bled for her favorite as she saw through what heavy conflict she was fighting her way back to peace. As day by day she watched her growing serenity, and saw the almost smiling cheerfulness with which she devoted herself to those around her, finding a kind of happiness in theirs, Hannah longed to take her to her heart, for she remembered the dark hours of her own life, when, with weak and trembling feet, she had walked the same rough path. In

all externals, in education and in habits of life, persons
more dissimilar than these two cousins could scarcely be;
but in the experiences of life and in the gradual changes
wrought thereby, they had, from widely-separated starting-
points, approached much nearer than any casual observer
could imagine. In their gentle endurance, in the brave,
kind, unselfishly cheerful spirit that governed both their
lives, there were strong points of resemblance. And with
the growing likeness came, if possible, a growing attachment. Lucy found one of her chief sources of happiness
in the companionship of her cousin. They were much
together; and though in their intercourse they never approached personal topics, yet each felt that she was understood by the other.

Thus the winter passed away. Few visitors came to
the Frasers', and those of the quietest kind; Mary and
Fanshaw once or twice, and oftener Singleton Burke. The
latter, by his assiduous but unobtrusive attentions during
Lucy's illness and lingering convalescence, had won a warm
place in the regard of her family, and even rendered himself, if not, indeed, a necessary, at least a valued source of
interest and pleasure in her own life. He stripped the
Colchester greenhouses of flowers to brighten her sick-
chamber; he ransacked the markets of three cities for
fruits to tempt her languid appetite. As she grew better,
and was able to resume her place in the family circle, he
brought pleasant books to entertain her, and made himself
a regular purveyor of the news of the outside world. All
that was most amiable and excellent in his character manifested itself now, and Lucy's esteem for him increased
with every interview.

Yes; little by little Lucy was winning her way to victory. The unconquerable spirit of her Scottish ancestors, the stout old stock of the Frasers, was asserting itself again. Their blood was in the veins of this gentle girl, and her spirit was, after its kind, as indomitable as theirs. Then, too, Lucy was a woman; and I do not deny that a certain maidenly pride lent its aid to her efforts to hide the deadly hurt which still bled within. She could not openly mourn one whom none knew as her lover; but secretly she cherished with tender exultation the knowledge of his love for her.

CHAPTER XXXVIII.

THE spring came slowly on. With the softer sky and warming winds, Lucy went abroad again, and found a pleasure in resuming her old habits. Long walks in gusty April days, and drives over heavy country roads, — rough means, perhaps, but effectual, — were slowly bringing the color again to her cheeks, strength to her step, and roundness to her limbs.

March and April were already gone, and May, with its pale, early green, and fragile, courageous wild flowers, had come. More than ever before, as Lucy watched the slow, annually-recurring change going on around her, she was reminded of her childhood. She would sit for hours together on the doorstep, luxuriating in the warm sunshine, and recalling, with a pensive smile, sweet May days come and passed long ago. The green fields and hill-sides, the tender foliage of the elms, with the building orioles flashing in and out, and the distant forest lines, were still the same. For all change in anything around her, it might have been but yesterday that she waded brooks and hunted wild flowers in the wet woods, an eager, happy child; but looking into herself, that time seemed so long ago, an interval like a lifetime appeared to stretch between.

One bright afternoon towards the latter part of May, Lucy had been sitting for some time in the doorway.

There was a slight moisture in her eyes, and her face wore the sweet, thoughtful expression which had come to be most habitual to it. She was thinking how good and merciful God is in that he has made the world so fair. When any great grief comes upon us, our hearts, in their blind, selfish sorrow, sicken at the sight of nature's brightness. We long to have the outward world put on a gloom in sympathy with ours. Its heedlessness of our pain seems cruel. We would have it always dark and cold. But the sun shines on, and the beneficent seasons come and go, doing with such sweet serenity their appointed work, that we are shamed out of our childish rebellion. Something of this thought was in Lucy's mind to-day.

"Surely," she said, "God did not make the world so beautiful for us to grieve in."

Lucy's reverie was interrupted. Her father, passing by, threw a letter into her lap. She looked up.

"Have you been to the Centre, father? Why did you not ask me to go, too?"

"There was no room for you, dear: I had the wagon full of bags. I will take you to-morrow morning."

"To-morrow I propose to drive with another gentleman."

"Indeed!"

"Yes. Captain Fraser has not precisely invited me, but I have invited myself to go with him to Edgehill."

"Are you going to Mr. Gore's?"

"Grandpa is. I am going to see Anna Marston, who is visiting her aunt there."

"Well, I think I will ask your grandfather to go round by Sam Moore's farm, and see about buying that horse for you. He has one that goes well under the saddle."

"Dear father, how kind of you! There is nothing could please me so much. I can ride every day."

"I hope you will, my dear child, and grow strong and well. Nothing could please *me* so much as that. But I forgot to say, as I came by Ben's house just now, Lydia called to me to ask you to go over. Ben is away, and she is alone."

"Very well; I will go when I have read this letter."

The letter which she now took up was from Horace Fleming, giving an account of his own wedding, which had just taken place, claiming her sympathy on that joyous occasion, and regretting that it could not "have been graced by her sweet presence." She was still smiling over the gay, brotherly epistle, when a light buggy drew up under the trees; and, raising her eyes, she recognized in its occupant Mr. Burke. He alighted, and came up the walk. Her greeting was frankly cordial.

He instantly noticed the unwonted brightness of Lucy's face, and glanced at the letter lying in her lap.

"I think," he said, as he clasped warmly the hand she extended to him, "that you must have had pleasant news in that letter."

"You are right. What should be pleasant news if a wedding is not?"

"A wedding past, or prospective?"

"This one is past, and the happy bridegroom writes to claim my congratulations. But," she added, rising, "I am forgetting the claims of hospitality, Mr. Burke. Will you not come in?"

"Not if you will allow me to stay here with you for a while."

"Willingly, if you prefer it."

She resumed her seat, and he took one beside her, and began telling her about Colchester and Mary.

It was very pleasant sitting there in the soft, warm air. Lucy seemed more like her own old self than Burke had seen her for a long time. The half playful, half pensive softness of her present mood was most attractive to him. He thought he had never loved her so well. He had not come that day with any purpose of making a final trial of his fate. How it came about he could never exactly tell; but somehow it was that after a little time he found himself speaking rapidly and earnestly, telling the story of his love, and pleading, with the eloquent incoherence of feeling, for a look — a word — which might encourage his hopes.

Lucy, when first she took the meaning of his words, had turned very pale, and made a half movement, as if to withdraw from his side. He had taken her hand, but she drew it from his clasp, saying, sadly, —

"My dear friend, I am sorry for this. Do not say any more, I beg. It is all idle, and can only pain us both. I thought I had made you see that before."

"Do not say so, Lucy. When, once before, you declined to hear, you did not reject my suit. Let me still hope that, if not now, yet at some future day —"

But Lucy interrupted him. Her tone was sad, but firm.

"No; I cannot allow you to pursue this subject. I repeat, it can only pain us both. Forgive me, but believe me, once for all; it can never be."

He saw that it was so — that her decision was irrevocable. He had been sanguine of success, and the sudden dashing of his hopes was a heavy blow; but he took it like a man. He rose to his feet, as if to go. She also rose, and stood beside him. Tears sprang, in spite of her, to her eyes, as she extended to him her hand.

"Do not let me think I have lost my friend," she said

"I can never be less than your friend, Miss Fraser," he answered, a little formally, but with no lack of generous fervor. He took the hand she gave him, holding it lightly for an instant, hesitated, as if he would have said something more, then, dropping it, with some nearly unintelligible words of farewell, hastened away.

After he was gone, Lucy sat for some time lost in rather painful thought. She had been quite unprepared for what had occurred, the perfect unobtrusiveness of Burke's recent attentions having not so much misled her into the belief that he had renounced his old hope as it had caused her to forget the subject altogether. She felt a deep regret for what had passed — regret at once for the disturbance of a friendship she found pleasant, and for the too evident pain with which her decision had been received. The interview had reawakened sorrowful thoughts and emotions which she was anxious to leave at rest.

Willing to drive away these painful reflections, she cast about in her mind for something with which to occupy herself, and remembered Lydia's message. Taking her hat and shawl from the rack just inside the door, she walked slowly down the hill. At the turn of the drive she met her grandfather.

"Where now, child?"

"Down to Lydia's, to play with the baby. I hope you have not been to Edgehill."

"Why do you care?"

"I heard you talk of going at dinner, and meant to ask you to take me with you."

"I shall go to-morrow. I must see Mr. Gore; and your father has been talking about a horse he thinks would suit somebody. I have promised to go and look at it."

"And will you take me along, grandpa? Anna Marston is at Edgehill, and I want very much to see her."

"Certainly; and you can tell me how you like the horse. Don't keep me waiting, though."

"Never fear. I'll be ready first, as usual;" and, waving her hand to him, Lucy hastened down the hill.

The air was still and sweet, and full of the scent of growing things. The sun was just setting, leaving a few flecks of golden cloud above the horizon, when she opened the white gate of Lydia's "front yard," and walked up to the door. She was met just within it by her cousin, who carried in her arms a fine, active boy of some four or five months.

"I am glad you came, Lucy," said Lydia. "Baby does not seem well; he has worried all day; and I am always so anxious about him when Ben is away!"

"Where is Ben?"

"He went to Kiffton early this morning, and ought to be back by this time. I expect him every minute. Hush, baby! Mamma is so tired! do let her rest a minute. He is such a tyrant, Lucy! He likes to be carried about, and he cries the moment I sit down with him."

"Come to me, little one," said Lucy, throwing aside her

bonnet, and reaching her arms to the child. Come to Lucy, for I know your poor mother's arms must ache."

The child, charmed with the sweet voice and smile, stretched out his tiny hands readily to Lucy, and rested his little head against her bosom, while Lydia, relieved, sank wearily into a rocking-chair. Soothed either by some gentle magnetism, or by the change of position, he lay perfectly still, and was soon sinking off to sleep. Lucy looked down tenderly for a few minutes into the baby eyes, and smiled to see how the soft haze of coming slumber was already creeping over them.

"Why don't you give this boy a name, Lydia?" she asked, at length. "It is a shame for him to be so neglected. If he were a girl, he should be called Lucy without further delay."

"O, we have decided upon a name at last. Indeed, my mind was set on it from the beginning, and Ben agreed with me; but every relative the child has in the world has proposed a different name for him, and been bent on calling him by it. We did not know but we should have to give up our own choice.

"And what is that?"

"We call him George, for Mr. Stafford; we don't put in the Stafford, but call him George Fraser, for grandpa. Don't you like the name?"

Lucy's face was turned towards the window, and therefore her cousin did not see the sudden quiver that shot over it, nor guess the effort with which, after only a few seconds' pause, she answered, quietly, —

"Yes, certainly. How much his eyes are like yours, Lydia!"

And then ensued a long talk on the one subject most interesting to the young mother — the baby and his belongings. The child had fallen asleep; and Lucy sat quietly in the gathering darkness, with his little form clasped close to her bosom, the name, which she could not yet bring herself to utter, a spell which endeared beyond description the unconscious sleeper. Lydia wished to relieve her, but she insisted that she was not tired, and refused to relinquish her sweet burden.

The evening wore on, but no Ben made his appearance; and Lydia, after the fashion of young wives, grew anxious and nervous. Her cousin suggested various causes which might have detained him. Perhaps he had found it late when his business was concluded, and had decided to wait until morning. His wife felt sure, however, that he would not fail to set out; and, in spite of all Lucy's suggestions, she grew constantly more nervous with thinking over the things that might have happened to him. She sat close by the window, her ear strained to catch the sound of his approaching wheels, and her fancy busy with visions of broken axletrees, treacherous bridges, and runaway horses.

It was past nine; the clock was nearing the stroke of ten, and he did not come. The hour struck, and the steady hands crept on. Half past ten, and Lydia's excitement was growing wild, when the welcome roll of wheels was heard in the distance. It came nearer and nearer.

"That is Ben! I know the step of his horse," cried Lydia; and the next moment they heard him driving into the side yard.

26

Lydia hastened to the door. "What *did* keep you so, Ben?" she asked, as the latter entered.

"I broke my wagon down below here, and had to stop and get it mended. Were you frightened, little girl? Good evening, Lucy. I am glad you were here. Lydia has the fidgets when I am gone."

"Do you want the lantern, Ben?"

"Yes, if you please. I will put the horse up, and then come and tell you of my luck."

"You are walking lame; what is the matter?"

"Only a slight sprain. I jumped when the wagon broke, and turned my ankle. It's a mere trifle — will be well to-morrow."

Lydia brought the lantern, and as her husband went out, she stood for a moment with the door open, watching him. When she returned into the room where she had left her cousin, Lucy had laid the baby in his cradle, and was putting on her bonnet and shawl.

"Why, Lucy!" she exclaimed; "you surely are not going home to-night."

"I must, dear. I am to go to Edgehill early in the morning with grandpa, and I have several things to do first."

"But at least wait till Ben comes in, and let him go with you."

"No; he ought not to walk to-night; he is quite too lame. I shall not let him go."

"But I can't bear to think of your going alone. It is eleven o'clock."

"Still it is quite light, and I know the way so perfectly. There will not be a soul on the road; and I shall be home in a few minutes."

"I know Ben will not like it."

"I'll come over to-morrow evening and make my peace with him. There, good night, dear; don't fret about me, for I shall do very well;" and, bending once more over the cradle to leave a kiss on the baby's velvet cheek, she went quickly out.

The night was very beautiful. There was no moon, but the sky gleamed thick with stars. A thin mist, breathed from the warm, moist earth, softened without obscuring their brilliancy. It was so light that Lucy could see all near objects, and so still that sounds she knew to be distant came distinctly to her ear. The air was warm, laden with soft odors, and with the subtile, delicious scent of the teeming earth. The road was, as she had predicted, wholly deserted; but the beauty of the night, the silence, and the lateness of the hour, made the solitary walk delightful.

She had a dim, sweet sense of being alone with nature, a feeling as if the great loving mother of us all were taking her to her bosom, hushing every sorrowful murmur, and smoothing away the wrinkles of old pain. What influence was around her she knew not; but as she walked on under the soft spring starlight, she seemed to pass out from the heavy shadows that had enveloped her into a region clear and bright. The past and the present seemed suddenly and widely divided; and she turned from that already fading behind to a future serene and clear.

So wrapped was she in thought, that she scarcely heeded the distance, and was surprised when she discovered herself within a few steps of her father's door. Looking up, she saw that a lamp was burning brightly in her own chamber, placed there, as she knew, for her convenience when she should come in. The hall was lighted, too; but all the lower rooms were dark. Everything was so quiet that she thought the family must have all retired; but as she approached the door she saw Jerry, the farm man, leaning against one of the elms that shadowed the grassy slope before the house.

The sight of him scattered at once her reverie, and she quickened her steps.

"A fine night, Jerry, but bad for your rheumatism," she said, as she passed him.

The man made no reply, and Lucy went on to the door-steps. Pushing open the door, she paused, and turned to take one more look at the lovely night. The hall lamp shot its rays far out, down the grassy slope, and she watched them gleaming on the gauzy wreaths of mist that were curling up from below, her figure framed for the moment in the brilliantly-lighted doorway. Only for a moment, however; then she closed the door, extinguished the lamp, and went softly up to her own chamber.

One of the windows was open, and she went to close it. A pale meteor went trailing across the heavens, and she leaned out to watch its course. She lingered till its bright-ness had wholly disappeared, and was again in the act of closing the window, when she was slightly surprised to observe that Jerry had not moved from the spot where she had passed him.

As the sash slid into its place, and the curtain fell over it, she could not help wondering what should keep the man out of his bed at that time of night. But other thoughts quickly claimed her attention, and Jerry and his nocturnal peculiarities passed from her mind.

Very soon her light, too, was extinguished, and darkness, silence, and slumber settled over all the house.

CHAPTER XXXIX.

LUCY was astir early next morning, passing quietly and quickly from one to another of the various avocations which she had made her own — opening windows, letting in the sweet spring air and the warm sunshine — brightening, freshening all that she came near. Once or twice she even sang at her tasks — not quite gayly, perhaps — not quite the old joyous, ringing song that rivalled the building birds; but strains that were clear, restful, and strong, that had in them a note of victory, as well as a reminiscence of conflict and pain.

They were on the road soon after breakfast, for the captain's business obliged him to make a wide circuit away from the usual road to Edgehill, and the morning promised to be warm for the season. It was a delightful day, and Lucy appreciated it with a keenness which showed how little the faculty of enjoyment was diminished in her. I dare say you do not like her for this. You think she must have been, to some degree, insensible or shallow that she still found her old pleasure in the gladness and glory of the day. She might seem more interesting to you, perhaps, were I to show her, as henceforth and for life, a pale, sad mourner over the grave of her love and its hopes. But that picture, though interesting, would not be true. She was not at all a heroine of romance, only a brave, good, gentle girl, who, having fought with and mastered her great grief, had found the peace which is born of such victories. For the rest, temperament would assert itself. She could not help enjoying, for she was born with the exquisite physical organization which imbibes pleasure at every pore. People with this happy natural endowment can never be wholly wretched, so long, at least, as youth, health, and fine weather remain.

The important business of Lucy's saddle-horse first demanded attention, and much discussion. It was finally settled to everybody's satisfaction; the horse was ordered over to Hillsboro' for trial before completing the purchase, and they turned their faces towards Edgehill. The morning was well advanced when they reached the village. They drove to the house where Lucy's friend was staying.

"You are not in such a hurry, grandpa, as to prevent your going in a few minutes. Mrs. Bird and Anna will want to see you."

"I will just look in and bid them good morning; and then I have some business to arrange with Mr. Gore. When that is finished, I may have a little time left."

They walked up the gravel path into a little veranda, and rang. The door was opened by a neat young girl, who, in answer to their inquiries, said Mrs. Bird and her niece were gone to spend the day at Colchester.

Here was a *contretemps* for Lucy. She pencilled a few words of regret upon the card she gave to the girl, and turned away with her grandfather.

"Well, Lucy, where next?" asked the latter.

"There is no one else I care to see."

"Then you may as well go with me to Mr. Gore's."

"Shall you be detained there long?"

"Half an hour, probably."

"Very well; we will go, then."

It cost Lucy some effort to give this assent. She felt strongly averse to visiting a house which must re-awaken so many painful associations; but it seemed difficult to avoid doing so without appearing unreasonable or discourteous, and she yielded. After all, she said to herself, what did it matter? She must learn to meet these shocks, one by one. They would, perhaps, be easier by and by. But she sat quite silent as they drove on to the other end of the village.

Ill success seemed to attend them this morning. On inquiring for Mr. Gore, they learned that he was confined to his room with a severe cold and an attack of rheumatism. The servant who gave this information knew them, and was quite certain that Mr. Gore, although he had excused himself to other visitors that morning, would wish to see the captain and Miss Fraser. Accordingly Lucy and her grandfather were shown into the drawing-room, while the man went up with their names.

He soon returned, saying they were to follow him. They were conducted up stairs to a kind of half study, half dressing-room, where they found Mr. Gore in an easy chair, with his right arm bandaged and stiff with rheumatism. He welcomed them cordially, apologizing to Lucy, as he warmly pressed her hand, for receiving her in such questionable shape.

Mr. Gore had not seen Lucy for a year; and, looking at her now as they talked together, his keen eye detected a change in her. There was the same soft grace he remembered before, the same bloom, the same enchanting smile; but over the sweet face seemed to have come just that haunting expression which looked out from the eyes of Anne Wycombe. He sighed as he saw that the resemblance to his ill-fated ancestress had become complete.

There were many topics to be touched upon; among them, one which Lucy knew must come up, and had braced her nerves to meet. They talked of Stafford. What was said she never could recall, but she only remembered thinking, through it all, how strange it was that these two gray-haired men should be sitting there and talking with tender regret of *him* who had been so young, so full of glorious life, — that he should be lying cold and dead, and they survive to weep for him. It seemed unreal — incredible.

After a time they passed to other things, and Lucy exerted herself to sustain her share of the conversation. The subject of Captain Fraser's business was alluded to, and dismissed by him as a matter which could well wait until his friend should be in better case. Mr. Gore remarked that he had been unable to attend to business for several days; he had then a number of letters of importance lying on his table unanswered. A young man in the village, who sometimes did writing for him, had been sent for that morning; but, unfortunately, he was away from home. The captain, with characteristic good-nature, immediately declared that he had the whole day at his disposal, and, if his friend would only make use of him, would be happy to write as many letters as the latter chose to dictate. The offer was accepted as frankly as it was made, and Mr. Gore turned to Lucy : —

"My dear young lady, what will you do while I take possession of your grandfather?"

"Pray do not be troubled on my account; I shall do very well, I assure you."

"You will find books in the library, and a piano in the drawing-room. I must beg you to order luncheon at what hour may suit you best. James,"— to the servant who answered his bell, — "bring the keys of the library to Miss Fraser, and see that she has everything she wishes for. Then remember, whoever calls, that I am too much engaged to see any one. I shall ring if I want anything; and don't come near me unless the house is on fire."

James held open the door for Lucy to pass out, and then the two old men were left alone.

Lucy lingered a while to look out of the large arched window of the upper hall, whence a wide and varied view was obtained; paused a moment before the picture of Mistress Anne Wycombe, to look into the painted eyes, whose expression perplexed her no longer, whose spirit seemed, indeed, to answer to hers, and, at length, went down to the drawing-room. She laid aside her bonnet, and, bringing from the library a portfolio of drawings, she buried herself in the recesses of a deep arm-chair, and began turning over its contents. But it was in vain she strove to fix her attention upon the pictures. Scenes widely different from any the artist had delineated filled her mind. She found herself recalling minutely the last occasion on which she had been in that room. Every incident was as fresh in her memory as the events of yesterday. Then, mentally, she went over the days which succeeded — those still, bright summer days before the sudden darkness came.

She lingered over them; she strove resolutely to hold her thoughts back from all which came after them.

In the midst of her reverie, the sudden ringing of the hall-door bell brought her sharply back to the present. Some one appeared to have inquired for the master of the house, for she heard James replying that Mr. Gore was particularly engaged, and had given orders not to be disturbed; but if the gentleman preferred to wait, he would show him into the drawing-room. Mr. Gore would be at liberty in an hour or two.

Lucy heard the person come into the hall. The idea of being intruded upon here, in her present mood, by a stranger, was intolerable; and, just as the new-comer entered the room, she made her escape from it by a French window opening on the terrace. She had passed out unobserved; and a few steps brought her to the head of the close-shaded walk running along one end of the garden. It was screened from observation on the side of the house by the line of locusts that bordered it, and on the edge overlooking the ravine by the old buckthorn hedge.

At the foot of the walk a sheltered seat invited her; but she was in no mood to desire repose. The excitement of her feelings demanded the relief of motion; and for a long time she continued to walk rapidly up and down.

The day had lost none of its beauty. The sun shone goldenly, and the water, rushing away through the ravine below, sparkled brightly in its light. The fresh spring wind came sweeping over the horse-chestnut trees, rustling their broad, just-opened leaves, and waving the fringy foliage of the locusts. On the rough face of the cliff fluttered gay, green streamers, and the swallows were

wheeling in dizzy circles over the great chimneys of the
old house. The air was full of perfume and pleasant
sounds. All around were the beauty and the gladness of
re-awakening life. But Lucy was unconscious of it all. In
her heart was swelling for utterance a great cry of agony.
The labor of months was undone in an hour; the half-con-
quered grief arose and faced her again, grim and terrible
as ever. All the resignation to which she had schooled
herself, all the strength and serenity which, little by little,
she had won, were swept away in a moment by the sudden rush of memory. A wild, passionate prayer for death
was on her lips.

A footstep on the walk startled her. She turned, and
stood face to face with George Stafford!

Both were, for an instant, motionless, — he pale, but
erect and haughty; she as if suddenly frozen. She stood
leaning forward, her eyes dilated, and on her forehead a
contraction as of physical pain. The next moment she
wavered, a mist swam before her eyes, and she would have
fallen, but that Stafford, springing forward, received her
insensible form in his arms.

Perhaps, if Lucy had not fainted away, this sudden and
unexpected meeting might not have led to an immediate
explanation between our two friends; but after such an
involuntary confession as that act amounted to, disguises
could go but little way. Indeed, when a young lady, after
a fainting fit, returns to consciousness to find herself in the
arms of a gentleman, to feel a strong heart throbbing near
her own, and to meet the close glance of eyes full of tenderness and anxiety, the situation is, on the whole, unfavora-
ble to the maintenance of artificial relations.

CHAPTER XL.

Two hours later, the two old men having finished their letters, Mr. Gore's bell rang loudly, and was answered by the same man who had appeared before.

"Has Miss Fraser had luncheon, James?"

"I think not yet, sir."

"Why, bless me, she will be starved! Is she in the library?"

"No, sir. I saw her go into the locust walk some time ago. And as I came past there just now I heard her talking with the gentleman."

"What gentleman?"

"One who called to see you, sir. I told him you were engaged, and he said he would wait."

"Who is he?"

"I never saw him before, sir. I showed him into the drawing-room; but I suppose he got tired of waiting, and went into the garden, where Miss Fraser was."

"Well, take my compliments to the gentleman, whoever he is, and to Miss Fraser also, and tell them I am at leisure, and shall be happy to see them up here. And bring the luncheon directly; we will take it here together. I shall treat you, captain, to a bottle of my father's choicest claret. Madison was president when the first cobwebs began to gather over it. What old fellows you and I are getting to be!"

"Yes; we shall be slipping off the stage soon, and the young folks will be filling our places. They will drink our old wine, and sit in our chimney corner."

"There, my friend, you are happier than I. You have a son to bear your name, and a lovely grandchild to gladden your old age. For me there is no one. My name dies with me, and my race, too, since that poor boy Stafford is gone. I had come to love him as a son, and to think that he would take the place of one to my lonely old age. But now — Great God! Do the dead appear when we speak of them?"

The last words of the old man were uttered in a scream almost like a woman's, as the door opened, and Stafford, with Lucy leaning on his arm, entered the room. The scene which ensued was all excitement and confusion. Mr. Gore, starting from his seat, clasped his recovered relative in his arms, and wept for joy. Lucy stole to her grandfather's side, and hid her agitated face in the shelter of his arm. James, coming in with the tray, was so overcome by the sight of his master, who had not taken a step unassisted for three days, thus suddenly restored to activity, that he was near dropping his whole burden upon the floor. Exclamations, questions, congratulations, and eager greetings resounded on all sides; and it was some time before any one had attained sufficient composure to listen to the wanderer's account of himself.

When the kind-hearted Lynch and his party turned reluctantly away from what they believed to be Stafford's lifeless body, the long and heavy swoon, consequent upon great loss of blood, into which he had sunk, did, indeed, so much resemble death that it was not strange they were deceived. And it had nearly ended in death. Had it not been for the half foolish boy whose life he had saved amid the snows of New England, the other attendants would have buried him, as the Englishmen had desired. But the lad showed such frightful rage when they offered to touch the body of his master, that they at length desisted from their efforts. Hours passed before there were any signs of returning life, and then they appeared so faint and feeble that it is doubtful if any civilized practitioner would have given the patient an hour's lease of life. But nature and her barbarian children were kinder to him. Their simple skill and primitive remedies, aided by the dry, pure air, and by the sound constitution of the wounded man, were victorious in the end. The process, however, was painfully slow. Six months wore away before he had regained sufficient strength to make travel practicable.

And then arose difficulties. All his money, papers, and what few valuables he had with him, he had parted with to Lynch. He was completely a pensioner on the kindness of the natives by whom he was surrounded. They had cared for him unweariedly; they took the most particular fancy to him; and they seemed to regard him as in some way belonging to them. They watched him so jealously, that the idea became fixed in his mind that he was virtually a prisoner in their hands. Whether it really was so or not he never learned, as he was careful, by a well-simulated appearance of perfect content with his situation, to avoid any such quickening of their suspicions as might lead to his being subjected to closer *surveillance*, or to restraint.

Another circumstance added to his perplexities. His hospitable though jealous entertainers were of a nomadic race; and once or twice, during the period of his sojourn with them, they had made a sudden flitting from one place of abode to another. Alarmed by the report that a hostile tribe living to the east of them were preparing for a raid upon their flocks and village, they would sweep up everything which they had, — households, herds, habitations, even, — and make a precipitate flight of many days into the interior. Stafford and Figaro were borne along with the rest. They could not well help it, even if they had known certainly that they wished to do so. But they were thus carried far away from any frequented route leading back to the country-whence they had come, and the difficulties and dangers of a return into India very greatly enhanced. From the best estimate which Stafford was able to make of their probable position, he was quite sure that some of the extreme outposts of the Russian government could not be far away. He believed that if he could but push forward in the general direction the natives were keeping, he could soon reach some trading post or military station, and have a chance of finding such assistance, and possibly companionship, as would enable him to penetrate into Europe through Western Asia. A careful computation of the chances convinced him that this route would offer no greater delays or obstacles than would attend an attempt to return by way of India. The novelty of the expedition, too, had a degree of attractiveness for him; and its dangers — which he probably under-estimated in some degree —did not detract at all from the favor with which he looked upon the plan.

It is impossible to repeat in detail the story of his long and weary wanderings, his dangers, hardships, delays, and detentions. He set out early in November, a short time before Brainerd's visit to Hillsboro', and about the middle of the following April reached Moscow, alone, save for the lad Figaro, without friends, credit, or money. Here a piece of good fortune befell him. He met an old London acquaintance, who supplied him with funds, and gave him information relative to his friends in England. This friend had heard the intelligence brought by Lynch, which of course no one doubted, the latter believing that he had seen Stafford draw his last breath. From Moscow Stafford wrote to his uncle, and arrived two days after his letter in England, where he was received by Colonel Ross as one risen from the dead.

He wrote at once to Brainerd, asking him to inform Mr. Gore of his resurrection. Brainerd, however, was absent in the South, and failed to receive the letter. Stafford, with all possible despatch, arranged his affairs, and sailed for New York. His disappointment was keen, on arriving, not to find Brainerd there to welcome him; but, sending a telegraphic despatch after his friend, he determined to employ the few days which must intervene before the latter could arrive, in a visit to Edgehill. He had reached Kiffton the previous afternoon. From the window of the hotel he had a glimpse of Ben Miller just driving away, but was too late to attract his attention. He took a horse and buggy about sunset to drive over to Edgehill.

"About sunset!" exclaimed Mr. Gore; "then, my dear boy, why did you not reach here last night?"

"In passing through Hillsboro', I was delayed some time,

27

misled by a light that shone before me, — a sort of *ignis fatuus*, I thought, — and in consequence I reached here so late that I would not disturb you, but went to the public house."

" An *ignis fatuus*, George, on those breezy hills! The idea is preposterous."

" I think so myself now, sir," answered Stafford, gravely. " It must have been a star, after all; but my vision was dim, and I could not tell its true character."

" What was it like ? " inquired the captain, curiously.

" It appeared to be shining from a window. I left my horse by the highway, and stood a long time under a tree to watch it. I have long been superstitious about the lights from Hillsboro' windows; but I do not think I ever realized until to-day their beneficent influences."

The captain stared and looked puzzled; and Mr. Gore shot at Stafford a keen glance of inquiry. The latter wore an air of such perfect seriousness that his kinsman's half-suspicion of "chaff" was allayed. But the meaning look that passed from Stafford to Lucy, and her conscious blush, were enlightening.

" Ah, ha ! " cried the old man. " Sits the wind in that quarter? I think you two have been making good use of your time in my locust walk this morning. Thomas Fraser, have you anything to say about this business? "

But the captain's perceptions had been quicker than those of his friend. He had drawn Lucy into his arms, and she was weeping there, quietly, but a little hysterically.

" My dear child," he whispered, " my precious lamb, I understand it all. Did you think, in all that time last winter, that your old grandfather did not guess what made the days so dark? Hush, child! Do not weep so. We are coming all right now."

Stafford, who had been shaking hands with his cousin and receiving his joyful congratulations, now approached. The captain still held one arm around his grandchild; but, reaching out the other, he gave Stafford's hand a cordial clasp. A twinkle of mirth shone through the suspicious moisture of his eyes.

"I see," he said, "you two have been making your arrangements without much reference to us old fellows; and now, I dare say, Miss Lucy relies on me to make her peace with her father and mother. But I warn you, sir, not to trust her too far. Another man holds her plighted faith; if she breaks it to him, she may to you."

"Grandpapa!" exclaimed Lucy, lifting her head with a flush of surprise.

"Well, child, is it not so? How many times have you solemnly pledged me your word to die an old maid for my sake?"

"My dear young lady," cried Mr. Gore, coming to the rescue, "give him the excuse of Benedick in the play: 'When I said I would die a bachelor, I did not think I should live to be married.'"

Lucy laughed softly; but the sweet seriousness of expression quickly returned to her face. She was standing before her grandfather, in one of her old childish attitudes, her two hands reached up, holding the lapels of his coat.

"Dear grandpa," she whispered, "I will never leave *you*. I will never have a home which you do not share."

It was a few minutes later, when the two elders were occupied with some discussion between themselves, that Stafford followed Lucy into a window recess, where she was standing, half screened by the drooping curtain. She looked up a little shyly as he came to her side.

"So, then, it was you, last night, and not Jerry," she said.

"It was I."

"But you have not given a true account of what brought you there."

"Why should you suppose that I have not? I had come up over the long hill, driving slowly, oppressed, in spite of all my efforts, by some heavy thoughts. It was already late when I passed the still and darkened home of the Pages, looking back with a blessing for all the kind, warm hearts within its walls. Rising the crest of the hill, I saw the distant light from your chamber window. Shall I tell you, dearest, what a wild, passionate longing took possession of me once more, for the last time, to be near you — perhaps, to gain a glimpse, if it were only of your shadow on the curtain, before going away forever? I could see by my watch, in the dim starlight, that it was nearly twelve o'clock. From my knowledge of the habits of your household, I felt sure that the family would all have retired; and, fastening my horse by the road-side, I proceeded towards the house on foot. The closed doors and the air of stillness everywhere convinced me that I had been correct in my supposition; yet the hall lamp was still burning, and your chamber, though lighted, was evidently unoccupied. I decided that you must be writing at your desk in the hall, and waited, thinking that when you should go up stairs, I might see you come to the window to close the curtain."

"You must have found it dull: weren't you very sleepy, sir?"

"It is fortunate for you that those two old men are in sight, or I would have my revenge for that speech. But I was just on the point of a confession. Will you laugh at me if I make it?"

"Perhaps."

There was gay malice in her tone, but the soft glance of her eye contradicted it. He went on:—

"Do you remember that night—now nearly two years ago—when you stood with me by that upper window in your father's house, and showed me, through the rain, the distant gleam of old Nancy's lights? You answered lightly and carelessly then, when I reminded you whose little candle, shining out into the gloom, had guided me from cold, and darkness, and death, into warmth, and light, and safety. But I dared not tell you then of the hope I had begun to cherish that the same hand would light me to a better, nobler life. I had not been a bad man, as the world goes; but O, Lucy, such a useless one! And I had such opportunities—I might have done so much! But my love for you had struck one sound, sweet root into the barren soil of my life. All the better and more unspoiled part of my nature quickened and swayed to you. You know that I am superstitious. I made an omen for my hopes of those shining lamps. The thought of their steady light burning on through so many years was full of encouragement to me. When they went out in sudden darkness, there fell upon me a cold fear that was never

quite banished from my thoughts, till, weeks later, its fulfilment came.

"After that I was reckless, desperate. I had staked so
much, and lost all! I had not even the relief of resentment; for I could not blame you. If your judgment
wronged me in one case, it was little. · What claim had
such a useless, selfish waif as I to be anything to you? I
think I never knew of how little worth my life had been
till I felt it ebbing from me in that dreadful solitude, and
thought how few would really care for my loss, how very
few would really be the better for the time which I had
lived in the world. That was the hardest of all, Lucy. I
loved life. Death was dreadful to me. Though in losing
you I had lost, I knew, the best that life could give me, yet
its tide was strong in my veins. I had so much strength,
so much capacity for living, — every quivering nerve in me
clung to this earthly life, and shrank from the stillness and
coldness of death. And to think that the existence so dear
to me was worthless to the world — that though I died
there, like a dog, in the desert, no one would be the loser!
A few kind old companions would drop a tear, and say,
'Poor fellow! he is gone;' and then everything would go
on as before I was forgotten. Darling, I know what that
look means. But I did not guess, then, the difference that
it would make to you. I know, now, why my life was
saved — it could not be valueless if you cared for it. It
has grown to be a precious thing, and should be put to
noble uses. Even when I stood, last night, hopeless of the
good this day has brought, looking upward to the light
which shone on me from your window, I knew that, though
you were lost to me, my guiding lamp was there. All the

past pain and sorrow were not lost. Your influence on my life would remain, and shape it to better ends. If the future should in any sense redeem the waste, and wreck, and folly of the past, it would be owing all to you. Your pure and steadfast light it would be which would shine before me like a star."

THE END.

www.ingramcontent.com/pod-product-compliance
Lightning Source LLC
Chambersburg PA
CBHW021329110726
47900CB00005B/1406